MIND MACHINES

Dima Zales

♠ Mozaika Publications ♠

Copyright © 2016 Dima Zales and Anna Zaires
www.dimazales.com

Published by Mozaika Publications, an imprint of Mozaika LLC.
www.mozaikallc.com

Cover by Najla Qamber Designs
www.najlaqamberdesigns.com

e-ISBN: 978-1-63142-199-0
Print ISBN: 978-1-63142-232-4

CHAPTER ONE

The gargantuan syringe approaches Mom's neck. Grandpa squeezes her hand and tries not to look at the rapier-sized needle as it breaks his daughter's skin.

"Misha," Mom tells me in Russian. "This hurts."

I take a step forward, my hands balling into fists as I glare at the white-masked surgeon.

"Why is it going into her neck?" I demand.

I see no hint of empathy in the doctor's reflective eyes, and I seriously consider punching him in the face. Since distracting him might worsen Mom's situation, I settle for a calming breath, though all I really get is a lungful of sterile, Clorox-filled air.

The operation room has bright surgical lights and torture-chamber surgical equipment sadistically displayed throughout.

"Why are all these frightening things around us if it's just a simple injection?" I stammer, taking it all in for the first time.

The doctor's knuckles whiten as he presses the giant plunger. A disgusting gray liquid whooshes out of the syringe into Mom's neck.

"Why do the nanocytes need to be delivered in such a terrible way?" I ask—mostly to prevent myself from fainting.

"They shouldn't be," Grandpa says in English.

Mom's round face is contorted with the kind of horror and desperation I've only seen on it once, when a scrawny mouse scurried into our living room in our first Brooklyn apartment. Just like on that day, an ear-piercing scream is wrenched from her throat.

I take another step forward. Maybe I'll just pry the doc away from her.

The bald spot on top of Grandpa's head is beet red, and I wonder if he's about to kill the doc with his shoe, employing the same violent swat he used against the culprit mouse.

The doctor steps away from us.

Mom's screaming turns into gurgles and fades away.

Gray liquid starts pouring out of her mouth.

I feel paralyzed.

The same liquid streams out of her eyes, then her nose and her ears.

"It's the nanocytes," I yell in horror, my vocal cords finally working. "But they can't be replicating!"

Mom's head disappears, replaced by a vague liquid shape of the replicating gray goo. In a violent heartbeat, the rest of Mom's body turns into the same fluid grayness.

With two gurgling screams, Grandpa and the doctor also melt into puddles of squirming, colorless protoplasm.

The enormity of these losses doesn't fully register before the substance creeps over my own foot.

A savage searing pain spreads through my body, and I know it must be from the nanos breaking my flesh into molecules.

This can't be real, is my last thought. *This has to be a dream.*

———

I jackknife into a sitting position on the bed. Either the gruesome deaths or the realization I was dreaming woke me.

My bedroom is darker than a naked mole rat's lair. Going by feel, I locate my phone on the nightstand and light up its screen.

When my eyes adjust and I can decipher the time, I fight the urge to toss the phone at the wall. That would be like killing the messenger—fleetingly therapeutic, but pointless. It's 3:00 a.m., which is probably my least favorite a.m.

I take a deep breath the way my yoga-obsessed ex-girl-friend taught me, and surprisingly, I feel a bit calmer. I guess things aren't so bad. If I calm down enough to fall asleep again soon, I can doze for another five hours and probably still be functional during the day.

Getting up, I go to the bathroom. The AC chills my naked body as I walk, so the first thing I do is vigorously wipe away all the cold sweat.

My breath evens out further.

As I make use of the facilities, I chide myself for freaking out over that unlikely dream scenario. Grandfather's been dead for two years, and even when he was alive, he didn't speak flawless—or any—English. Also, the nanocytes we're using on Mom are the non-replicating kind, which is partly why each dose costs an obscene amount. Future replicating nanotechnology will build itself out of raw materials, so it'll only cost as much as those materials do, but that's not the case with this experimental batch. Finally, the injection procedure is noninvasive and *won't* require a surgeon, or even a doctor, to be present. This nightmare was just a manifestation of my irrational anxieties.

What I need now is sleep. As one of my family's favorite Russian sayings goes, "Morning is wiser than evening."

Yawning, I get back into bed and fall asleep half a second before my head touches the pillow.

CHAPTER TWO

"A cure for dementia and Alzheimer's?" Uncle Abe's gray eyes pulse with excitement, the way Mom's often do.

"It's not exactly a cure," I say at the same time as Ada says, "It's mostly a treatment for the symptoms."

"How cute," Uncle Abe says in Russian. "Your chick is already finishing your sentences."

As though she understood the Russian words, Ada's face lights up with an impish grin.

"We're not a couple," I tell Uncle Abe in Russian.

"Yet?" He gives me a knowing wink.

"It's not polite to speak in Russian in front of Ada," I say in English.

"I'm okay," Ada says. Only the shadow of a smile lurks in the corners of her eyes now, making her look like a punky version of the Mona Lisa.

"Still, I'm sorry," Uncle Abe tells her, his accent softening the *t* and the second *r*.

As we stroll through the hospital corridor, Ada takes the lead. She's a typical New Yorker, always twitchy and multitasking. I surreptitiously look her up and down, my eyes lingering on one of my favorite assets of hers—that special spot between the soles of her Doc Martens boots and the tips of her spiky hair.

Ada glances over her shoulder, her amber eyes meeting mine for a second. Did she feel me gawking at her just now? Before I can feel embarrassed, she stops in front of a green door and says, "This is the room."

The three of us walk in.

Unlike my dream, this isn't an operating room. It's spacious, with big windows and cheerfully blooming plants on the windowsills. At a glance, it's reminiscent of my stylish Brooklyn loft—if a mad scientist's wet dream was used as inspiration for the interior design.

Staff members from Techno, my portfolio company that designed the treatment, are already in the back. Mom is sitting on an operating chair in a white hospital gown, with a plethora of cables attaching her to a myriad of cutting-edge monitoring tools. Completing her getup is a headset—something straight out of the old *Total Recall* movie. It must be the "latest in portable neural scan technology" that JC, Techno's CEO, mentioned to me. I make a mental note to define *portable* to him.

I hear a "hi" from the farthest corner of the room. The person who spoke must be hidden behind the wall of servers and giant monitors. The other Techno employees keep working silently, though it isn't clear whether they didn't hear me come in, or if they're being antisocial.

Many folks at Techno could stand to improve their social skills. A psychiatrist might even label some of them as borderline Asperger's. Personally, I find those types of labels ridiculous. Psychiatry can sometimes be as scientific and helpful as astrology—which I don't believe in, in case that's not clear. A shrink back in high school tried to attach the Asperger's label to me because I had "too few friends." He could've just as easily concluded I had Tourette's based on where I told him to shove his diagnosis. Then again, maybe I'm still sore about psychiatry and neuropsychology because of how little they've done for Mom. Pretty much the only good thing I can say about psychiatry is that at least they're no longer using lobotomy as a treatment.

I look around the room for JC. He's nowhere to be found, so he must be in a similar room with another participant of the study.

Mom turns her head toward us, apparently able to do so despite the headgear.

My heart clenches in dread, as it always does when Mom and I meet after more than a day apart. Because of the accident that damaged Mom's brain, it's feasible that one day she'll look at me and won't recognize who I am.

Today she clearly does, though, because she gives me that dimpled smile we share. "Hi, little fish," she says in Russian. She then looks at her brother. "Abrashkin, bunny, how are you?"

"Mom just used untranslatable Russian pet names for us," I loudly whisper to Ada and wave hello to the still-uninterested staff in the back.

Mom looks at Ada without recognition, and I inwardly sigh. They've met twice before.

"Who's this boy?" Mom asks me in English. "Is he an intern at Techno or something?"

"She's not a boy, and her name is Ada," I respond, trying my best not to sound like I'm talking to someone with a disability, something my mom deeply resents. "She's not an intern, but one of the people who programmed the nanocytes that'll make you feel better."

"Nice to meet you, Nina Davydovna," Ada says as though they haven't done this before.

Mom's eyebrow rises at either the girlish resonance of Ada's bell-like voice or her proper use of the Russian patronymic. She quickly recovers, though, just like the last time, and also like the last time, she says, "Call me Nina."

"I will. Thank you, Nina," Ada says.

I realize Ada addressed my mom so formally on purpose—to lessen Mom's stress—so I give her a grateful nod. Of course, if Ada wanted to go the extra mile, she could've worn different clothing or changed her hairstyle to eliminate Mom's confusion about Ada's gender. Then again, Mom's confusion might be part of her condition, because to me, despite the leather jacket and black hoodie obscuring much of her body, Ada is the epitome of femininity.

"Is she his girlfriend?" Mom asks Uncle Abe conspiratorially in Russian. "Have I met her before?"

"I'm not sure, sis," Uncle Abe says. "From the way he looks at her, I suspect it's just a matter of time before they hook up."

"Oh yeah?" Mom chuckles. "Do you think she's Jewish?"

Blood rushes to my cheeks, and not just because of this "Jewish or not" business. It's something that became important to Mom only after the accident—unless she's always cared but only started voicing it after the brain damage lowered her inhibitions. My grandparents certainly often spoke about this sort of thing, going as far as blaming the situation with my father on him being non-Jewish—something I consider to be reverse anti-Semitism.

It's unfortunate, but their attitude was forged back in the Soviet Union, where being Jewish was considered an ethnicity and used as an excuse for government-level discrimination. Since one's ethnicity was written in the infamous fifth paragraph of one's passport, discrimination was commonplace and inescapable. My mom was turned away from her first choice of universities because they'd hit "their quota of three Jews." She also had a hard time finding a job in the engineering sciences until my father helped her out, only to later sexually harass her and leave her to raise me on my own. Even I was affected by this negativity before we left. When my seventh-grade classmates learned about my heritage from our school journal, they told me that with my blue eyes and blond hair (which darkened to brown as I got older), I looked nothing like a Jew. Though they used the derogatory Russian term, they'd meant it as a big compliment.

What makes the topic extra weird is that in America, where Judaism is more of a religion than an ethnicity, we're suddenly not all that Jewish. I mean, how can we be if I learned about Hanukkah in my mid-teens and when I had a very non-kosher grilled lobster tail wrapped in bacon last night?

Yeah, I also learned what *kosher* means in my mid-teens.

Either way, I couldn't care less about Ada's Jewishness—though, for the record, with a last name like Goldblum, she probably is Jewish. I don't know what that term means to her either, since she's just as secular as I am. I think my biggest issue with Mom's question is that I simply loathe labels applied to entire groups of people, especially labels that come with so much baggage.

"It's hard to say," Uncle Abe says after examining Ada's dainty nose and zooming in on her pierced nostril. "With that hair, she's definitely not Russian."

Here we go, another label. To my grandparents, the term *Russian* was interchangeable with *goy* or *gentile*, but I don't think my uncle is using it in that context. Though in Russia we were Jewish, here in the US we're Russian—as in, the same as every Russian speaker from the former Soviet Union. I'm guessing my uncle is saying that Ada doesn't look like she's from the former Soviet Union, since a certain way of dressing and grooming typically accompanies that, at least for recent immigrants.

I decide to stop this thread of conversation, but before I get a chance to put a word in, Mom says, "When I was young, that kind of haircut was called an explosion at the noodle factory."

They both laugh, and even I can't help chuckling. I know the haircut Mom is referring to, and it's an eighties hairdo that may well be a distant ancestor to what's happening on Ada's head. The bleached, pointy tips make her look like an echidna with a Mohawk—an image reinforced by her prickly wit.

The door to the room opens, and a nurse walks in.

Seeing her scrubs raises my blood pressure, though I'm not sure if it's from the standard white coat syndrome or a flashback to my earlier nightmare. Probably the former. There was no anesthesia in Soviet dentistry when I was growing up, so I developed a conditioned response to anything resembling dentist clothing. Anyone in a white coat gives me a reaction akin to what someone suffering from coulrophobia—the irrational fear of clowns—would experience during a John Wayne Gacy documentary or the movie *It*.

The nurse walks over to Mom and reaches for a big syringe lying stealthily by Mom's chair.

The Techno employees in the back collectively hold their breaths.

The nurse doesn't seem to understand the auspiciousness of the occasion. She looks like she wants to finish here and move on to something more interesting, like watching a filibuster on C-SPAN. Her nametag reads "Olga." That, combined with her circa late-eighties haircut and makeup, plus those Slavic cheekbones, activates my Russian radar—or Rudar for short. It's like gaydar, but for detecting Russian speakers.

I bet Mom is insulted by the hospital assigning this nurse to her. It implies she needs help understanding English. Having earned a Bachelor of Science in Electrical

Engineering after moving to the States in her mid-thirties, Mom takes deserved pride in her skills with the English language—skills the accident didn't affect.

In the silence, I can hear Mom's shallow breathing; her fear of medical professionals is much worse than mine.

Olga grips the syringe and raises her hand.

CHAPTER THREE

Uncle Abe looks away. I'm tempted to follow his lead but decide against it.

To my relief, instead of Mom's neck, Olga connects the syringe to the port below the IV bag. This makes sense, since it's the easiest way to access Mom's vein.

Reality further diverges from my nightmare as I note the clear liquid carrying the nanocytes and the fact that Mom doesn't even wince throughout the whole ordeal. And she's operating on senses heightened by fear, so if there was a reason to wince, she would have, and she probably would've screamed as well.

The people scanning the monitors murmur amongst themselves, but no one sounds alarmed. Excitement permeates the air.

The nurse double-checks the vital signs and makes a Grinch-like face. In a Russian accent that confirms my Rudar's suspicions, she says, "I'll be around if I'm needed."

Without waiting for anyone to respond, she exits the room.

"How are you?" I ask Mom.

She shrugs, clearly overwhelmed by all this activity.

"You'll be fine, Nina," Ada says. "I'm sure of it."

I've read through countless reports and studies on the treatment, so I should be as confident as Ada is. But I worry, because as the poem goes, I only have one mother.

"I feel a slight burning in my arm," Mom says. "But it's not too bad."

"That's normal with intravenous delivery." Ada plays with the silver stud pierced through two spots in her ear cartilage. "It would've been worse if you'd gotten all the liquid at once. You might've felt nauseous."

I wonder where Ada learned all this medical info. Her background is in software, like mine, though I haven't written a line of code in a decade. In contrast, Ada is the most genius programmer I know, and that's saying a lot. As part of my job, I meet tons of talented software engineers—not to mention I'm besties with a world-renowned techie.

As though she read my mind, Ada says, "I was in the room with a few of the other participants, so I know what to expect."

This is yet another example of Ada's strange behavior around me, which began when I broke up with my ex a few months back. Is she hinting that she disapproves of my apparent lack of interest in the other participants? If so, she might actually have a point there, but she has to understand that all this—from investing so much of my own and my venture capital fund's money into Techno, to getting my friends in the industry involved in the Brainocyte research and development—is to help my mom. At least, that's my primary motivation. Of course I'm glad this technology will also lead to great things for other people, but I hope Ada can forgive me for focusing on the most important person in my life.

"How are things looking?" Ada asks loudly enough that the people in the back can't ignore her.

David, part of Techno's army of engineers, gives her a thumbs-up and says, "So far so good."

Ada nods at David, then looks at me. "Don't worry," she says. "Nina is still set to be the first participant to proceed to Phase One."

Looks like my suspicion was right. It must irk Ada that I'm not showing interest in any of the others. Once I make sure Mom is doing well, perhaps I'll pay some of the other participants a visit, starting with Mrs. Sanchez.

"What exactly is this treatment?" Uncle Abe asks and sits down on the couch—the only surface not covered by wires.

Ada looks at my mom, who doesn't reply, leading me to believe she forgot the details of the treatment. Usually, that would upset me, but since we're doing something to fix this very problem as we speak, I remain optimistic.

"That liquid contains Brainocytes," Ada says when she's sure neither my mom nor I want to take the lead. "They're the product we're testing."

My uncle and, sadly, Mom look at Ada with blank expressions, and Mom mumbles a paraphrase from a Russian proverb about how eggs are about to teach the hen.

"Okay, let me start over," Ada says and takes a seat on the other end of the couch. "Brainocytes are a type of nanocytes designed to penetrate the blood-brain barrier and create the most powerful brain-to-computer interface—BCI—ever made."

The blank looks don't change, so she says, "How much do you know about nanotechnology and neuroprosthetics?"

At the mention of nanotechnology, Mom's eyes shimmer with recognition. "After I finished college the first time, we had a scanning tunneling microscope where I worked, so the idea of molecular machines was often discussed, especially when the translations of Eric Drexler's work became available."

"Why do I have a feeling I'm about to regret my question?" Uncle Abe mutters.

In his defense, he must've heard Mom talk about her old job more often than I have. That old job is closely intertwined with the whole affair involving my father, so those memories are like emotional dynamite for Mom. Since I can tell my uncle is about to say something that might really upset her, I stop him by plopping down on the couch between him and Ada.

Smiling at Mom, I say, "The simplest way to explain Brainocytes is to say that they're a bunch of super-tiny robots. They're currently swimming through your bloodstream into your brain, where they'll plug into your neurons. This will allow for all sorts of interesting interactions."

I've seen this exact expression on Uncle Abe's face when he tried uni sushi and learned that *uni* is Japanese for a sea urchin's gonads. Once he's won the yuck battle with himself, he says, "That sounds pretty invasive and creepy, but if anyone was going to agree to such a treatment, it would be our Nina."

It's true. Mom is more adventurous than her brother in every way, including her choice of foods. She loves uni.

Through the couch cushion, I feel Ada stiffen as though she's preparing to spring into action. I'm not surprised. The topic my uncle hit upon is Ada's pet peeve.

"It's not invasive at all," she says, her tone veering dangerously close to patronizing territory. "Nina is getting the safest neural interface of its kind. By not requiring the opening of the skull, as other similar technologies do, we avoid the risk of infection, not to mention leakage of cerebrospinal fluids—"

"This isn't the first time someone's tried to work directly with the brain," I interject before Ada can smack my uncle with a technical treatise. "Parkinson's and epilepsy patients already receive special brain pacemakers. Other products on the market—like retinal implants, for instance—allow the blind to regain some rudimentary sight, and cochlear implants allow the deaf to hear. Some implants turn thoughts into computer commands so quadriplegic patients can control their prosthetic limbs. Brainocytes can replace all these brain-implanted devices and, as Ada was saying, in a much safer way."

"I understand," Uncle Abe says, but his tone makes me doubt that he actually does.

Pretending I'm still explaining things to him, I continue for the benefit of Mom's failing memory. "The

Brainocytes are the hardware. They'll lodge themselves all over Mom's brain, and once that's done, we can use the right software"—I incline my head toward Ada, acknowledging her key role in the creation of the necessary apps and interfaces—"to treat Mom's condition by stimulating the correct neurons in the carefully selected portions of her brain, all with the aid of external supercomputers. The idea is to simulate brain regions to supplement any missing functionality in the heavily damaged parts."

Ada sighs, and under her breath, she murmurs something along the lines of, "So this is how much you have to dumb things down for investors?"

"Sorry." I gently poke Ada with my elbow. "Do you want to take a stab at explaining Phase One to my uncle? I'm sure you can go over it without insulting anyone's intelligence."

"Don't mind if I do," Ada says, "especially since Phase One is very easy to explain. We'll primarily be working with neurons responsible for vision, specifically the ones within the ventral stream. My Augmented Reality Information Overlay suite of services will evoke Einstein's API—"

Uncle Abe chuckles, interrupting Ada, and even Mom's eyes appear glazed over. Despite all of Ada's prodigious cognitive abilities, adjusting to her audience isn't her strong suit.

Sighing in defeat, Ada says, "Why don't you have a go at it, Mike? Meanwhile, I'll make myself useful by checking the monitors."

She gets up and trudges to the other side of the room.

Unpeeling my eyes from the tightness of Ada's black jeans, I say, "Ada had one thing right. Phase One *is* really simple to explain, especially in comparison to the other stages. In a nutshell, you'll see text boxes hanging in the air, like thought bubbles in cartoons or dialog in comic books. These notes will be provided to you by an advanced artificial intelligence called Einstein, which is like Siri in your phone"—I look at Mom—"or Cortana in yours"—I look at my uncle—"only a thousand times more versatile and way smarter. By the way, Mom, Einstein was designed by my friend Mitya. You remember him, right?"

"Yes, I do," Mom says in Russian, and I see the grateful smile she adopts when her memory works like it should. "He's such a good boy and a wunderkind to boot."

"If you say so," I say, feeling a pang of jealousy at my mom's unabashed admiration for my friend. Though she thinks very highly of my mental capabilities, Mom is biased toward people whose work results in actual products. She calls them "doers." As a result, she admires software wizards like Ada and Mitya, since she can see the apps they write. Because I merely invest money in companies, I'm not a doer and thus don't make her as proud. Never mind that without me, a lot of doers wouldn't get their ideas into the market at all.

"You didn't see the debauchery your good boy Mitya partook in at MIT," I tell her, then stop, realizing I almost incriminated myself. Mom might correctly deduce that as Mitya's former roommate, I was also involved in said debauchery.

"Everyone does something stupid in American colleges," Mom says, not missing a chance to brag about her personal experience with this venerable institution. "Now can we please get back to explaining what's happening in my head?"

"Right," I say. "At first, you'll have extra information about everything around you, consisting mostly of notes on new people you meet or new places you visit. It won't be that different from me walking around with you, giving you reminders. Of course, we wouldn't give you Brainocytes just for this phase, since special glasses or contact lenses can be used for this type of memory assist. Another company my fund's invested in is actually aiming to do just that. But Phase Two takes things in a far more interesting direction, one that can only be achieved with Brainocytes."

"We're ready," Ada says excitedly. "Just waiting for JC to join us."

The door opens, and JC prances in.

"I always thought CEOs were like the devil," Ada tells him. "I was just talking about you, and here you are."

I inwardly smile. JC's lucky Ada isn't Russian, since the equivalent of "speak of the devil" in Russia is "remember the shit, and here it is."

"Hello, Adeline," JC says, using Ada's full name as a small retaliation.

Ada hides her face behind the screen, but I can tell JC won this round. Ada hates her full name almost as much as she loves her nickname. The latter honors her namesake, the Countess of Lovelace. Ada Lovelace designed the first-ever algorithm for a mechanical computer that

Charles Babbage was planning. The machine was called the Analytical Engine, but sadly, Babbage didn't actually build it, so the historical Ada never saw her programs run on it.

JC ignores Ada and gives my mom a creepy smile that, combined with his red hair and rounded face, makes him look like a lecherous leprechaun. Well, the smile is creepy in my opinion. Mom glows in response, so as icky as it seems to me, she appears to like it. Again.

In his late forties or early fifties, JC is the oldest employee at Techno, a place where some people call me, a thirty-five-year-old guy, "sir." But his age isn't why JC is the CEO. He's the CEO because he has an uncanny knack for motivating the people around him. JC's weapon of choice is getting folks as excited about technology as he is, a technique that doesn't work on Ada because she doesn't think JC is excited enough—which, compared to her, he isn't. I wonder if Ada would make a better CEO because of that. Not that she would want the job; she doesn't like managing people. Just getting her to lead a team of super-bright software engineers was an epic effort that required bribes and pleading.

"Your name is JC, isn't it?" Mom says.

"Yes. May I call you Nina, then?" JC walks up to her and touches her IV-free elbow.

"Please do," Mom says.

Maybe it's me, but her remembering him when she forgets most other people makes JC look smug, and I'm tempted to tell him my mom's favorite saying about men:

"To a Russian woman, a man needs to be only slightly more attractive than a gorilla."

"Can we please start Phase One?" Ada asks.

Interesting. Ada interrupted this weird exchange. Maybe that means I'm seeing things that aren't there? Ada is no expert when it comes to social interactions, but she isn't rude. If she noticed older people flirting, she wouldn't have intruded. She must not have picked up on the same vibes.

"If Nina is ready," JC says, "I think that's a great idea."

"I'm ready," Mom says.

JC nods at her solemnly and walks over to stand next to Ada.

I get up from the couch and join them.

"Okay, when I press this button"—Ada brushes her finger against the Enter key—"Phase One will begin."

"Do it," Mom says and closes her eyes.

Ada's finger dramatically hovers above the key for one long moment. Then she presses the button with a flourish.

CHAPTER FOUR

Mom opens her eyes and blinks so fast I wonder if she's trying to communicate in Morse code.

At first, the screen displays only static.

As Ada frantically types on the keyboard, the picture becomes clearer. Soon after, I see a ghostly outline of the room from Mom's point of view.

"This part will be encrypted shortly," Ada says to no one in particular. "For now, it'll help us get an idea of what Nina sees."

I make out shapes that correspond with the people in the room. Since this is Mom's neural data we're looking at, I half expect to look taller and handsomer—and maybe even have a halo over my head—but I'm just a shapeless blob, same as everyone else on the screen. I think that's from our algorithms, though, and not my mom's true perception of me.

The metadata shows up next to the shapes, just like the thought bubbles I expected. I don't know about Mom, but I find these bubbles helpful. They make me recall the names of a few of the shyer engineers in the room.

Mom attempts to remove the brain-scanning contraption from her head as she looks around. Uncle Abe rushes in to help her. Some of the nearby monitors go berserk, but no one seems worried about it.

"This is so weird." She waves her hand next to where her brother's nametag data must be. "I feel like the Terminator."

Uncle Abe helps Mom gain a greater range of motion by removing more monitoring equipment.

"Can I change what these subtitles say?" Mom asks after a few seconds. "Can some of them be in Russian?"

"You'll have to learn how to use the mental computer interface first," Ada says. "That's something we'll work on for the rest of the day." When Mom frowns, she adds, "If you want to change a couple of them manually right now, you can. In fact, it'll give us a small head start since we were going to have you type on a keyboard during the interface portion anyway. Let's remove that IV and the rest of the gear so you can be more comfortable."

"I'll go get the nurse," Uncle Abe says. "It's safe to take all this stuff off, right?"

"Quite safe," JC says. "Most of that equipment is meant to collect data for us, but we have a dozen more subjects to go. We'd need to remove all those devices to take the brain scans in a few minutes anyway. Besides, the Brainocytes are now collecting the most important data."

When my uncle leaves, Ada tells Mom, "We'll teach you how to keep your Einstein database up to date. It uses face and voice recognition technology, and it'll know when you meet someone for the first time. From there, you'll learn how to store a new person's information. Relatedly, for future phases of your treatment, your Brainocytes will start monitoring your brain activity at crucial moments, such as when you interact with people you know well. Should your condition worsen, the Brainocytes will help your brain by recreating these healthier brain states when you meet that person again."

"She means you won't just see text, but also feel the right feelings," I chime in.

The door opens, and the nurse, Olga, lumbers in, followed by my uncle.

She frees Mom from the IV, the blood pressure monitor, and all the other medical equipment. With a lack of curiosity bordering on the pathological, the nurse once again leaves the room.

Mom shuffles over to the monitor.

"Here," JC says. "Touch the text box you want to edit and type in your custom information."

"Wait," Ada says. "If she's going to use the keyboard anyway, why don't I start the BCI learning algorithm?"

"We won't gain much by capturing these few keystrokes," JC says, "but go ahead if you want."

Ada's fingers dance over the keyboard, something pings, and she gives Mom a thumbs-up.

Mom proceeds to edit the metadata bubbles.

"That's not funny," Uncle Abe says when he sees the bubble she changed above my head. She replaced "Mike Cohen" with Russian text that roughly translates to, "Dear self. If you ever need this reminder and can no longer recognize Misha, your only son, it's best for everyone if you arrange for yourself to be euthanized."

Above Uncle Abe's head is something similar.

After I read JC's bubble, which says, "Interesting young man," I realize we're literally intruding on Mom's private thoughts.

"When will you turn on the encryption?" I ask Ada.

"Now, actually," Ada says and presses a few keys. When the feed from Mom's vision goes static, she adds, "The data going to Einstein and other servers was already encrypted, so there's nothing to do there."

"You didn't have to do that," Mom says. "If I need to sacrifice my privacy to help with the study, I'm more than happy to do so."

JC and Ada exchange looks. I strong-armed everyone into letting Mom into the study because she's my mom, but I also knew she'd make an outstanding participant—as her willingness to let us spy on her demonstrates. Not that I would've done anything differently had she been the worst patient in the world; when it comes to Mom, filial loyalty trumps all.

"You don't have to do that, Mom," I tell her. "We have a protocol. After the initial setup is complete, we want to make sure the participants enjoy the privacy they deserve."

"Are you ready to work on the BCI?" Ada asks, looking eager to change the subject.

Mom glances at me questioningly, so I decipher the Ada-speak for her. "She means learn how to use your new Brainocytes as a computer interface."

"Right," Ada says. "Though I think Nina understood me." Facing Mom, she says, "To be more specific, you'll work on learning how to type with just your mind. It'll be easy. First, we need the Brainocytes to observe you typing for real for a few hours. Afterwards, you'll learn to type mentally, using your imagination. If all works as planned, my team's algorithm will catch your imaginary keystrokes, since mental actions light up the same parts of the brain as physical actions."

The door opens, and a big, dark-skinned man in scrubs walks in, pushing a wheelchair along.

"I'm here for Nina Cohen," he says.

"That's me," Mom says.

"You're scheduled for an MRI," the guy explains and steers the chair toward her.

Mom leans away and says, "I'm not getting into that."

The guy looks confused.

"She can walk to the MRI," I tell him. "You can leave the chair here. Will that be a problem?"

"No," the guy says, "but Dr. Carter said—"

"Such an overly litigious country," Mom cuts in. "These doctors like to cover their asses to the point of insanity." She stubbornly folds her arms and gets up. "I won't be a part of this foolishness. Please lead the way, young man."

The guy folds the wheelchair and leaves it by the wall. Under his breath, he mutters, "Okay, but the doc said to use the chair."

"When will she be back?" I ask the guy.

"In about an hour and a half," he says.

"Do you want anything to eat afterwards?" I ask Mom.

"A turkey sandwich," she responds, "with extra mayo."

"You got it," I say and suppress a smile at the look on Ada's face. I could've predicted she'd cringe at Mom's food choice.

Mom and her disgruntled guide exit into the corridor.

"A sandwich sounds good," my uncle says. "Especially one with extra mayo."

Ada takes this one in stride. I guess she's more invested in my mom's health.

"Anyone else hungry?" I ask, looking around the room. "I'm buying."

Pretty much everyone takes me up on the offer, supporting my theory that most people—even if they're fasting or on a strict diet—will gladly gobble down free food.

When we get to the cafeteria, I realize the staff in Mom's room must've texted or emailed the majority of the other Techno employees, because most of them are here. Grinning, I extend my offer of a free lunch to them as well.

Grabbing a tray, I pull my uncle along and stand behind Ada.

She loads her tray with a salad, an apple, two bananas, and a heap of steamed vegetables.

Uncle Abe gives her tray a dubious onceover. "What about meat and bread?"

JC chuckles, and I fight a smile of my own. For the second time today, my uncle is about to regret his question.

To Ada's credit, this particular optimum nutrition lecture is the shortest one I've heard her deliver. It only takes her a couple of minutes.

"So the easiest formula," Ada concludes, "is to maximize your micronutrient intake while eating as few calories as possible. The best route to that is whole, unprocessed, plant-based foods."

My uncle demonstrates how little Ada's spiel influenced him by getting a very processed and not very plant-based ham sandwich. He believes in the Russian proverb that states, "Bread is the head of everything," and worships meat to the point that ham is probably enshrined in his kitchen.

As I make my own selections, I wonder why Ada decided to trim down her pitch. Is she finally learning to adjust to her audience? She didn't even go into her reasons for eating this way—reasons that have little to do with vanity. She wants to maximize her lifespan so she can, and I quote from having heard this a dozen times, "catch as many transformative paradigm shifts in technology as possible and, hopefully, live long enough to catch mind uploading."

Ada's nutrient logic must've rubbed off on me, because my meal contains half the calories I might've chosen otherwise. I also get Mom's extra mayo in packets instead of slathered on the bread. This way, Mom can decide for herself how junky she wants her meal, leaving my conscience somewhat clean.

We sit down and start eating. Inevitably, the conversation returns to the topic of Brainocytes, and Ada says,

"As much as I try, the implications of this technology are difficult to wrap my head around."

"If it's hard for you, imagine what it's like for us mere mortals," I say.

"We can help so many people," JC says, his green eyes shining fervently in his freckled face. "We can restore vision to the blind, hearing to the deaf, and memory to those who've lost it."

"All wonderful, but just scratching the surface of what's possible," Ada says. "Eventually, we'll be able to take a regular person and enhance the very thing that makes us human—intelligence, memory, empathy. Can you imagine the impact on the world if much smarter human beings populated the planet?"

JC bites into his burger, Twix-commercial style. Like me, he knows and understands Ada's transhumanist views. I agree with some of them, as do three quarters of Techno employees. JC probably also agrees, but he doesn't like these ideas bandied around in front of laymen. According to him, talking about human enhancements is bad for business, thanks largely to Hollywood's obsession with cautionary tales about human hubris.

"Fine, if you want to keep things prosaic," Ada says, "just the virtual and augmented realities alone could revolutionize the entertainment and educational systems. Once people start seeing the internet in their minds and watching movies and playing video games in their heads, the daily life of the average person will be unlike anything in history."

"Right," JC says. "We'll turn into a completely self-centered society. I can't wait."

"You're wrong," Ada says, though she knows JC likes to play devil's advocate. "When text and email will be done in people's heads, we'll end up with technology that's indistinguishable from telepathy. Being able to communicate through thought will connect the human race more than ever before. Though all that is short term. Having this unprecedented look inside the brain will lead to—"

"—brain simulations," I say, imitating her voice. "Which will lead to better AI and brain uploading."

"Which will also lead to fear," JC picks up, though his voice sounds like Yoda's instead of Ada's. "Which will lead to anger, which will lead to hate, which will lead to suffering, and all this leads to the dark side of the Force."

"That's not the exact quote," Ada says, and I have no doubt she's right. She has an eidetic memory when it comes to pop culture references.

Everyone except my uncle laughs at JC's joke, but it's nervous laughter. They all know this work really *is* scary to some people. This is why JC wants to keep the focus on correcting debilitating conditions for the time being. Even the worst luddites wouldn't deny Alzheimer's patients the chance at living a normal life, or quadriplegics the ability to control their environment, or blind people their vision. But as soon as the topic veers into Ada's favorite territory, improvement of normal function, things get thornier.

My uncle's pocket rings.

He gives us an apologetic look before taking out his phone and glancing at the screen. Whatever he sees there makes him frown. Getting up, he explains, "It's my son. I have to take it. Misha, I'll meet you in Nina's room."

With that, he walks away from our table. As someone who knows his son, I shudder and mentally wish Uncle Abe good luck.

The rest of us talk shop for the remainder of the meal, and I learn that Mrs. Sanchez is the next person scheduled to get Phase One enabled. We all know how little this first phase will help her, so the plan is to expedite her treatment and see if the phase that simulates missing brain function will help her more. Ada says she wants to oversee the beginning stages of this, so I volunteer to join her, in part to prove that I do care about the other participants, but also because I don't have to fake it. Given Mrs. Sanchez's situation, I genuinely do care about her.

Like Mom, the reason she's in this study is because of me. In fact, her life was affected by the same event as my mom's—that fateful car accident. Mom doesn't remember what happened, so I had to read about the crash online and in police reports. That's how I learned that a mentally unstable man was waltzing across the Belt Parkway highway. Mom hit the brakes in an effort to spare his life, and she succeeded in that. Unfortunately, she traded hitting the man for hitting the metal curb. What's even worse is that an SUV swerved to avoid colliding with Mom's car.

It was Mrs. Sanchez's son, daughter-in-law, and two grandchildren in the SUV. Instead of hitting the guardrail on the left, their car went down the hill on the right side and flipped multiple times. They all died, but the poor woman, Mrs. Sanchez, still doesn't truly know this. Her Alzheimer's was already in full swing by that time, and the tragic news about her family doesn't register when someone informs her of what happened. The problem with *not* informing her, however, is that she repeatedly asks for her son and his family. She's a widow, so after the accident, the only family she had left was an older brother who passed away a few months ago. I've been paying her bills ever since, and when I got the chance, I convinced JC to include her in the study despite her poor health.

"Let's get Mrs. Sanchez something that's safe for her diabetes," I suggest.

Ada gives me an evaluating look. "She likes her junk food, so that'll be tricky."

"We'll get something healthy and something fried, but only show her the healthy choices first," I say. "We used to do this with Grandpa."

"Sounds like a great plan," JC says. "You two go do that, and the rest of us will run ahead."

I get up, and Ada follows.

"It *is* a good idea," Ada says. "Why don't I get the healthy choices and you get the rest?"

"Sure," I say.

"Just don't get her anything with too many carbs," Ada warns. "She could go into a coma."

"Deal," I say and walk back over to the tray line. "We'll drop off Mom's sandwich in her room on the way."

"This tastes like hospital food," Mrs. Sanchez complains as she eats Ada's healthier choices.

It *is* hospital food, but since Mrs. Sanchez doesn't recall where she is and hates hospitals on top of that, I see no need to remind her. She'll realize she's in a hospital when she looks in the mirror and sees her outfit, which is the same white hospital gown Mom was wearing earlier today.

Making a face, Mrs. Sanchez looks at Ada. "Are you sure they didn't have ice cream?"

"I'm sure," I lie. "But they did have Jell-O."

If I left the answer up to Ada, she might've blurted out the truth. She's almost pathologically honest, a bit like young George Washington, though I have my doubts about him. In Russia, we have an identical story about a young kid never telling a lie, only in that version, it was Lenin, the communist revolutionary leader.

"Is the Jell-O sugar-free?" Mrs. Sanchez's kind, chubby face twists in disgust at the very idea of sugar substitutes.

"No," I lie again. "So don't eat too much of it."

The real reason I said she shouldn't have too much Jell-O is because Ada might have an aneurism from watching Mrs. Sanchez eat something chock-full of aspartame, or whatever the name of the "evil" artificial sweetener is in Jell-O.

When Mrs. Sanchez tastes her gelatinous treat, she rubs her lips questioningly, and I'm ready for her to catch me in another lie, the way she did with the soda earlier. In that case, she got suspicious because Ada had peeled off the label; misleading someone doesn't count as lying in Ada's book. Fortunately, Mrs. Sanchez doesn't say anything this time and continues consuming her Jell-O.

I study Mrs. Sanchez as she eats, and worry overcomes me again. She and Mom are the same height and age and have similar apple-shaped body types. According to Ada, this increases my mom's risk of diabetes. Sure enough, Mom's sugar has been creeping up. Sooner or later, I might have to unleash the full wrath of Ada's dietary philosophy on her in the hopes that she starts eating healthier—unless the Brainocytes can be used to curb cravings?

While I'm pondering that, a nurse comes in carrying a syringe and a tray of food.

"Didn't Mrs. Sanchez already get her Brainocytes injection?" I whisper to Ada, then realize the syringe is too small.

"She did," Ada replies. "This is probably her insulin."

"Oh, good. You're already eating," the nurse says to the older woman and nods gratefully at Ada. "I'll be back in a few minutes to give you your insulin."

Mrs. Sanchez looks as excited at the prospect of getting a shot as a toddler would. She nervously twists her giant emerald ring, a treasured gift from her older brother, who, shortly before his death, gave her a much better gift in the form of his consent for her participation in this study. I hope the ring doesn't make her ask about her brother again—a topic as painful for her as the inquiries about the rest of her family.

My phone vibrates, and I see it's a text from Uncle Abe telling me my mom is back from her MRI. I want to hurry back, but I decide to stick around a little longer.

"If it's your mom, you should go," Ada says, and to my shock, she gently brushes her fingers against my elbow.

"My minions are working on the BCI with her, and it'll be useful if someone with a brain is there."

Ada is a Team Lead for the software developers at Techno, and she refers to them as minions, even to their faces. Contrary to Ada's statement, they have more than enough brains and are paid triple what they'd earn at a hedge fund, the usual path for New York experts of their caliber.

"Good luck, Mrs. Sanchez," I say. "I hope this treatment helps you in the long run."

Mrs. Sanchez nods, and I head over to Mom's room.

As I walk through the white corridors, I pass the rooms occupied by the other participants. I continue to Mom's room without stopping because I want to catch her before she finishes her lunch.

"Hi, kitten," Mom says in English. Though her English is good, sometimes she overlooks certain subtleties, like the fact that this literal translation of what sounds cute in Russian comes off as fairly emasculating in English.

David, one of Ada's brightest minions and a second-generation Russian immigrant himself, gives me a sympathetic smirk.

Mom is sitting on the couch with a keyboard on her lap, so it looks like she's done with lunch after all.

"Your uncle left," she says, "and you should go too. David tells me I'll be typing for hours and learning how to control an imaginary dot for the rest of the day after that."

"That's nonsense, Mom. I'm not going anywhere."

"Surely you have some important business to deal with? Or a girl to take out?"

"If you insist, I'll check in with my secretary and maybe read up on some companies on my phone later," I say, knowing if I don't give in to this Jewish mom business of "don't worry about me" at least a little, she'll keep it up for a while. Besides, my mom is right. A multibillion-dollar fund doesn't run itself. As good as my analysts are, I still have to vet all investment ideas, not to mention deal with the investors. I cleared my schedule to be with my mom for this treatment, but there's always work to be done.

"Good," she says and picks up her keyboard. "So, David, what do you need me to do?"

The rest of the day passes the way Mom said it would. Under David's tutelage, she masters the art of typing with her mind. Sometimes, her fingers twitch as though she's really typing, but most of the time, it looks pretty eerie as text shows up on the screen without any outward action. She simply has to imagine herself typing the words.

The "mental mouse" portion of BCI training is a lot trickier for her, but David assures her she's doing well and that she'll have it down in a day or so.

"Why do I have to sleep here?" Mom asks after everyone's done eating dinner.

"Just in case," David says. "Dr. Carter agreed to assist our research on the condition that we take every safety precaution."

"I haven't even met this Dr. Carter," Mom says, "but when I do, I'll give him a piece of my mind."

She has met him, and I know because I was there. She actually gave him more than a piece of her mind, which is probably why he stayed away today.

"It'll be fine, Mom. I'll be around if you need me. Everything will be fine."

"You're not staying in the hospital." Mom takes her ultimatum stance, planting her hands on her hips. "If you stay here, I'll leave, Dr. Carter or not."

"I won't stay in the hospital," I say, knowing this is a fight I can't win. "But I'll be here first thing in the morning."

Mom considers this for a moment, then shows her approval by removing her hands from her hips.

What I left unsaid is that I'll be nearby. I booked a room at the HGU Hotel so I'll be within walking distance, just in case something goes wrong tonight. If Mom knew this, she'd be upset, especially since I booked the six-hundred-dollars per night King Suite, the only room they had available on short notice. Though she knows I make insanely large sums of money, she can't turn off her legitimate concern over finances, a response she developed when we first moved to the United States. Since I was thirteen then, I didn't internalize the situation as much as she did. I understand her feelings on the matter, though. We came to the US as refugees with a few hundred dollars in savings, if that. Between the help from Uncle Abe, who let us stay with his family in the beginning, the special immigrant-aid program called NYANA, and the very generous help from the American welfare system, we had just enough to survive while we got settled. Eventually, though, Mom felt uneasy about receiving "government charity" and found a home attendant job on Brighton Beach. Juggling English lessons and a Bachelor's degree with her grueling job must've been a nightmare. I still can't believe she went through it all. To me, the idea of picking up my stuff and moving to a place where I don't speak the language and don't know anyone or anything—say, Spain or Japan—is unthinkably frightening.

What's even more impressive is that Mom essentially did it for me. Besides the possibility of new pogroms, Mom's biggest fear was the looming prospect of me getting drafted into the nightmarish institution that was the army in the former USSR. It was a place where being Jewish would've made the already horrific hazing practices borderline deadly. I'm glad I didn't have to go through that. The NYC public school system isn't the army, but the bullying I experienced there has led me to believe I have very little tolerance for humiliation and pain.

My reminiscing is interrupted by a pair of guys who wheel in a bed for Mom to sleep in. David and the rest of the Techno peeps take this as their cue to leave for the day.

I stay for a bit to chat with Mom about anything she might've been embarrassed to bring up in front of strangers. When she demonstratively yawns for the fifth time, I get up, kiss her cheek, and say in Russian, "Bye, Mom. I'll see you in the morning."

"Yes," she responds with a yawn. "Morning is wiser than evening."

"Indeed it is." I smile at her and leave.

When I make my way down to the first floor of the hospital, I consider moving my car from the hospital parking lot to the hotel. I decide against it, since the hotel probably has valet service, meaning I'd have to wait to get my car if

I needed it in a hurry. Besides, I'm just three measly blocks away, and the hospital has better security.

It's a new development, me worrying about a car. I was never into cars, and I'm still not, but I've grown to love mine, even though it started off as a joke. My car's nickname is Zapo, short for Zaporozhets, in honor of a horrific Soviet-era car my grandpa was constantly lying under and repairing when I was growing up.

Zapo isn't an authentic recreation of that ugly car, of course. In terms of energy efficiency, they're actually polar opposites. I'd say they're spiritually connected by their fugly exterior designs. Zapo is a Prius, but the inside is modified so drastically that it cost me almost as much as an entry-level Bentley. Additionally, Zapo has a beta prototype of the Einstein navigational system that Poisk, Mitya's company, is working on, plus other mods and an engine that would make the cars from *The Fast and the Furious* jealous. I half-jokingly call Zapo my "super-expensive gold-digger repellent."

Exiting the large automated doors, I turn onto 30th Street and spot Ada trying to hail a cab without any success.

Now I'm truly glad I didn't decide to drive. I rarely get a chance to talk to Ada outside of work.

When she sees me, she lowers her arm and says, "David emailed me about Nina's day so far. She looks to be the furthest along. I'm very pleased we're making such swift progress."

"You can take most of the credit for this," I say. "You and your minions wrote such an intuitive user interface that even my grandpa would've mastered it—and he had trouble working the VCR."

"Everyone had trouble with those clunky VCRs," she says, but I can tell she likes the praise. I think she's even blushing, and I've never seen her blush.

"Do you want to stay at the hotel with me?" I ask. Her eyes widen, and I realize what I just said. "I mean, in the same hotel as me. In a separate room."

"Right." Her shock turns into a grin so wide her eyes almost close. "I'm sure that wasn't a Freudian slip."

My face feels hot enough to cook an egg on. Trying to lessen how foolish I look, I say, "I just pictured you schlepping all the way back to Williamsburg and wanted to offer a better alternative."

"I get that, and thank you, but I can't," she says. "I have to feed my rats."

"Your what?" I ask, wondering if it's possible to mistake the *c* in cats for the *r* in rats.

"I adopted a bunch of rats once they weren't needed for experiments anymore," Ada explains. "A lot of the Techno folks did. My cuties aren't as needy as a bunch of dogs, but I can't *not* show up without notice or setting up a long-term feeder for them. Plus, it's bath day today, and they love it so much. Rain check?"

"Sure," I say. Would it be impolite to ask her how many rats she actually owns and how many it would take for her to qualify as a rat lady? "I'll put you up in a hotel room of my choice some other day then."

We look at each other and laugh.

Ada sees a cab in the distance and waves at it. The cabby stops in front of us, and I hold the yellow car door open for her. "I'll see you tomorrow at nine, right?"

"Yeah," she says, getting inside the cab. "I'll check on Mrs. Sanchez first, and then go to your mom's room. I'm sure we'll get to Phase Two with her, and I'm excited."

"Yeah, me too," I say and shut the door.

On the way to my hotel room, I wonder if it was just my imagination, or if Ada was a little friendlier toward me. For a few months now, Ada's been acting a bit distant around me. Since the start of this behavior coincided with when my ex dumped me, I figure Ada is just dreading the uncomfortable conversation where I ask her out and she has to turn me down. Since our working relationship is hard to define—as a major investor in Techno, I'm someone her boss, JC, answers to—I've been wary about pursuing anything. Not only am I sensitive about the issue of workplace sexual harassment, but Ada is the most irreplaceable person on the Brainocytes project. I knew she was bright when she first joined Techno, but around the time she started growing distant, I noticed how much of a genius she truly is. Maybe it's my infatuation goggles at work, but the leaps she's singlehandedly made with the Brainocytes software shaved off at least six months of work from the project.

I think about Ada on and off for the rest of the evening. As I fall asleep, I decide that once the study is complete, I will ask her out, consequences be damned.

CHAPTER FIVE

I walk down the hospital corridor, munching on an egg-and-cheese croissant. In my free hand, I'm holding a bag with a breakfast sandwich for Mom, oatmeal for Ada, and a diabetes-safe omelet for Mrs. Sanchez.

Figuring I'll leave Mrs. Sanchez's food with her, I make my way to her room.

When I enter, I realize I'm the first one here and look at my watch. It's 8:50 a.m., a little before the usual workday starts, even for a bunch of workaholics like the folks at Techno.

Then something odd becomes apparent. Though it looked like Mrs. Sanchez was in her bed at first, she actually isn't.

I look around the room as though she might be hiding behind all the hardware in the back.

Obviously, she isn't here.

I exit the room and bump straight into Ada.

"Hey," I say. "Do you know where Mrs. Sanchez is?"

"She should be in her room." Ada looks at Mrs. Sanchez's door. "She isn't?"

"Excuse me," an unfamiliar nurse says, approaching the door. "I need to get through."

"Are you here to see Mrs. Sanchez?" I ask, not moving out of the nurse's way.

"Yes," she says. "I'm here to give her her insulin."

"She's not in her room," I say. "I was just there."

The nurse looks at me doubtfully, so I ask, "Do you have any idea where she could be?"

"She's supposed to be in her room," the nurse says.

"Could she be in the bathroom?" I ask.

"The nearest one is in her room," Ada says and goes into the room.

"If she left the room to use the bathroom, it's two doors down," the nurse says.

I head down the corridor and find the bathroom empty.

When I get back, Ada and the nurse are walking toward me.

"She's not in the room bathroom," Ada says.

"And she isn't in the one down the hall," I respond.

"She couldn't have wandered off too far," the nurse says. "They would've spotted a patient at the nurses' stations at each end of the floor."

"Maybe she walked into one of the nearby rooms?" I ask.

The nurse shrugs.

"Why don't you go check," I suggest. "Ada and I will make sure Mrs. Sanchez didn't somehow join one of the other participants in our study."

The nurse leaves, and Ada and I split up to search the rooms of the two nearest participants.

I enter Mr. Shafer's room.

He isn't in his bed.

I check the bathroom and find it empty.

On a whim, I walk up to the bed and touch it.

The scratchy, over-starched hospital sheets are still warm. Wherever Mr. Shafer went, he left recently.

Ada is waiting for me in the corridor, looking worried.

"Mrs. Stevens is gone too." Ada runs her fingers through her bleached Mohawk.

"So is Mr. Shafer. Maybe it's something JC organized? Maybe he's giving a lecture or something to the whole group? Or maybe Dr. Carter—"

"No," Ada says. "I would've been notified if someone from Techno had planned anything. I don't see how Dr. Carter could be behind this; he clears everything with JC. Besides, he knows Mrs. Sanchez needs her insulin."

I consider her words carefully and find no flaw in her logic. There's no reason these three participants should be missing from their rooms. If only one person was missing, especially Mr. Shafer, we could maybe brush it off as him going for a walk despite us explicitly telling him not to. That the relatively sedentary Mrs. Stevens is also missing is a lot stranger, since she wouldn't go for a walk to literally extend her life. And the fact that Mrs. Sanchez, with her foot problem, is also gone pushes this incident firmly into the realm of the impossibly anomalous.

My mind leaps to another thought. Are the others missing as well? Though it's not completely rational, my gut turns into tundra-like permafrost, and I quickly say, "Check on the others. I'm going to Mom's room."

Hoping I'll feel like a paranoid fool in a minute, I sprint down the corridor and stab the elevator button with my finger.

The elevator doesn't instantly open, so I dump the food I'm still holding into a nearby garbage bin and punch the button again.

Then I notice the elevator has a light indicating where the car is, and that happens to be on the fifteenth floor. The number changes to fourteen far too slowly, so I decide to run down the two floors instead of waiting.

The staircase is musty. It probably doesn't get used much. I whoosh down, trying not to inhale too much stale air as I take the stairs two at a time.

When I exit the staircase, I get strange looks from the nurses at their station. Ignoring them, I zoom down the corridor.

My breath is ragged by the time I reach Mom's room. As I twist the handle, I will Mom to be there, going so far as picturing her reaction to seeing me disheveled and out of breath.

Cracking the door open, I'm confronted with a bizarre view.

Mom is sitting in a wheelchair, eyes closed as though she's asleep.

She's being wheeled by a guy I've never seen before—though now that I have, I won't soon forget him. The hands holding the wheelchair handles are covered in tattoos, as is all the skin peeking out from under his scrubs. With his nearly seven-foot bulky build, protruding forehead, and quarter-pounder jaw, he's living proof that humans are closely related to apes, and maybe even bison.

"Where are you taking her?" I ask loudly, hoping they'll hear me at the nurses' station. "Who are—"

I register a whirlwind of movement, and a tattooed fist crashes into my cheekbone. The shock of pain sends me reeling, and the playing cards tattooed on the ape-bison's knuckles dance in my vision as the world starts to fade.

CHAPTER SIX

Fighting unconsciousness, I attempt to curl my hands into fists.

All I accomplish is gaining enough self-awareness to feel an oversized arm grab me and throw me.

My back slams into a small table, and air wisely decides to vacate my lungs. Gasping, I slide down. Junk clatters on the floor around me, releasing the powerful stench of medicine.

With a monumental effort of will, I struggle to not pass out.

The ape-bison guy slams the door shut behind him.

I keep gasping for air and fighting for lucidity.

Pushing up with shaking hands, I wonder if this is how boxers feel when they try standing after getting knocked down. If so, why didn't they pick another profession? For me, this decides it here and now: I'd prefer a career as anything else, even a politician, to that of a boxer.

Slowly, I gather my legs under me. I figure the boxing referee would've counted to nine by now.

Fighting nausea, I tentatively put weight on my jelly-like legs. Instantly, vertigo seizes me, and I fall on all fours, losing my breakfast on the floor. In a detached manner, I wonder why I've never heard of a boxer throwing up during a match. On a positive note, despite the acidic taste in my mouth, I feel a minuscule dose of relief.

Struggling to my feet again, I stumble toward the door. By the time I grasp the doorknob, I feel like I've regained some rudimentary hand-eye coordination.

When I exit the room and look around, I see my attacker at the end of the corridor to my right. He's blurry, as though I'm seeing him through a fog—like the hedgehog from the Soviet cartoon of my childhood.

"Stop him," I yell, or try to. The sound comes out raspy and weak. Worse, the attempted yell messes with my already unsteady breathing.

Holding on to the wall as I stumble forward, I will my breath to stabilize.

When I feel like I can survive expending the air, I yell, "Stop that guy!"

This time, my voice carries better, but I hear the elevator doors *ding* at the end of the hall.

My adrenal glands go into overdrive, and I jerkily increase my pace.

A nurse looks up at me from her desk. "Are you okay? Why are you screaming?"

Unable to yell again, I close the distance between us and choke out, "That large man with a wheelchair?"

"He got into the elevator before you started yelling," the nurse confirms. "What's going on?"

"Call the police," I gasp. "Someone kidnapped my mother, Nina Cohen."

The look on the nurse's face reminds me of a squirrel facing a bicyclist in Central Park.

I don't stop to calm her down and stagger toward the elevator.

One car is on the twentieth floor, while the other is already on the ninth.

I quickly assess my options. I can summon the elevator, or I can walk down. It's nearly nine in the morning, and I don't know if that means the rush hour for the elevators has begun, especially when it comes to going down. On the other hand, am I in any condition to attempt the stairs?

I punch both buttons and turn toward the stairwell, figuring I'll go down to the next floor before making a decision. If I can't get down on foot, at least I summoned the elevators closer to the floor below.

"You're bleeding," the nurse yells when I'm halfway through the door. "You should let me—"

Whatever she said I'll never know, because the door closes behind me as I begin my descent.

I'm feeling slightly better, though I suspect it's from the adrenaline. I can't take the stairs two at a time like I did a few minutes ago, but at least I don't stumble and I can let go of the handrail once in a while.

When I get to the eleventh floor, I'm still not sure whether I'll be better off taking the elevator. I hurry to the door and stick my head out. One elevator is on the fifth floor, and the other made it all the way to the twelfth. I decide it's definitely worth the wait and jab my finger against the elevator button, wishing it were the ape-bison's eye socket.

Milliseconds stretch into ages, and I decide to multitask so I won't go crazy. I command Einstein in my nifty phone to dial Ada before I even take it out of my pocket.

"Mike," Ada shouts as soon as the call connects. "I didn't find a single participant. I'm talking to JC right now, and he has no clue—"

"Someone's kidnapped them," I blurt out. "I saw a man taking my mom. Call the police. I'll try to get you more information."

"Wait, who—"

The elevator doors open, and I rush inside, ignoring the call for the moment.

I have a new choice to make. What floor do I press? Given the wheelchair the guy had my mom in, and since Ada said everyone else is missing too, I can only assume the kidnapper is putting all the participants in a large vehicle, maybe even a bus. Given Manhattan rush-hour traffic and hospital zoning rules, it's safe to assume he wouldn't park near the front doors. No, doing something as nefarious as loading unconscious people into a vehicle is best done in the relative privacy of the parking lot. Thus decided, I press the basement-floor button. There could be flaws in my logic or other variables I'm missing, like they, whoever "they" are, might have an ambulance or diplomatic plates, but I have to act on my best guess.

The doors close, and my call disconnects.

I keep my thumb on the close-door button as the elevator starts moving. Supposedly, holding this button will make the elevator travel without stopping, an express feature designed for emergency personnel. When I first heard this, I didn't really believe it and was never selfish enough, or in a big enough rush, to test it. I do know that pressing the close-door button doesn't shut the doors any faster and might just act as a placebo, like those walk buttons at pedestrian crossings in NYC.

The elevator crawls past the tenth floor, then the ninth. I look at the door's reflective surface and see the nurse was right. My shirt is covered in blood. Fortunately, most of the blood is from a nosebleed. I've been prone to nosebleeds since I was a kid, and I've learned not to worry about them. At MIT, I used to get nosebleeds from the dry air caused by the dorm's central air system. Mitya, my then roommate, used to tease me about it, saying the reason I get so many nosebleeds is because I have such a large schnoz. I'd retort that big noses are considered a sign of virility in many cultures and that they also accurately correlate with a certain part of a man's anatomy, similar to shoe and hand sizes.

Besides the blood, the right side of my face has a bruise so big I think it might develop a few bruises of its own. On the plus side, the nausea has subsided, or maybe I'm just getting used to it. Overall, the pain in my body has gone from agonizingly burning to unpleasantly pulsing.

I pass the fifth floor without stopping and start thinking the elevator might make it all the way down without interruption. Is this trick with the close-door button actually true? Or is everyone coming to the hospital at this hour going up? Whatever the cause, I hope this continues.

I pass the fourth floor, then the third. When the elevator passes the second floor, I let go of the button and all my muscles tense, ready for action.

As soon as the door opens, I try to sprint but end up staggering out of the elevator. Ignoring the returning lightheadedness, I hurry toward Zapo and look around.

I don't see anything, but I do hear a large-vehicle engine starting in the distance.

Fishing my car keys out of my pocket, I press the Start Engine button that was originally meant to warm up my car in the winter.

Most Priuses start so quietly I wouldn't be able to hear my car from where I'm standing, but Zapo isn't a typical Prius. I can make out its tricked-out engine quite distinctly.

I also hear the sound of screeching tires from the same place I heard the other vehicle's engine start.

Picking up speed, I swallow my heart back into my chest and say to both the AI on my phone and in the car, "Einstein, I'll be driving on manual."

"You asked me to remind you to never drive drunk or tired," says Einstein's voice. For the sake of understandability, the AI's German accent is subtler than the one the famous physicist actually possessed.

I fight the urge to curse at the AI, as that would simply waste valuable seconds. Besides, worrying about my safety *is* something I usually want Einstein to do; it's just that today, it would be better if Einstein were smart enough to worry about my mom instead, a task that's still too generic for Einstein to tackle, no matter how much I anthropo-morphize the AI by calling it a "he."

At least, as always, Einstein saves me a few precious seconds by pulling my car out of its parking spot and slid-ing the door up. Yes, Zapo's door opens vertically, like the DeLorean from *Back to the Future*.

"I'm not drunk or tired," I say as I leap inside. "I'm in a big rush."

Before I can get a lecture, I buckle up.

"According to my settings, you also asked me to be wary of you being in a rush," Einstein says.

A cartoony version of the famous old man with fluffy white hair shows up on the large dashboard screen and looks at me with carefully calculated grandfatherly con-cern.

"Activate manual drive," I demand. "This is an emer-gency override. Code red. 911."

One of the code words must work, because Einstein says flatly, "Manual controls activated."

I grab the wheel and slam on the gas pedal.

"The speed limit in this parking lot is eight miles per hour." Einstein stares at me with unblinking disapproval from the screen. "You're going twenty-one miles per hour."

"Get used to it," I say, though I know full well he won't. "This is why I needed the emergency override."

"It's not safe." Einstein's white hair seems to get wilder as he frowns. "Please consider slowing down."

I swerve toward the exit, all my focus on catching up with the bigger car I heard.

When I see the parking lot exit a few moments later, I become the first New Yorker in history to be grateful for traffic.

A line of four cars is waiting to leave the lot, and the second from last is a large black minibus I strongly suspect is the vehicle I'm after.

I try to see its license plate, but the Honda behind it is blocking my view. I text Ada what I know about the car so far, typing out, "Tell the cops the perps are driving a Mercedes Metris minibus. I'll text you the license plate number when I have it."

The cars move, so I pull up close to the Honda before clicking send.

"One out of every four car accidents in the United States is caused by texting while driving," Einstein says. As always, his German accent is almost undetectable when he's doing his favorite task—quoting stats.

"I'm not driving now." I try not to sound defensive. "I'm sitting in traffic."

"Texting while driving causes a four-hundred-percent increase in time spent with eyes off the road," Einstein retorts. In many ways, he's just an advanced version of those annoying customer service answering machine AIs, and his arguments can be just as circular.

"What are the statistics of accidents caused by people who are arguing with their navigation systems?" I move forward to take the space created by another car moving up.

"No data," Einstein says.

"I bet once more people have something like you in their cars, those stats will be high." I drum my fingers on the dashboard.

Einstein doesn't argue—yet another bit of proof that he isn't that clever. If he possessed a generalized intelligence, he would've noted that it's him, not me, who usually does the driving, and since an AI can multitask better than I can, no accidents would occur.

When the minibus pulls up to the exit, my whole body tenses and I forget about Einstein. As soon as the Metris starts moving, I do the most dickish parking lot maneuver I've ever done. I floor the gas and circle around the Honda, pulling my nose into the opening the minibus just left.

I can practically hear the woman cursing over her blaring horn, but I don't care. Mom's safety trumps social mores. As soon as the Metris moves a few inches forward, I boldly cut in front of a Crown Vic, following my prey. This time, it's a guy who curses at me, so I keep an eye on him in my rearview mirror. If he's aggravated enough, he might exit his car to start a fight with me, and that's the last thing I need.

The guy doesn't get out, but about a dozen cars behind him join in on the honking, their joint blaring synchronizing with my pounding heartbeat.

Ignoring the noise, I orient myself. This is First Avenue, and all four lanes are jammed. At least I'm right behind the minibus, even if neither of us can move.

I use this chance to text the license plate to Ada. I also consider leaving my car and running up to the Metris. Before I can do so, the cars inch forward. The left lanes are moving a bit more freely, causing everyone from the right lanes to make matters worse by trying to switch over there.

A few cars up, I see the source of the traffic—a double-parked car. I've lived in this city long enough to loathe people who double-park. This particular offender is a Poland Spring water delivery truck, as evidenced by the paint job on the sides and the man wheeling an empty water container into the vehicle.

I've never wished for a cop to appear this badly. First, this imaginary cop would help me stop the kidnappers. Then, once my mom was safe, he'd write this idiot a juicy ticket, since even commercial vehicles aren't allowed to double-park and block traffic in Midtown. Then I remind myself that this Poland Spring guy is why I'm able to follow the minibus, so in a way, he's doing me a favor.

When the Poland Spring truck starts moving, so do all the other cars.

"The speed limit is twenty-five miles per hour," Einstein chimes in.

"That's my speed."

"You're going twenty-six miles per hour," he says.

Since we're approaching an intersection, I ignore the AI and tighten my grip on the wheel.

The Metris turns right onto 34th Street and cuts off three cars as it slots itself into the leftmost of the three available lanes.

Tires screeching, I attempt to duplicate the minibus's rude maneuver and pass a Lexus and a Hyundai. When I screech by a super-aggressive NYC yellow cab, I'm not surprised that the idiot scrapes my bumper. At least the touch is so light it doesn't impede my turn.

"You've been in an accident," Einstein says. "You should pull over."

I contemplate hitting the LCD screen, but figure it's best to just ignore him, especially since the Metris cuts across traffic again to get to the rightmost lane.

I follow him, and we pass by the ever-present orange cones that seem to proliferate in Manhattan. When I spot the nearest green directional sign, my stress level climbs. I can guess why the Metris turned into the rightmost lane. In a few feet, it's going to make a right to get onto the FDR Drive, one of the Manhattan highways. I should've thought of this back in the parking lot—not that it would've helped. Langone Medical Center is right next to the highway, so any kidnappers worth their salt would take advantage of that fact. On some level, I hoped to chase them through the congested streets until we passed a police car. It doesn't matter, though. I'll follow them into the surrounding ocean if I have to.

My knuckles go white on the steering wheel, and my calf muscle tenses as I hit the gas again. In an instant, I catch up to the minibus, and our bumpers nearly kiss.

"We're too close," Einstein whines and blurts out more safety minutia, but I ignore it all because my already hyperactive heart is threatening to jump out of my ribcage, *Alien* style.

In the tinted glass of the Metris's back window, I see the protruding forehead of the ape-bison asshole.

He locks eyes with me and shouts something toward the front of the car.

With smoke coming out from under the minibus's tires, the vehicle shoots forward and makes a sharp right turn, ignoring the red light in front of us.

CHAPTER SEVEN

I nearly floor the gas pedal as I turn the steering wheel all the way right.

The tricked-out motor roars to life, and Zapo accelerates like no other Prius before it.

"You're passing the red light at double the speed limit," I hear Einstein say over the screeching tires and the pounding in my ears.

I ignore him and focus on the road.

The minibus is already merging onto FDR, and I fly onto the highway after it.

The middle and fast lanes are unusually free today, though the rightmost lane is beginning to clog up.

The kidnappers cut in front of a black Jeep Wrangler in the middle lane.

I let the Jeep pass and look in my rearview mirror. A red Cadillac is gaining on me on the left. I normally wouldn't dare switch lanes in this kind of situation, but today, I signal the turn, say a prayer to the Cadillac's brakes, and swerve into the middle lane.

The Cadillac's burning tires make an unhealthy squeal, but nothing hits me.

Einstein spews a laundry list of infractions, but I tune him out so I can focus on the minibus as it switches lanes again.

After successfully swerving in front of the Cadillac, I decide to really push my luck with the Honda Accord in the fast lane. Though it's at least a couple of feet closer, I'm hoping the driver saw my earlier stunt and started driving more cautiously.

I signal again and swerve.

There's a loud thump as the Honda's bumper crashes into mine.

1 0 1 1 0 0 0 1 0 0 1 0 1 0 1 0 0 1 0   1 1   0 0 1   1 0 1 1 0 1 0
1 0   0 1 1 1 0 1 1 0 0 1 1 1 0 1 0 0 0 0 1 0 1 0 1 0 0 1 1 1 1 1 0 1
1 0 0 0 1 1 1 0   0 0 0 0 1 1 0 1 1 0 0 1 1 1 0 1 1 0 0 1 1 0 1 0 1
0 0 1 1 1 0 1 0 1 0   0 1 0 0   1   1 1 0 0 1 0   0 1 1 0 0 0 0 0 0 0
1   1 1 0 1   0 1 1   0   1 1 0 0 0 0 0   1 0 1   0 1 0   1 0 1 1 0 1
1 0 0   0   0 0 1   0 0 1 0   1 0 0   0 0 1   0 0 0   1 1 0 1 0 1
0 1 0 0 0 0   0 0 1   0 1 0 0 1 0 1 1 0   1 0 1   0 1 0   0   0 0   0
0 1 1 0   1   0 0   1 1   1 0 1 0 0 0   1 0 0   0 0   0   1 0 0
0 0 0 1 0 1   0 0   1 1 0   0   1 1 0   0   0 1 1   0   1
0 0 1 0 1 0   0 1 1   0   1 0 0   1   0   1   0   1 0 1 0
1 0   0 1 0   1 1   1   1 1 1 0   0   1 0   1   1 1 1
0   0 1 0   1   1   0 1 0   1   0   0 1   1   0 1 1
0 1   0 0 0   1   0   0   1   1   1 1   1   1 0 0
0   0 1 1   0   0   0   0   1   1 1   0   0 0 1
1 0   0   0   1   0   0   0 0   1   0 0 0
0 1   1 0   0   0   0   1   0   0   1 0
0 1   1   0   1   1   1   1 0
0 0   0   1
0 1   1   0 1
0
0

CHAPTER EIGHT

"You've been in an accident," Einstein complains again.

"No shit," I grit out and push the pedal harder. Something clangs behind me, and a look in the rear-view mirror confirms what I already suspected. My back bumper fell off.

If I had time for caution, I'd probably pull to the side of the road. Instead, I slam on the gas.

My tires squeal. The car pulls left, and Zapo leaves its paint on the shoulder of the highway. At least I didn't go over the rail and fly into the ocean.

"The car alignment is off," Einstein says.

"Now you tell me," I say and do my best to adjust to the constant leftward drag of my ride.

For the next few minutes, the minibus continues to speed up and jump from lane to lane. I follow, and given my lack of bumper and the car's misalignment, the fact that I only lose my right mirror is some kind of miracle.

Einstein doesn't agree with my assessment. Throughout the chase, he unleashes a torrent of complaints about my driving. The highlights include going triple the speed limit, leaving the scene of multiple accidents, not signaling when switching lanes, and driving in a damaged vehicle.

As we get closer to downtown, I feel a glimmer of hope, and when we pass the Brooklyn Bridge, the hope congeals into a possible plan. The kidnappers are likely heading into the Battery Tunnel. Their only other option is to get off the highway and face downtown traffic. If I'm right, after they exit the Tunnel, they'll encounter the tollbooths, and with any luck, there'll be cops around. Even if the cops aren't present, I can make a big scene once we get there, maybe by crashing into the minibus or one of the booths—whatever it takes to get attention. There's even a small chance I won't need to do anything. If Ada gave the police the minibus's license plate, the cops at the toll stop—assuming there are any—may simply do their jobs.

My target goes around the diminutive Smart Fortwo car in the middle lane, so I swerve after it, hoping the environmentally conscious hipster chick inside that tiny coffin doesn't get a heart attack. The minibus whooshes into the Tunnel on the left side, and I nearly crash into the wall as I squeeze in behind it.

Handling my damaged car was difficult up to this point, but it'll be particularly tricky in the enclosed space up ahead.

When my eyes adjust to the Tunnel's darker environment, I blink repeatedly, as though that'll change what I see.

The left-side window in the minibus is open, and the now-familiar ape-bison hybrid is sticking his head out. Then his tattooed hand pulls out a gun as big as my head—which is where the weapon's barrel is now pointed.

On pure instinct, I duck in a move worthy of a Ninja Turtle as a shot rings out.

The Tunnel must somehow amplify the sound, because this is what a cannonball would sound like if it were fired directly into my eardrum.

Scenes from my early childhood don't flash before my eyes, and I'm not hit with the pain of getting shot—all good news. Somehow, the guy must've missed, though I have no idea where the bullet ended up.

When I look up, he's still there, aiming the gun in my direction.

A new spike of adrenaline rekindles my body's last reserve of energy, and the world gets sharper and clearer. Trying to make myself a more difficult target, I turn the wheel toward the orange cones that separate the lanes inside the Tunnel. The nearest cone flies up behind me and hits the green Ford Mustang on my tail.

Alas, my reprieve only lasts seconds. The shooter leans out of the right-side window, and without much ado, he fires at me again.

My ears ring and my windshield explodes, raining tiny shards of glass all over me.

I slam my foot on the brake so hard I hurt my ankle. Or at least the brake is what I meant to slam. In the heat of panic, I must've pressed on the gas, because Zapo suddenly lurches forward.

I hear another shot.

My shoulder feels like it was hit with a burning-hot baseball bat, then skinned with a potato peeler and sprinkled with alcohol and salt.

At the same time, the steering wheel jerks in my hands, and I register the weather-beaten wall of the Tunnel rushing toward my face with the inevitability of tax season.

Somehow, in that brief moment, many thoughts rush through my head, but the highlights are: "A bullet must've hit my tire" and "I'm going to die, and I haven't saved Mom."

Zapo smashes into the wall, and I see it start to pancake before the world becomes one violent explosion of whiteness, followed by the nothingness of unconsciousness.

CHAPTER NINE

"Where am I? What the hell is happening?" I try to say, but my lungs are empty.

I gasp for air, but something is obstructing my nose and mouth. It feels like someone is smothering me with a pillow after an elephant sat on my face.

I hear the creaking of plastic and metal as someone's thick-gloved hands grab me. Pain explodes throughout my body, and oblivion reclaims my consciousness.

I feel like I'm inside a meat grinder. I open my left eye a sliver and close it before the blinding light can ruin my retinas.

"Damn," I attempt to say, but my lips feel stuck together. "How much did I drink last night?"

"You're going to be okay," says an unfamiliar voice. "We're taking you to the hospital. I gave you something to make you more comfortable."

I feel warmth spread from my arm, an itchy sort of warmth that takes the pain away.

A splinter in my brain doesn't let me enjoy the relief. My mind resembles scrambled eggs, but I remember the problem and try to say, "No, I need to stay conscious. My mother was kidnapped. They shot at me—"

Realizing I'm just mumbling, I focus on not letting the drugs put me under, but the warmth spreads above my neck and my awareness slips away.

I try opening my eyes, but I feel like I'm too stoned. What the hell did I smoke?

"Will he be okay?" asks a familiar female voice from somewhere far away. "What's wrong with him?"

"He was shot, but the bullet only grazed his shoulder," an unfamiliar male voice responds. "He was also in a car accident, so he has a mild concussion, bruised ribs, whiplash, and a slew of other minor injuries."

Even in my confused state, I know that list isn't complete. With pride, I recall that I also got punched in the face and didn't cry afterwards or anything.

"He looks like aged steak," the female voice says, and through the haze, I feel like her name is on the tip of my tongue, along with the iron taste of blood and medicine. Something tells me this woman doesn't eat meat and wouldn't compare me to steak, or any other non-vegan dish, as a compliment.

"The police officers want to ask him a few questions," the male voice says. "Maybe you can shed some light on this situation for them instead? I don't think he should be disturbed."

"I already spent a few hours talking to them in circles," the woman replies, and I'm finally clearheaded enough to connect the dots and name her as Ada. "I just wish the cops would focus on looking for Nina and the rest of our test subjects instead of hounding us. The last thing Mike needs is an interrogation."

I will my eyes to open, and they grudgingly oblige, though I immediately close them again when the bright hospital light pounds the rods (or is it cones?) in my eyes like a sledgehammer. Trying again, I manage to keep my eyelids open long enough to glimpse a disheveled Ada standing next to some guy in a white coat—the sight of which instantly triggers my dentist/doctor phobia.

During my next eye-opening attempt, I take in my surroundings. The sterile whiteness reminds me of my recent nightmare. I try to focus my thoughts but find it much harder than controlling my eyes.

My throat feels like sandpaper, but I still try asking, "Where am I?"

This is when I realize a mask is covering my face and muffling my words.

"I think he's awake!"

Ada's exclamation is too loud for my hurting brain to deal with, so I mutter, "Too loud."

"He tried saying something again. You should take off that oxygen mask," Ada tells the doctor.

The doctor studies me skeptically.

Ada steps closer to me and softly says, "Mike, Mishen'ka, how are you feeling?"

That assault on my ears must've made my mind fuzzier, because I don't believe the gentle way Ada is touching my hand is normal, and I've never heard an American properly use the diminutive Russian form of my name before.

The white-coat man finally feels the need to remove the obstruction from my face.

I try speaking again, almost instinctively. "Where's Mom?"

Once the question leaves my lips, I realize that's the reason I'm fighting the drugs or whatever it is that's making me want to nap.

"The police and FBI are looking for her," Ada says, and I note that her tone is indeed uncharacteristically soothing. "They've been grilling me and the other Techno employees about everything. They've also collected information on every study participant and even asked about the research."

A wave of disappointment crashes against the sudden tsunami of nausea. My breathing speeds up, and I overhear Ada say, "I think he's in pain. Give him something. Please."

The doctor must agree with her, because he does something and a new wave of pleasurable warmth arrives.

Ada leans in and strokes my hair.

"Wait," I say. "I don't mind the pain. I want to—"

Before I can finish the sentence, the drug knocks me out.

This time, I wake up remembering everything. I guess it's an improvement. I lie there trying to master my mind before I let anyone know I'm awake, lest they knock me out with painkillers again.

Somewhere, Ada is having a heated discussion with who I assume are members of law enforcement.

"He might know something critical," a man says. "His own mother is—"

"I'm awake," I half moan. "And I want to help in any way I can."

I pry my eyes open and see Ada's face as though through a haze. Her forehead is creased in worry, which I find both comforting and surprising.

Next to Ada are two vague shapes that must be the cops, though they aren't wearing NYPD uniforms.

"Mr. Cohen, if we could ask you a few questions," says the guy on the left, and I can't help but think he looks like a German Shepherd.

"This is very important," adds his partner. This one, perhaps inspired by my foggy brain, reminds me of a root vegetable—something between a beet and a potato.

"Of course," I say and swallow to clear the needles from my throat. "Ask away."

So they ask. With the combination of drugs and adrenaline in my system, I feel like a captured spy pumped full of truth serum. Constantly fighting for lucidity, I answer all their questions as accurately and methodically as I can, which in my condition isn't saying much. Eventually,

I ask my own questions and learn the authorities haven't made any headway in locating Mom and the others. No one stopped the minibus outside the Tunnel. There weren't any cops there, and the tollbooth clerks were out of their depths after hearing the gunshots.

"We think they changed the plates shortly after passing through the tollbooths," says the German Shepherd guy.

"But rest assured, we will stop every black Mercedes Metris driving in the New York metropolitan area," says the beet-potato guy.

They're interrupted when my old pal, the dread-inspiring white-coat guy, walks in and says, "Gentlemen, you said this would take two minutes."

Ada puts her hands on her hips and gives my interrogators a look she usually reserves for people who don't bother getting their code peer-reviewed.

"I'm okay," I say, but even to my own ears I sound like an anemic anorexic.

The doggie guy gives me an unsympathetic onceover and says, "If we can just have one more moment."

His veggie partner brings something up on his phone, places it in my hands, and says, "We got these from the hospital security footage."

To my relief, I can lift the phone to my face, though it feels like it's filled with osmium, an element denser than lead.

When I see the screen, I forget the strain of holding up the phone and fight for the energy to look through the photos in front of me.

There's a different person on each of the three images. Two are caught at very odd angles, but it doesn't matter since I already know I haven't seen them before. The remaining photo is distinguishable, and the mug on it is very familiar.

It's the guy who punched me in the face.

"Have you seen any of these men before today?" the second guy asks.

I shake my head but don't stop looking at the ape-bison asshole.

I guess the beet-potato guy notices me burning holes into the screen with my eyes, because he leans in and looks at the image. "Is that the man who attacked you?" His voice is almost soothing.

"Yes." My arm stings, and I realize I've clenched my fingers around the phone so hard the IV entry into my arm got messed up. "But I don't think I've seen the others, and I'm sure I've never seen him before today." I tear my eyes away from the screen and look up at the man leaning over me. "What about you? Can't you look them up using facial recognition software?"

"No," says the canine policeman. "I mean, yes, we tried. Two of the images didn't capture enough of their faces to allow a lookup; the picture of the man who attacked you did allow for a scan, but he didn't pop up in any of our databases."

I shake my head and wince at the agonizing throb in my skull.

I hand the phone back to its owner, and he takes it. He must see the despair on my face, because he looks questioningly at his partner. It's as though he's trying to telepathically check if he should say something.

His partner gives him a slight nod. The beet-potato guy clears his throat and says, "The tattoos on the man who shot you are common within certain Russian criminal elements…"

Now that he mentions it, I realize he's right. I'm no expert, but I've seen enough movies featuring the Russian mob—almost all the action flicks nowadays—to notice certain patterns when it comes to the ink Hollywood puts on its villains. It's possible there's a correlation between the tattoos in those movies and the ones in reality, at least if the studio people did any research. The latter isn't a given, since everything else related to Russians in American films is far from accurate. The vast majority of the time, the atrociously spoken language doesn't match the subtitles, and the actors who play the Russian characters don't look remotely authentic, like the stereotypically Swedish-looking Dolph Lundgren from *Rocky 4*. And yes, as much as I don't like terms like Slav, Aryan, Semite, and so on, I believe a movie should look realistic.

In any case, armed with this idea, I see that my attacker could easily be Russian; he has a rounder face with a brick-like jaw similar to my elementary school janitor. I can't believe I didn't pick up on it earlier, but I guess my Rudar isn't impact resistant.

The German Shepherd guy takes me out of my musings by saying, "You mentioned your uncle was there at the hospital, but you never mentioned your cousin."

Finally understanding why they've been tiptoeing around this Russian-crime connection, I say, "Joe wasn't there at all. Do you actually think he could have any connection to this? You think he would kidnap his own aunt?"

"Or someone who wants to get to him might've taken her," the vegetable guy mumbles defensively. "We need to think of every possibility. Your cousin is—"

"Thank you for your time," his partner interrupts. "Here." He hands Ada a business card. "If either of you recalls anything of note, please give us a call. We have your information, and we'll stay in touch."

"Wait," I shout at them, but they're too far away to hear me. To Ada, I say, "Why would Joe's enemies, if that's whom they suspect, take a dozen strangers and Mom?"

Ada shrugs. "Your cousin did call your uncle when we were having lunch…"

"What are you saying? That my uncle is part of this?" I stare at her. "That's crazy. My uncle adores his sister. In fact, that reminds me. He needs to know what happened."

"I believe they already talked to him," Ada says. "They spoke to everyone who was at the hospital and the families of every participant. I guess they're still trying to reach your cousin."

"Look, Ada, about my cousin…" I pause, searching for the right words, then end weakly with, "He's a complicated person."

Okay, so maybe that's the understatement of the century. The labels people use when referring to my cousin are *psychopath* and *sociopath*. Though I hate those psychological terms, in this case, it's quicker than saying, "He who flouts the law while being prone to aggression, and who shows little remorse over any of the atrocities he's committed."

Gathering my thoughts, I start over. "Okay, he's not a nice person—maybe even a horrible person—but I believe he has a code, or something that passes for ethics, and in his own way, he has deep respect for my mom, who helped him—"

"I didn't mean to imply anything," Ada says. "I'm sorry."

I nod, accepting her apology, and wonder if I'm giving Joe too much credit. Past events replay in my mind. The time I found him beating a bird with a rock when we were kids. The time in Sheepshead Bay High when he put that big kid in the hospital with five broken ribs for using the funny Russian nickname of *Josya* instead of *Joseph* or *Joe*. Then again, I also recall Joe's face at the hospital after Mom's accident. He looked like he might strangle one of the nurses. At the time, I took that to mean he didn't like his aunt being in that situation.

"I think your conversation is too stressful for Mr. Cohen," the white coat suggests to Ada, and I remember he's still here.

I shift in the bed and grimace, unable to fight the rush of pain made worse by my dread for Mom.

"Do you want me to give you something for the pain?" the white-coat guy offers.

I look at him and finally get around to reading his nametag. His name is Dr. Katz.

"No more painkillers," I say. "I want to clear my mind so I can focus on the kidnapping."

The doctor looks momentarily surprised. I guess he thought I was too wimpy to refuse painkillers. In the next moment, however, he returns to that professional detachment they teach in medical school. "You'll have difficulty breathing without medication. Your ribs are—"

"I'm actually feeling much better," I lie. "When and if I'm in pain later today, I'll take something."

To create the illusion of vigor, I try to sit up, hoping it'll also help with my sudden bout of lightheadedness.

I have to almost literally bite my tongue to keep from screaming in pain. When my head stops spinning, I glance guiltily at the doctor. He either didn't notice or doesn't care—no doubt another thing they teach in medical school.

Ada grabs the remote control for my bed and helps me get into a half-sitting position. When I'm more upright, I'm surprised that I don't projectile vomit, shout obscenities, or lose bowel control. The performance must be convincing enough, because Dr. Katz looks mollified.

Pushing my advantage, I steady my voice and say, "Thank you, Doctor, for all the help so far. I really don't like hospitals, and I hope I can get out of here as soon as possible. For now, maybe you could give me a few pills I can take as needed? Perhaps Percocet?"

Dr. Katz considers this. His expression implies he doesn't approve of his patients deciding what painkillers they should take, but since I must have suggested the right one, he simply says, "Sure. I'll write the prescription," and walks away.

As soon as Dr. Katz is out of sight, I let my shoulders stoop slightly, but for Ada's benefit, I don't slouch in proportion to the agony I'm feeling. She's staring at me with the intensity of a jeweler pricing out a diamond, so I say, "I'll need your help getting out of here as soon as I can walk."

"What good will that do?" Ada crosses her arms. "Besides make things worse."

I hold her gaze. "I might come up with a way of locating everyone."

She looks away for a moment, then touches my IV-less left elbow. "Look, Mike," she says softly. "I can't even imagine how you must be feeling, but you have to realize the cops are professionals at this, and you—"

"I care about this more than they do," I say. I know it's an illusion, but I feel healing energy spreading through my arm from where Ada's tiny hand is resting. "More importantly, I can approach this analytically, like an engineer."

It might be another drug-induced delusion, but as soon as I say those words, an idea forms in my head. It must illuminate my face like the proverbial light bulb, because Ada pulls her hand away and looks at me intently. "What is it?"

"The engineering approach," I say, stressing every syllable. "I think I know how to find Mom."

CHAPTER TEN

I must've given Ada a clue, because she looks thoughtful for a moment. "If it's what I think—"

"Do you know where my phone is?" I pat down my gown-clad body, realizing for the first time that I'm naked under the thin layer of cloth.

Ada grabs my phone from a random pile of objects on the side table and hands it to me.

"Wow," I say as I examine the sleek device's flawless surface. "There's not even a scratch on it."

"You were overdue some good luck," Ada says. "Let's hope it holds."

"The sense of relief I feel is disproportionate," I say, the phone shaking along with my hand.

"You could be projecting something onto it," Ada suggests.

"Maybe. Then again, I did nickname my phone 'Precious.' I bet you didn't know that."

For the first time since I woke up, mirth twists the corners of Ada's lips. "I like that," she says. "Only you do realize that instead of prolonging your lifespan the way Precious did for Gollum, yours just shortens your attention span?"

"It's a prototype," I say and unlock Precious. "The first wave of super-smart phones from SandoMobile, a firm my fund is invested in. These puppies will cost two grand when they come out, and not because they have any gold or diamond bling built into them, like other luxury cellphones. The cost is all due to its fancy hardware, most of which I can't even leverage because of the lack of proper software."

"If you want me to write software for this thing, you can forget it." Ada's smile touches her eyes. "Brainocyte apps will keep me busy for a couple of years."

I mumble that it wasn't what I meant and check the screen. Precious is already on the hospital's Wi-Fi.

Einstein's tiny face looks at me from the screen, his cartoon eyes wise and patient.

"Einstein," I enunciate, "start a video call with Mitya."

"Done," the AI responds in his German-accented voice, and Mitya's company's video conferencing app launches.

"Let me hold that for you," Ada offers and leans in so close I can smell her coconut shampoo.

"Thank you." I hand her the phone, and our fingers touch for a second, generating a spike of oxytocin that goes from my hand straight into my brain.

She sits on the bed next to me and holds the phone as though we're about to take a selfie.

To my relief and surprise, it only takes twenty seconds for the app to indicate that someone has picked up the call.

Considering we're about to chat with a multibillionaire C-level honcho of multiple corporations, I'd say I just got lucky.

The rest of the world knows Mitya as Dmitriy Levin. Unlike my name, Dmitriy isn't easy to Americanize, but it does have two short forms—Mitya and Dima. My friend prefers the less commonly used version of the two. As I look at him now, I recall how people thought we were related back at MIT, calling us the M&M brothers. I'd like to pretend it's because of the same keen intellect in our eyes, but I suspect it's really because we have the same brown hair, which we still keep equally short, and the fact that we're both allegedly immigrants from Russia—even though that last part is inaccurate, since Mitya is from a part of the former Soviet Union that's now Ukraine.

"*Zdorovo.*" Mitya's booming voice sounds like he's here in person, thanks to Precious's fancy new speaker technology. "I can't see you yet."

"That's 'hi,'" I whisper to Ada, and to Mitya, I say, "Hey, I have Ada here with me."

Mitya stares at his screen intently. He's sitting in some cushy conference room, wearing his signature blue hoodie. The video must finally turn on on his end, because he exclaims, "Wow. What the hell happened to you?"

"You won't believe it," I say and explain the events of the day to him, occasionally letting Ada fill in the gaps on parts I didn't know, like the total loss of my poor Zapo.

"Bro," Mitya says at the end of the tale. "What can I do to help?"

"I have an idea," I say. "It requires leveraging the servers you've been donating to the project."

Mitya is hugely invested in Techno, second only to me. Besides money, he's also given Techno a lot of technology and other resources, the most expensive of which might be his time. And, naturally, he's provided the servers that the Brainocytes communicate with. Who else has custom-designed supercomputers lying around?

Mitya must understand where I'm going right away, because he says, "Are you forgetting the privacy stuff? My people worked with hers"—he nods at Ada—"to make all the connections completely anonymous. JC didn't want people feeling like we could track their whereabouts from the backend—"

"I'm not a noob like JC." I tilt my head. "I know you can hack whatever crypto Ada's minions and your peeps put together. You got into—"

"Hey," Mitya interrupts in Russian and looks meaningfully at Ada. "I got this," he adds in English. He looks thoughtful for a moment, then starts typing on his very loud mechanical keyboard. Judging by his focused expression, he's no longer looking at Ada and me. He probably minimized our image to go through the privacy code.

"They did a good job," he mutters, his eyes scanning the screen. "Someone's getting a promotion."

"That's nice. I'm glad you're happy with your peeps." I have a hard time taming my sarcasm. "Now can you please help me locate my mother?"

He doesn't respond for a few minutes, but his keyboard sounds like machine-gun fire. I half expect to see smoke surrounding him.

"I can probably do it," he finally says. "In a few days, if I'm lucky. A week in the worst case."

"I don't have a few days." A wave of nausea hits me, causing the room to spin. "It needs to be minutes, or hours at the most."

"I'm sorry." He grimaces. "Locating people using Brainocytes wasn't in the specs. Quite the opposite, actually. All I can say is that *something* is running on those servers, so at least it's proof of life."

"That something could be the backups," Ada whispers. "Or even my—" She stops talking and looks at us sheepishly, probably feeling bad over shattering my "proof of life" hopes.

I fight the urge to scream in frustration, partly because I don't think it'll help, but also because I don't have the strength for something so strenuous. Inhaling deeply, I let out the breath and say, "Is there something we can do to locate them? You two are the smartest people I know. Can't you think of something?"

I stare pleadingly at the phone, then lock eyes with Ada.

"Well." Ada looks away and nervously rubs the buzzed part of her head. "When you first brought this up, I thought you had a more complicated idea in mind. It, too, would require some coding, but not as much as what Mitya quoted. I think I could write this app in a few hours or so. It's just that it kind of goes against every Techno policy we have."

"I promise if those idiots fire you for this, you can come work for me." Mitya's green eyes blaze with avarice. "What did you have in mind?"

"Dude," I say. "You promised not to poach her, remember?"

"Wait." Ada looks from me to the screen. "You guys talked about me?"

Mitya does a poor job suppressing a snicker, and I give him a warning glare. We have talked quite a bit about Ada, but almost never in a professional context. Usually, I just tell Mitya how close I'm getting to maybe, probably, possibly asking her out, and he tells me how much of a wuss I am.

"That's not important now," I say. "Tell us your idea."

"Fine." Ada moves the phone to her other hand. "We can use the backups."

"Yeah, you mentioned those before," Mitya says. "What do you mean?"

"In computer science, a backup is the practice or a set of procedures for making extra copies of data or hardware in case the original gets lost or damaged," Ada deadpans.

"This is serious, Ada," I say. In case she wasn't kidding, I add, "We obviously know what a backup *is*, just not what you mean in this context. Is there a backup of the secured data that's easier to hack?"

"No, it's the Brainocytes themselves," Ada says. "Doesn't anyone ever read the documentation?"

"I think I understand," Mitya says. "The hardware is redundant."

"Exactly," Ada confirms. "If any one Brainocyte goes out of order, an identical one can replace it."

"And you've kept double the Brainocytes, meaning for every test subject that was injected, you have an extra batch on standby." Mitya pushes his amber-tinted computer glasses up his nose—his poker tell.

"I know all that," I say, not caring if I sound defensive. "I don't see how those extra Brainocytes can help us, though."

"If we activate any of those backup Brainocytes," Ada says, "there won't be any security issues, because these Brainocytes all share the same IDs. So I can write an app that will leverage your mom's backups to locate her primary Brainocytes, or her, in other words."

Even with my less technical know-how, I recognize the simplicity and elegance in this solution. I also see the problem. "I thought Brainocytes only activate when inside a subject's brain."

"Hence the procedure issues I mentioned earlier," Ada says. "Not to mention privacy—"

"I volunteer," Mitya cuts in. "We don't have to tell anyone about it if you think you'll get in trouble."

"Wait." My head is spinning again, but this time, it's not just from the concussion. "It can't be you, Mitya. Even with your private jet, wouldn't it take you about a day to get here from the West Coast?"

"I can cut that down to—"

"No," I say firmly. "I need you in your office, helping write the app Ada mentioned and working on hacking the security in case this new Plan A doesn't work."

Mitya nods disappointedly. I've always known that my friend was helping with this project because he, like Ada, wants mature Brainocyte technology inside his head. I can't even blame him, since I've thought about it myself. It doesn't take much of a leap to picture how cool it would be. I mean, I have techno-orgasms just using Precious. Brainocytes integrate with your *mind,* so it would be like my phone on steroids and amphetamines. It's just that I never allowed myself to dwell on this because it makes me feel like a selfish, lousy son—like I'm investing in Techno for reasons other than helping Mom get better.

Thinking of Mom tightens my chest. I wonder if the kidnappers fed her and whether they're treating her okay.

I'm pulled out of my thoughts by Ada loudly clearing her throat.

I expect she's about to volunteer to receive the Brainocytes, but she doesn't. She just looks at me expectantly while tapping her steel-toed boot.

"It should be my head," I say with a confidence I wish I felt. "It's my mom we're trying to save."

"You just went through an ordeal," Mitya objects.

"Which just means I'm already under a doctor's supervision," I counter. "I even have an IV in my arm and everything. If we want to do this on the down-low, it doesn't get any stealthier."

"I think it'll work," Ada says. "The Brainocytes are pretty harmless. If I thought they could hurt Mike, I'd veto this plan, but I think this is the best resource distribution. Mitya works on a secondary solution, and I go get Nina's backup batch and start writing the locator app in the cab."

Her confidence unknots my stomach. "Thank you," I say, touching her hand.

"Fine. I'll take a crack at this security for now." Mitya says. "Keep me posted on your progress, and let me know if there's anything else I can do to help."

"We will," Ada says.

"*Spasibo*," I say, thanking him in Russian.

"Don't mention it," Mitya replies in Russian. "Good luck, guys," he adds in English and disconnects.

Ada hands me my phone and says, "Do you want me to get you anything on the way?"

"No. Just get me a batch of nanotechnology, the less tested on humans, the better."

Ada chuckles. "Try to get some sleep while I'm gone. I'll pick up your Percocet prescription as well."

Without waiting for my response, she leans in and gives me a loud smooch on the forehead.

I'm so stunned I only recover from the kiss once she's gone. Her lips are officially the softest things to ever touch my forehead—not that I make a habit of checking textures that way. I wonder what the kiss actually meant. Was that more than a friendly kiss, or does Ada always act that way when a male colleague is in pain in the hospital?

The nap idea is a good one, so I let myself close my eyes, just for a second. My breathing evens out, and I'm about to drift off when I hear someone approach my bed.

I open my eyes, and blood drains out of the big bruise I call my face.

"Hi, Mike," my uncle says. "I'm sorry if we startled you."

"You didn't," I say, staring at the person accompanying my uncle—the guy I used to think of as a friend, until he scared the shit out of me with his antisocial behavior.

"Hi, cousin," I say in Russian, meeting Joe's lizard-like gaze.

CHAPTER ELEVEN

"Where's my aunt?" my cousin demands with an intensity that implies I'm the one responsible for my mom's disappearance. "Speak. Now."

"The cops were here," I reply tersely. "They thought *you* might know where she is."

Joe steps toward the bed. His blue eyes glint with ice that reminds me of Hannibal Lecter's signature stare. I glance at my uncle for help, but he's clearly petrified.

"They also hinted that this could be the work of an enemy of yours." I wait one frantic heartbeat, then ask, "Is it?"

My cousin stops his onslaught, considers the idea for a moment, then confidently shakes his head. "No. They got it wrong. No one who knows me would dare fuck with my family."

The words aren't spoken with any bravado, but his sheer calmness is what bothers me. He's just stating a fact. Of course, there's a subtext to his words, a threat to whoever the kidnappers are. In this moment, it's all too easy to picture Joe going complete Keyser Söze on their asses and killing their kids, their spouses, their parents, their cats/dogs/parrots/goldfishes or whatever.

"How bad is it?" Uncle Abe asks, studying my face. His voice is so kind it's hard to believe he and Joe share half of their DNA. "Does that hurt?"

"Not much," I reply. I probably would've sounded more sincere if my voice hadn't cracked and if I hadn't cringed.

"Are you ready to tell me who did that to your face?" Joe asks. It might be my imagination, but did his intensity dial down from eleven out of ten to a mere ten?

"It was this big Russian guy," I begin and tell my uncle and cousin the whole story, only without going into the nitty-gritty details of the Brainocytes—specifically that they'll go into my head. Instead, I say there's a technical solution.

My uncle looks petrified as I go on, while Joe's features simply darken, an impressive feat given his semi-permanent somber expression. I fleetingly wonder if this whole situation is bringing back memories for them of how they lost Aunt Veronica. She had a heart attack before I came to America, so I don't know many of the details surrounding her death, but I suspect both men were forever changed by it.

"This technical mumbo jumbo," my uncle says. "Do you think it'll help us find her?"

"It sounds promising," I reply. "Plus, there's this other solution Mitya is working on."

"I don't have much faith in these solutions," Joe says, his expression unreadable. "And I don't have any faith in any solution that involves the pigs." He looks me over; then, perhaps deciding it's too harsh to compare me to the cops, he adds, "Especially the pigs."

"So what do you suggest?" I do my best not to sound challenging, since I need to keep my head to put the Brainocytes in.

"I'll look into this myself," my cousin says. "Whoever these fuckers are, they're making me—" His jaw muscles spasm, and he stops talking. Taking a calming breath, he pulls out his phone.

His face is back to its expressionless state, but I think I briefly glimpsed some emotion there. Was he about to say, "They're making me mad" or "They're making me look bad"? I don't mind if it's actually the latter. Maybe if he thinks these criminals don't respect him and are about to ruin his reputation by taking his aunt, he might be more motivated to help her. Or maybe I'm being unfair, and he genuinely cares about his aunt.

"You mentioned there was a Russian nurse at NYU Langone," Joe says. "Her name was Olga, right?"

"Yes," I say cautiously. "Why? Do you think she had anything to do with this?"

"Put in your number," Joe says instead of answering and hands me his iPhone.

I take the phone and note he created a new contact in his phonebook, calling me "bro2." I doubt it's because he's particularly fond of me. It's far more likely he used that term because there's no word for *cousin* in Russian. Instead of cousin, you use the word *brother,* but add a degree of separation to it. For example, Joe and I are *secondary brothers*, because our parents are brother and sister—kind of like how the term *first cousins* gives the same information. I wonder if this nomenclature results in cousins feeling more like family in the Russian-speaking part of the world. I certainly felt like Joe was my brother when we arrived in the US, but that quickly changed. Having said all that, Joe speaks English much better than Russian, having arrived here when he was just a kid. So maybe he meant "bro" as a kind of English slang, since he has another "bro" in his phone already. Still, even that suggests a closeness we don't really share, at least as far as I know.

Seeing the irritation on my cousin's face, I focus on the task at hand and put in my phone number.

"Check if you got my text," he says and types something into his phone.

"You have a text from Joseph Cohen," a German-accented voice says from my phone.

My uncle raises an eyebrow. "Should I read it?"

"No," I respond and tilt the phone toward me. Joe's message is just an ellipsis. "Einstein, please save this as a new contact and rename it Joe."

"I'll be in touch," Joe says and turns on his heels. When he's almost by the door, he says over his shoulder, "I expect updates on the technical solutions when you have them."

Before I get a chance to come up with some witty but safe reply, Joe is gone.

My uncle is left standing with an uncomfortable expression on his face. I know this isn't the first time his son has put him in an awkward position. Probably more like the millionth time. I can't even fathom what it must feel like to be the father of a guy like Joe, especially when you're as chill of an individual as Uncle Abe is. In that family, the apple fell so far from the tree it didn't even land in the same garden.

"I think he'll help," my uncle finally says. He looks like he's trying to think of the right words, but he ends up only adding, "Just be careful."

I nod, ignoring the throbbing in my temples.

"Did you eat?" my uncle asks, and I recognize an attempt to change the subject.

"No," I say. "Think you can bring me something light?"

Looking relieved, Uncle Abe asks me what I want, and I request fruit and Jell-O. In truth, I don't think I can stomach something even that low-cal, but I'm too exhausted for any more conversation and could use a moment to close my eyes.

As soon as he leaves, I fumble with the bed controls to make the mattress flat and doze off.

―――――――――

I wake up to voices and a sharp pain enveloping my whole body. Breathing hurts, shifting on the bed hurts, and even thinking hurts. All remnants of the pain medication must've gotten flushed out of my system while I was sleeping. As a cherry on top, I also feel my bladder starting to complain.

"He's been sleeping since I left to get food," my uncle says. "Dr. Katz suggested I let him sleep, so I stepped out to buy him some clothes to replace the ones he bled on."

Ada nods. "Good thinking. He might want to be awake for this, but maybe we should let him sleep a little longer."

"I'm awake," I croak and open my eyes. "How did it go?" I give Ada's messenger bag a meaningful look.

"I'm almost done with the app," Ada says. "I submitted the code to my own personal Git repository and asked Mitya to review it. Do you want to take a look? I can walk you through it."

"Yes, please. Anything I can do to help."

Ada gets her laptop out, and I put my bed into a sitting position. She places the computer in front of me, and I examine her code.

Now, I'm no programing novice. My MIT Bachelor's degree was in Computer Science, and they don't give you that without forcing you to get your hands dirty. More importantly, my very first job was as a C++ developer at a startup. I did that for a few years before I made enough money to start my venture capital fund. Though I was a good programmer, I admit the money had less to do with my coding skills than luck—or rather my uncanny skill at picking good companies, as I prefer to think of it. That startup gave me a load of stock options, which went through the roof when they had an IPO.

This is all to say that when I think Ada's code looks too clever, it doesn't mean I'm too dumb to get it, though I guess someone too dumb might say something similar. It's just that, like with some of her speeches, Ada didn't bother making this code easy to read. To be fair, as a bit of code that's meant to be used once and thrown away, its illegibility might be excused, especially since she wrote it in a rush.

But part of me cringes whenever I see her use the more obscure "?" format for her conditional statements instead of "If, else." Call me lazy, but something like "if statementVar==true, consequenceOfTruth, else consequenceOfFalsehood," reads much better to me than "statementVar?-consequenceOfTruth:consequenceOfFalsehood." She also didn't include any comments explaining her code. Yet despite all these minor gripes, I get the feeling I'm looking at the work of a genius as I review line after line of the app.

I get so engrossed in the code that I automatically accept and eat the fruit salad my uncle brought me and then gobble down the Jell-O.

"I don't know what any of the APIs you invoked do," I say at the end. "But aside from that, this all looks good to me."

What I don't say is that I'm slightly disappointed by how error-free it all is. Had I found something wrong with her code, I could've shown off my skills. Then again, since this stuff will be running in my head, and since its purpose is locating Mom, Ada's competency is a good thing.

"Great," she says. "While we wait for Mitya's feedback, should we proceed with the next part of the plan?"

She glances at my uncle. Her unasked question is obvious. Do we want to do the Brainocyte thing in front of him?

"Uncle Abe, can you please get me more food?" I ask. "Maybe mashed potatoes?"

If my uncle caught on to our scheme, he doesn't show it. He simply says, "Ah, you're getting your appetite back."

In the Russian culture, having a good appetite and, relatedly, being slightly overweight is a sign of health. As a result, my grandmother had always tried to overfeed me.

"Yes," I lie. "Starving."

"How about you, Ada?" my uncle asks. "Can I get you anything?"

"I had a smoothie on the way, thanks," she says. She watches my uncle leave before retrieving the giant syringe from her bag.

"Ready?" she asks and approaches my IV bag.

"I guess." I look at the needle in her hand with distrust.

"Look, Mike, I can see you don't like hospital stuff. I understand. I don't like it either. After my mom got sick…"

Ada's eyes look distant, and it's clear she's reliving the day her mom succumbed to cancer. I want to jump up and give her a comforting hug, but since I don't think it would be appropriate, I just say, "It's okay. Let's do this."

"You sure?" she asks, regaining her composure.

"Just one question," I say. "Do you know what you're doing?"

"Yes, I've done something like this before." She rubs the corner of her eye with her finger. "You'll be fine. I promise."

She puts her hand on mine and gives it a gentle, reassuring squeeze. In an ironic turn of events, she's the one comforting me.

I wish I knew where Ada got her unshakable optimism from, but I do feel a modicum better. Capitalizing on this, I remind myself that what's about to happen is critical to locating Mom. I also tell myself that my fear of all things medical is irrational, a condition I developed from getting my teeth drilled without anesthesia—something that isn't relevant to my current situation.

When I feel like my voice won't quiver, I swallow and say, "Yes, I'm ready."

Ada doesn't give me a chance to change my mind. In a swift, confident move, she sticks the needle into the IV the way I saw the nurse do to Mom what feels like a year ago.

The clear liquid fills the bag, and the Brainocytes start their trek up my veins.

CHAPTER TWELVE

As soon as I picture the stuff swimming in my bloodstream, my already bad nausea intensifies.

"It's making me lightheaded," I gasp. "There are also all these odd sensations in my body."

"Lightheadedness is normal, but I doubt you can feel more than that. It's not possible to actually feel the nanobots swimming through your bloodstream," Ada says. "But you might feel a slight burning at the entry point."

As soon as she says it, I notice there's indeed a burning sensation around the spot where the IV connects to my arm. And then my lightheadedness evolves into something worse, and the hospital room spins around me faster than my dorm room did on the morning after I drank half a bottle of vodka with Mitya.

"You're turning white," Ada says worriedly. "Breathe."

I take quick, shallow breaths, in and out, figuring what works for panic-attack victims should work for me. The breathing helps a little, though I can't inhale too deeply without feeling pain in my ribs.

"That's good," she says. "Keep doing that. It'll be okay. Trust me."

I keep breathing and try to relax. When I put Mom through this yesterday, I didn't stop to think how I would feel about tiny machines messing around with my brain. Now I realize I'm terrified, but of course, it's too late.

"When can we test the app?" I ask, desperate to distract myself.

"After Mitya is done reviewing the code," Ada says. "But before we get to that, there's something I need to tell you. Something important. I—"

She stops talking when my uncle enters, carrying a tray of food.

"You were saying?" I say to Ada.

"Later." Ada's lips press together in a slight, but surprisingly adorable grimace. "You should eat first."

I look at the tray of food and realize my appetite is also similar to that hangover incident. Nevertheless, I reach for the mashed potatoes and valiantly swallow as much of it as I can, figuring food should help me heal faster. I wash it all down with a little square box of whole milk while Ada mutters something negative about dairy consumption.

"I want to try standing," I say when I can't ignore my bladder anymore. "Uncle Abe, can you please give me a hand?"

Ada frowns. "Is that a good idea?"

"I need to use the restroom," I explain. "I wanted to try getting up anyway."

"The doctor said it was okay." My uncle looks at Ada to see if she'll contradict him, and when she doesn't say anything, he extends his hand to me.

I lean on him and place my feet on the floor. My head is pounding with agony, and the pins and needles in my legs join the already crowded party of unpleasant sensations in my body.

"I think I need a nurse or a doctor," I say, realizing I'll have to pull the IV with me to the bathroom otherwise.

Ada walks off to get someone, and I use this chance to wince in pain.

"Maybe you should use one of those metal bucket things instead?" my uncle suggests. "I can see you're hurting."

"I'll be fine," I grit out through clenched teeth and attempt to put the least amount of weight on my uncle's hand as I stand up.

Just as swiftly, I sit back down again.

"I'm just warming up my legs," I say defensively. "They fell asleep."

The second attempt hurts more, but the room doesn't spin as fast and I can stand straight for a few beats before I need to rest again.

"What are you trying to prove?" my uncle asks in Russian. Then, more conspiratorially, he adds, "Are you trying to show off in front of the girl?"

"To help Mom, I need to be on my feet," I say and get up again.

Grabbing the IV stand, I take a shuffling step. The worst pain is coming from my side, as if something isn't letting me take in a full breath. Must be the bruised ribs. My left elbow hurts too. I don't recall why, but my shoulder and face are particularly painful. My face is also burning from the blood that, for some reason, rushed to my head. On top of that, I feel like I'm about to lose both the food I just ate and my bladder control. Otherwise, I'm feeling great.

A male nurse I don't recognize comes in with Ada. With unprofessional surprise, he says, "You're standing."

"Yep. And please tell Dr. Katz I'm checking out. Also, can you take this out?" I shake the IV tube.

The nurse looks at me suspiciously but does as I requested.

"Help me get him to the bathroom," my uncle says and grabs my right elbow.

"I don't need help," I say and take a firm step.

My next step is far less firm, but I make it anyway. The less I shake, the better I seem to feel, so I shuffle forward slowly.

By the time I make it to the bathroom, I'm ready to spill national security secrets just to make the pain stop. Though I only need to go number one, I do my business sitting down so I can catch my breath.

My nose decides to bleed again, or, more specifically, my left nostril. I stuff it with rolled-up toilet paper, a trick I learned when I was a teen.

"Is everything okay in there?" the male nurse booms from outside the door.

"Loving it," I yell back. "I got this."

Cutting short the toilet rest, I get up and wash away any sign of my nosebleed, which has already stopped.

I examine myself in the mirror and chuckle humorlessly. My face looks way more purple than it feels.

Leaving the restroom, I refuse the nurse's help again. The trip back to my bed hurts a tiny bit less—maybe because my brain is adapting to the constant pain.

"Where's my uncle?" I ask when I lie back down.

"I'm not sure," Ada answers. "I think he left to make a call. I tried explaining how we'll find your mom, and he seemed excited."

"Well, we're not waiting for him to return," I say, "assuming we can use the app already. Or do I need to call Mitya and hurry his ass up?"

"No," Ada says, her forehead wrinkling. "He finished the review."

"But?"

"No buts." Ada clears her throat. "It's just that I only have the most rudimentary tools on this laptop. I'd be far more comfortable if we could get you to the Techno headquarters or the NYU Langone Center, though the most optimal option is my apartment. This way, I'd get to keep my job in the end."

"Are you saying you don't have what you need to make the app work?"

"No, I can make it work," Ada says, "but just barely. You'll get the most vanilla build of the interface, and you'll have to use the laptop inputs to work with it. No debugging will be available, and the worst part is this version doesn't collect much data. I figured since you're doing this anyway, we might as well learn as much as we can about—"

"Time is of the essence," I remind her. "No offense, but I couldn't care less about Brainocyte research right now. Once we locate my mom, you can collect all the data you want."

"Okay," Ada says and sits next to me on the bed. "Here goes."

She does something on the laptop.

"Did it work?" Ada asks after a few seconds of silence.

"I feel *something*," I say. "Like the world is getting a little clearer."

"I think that's a purely psychosomatic response," Ada says, waving dismissively. "Can you see it?"

She points at the screen, but I can't tell what she's pointing at from my angle.

"See what?" I ask, but then I do see it.

The "it" in question is a golden sphere floating in the middle of the room. It doesn't look like a hologram or a computer image. It looks solid and very real.

"I see it," I say. "What is it?"

"Just an icon you need to click." She puts her computer on my lap and points at the trackpad, saying, "You'll be able to do this with your mind after some training, but for now, you should use that."

I drag my middle finger across the trackpad's cold surface and notice another artifact move next to the base of my bed. This object looks like a square piece of white marble the size of a matchbox. When I study it more closely, I realize it has a triangular shape that leads its movements.

It's a three-dimensional version of those classic computer arrows I've used all my life, only bigger.

"The pointer," I say. "It looks so real."

"We're dealing with your vision center," Ada explains. "It doesn't take a lot of effort to make things look solid."

Determined to locate Mom, I suppress my awe and use the trackpad to move the white arrow toward me, then away from me, then left and right. It looks kind of spooky when it passes through my body like a ghost on its second trip toward me, but that's how it should be since the arrow is simply in my mind.

"Use the up and down key to make it move vertically," Ada suggests.

I do as she says. The process reminds me of flying my Phantom 3 drone or playing some kind of video game.

"Press the Enter key or left-click to initiate the icon," Ada says before I get a chance to ask her what to do.

"Okay." I navigate the white pointer to the middle of the room so it touches the golden sphere. "Done."

As soon as I press Enter, the room disappears and the world falls into a bright tunnel of static and colors.

The tunnel ends abruptly, and I'm back in the room. A text box that resembles a street sign hangs in the air. I guess this is how Mom's Phase One reminders must look from inside her head. The box says, "Connection failure."

I explain what happened and see Ada's face drain of color. I know what she's thinking—I saw the code after all—but given the gravity of the situation, I say, "Please tell me what this means."

"A connection failure message can mean many things." Ada's voice is unsteady. "It could be a problem with the hospital Wi-Fi, for example."

"My phone is on the same network, and it's working fine," I counter. "Besides, doesn't cell connection kick in when Brainocytes aren't on Wi-Fi?"

"You're either on Wi-Fi or a cell network, and when on Wi-Fi, the firewall can still create this situation," she mutters. "Let me try a different port."

She appropriates the laptop, changes a variable in her code, recompiles the app, and—I'm guessing—reloads it into my head.

"Let's try again," she says. "The new icon should show up in a moment."

The golden sphere returns, and I repeat my earlier actions.

The result is the same: connection failure.

"It's happening again," I say, a heavy feeling growing in the pit of my stomach. "What else might be causing it?"

"It could still be the hospital firewall," Ada says. "But it could also be an issue with the connectivity on the other end. It's hard to say. I doubt it's because your mom's Brainocytes are disabled."

The hairs on the back of my neck stand up as though I got electrocuted. "Ada… the only way the Brainocytes can be disabled is if the host brain is dead, right?"

This is when I notice my uncle is standing there. I'm not sure when he returned, but judging by the stark paleness of his face, he at least heard the last thing I said.

I stare at him, icicles floating in my blood, and he stares back at me. Through all the mishaps of the day, I didn't let myself consider the possibility that my mom might not survive her kidnapping. Yes, it would've been a rational thing to worry about, but I just couldn't dwell on it, maybe because the idea is too unthinkable. Now that I'm forced to consider it, though, dark specks dance in my vision.

Despite Ada's reassurances, the evidence we have points to this horrific possibility.

Mom might already be dead.

CHAPTER THIRTEEN

Seeing our faces, Ada quickly says, "Those are just a few possible explanations. Instead of speculating, let's rebuild the app with debugging capabilities and maybe expand it so we can see where the connection is going awry."

I swing my legs off the bed. My aches and pains somehow fade into the background, perhaps because I'm so terrified.

"Okay," I say, grasping at the thread of hope Ada gave me. "We have to get to your place to retry this, right?"

"Ideally, yes," Ada says. "Though it might be closer to—"

"I don't want to get you into trouble," I cut in. "So as long as you have all the tools you need at your place, that's where we'll go."

"I might be even better equipped there than at Techno," Ada says. "I was going to tell you—"

I make a slicing gesture through the air. "I'm already sold on going. Uncle Abe, did you drive here?"

"Yes," my uncle says.

"Can you give us a lift to Williamsburg?"

"Of course," he says. "But—"

He stops and I follow his gaze to the somber countenance of the law enforcement official I labeled as the beet-potato guy. Now that my mind is no longer under the influence of drugs, I see that he doesn't really look like either one of those vegetables, per se. He looks more like the Mr. Potato Head toy—which only vaguely resembles a potato—and his complexion is a lighter shade of red than a beet.

"Detective Sawyer," my uncle says, his voice turning hopeful. "Do you have any new information for us?"

At the detective's expression, my hands and feet turn colder than when I nearly got frostbite in Moscow.

He's got bad news, I can feel it.

"There's something I want you to look at," Sawyer tells my uncle, and his tone intensifies my fear. Taking out a large phone from his jacket, he approaches Uncle Abe. "We found the black Mercedes Metris minibus," the detective explains. "There was one body discovered inside it, and I'd like you to take a look at it. My partner is on the other end; he'll point the camera for you."

My uncle takes the phone and looks at it for the ten longest seconds of my life. Then he screams the Russian equivalent of bloody murder, drops the phone on the floor, and covers his mouth with both hands as he doubles over. I look incredulously at my tough-as-nails uncle as he whimpers softly. This is a man who fought in Afghanistan, and the Soviet version of that conflict was a nightmare.

I jump to my feet, a surge of adrenaline turning the pain into a distant buzzing.

Before I can bend down, Sawyer retrieves the phone and hands it to me. "I'm sorry," he murmurs.

I look at the screen.

The camera scans the inside of the car, and I see a body sprawled on the seat in an unnatural position. It's a woman dressed in a white hospital gown—a woman who possesses an achingly familiar apple shape.

"No," I whisper. "It can't be."

The camera only captures the body up to its shoulders, so despite my uncle's reaction, it could be someone else. Of course, denial *is* one of the major stages of grief.

"Move the camera up," I instruct Detective Sawyer's partner on the other end. "Let me see."

The view begins to move.

With all my might, I will this person not to have Mom's face. I feel like I'd make a deal with the devil for it to be anyone but my mom.

The phone's owner finally lets me see her upper body, and I feel myself getting welded to the ground.

This body has no face.

Of any kind.

I blink, horror clouding my thinking.

It's not just the face that's missing.

It's also the scalp and the ears.

This body has no head.

CHAPTER FOURTEEN

Hypnotized by the atrocity on the screen, I can't look away.

My fingers loosen for a second, but I tense my grip before I can drop the phone like my uncle did.

I feel the half-digested mashed potatoes in my throat.

The person on the other end of the phone must understand the reaction the headless upper body generates in people, because he lowers the phone again, and this is when I see it.

On the body's right hand is a ring.

A giant emerald ring that changes everything.

"This is Mrs. Sanchez," I say hoarsely. "That's her ring."

I hand Ada the phone since she's seen the ring as well. Ada looks at the screen and nods. Then the phone on the other end must move again, revealing Mrs. Sanchez's headless body, because Ada turns translucently pale and clutches at her mouth as though she's about to lose her smoothie.

"It's not Mom," I say, this time in Russian, because I think my uncle is so lost in grief he didn't hear me identify the body. "It's this poor lady who was part of the experiment."

Relief relaxes the worry lines in my uncle's face. I realize I, too, must look relieved and feel a pang of guilt. A better person wouldn't be so glad to see Mrs. Sanchez dead in Mom's place.

Detective Sawyer takes out a notebook and pen and says, "Tell me about Mrs. Sanchez."

A half-coherent conversation follows, where I tell him about the poor woman, her family situation, her Alzheimer's, and her diabetes.

"Maybe she went into a coma," Ada says in a shaky voice. "She didn't get her shot this morning, and I doubt the kidnappers brought insulin with them."

"You're right," I say. "They might've finished her off, not wanting to take a comatose patient with them."

"But why take the head?" my uncle asks. "Is this some crazy cult? Or terrorists? Is there going to be a beheading video on YouTube?"

As soon as he asks this, a piece of the puzzle falls firmly into place.

Ada beats me to verbalizing my suspicions. "It's about our research," she says. "They took the head because that's where the Brainocytes are."

I've been too busy to think about the kidnappers' motives until now, but what Ada suggested is the best explanation, especially in light of the missing head.

The detective must also see it, because he asks us to explain the research to him again. I let Ada handle it while I take my uncle aside.

In Russian, I whisper, "Can you get rid of the cop for me? I want to go to Ada's house and retry the technological solution, but I have a feeling he might insist I identify Mrs. Sanchez in person or something. Afterwards, tell the hospital people I checked myself out and that they can send me my bill whenever it's ready. And don't worry, whatever Ada and I uncover, I'll keep you in the loop."

My uncle bobs his head, and as soon as Ada finishes her explanation, he turns to the detective. "Can I buy you a cup of coffee?" In a lower voice, but still loud enough so I can overhear, he adds, "There's a private matter I'd like to discuss with you."

The detective's eyebrows go up in an uncanny imitation of Mr. Potato Head. He probably thinks my uncle might tell him something about his son. The proposition is tempting enough that the detective says, "Sure. Thank you."

As soon as they walk off, I tell Ada, "We're leaving. Now."

Ada looks a little shell-shocked. She might still be processing Mrs. Sanchez's demise. Figuring she can sort out her emotions on the way, I grab the clothes my uncle got me and go into the bathroom.

Again, I'm amazed at the effects the adrenaline is having on my pain sensitivity. I almost feel normal as I take off the hospital gown, but when I put on the street clothes, the pain breaks through with such vengeance that I consider taking a Percocet. In the end, to keep my mind as clear as I can, I decide to tough it out.

"Let's go," I tell Ada when I leave the bathroom. "We'll have to cab it."

"Please, come in," Ada says after unlocking the reinforced door to her apartment.

I follow her, wondering if she was the paranoiac who installed it. Since her building is smack in the center of the most bohemian, and thus costly, part of Williamsburg, the neighborhood should be pretty safe, though I guess this door might predate the gentrification. I'm not surprised Ada chose to live here. She fits the neighborhood's flair perfectly, and her exorbitant salary is proportional to her brilliance.

Personally, I don't see the benefit in living in trendy neighborhoods unless they come with great restaurants and improve the commute. If I were in Ada's shoes, Williamsburg wouldn't work for me. Though it does have great food options, it's much too far from the Techno headquarters.

I myself live in Brooklyn Heights. It isn't the cheapest place in the world, but since I can afford a penthouse in NoHo (and thus anywhere in Manhattan), I rightfully consider my current multimillion-dollar brownstone a humble abode. In fact, I often feel like I'm following the advice in the book *The Millionaire Next Door*, which talks about self-made rich people living below their means. In my case, I'm more like a billionaire living next door to millionaires, but that's still below my means and within the spirit of the book, I think.

"My office is this way," Ada says and leads me through a sleek kitchen with modern-style cabinets and appliances that look like she got them at the MOMA museum. When we pass through the long, high-ceilinged corridor, I note a strange mix of punk bands and sci-fi movie posters occupying every inch of wall space.

"This is it," Ada says proudly as we enter a room that was originally meant to be the living room. What Ada created here looks a lot like a cross between a data center, a gadget lover's wet dream, and a mad scientist's lair.

In the cool air conditioning of the room, racks of servers hum computations and two enormous TVs are hooked up to the latest Xbox and PlayStation. A row of about a dozen different monitors occupies the wall to my right. At the center of it all stands a desk with five monitors and a keyboard that's split in half, with each half about a foot apart. A large trackpad sits in the middle, with a mouse to the right and a trackball to the left. A giant pair of headphones hanging over one of the screens completes the picture.

"Well, you got your input and output devices covered," I say, noting the row of video game controllers sitting on a large computer tower by the desk.

"Please, have a seat." Ada points to a large beanbag chair that could just as easily serve as a dog's bed.

I sit there, and she plops into a blue Herman Miller chair designed for ergonomic work. It's identical to the ones they have at the Techno offices.

"Give me a minute." Ada puts on the ginormous headphones and starts typing.

Her keyboard must be mechanical, with either blue or green switches, because every keystroke is loud enough to make me daydream about Percocet.

I might've dozed off, I'm not sure, but she startles me when she clears her throat and says, "I'm going to give you a custom-made environment I designed to work with the Brainocytes. I dubbed it AROS, which you can pronounce as Eros. It stands for Augmented Reality Operating System."

The room around me momentarily brightens, and a bunch of floating holographic images appear in the empty and, in some cases, not-so-empty space.

"Don't worry about the unfamiliar icons," Ada says. "Here"—she hands me the Xbox controller—"control the arrow with this."

Sometimes I get depressed when I think about how many video games I've played in my life. It's especially sad when I consider it within the context of, "Time is money." I feel like I'd be twenty times richer if I'd worked instead of playing Xbox for hours. Then again, I could say the same thing about binge-watching TV shows and other entertainment.

The controller sits comfortably in my hands, as only an object held for thousands of hours could. I twiddle the right stick, and the familiar white arrow appears, only this one is ghostly like everything else in this so-called AROS. It also moves much faster than the one at the hospital. Using the right stick, it takes me only a second to fly the pointer to the familiar sphere icon in the middle of the room, which also isn't solid in this instantiation.

I click it, and the result is the same as back in the hospital, only the "connection error" sign is see-through.

"Okay," Ada says without turning. "I traced it this time. The packets definitely left your head and reached Mitya's LA datacenter. There are no problems with the security there as far as I can see. The issue is that the server can't shake hands with your mom's hardware."

A cold fist grips my heart again. "So she's either not connected, or she's dead?"

CHAPTER FIFTEEN

"I don't think she's dead," Ada says. "I piggybacked on her ID and tried to ping the other participants. I got the same results each time."

"Which could just mean they're all dead, like Mrs. Sanchez," I say, but the tightness in my chest loosens at the ray of hope.

"That doesn't add up." Ada turns her chair to face me. "Why leave only Mrs. Sanchez's body behind? If they killed everyone, they would've taken their heads too and dumped the bodies. Heads are easier to transport."

Thanks to Ada's logic, I feel like I can stop hyperventilating a little and gather my thoughts. Getting an idea, I ask, "Is there a log somewhere on the server? Something that can tell you where my mom was at any given point? As they drove around, she probably got onto a couple of Wi-Fi spots before switching back onto the cell network. Wouldn't those events be logged somewhere?"

"Of course." Ada smacks herself on the forehead, swivels her chair back around to face her monitors, and clicks away for a few long minutes.

"You'll have to run the app again," Ada says when she stops working. "I'll be able to access the log afterwards."

The sphere icon shows up, and I click it.

"Yes," Ada says excitedly and attacks her keyboard once more. After a few minutes of frantic typing, she says, "Come take a look."

On the biggest monitor on her desk is a zoomed-out map of New York and its boroughs, with dots spread across it.

"You're a genius." Ada looks up at me. "Whenever Wi-Fi was available, the event was logged, with timestamps and GPS coordinates. That right there"—she indicates an area on the outskirts of Long Island—"is the last location that was logged."

She plays with her trackpad, and the map zooms in on the area, switching to satellite view.

"It's a private airport," I say, examining the greenery, the runways, and a couple of sleek planes.

"This explains why there isn't a connection." Ada swivels toward me again. "They must be in the air without a Wi-Fi connection."

Though I should feel relieved, the idea that someone is flying my mom to who-knows-where is deeply unsettling.

"We have to tell the police," I say. "They might be able to narrow it down to which plane and when."

"Maybe." Ada pinches her bottom lip. "It's certainly worth a shot."

"Can you write a version of this app that'll keep trying to connect and notify us when it succeeds?" I ask. "This way, when they land or drive into an area with cell service or Wi-Fi, we'll know right away."

Ada's dimple shines in full force, and she says, "I was just thinking along those same lines. I've got to say, I'm impressed you thought of it. Unlike me—" She suddenly stops, her dimple disappearing, and looks at me guiltily.

"Thanks, I think," I reply, frowning.

"I didn't mean to make that sound like an insult." Ada looks at her hands. "I've been trying to tell you something, but it can wait until we do this."

Before I can inquire further, she pointedly turns around, puts on her headphones, and begins writing code.

While she's working on that, I get in touch with the detective, explain why I had to leave the hospital in a hurry, and share the airport information. At the end of the call, I don't get the warm, fuzzy feeling that my extra bit of information might magically solve anything. Still, I promise to keep them in the loop on our end, get a reciprocal commitment in return, end the call, and contact my uncle to give him an identical update.

Before I get a chance to check if Ada is done, my phone lights up from an incoming video call.

A jolt of adrenaline hits my already overloaded system. It's Joe.

He wanted me to keep him posted, and I forgot to do exactly that. Did Uncle Abe tell Joe what he just heard, and does my cousin now want to berate me, or worse?

"*Privet*, Joe," I say, though the Russian "hello" and the very Americanized "Joe" go together about as well as an American eagle and a sickle and hammer. Although, strictly speaking, an eagle (albeit a double-headed one) *was* the main coat of arms of the Russian Empire before it went all Soviet, and I think they brought it back later in the nineties, but that was after I'd left. Some think of bears when they think of Russian symbols, but I've never understood why. There aren't any bears on any of the Russian or Soviet regalia, and if any nation should be associated with bears, it's probably China, given their fascination with pandas.

"Hey," Joe responds tersely. "Is this the Olga you told me about?"

The screen switches to the front-facing camera, and the face of the nurse who was working with Mom at NYU Langone fills the screen.

Instead of her usual uncaring expression, Olga looks disheveled and terrified, like a pigeon facing a rabid tomcat. She's standing in a dingy hallway, and I see a door broken off its hinges to her left.

"Yes," I say, doing my best to disguise my unsteady voice. "That's her."

My cousin perches the phone on something—probably a shoe rack, judging by the boot blocking part of my view. Then he walks into the frame and up to Olga and grabs her by her throat. "Tell me who took Nina Cohen if you want to live," he growls at her in Russian.

I'm almost too petrified to notice the *Terminator*-ish line Joe accidentally quoted. If my cousin were sane, he'd wait for an answer before blocking her speaking apparatus. But this is Joe, and he squeezes her neck until the woman's eyes bulge out of her head. When he lets go, she gasps for air but doesn't scream out answers the way I would have in her place.

Suddenly, a man sticks his head into the open doorway of the apartment. He's big, and his face is contorted in fury.

"What the fuck is going on here?" the guy says in accented English. "I'm calling the—"

Without a single word, Joe leaps at the newcomer.

In a smooth motion, my cousin punches the guy in the stomach. He must catch him straight in the solar plexus, because the big guy doubles over and gets a knee to the face.

"*Nyet*," Olga screams as she looks down at the fallen guy, and I realize Joe just took down her husband or boyfriend.

My cousin must realize this too, because he cruelly kicks the man in the ribs and says, "Speak, bitch, or you're scrubbing him off the floor."

Olga looks too stunned to speak, but Joe doesn't care and gives the guy another vicious kick, this time in the face.

Blood pours from the man's face. Seeing it, Olga frantically cries, "Stop!"

She starts speaking quickly, stress making her mix English and Russian together.

"*He spoke Russian,*" I puzzle out, "*but he had an accent, like he just arrived from there. He paid five grand for the information about the Russian woman, Nina Cohen, and the rest of the people. I don't know who 'they' are. I'll give you the money he gave me. I'm sorry. Please don't kill me. Please don't kill Grisha."*

"I want a name." Joe's hand is back around her neck. "Give me a name, or I'll break your fucking neck."

"He said to call him Anton," Olga gasps. "I don't know his last name. I don't know anything else."

"Describe Anton." Joe loosens his grip on her neck.

She frantically describes a man who sounds suspiciously like my attacker. Joe, who heard the description from me, must recognize that, because he's convinced enough to let go of her neck and pull out a bunch of computer printouts from his pocket.

"Which one?" He shows her the images.

My guess is he has the pictures the cops showed me earlier. I wonder how he got them. Joe's official line of work is private security, so maybe he has connections on the force? At least I hope that's what it is.

Olga points at an image, and in a gesture of uncharacteristic thoughtfulness, Joe turns it my way.

"That's the guy I saw," I say, disguising my voice again.

"Okay," he says to the woman. "Are you sure you don't know anything else? If I find out you do, if I think you lied to me, I'll come back and—"

"I told you everything," Olga whimpers. "I swear on my mother's health."

She rambles some more until Joe stomps on Grisha's leg, causing a loud crunch, and says, "Shut the fuck up."

Olga stops talking, and the silence is broken only by the man's ragged breathing from the floor.

"If you speak to the cops, everyone you know dies," my cousin says with as much emotion as someone complimenting her kitchen. "I'll start with him." He gives Grisha another kick.

Tears stream down Olga's face, but she keeps quiet and simply nods.

Satisfied, Joe steps over the broken body and looms over the phone. Then his palm gets huge, which I take to mean he grabbed the phone. He walks out of the apartment, and the screen shows blurry movements for a while.

The glimpses I get of the building's hallways and windows have a distinct grayness about them. That, combined with Olga's nationality, screams to me "somewhere on Brighton Beach."

My nausea makes a comeback and not just because I'm seeing the world spinning on the screen.

Taking in deep breaths, I unpeel my eyes from the phone and glance at Ada. She's still wearing her headphones and clicking away as though nothing's happened.

I turn off the video on my side so Joe doesn't spot Ada and say, "Joe, you realize I'm still on the line?"

My cousin stops walking and says, "Looks like that was a dead end."

I resist the urge to yell, "It almost literally turned into a dead end, you maniac." Instead, I say, "Not really. The fact that they paid for information supports our earlier suspicion that they want the technology. I was actually about to call you with an update of my own."

In the heavy silence that follows, I tell Joe what I know so far and finish with our airport findings.

"A private airport." He grunts. "They have money. I don't like the sound of this at all. Do you know who owns that place?"

"No."

"Fine. I need to talk to a few people. I'll call you back. Let me know if you find out where they flew to."

"Okay, I will," I say. "But before you go, can you email me the pictures you showed Olga? The ones with the kidnappers?"

"Sure," my cousin says and hangs up without so much as a goodbye.

CHAPTER SIXTEEN

I put my elbows on my knees, cradle my head in my hands, and wait until my breathing evens out.

This is exactly what I needed on top of everything else, to become an accessory to a crime. The righteous part of me wants to call the cops, but a more practical part vetoes that idea. First, if Joe found out—which is likely—he wouldn't hesitate to do something worse to me than what he did to that poor schmuck. Second, rightly or wrongly, Joe had good intentions, or at least intentions that will benefit my mom, and Olga certainly wasn't innocent in this mess. Plus, Grisha looked like he could've kicked Joe's ass, so that makes the beating somewhat defensive. Of course, the latter rationale is more of a rationalization, since self-preservation is more than enough to persuade me against ratting on Joe.

I briefly wonder if I should at least call an ambulance anonymously, but then I remember I don't even know where to send help. Olga can call 911 herself. Plus, since she's a nurse, she can give Grisha first aid if he needs it.

My conscience more or less appeased, I check my phone for the kidnappers' images and find that my cousin came through. I recognize the pictures from earlier, particularly Anton's, the guy who attacked me. Encouraged, I call Mitya and give him the rundown—minus Joe's interrogation of the nurse.

"So I can stand down?" Mitya's desk is filled with unopened bottles of Red Bull, bags of Cheetos, and a jar of green M&Ms, reminding me of our MIT days. "Sounds like you don't need the Brainocytes' privacy bypassed anymore."

"Yeah, that's the main reason I called," I say. "I didn't want you pulling an unnecessary all-nighter."

"I appreciate it," Mitya says. "Let me know if there's something I *can* do."

"Is that Mitya?" Ada asks from her desk, pulling off her headphones.

"Yep," I reply. "I was about to let him go."

"Wait a minute." She walks over, kneels next to me, and leans in close so the phone camera can see her. "Hi, Mitya. I need a favor."

"What's up?" Mitya clearly noticed Ada's proximity to me, and I can see he's itching to say something, so I surreptitiously show him my fist while pretending to rub my chin. He notices, winks, and just says, "What can I do for you, Ada?"

"You know the brain simulations we run on your STRELA servers?"

Strela means arrow in Russian, though I believe Mitya has a clever acronym behind it. Next to his personal time, the STRELA servers is the most generous resource he provides to the Brainocyte project. As of last year, this stupendous hardware topped the list of most powerful supercomputers in the world—or it would have if Mitya had disclosed the exact specs to anyone, which he hasn't. However, he did hint that it's multiple orders of magnitude more powerful than China's famous Tianhe-2, and that behemoth can do a whopping 33.86 petaflops. The plan is to use STRELA to run brain simulations that will allow Brainocytes to make the rest of the brain think the damaged tissue is up and running. It's at the core of Mom's later treatment.

"Yeah," Mitya says, his eyes glinting curiously. "Pricey buggers. What about them?"

"Can you double our allotment?" Ada asks.

"Mind if I ask why?" Mitya pushes up his glasses, and I know that means he's excited.

"Would you *not* do it if I refused to tell you?" Ada tenses up next to me.

"I'll do it since it's to help Mike," Mitya says. "But if you don't tell me why, I'll be pretty disappointed."

"I want Mike to hear the reason why first," Ada says. "Then, when things calm down a bit, I promise I'll explain, especially if you promise to keep quiet about it."

"Mike knows I can keep a secret," Mitya says. "Regarding more STRELA resources, consider it done." He grabs a handful of M&Ms, chews noisily, and adds, "Because it's *already* done. My old mentor at MIT gave up his research with their neuroscience department about a week ago, and since that was the only thing sharing your STRELA servers, those cycles are yours in one, two…" He starts typing on his computer—way too long for a three count, if you ask me—and finishes with, "Now."

"Sneaky." Ada's shoulders relax. "But thank you anyway."

"Yeah, thanks, dude," I say, pretending I'm not completely clueless about the reason for Ada's request. "I owe you big."

"We'll continue this conversation when I see you in person," Mitya says. "Now if you'll excuse me, I'm going to jump into my limo and read the thousand emails that have piled up thanks to you."

"Wait, what do you mean in person?" I nearly shout, trying to catch him before he signs off.

"Oh, I've had my private jet prepped, and my driver is on standby. In less than ten hours, I'll be in NYC."

"I really appreciate your help, but it's too much. You're—"

"Your best friend, and I didn't say I was flying out just to help you," Mitya says. "There's some business I need to take care of on the East Coast, and I want to visit Gramps, so don't worry about it."

"Still. Seriously, thank you," I say. "Is it possible to reach you in your jet?"

"I had to spend a quarter mil, but I now have Gogo's Wi-Fi on my plane." He gives us a smug grin. "And even if I didn't, didn't I show you this?" He takes out a clunky satellite phone and dangles it by its long antenna.

He didn't, and he knows it. When it comes to gadgets, Mitya loves showing off.

"Happy flight," I say, translating the traditional Russian farewell for Ada's benefit. "I owe you so big I don't even know where to start."

"I'll take your *Tales of Suspense* #39 and call it even," Mitya says. "Or your Kamakura katana."

"They're both yours," I say without hesitation.

"You know I'd help without any rewards," Mitya says, his tone turning unusually ceremonial.

"Of course. I know that," I say.

"Oh, and there's actually something Ada can do for me when I arrive," he says, his voice back to normal.

Jealousy floods me in a kind of "protect Ada's honor" alpha maleness that makes me want to reach through the phone and flick my friend on the nose.

"Get your mind out of the gutter," Mitya says when he sees my expression. "I mean she can give me the Brainocytes too. That lady who died, her backups are now useless, so…"

I feel a slight pang of disappointment. He really meant it when he said he's not just coming here on my behalf. *This* is probably what he wants most out of the trip. I should've guessed. With Mitya, everything he does has layers of benefit for him, but—and this is key—also for the people close to him, which includes me.

"We'll discuss that when you get here," Ada says evenly.

"Sounds good," Mitya says. "You should know that I already figured out why you want those extra STRELA servers. If it's for what I think it is, did you know I have more where those came from? In a matter of months, I can do better than double those resources; I can put a couple of zeroes behind what you have today."

Ada's eyes shine so brightly with avarice I bet Mitya can see it through the phone. She'd make a terrible poker player.

"It sounds like we do have things to discuss," she says, her voice betraying her almost as much as her eyes.

"We sure do," Mitya says and signs off.

I look at Ada, who only now realizes how close she is to me. Or I assume that's what happens, because she jumps to her feet and returns to her chair.

"That *Tales of Suspense* is when Iron Man first shows up in the comics, and it's in pristine condition," I explain. "And that katana is from the thirteenth century."

"I knew all that, except for the condition of the comic," Ada says, and I'm not sure whether she's boasting.

"Anyway," I say. "Let's get back to the reminder app."

"Right, that," Ada says. "To make my life easier, I'll give you a different build of AROS that will, among other things, include that app. Afterwards, we'll talk."

Before I can reply, she clicks Enter and I feel that slight "disturbance in the Force" that happens every time she reloads the software in my head.

More icons fill the room. In the middle of it all is the same sphere.

"Load it." Ada gets up and hands me the Xbox controller again.

I do as she says and tell her, "Nothing happened."

"And nothing *will* happen until your mom connects to a cell tower or a Wi-Fi hotspot," Ada says. "Once she does, not only will you get an alert, but so will I."

"Good. Is it loud enough to wake us up?"

"Oh yeah," Ada says mischievously. "It won't be easy to ignore, I assure you."

"Okay," I say. "Now tell me whatever it is you've been teasing me about."

Worry replaces the mischief on her face. "You must be hungry," she says. "Let's talk in the kitchen. You can press the A button to dismiss the icons."

I press A, and all the AROS images go away. When I get up, my legs and body want to scream, but I don't let Ada see it. She leads the way, and I scramble after her into the modern-artsy kitchen.

"You can sit there." She points at the metallic barstool.

After I sit, I tell her, "I'm still not that hungry."

"I have something very light in mind," she says. "Banana ice cream. You'll love it."

I raise my eyebrows at the idea of ice cream being light, especially for a health-obsessed vegan like Ada, but I don't say anything. I'm determined not to get sidetracked from whatever secret she's been building up to.

Ada goes to the freezer and takes out a plastic-wrapped packet filled with frozen, peeled bananas. The freezer is actually chock-full of these, making me wonder if she has a monkey living in her apartment somewhere. Ada takes out four bananas, walks up to a big blender, and puts them in. Before I can object, she starts the machine, and its roar sounds like it has either a chainsaw or a Harley Davidson motor inside. My brain tries to jump out of my skull, and I cover my ears as tightly as possible.

The noise stops, and Ada worriedly says, "I'm so sorry. Your concussion—I didn't think. Are you okay?"

"Sure." I cautiously let go of my ears, though they're still pulsing in pain. "Please don't do that again, or at least not for a couple of years."

"Sure," she says. "I don't know if it'll be worth the literal headache, but here you go." She scoops two-thirds of the smoothly blended banana into a pretty bowl. It looks a lot like ice cream, and I reach in with my finger, curious to taste it.

"Wait," she says and rummages through a cupboard. She pulls out a bag of mixed nuts and sprinkles them over the ice cream.

Before I can use my finger again, Ada places fancy spoons into our bowls and nods approvingly.

I taste the dish. The texture is spot on, but I'm not sure I'd go so far as calling it ice cream in terms of taste. Then again, it could easily pass for some kind of gourmet banana-flavored gelato, and given the simplicity and healthiness of the recipe, that's pretty impressive.

When she looks at me questioningly, I say, "It's yummy, but I think you've danced around the subject you're hiding long enough."

"All right." She licks her spoon nervously. "I'll just come out and say it." There's a long pause, and then she solemnly says, "I have Brainocytes in my head."

I nearly choke on a walnut, cough, and then stare at her, unable to shake off my incredulity. Of all the things

I expected to hear, this wasn't on the list. In all honesty, some part of me was hoping she knew something about the kidnapping and was about to tell me Mom was safe and sound. I guess I'm kind of single-minded that way.

Clearing my throat, I put my spoon down and ask, "How? Why?"

"Early on, during primate testing, I stashed a prototype set before we added all the ID security stuff to them." Ada looks down at her quickly melting ice cream. "I guess that makes me an embezzler. I used my position to—"

"Look, Ada," I interrupt. "If you're feeling bad about this, you shouldn't. I don't care about the costs. I'm one of the primary investors, so whatever you took, it was mainly my money. But if you wanted Brainocytes, all you had to do was talk to me."

She looks at me, her eyes glinting with hope despite the suspicious moisture there. "I was impatient, and I didn't think anyone would understand."

"So you put hardware that was meant for a chimp inside your head?" I chance another small spoonful of dessert.

"Aside from security, the Brainocytes haven't changed since then," Ada says with a sigh.

Epiphanies explode in my head, and I say, "So that's why you kept insisting how safe the treatment is." I rub the bridge of my nose. "You already went through it."

"It's also where all these advanced apps and the custom OS for the Brainocytes came from," she says. "Or did you think what I gave you was just meant for your mom?"

"I wouldn't know the difference," I say, but realize that it does explain why her home office is set up better than the one at Techno. "When exactly did this happen?"

"A few months back, right before Kathy broke things off with you. The timing was poor." She looks at my bowl and says, "It's melting."

I shove a couple of spoonfuls of ice cream into my mouth and ignore the resulting brain freeze. So this is why Ada was acting so strangely around me. I was wrong when I thought it was because she was wary about me asking her out; it must've been her guilt about the Brainocytes. I swallow the pulverized banana and say, "Okay, I guess I get the how part, and I can probably guess the why, but I want to hear you say it."

"That part's simple." Ada looks at me steadily, almost challengingly. "I did it for the same reason Mitya is helping us, for the same unspoken reason everyone at Techno is working on this technology. I simply didn't want to wait." She takes a deep breath. "I did it so I can transcend being human."

CHAPTER SEVENTEEN

Maybe I expected Ada to use slightly less pompous verbiage, but I did suspect that transhumanism was behind it all.

"Can you be more specific?" I scrape the bottom of the bowl for the last bit of ice cream. "What exactly did you do to yourself?"

"Well, for starters, I can almost seamlessly do anything that usually requires a computer with just my mind, at nearly the speed of thought," she says. "They say a modern cellphone allows its owner to have access to more information on the internet than President Clinton had during his presidency. My abilities are those of this modern cellphone owner, only taken much further. I can do advanced calculations, access Wikipedia, and Google any question, all in my head. You get the idea?"

The implications are truly incredible, but I put all that aside and say, "Okay, it's not *that* far removed from Phase Three, which Mom and the others were about to get."

"True. Working on my own, I never really went far beyond what we were going to do for your mom. I just expanded on it," Ada says. "But it was enough of a starting point. Mind-computing access aside, when you combine our brain region simulations with a healthy brain, you get a boost in intelligence, and not the metaphorical kind based on apps like I was just talking about. A much more literal one. You know, the topic JC never likes to talk about."

"Okay, neuroscience isn't my strong suit, but I get the gist of how we can simulate certain key brain regions to bypass my mom's trauma," I say, thinking out loud. "The Brainocytes will make the right neurons think a healthy version of that broken brain tissue is in place and firing. I knew enhancement was theoretically possible, but—"

"It'll use that same basic premise," Ada interrupts, "but it'll essentially provide the brain with extra brain regions, as well as faster versions of the original regions. Eventually, neuroplasticity will kick in, and the brain will learn how to really use the extra power. Though even out of the box, I was able to give myself a certain boost—"

"Wait," I say. "I just realized something. This is what's been behind your off the charts coding lately, isn't it? I was just thinking about it earlier today."

"Probably. The brain boost helps with everything, but in this case, my coding improvements might also be due to the integrated development environment—aka AROS IDE—that I've developed. I can literally write code in my head." She beams at me. "I'm so glad I can finally share this with someone. It's so amazing. After a while, typing mentally and using the IDE turns spooky, and I almost feel like the apps get written by me just willing it."

"Hold on." I cross my arms. "So why did you use that super-loud keyboard today?"

She bites her lip. "I was waiting for a good moment to tell you. Sorry. I didn't do it just to fool you. I use the thing for practice sometimes, and for cover at the office. In any case, it's good for me to stay sharp with older tools, because who knows what could happen one day. In general, this enhancement does have a small flaw—you have to be on Wi-Fi or a cell network, though the latter offers reduced capabilities."

"That's true." I uncross my arms and study her with wonder. "So you'd get dumber if you went camping? But how does the keyboard help you with that? I don't see why you'd ever need a keyboard again—once you come out to your coworkers, that is."

"It's like eBooks versus paperbacks." She picks up our bowls and puts them in the dishwasher. "Some people like one or the other. I still like both, even though I can now read books without any devices at all. Still, even when I used the Kindle, which I loved, sometimes I'd want to read a paperback, and I still do. There's something about the feel of paper in my hands and the smell of ink on the pages. Using a keyboard is like that—a sentimental activity, I guess. As to getting dumber if I'm not around a cell tower or connected to Wi-Fi, you're not that far off. I hate not being on the internet. It's more debilitating than being drunk or stoned, and it's why I never take the subway anymore—even above ground, the reception is abysmal."

"Wait a minute." I decide to voice a concern my mom once raised when I explained the brain simulation stuff to her. "These simulated brain regions aren't simulating your own brain, right?"

"Right," Ada says. "In theory, the Brainocytes can be used to map out my brain, but that isn't what I did. I just used the more generic simulations based on the ones your mom was going to utilize."

"So this is like having parts of someone else's brain in your head?"

"Sort of, I guess, but that isn't an issue. I think of it as having extra neurons supplementing my brain," she explains. "The simulated regions adapt and learn to work together with my biological brain, which means I'll make them my own over time. But I see where you're going with this. Are you worried about the slippery question of identity? Like what happens when the supplemental brainpower gets more powerful than my biological brainpower? Will I be a mind running on a computer server using my body as an avatar? Are you worried about what will happen if I lose connection in that scenario? If I will feel as dumb as a rock in comparison to my normal self?"

I didn't mean to ask her any of the interesting questions she just raised, but since we're going down that road, a big question pops into my head. "What about consciousness? Given the scenario you're describing, if you had more of a simulated brain than a meat one, would you still be conscious?"

"If the brain regions are properly simulated, you won't be able to tell the difference between them and the biological versions, so why wouldn't the whole be conscious? I imagine the resulting Ada would be *more* conscious than I currently am, with her mind expanded and all that. Anyway, we don't need to worry about all these philosophical questions, since the hardware required for even a fraction of the human brain is enormous. The STRELA servers are the best hardware in the world, and they can only simulate small regions. So yeah, so far, I can assure you I'm still conscious." She winks at me.

"But wouldn't it have been better to have these answers before you jumped in and used the technology on yourself?" I ask.

"No." Ada's forehead crinkles. "Doing this now will actually help me bring about more powerful advancements, since the smarter I am, the more capable I am. I see each future mind boost as an incremental update, akin to what's already happened to me. It's not scary at all. So in the future, say when the STRELA servers' capabilities double or triple, I'll easily be able to imagine how things will turn out. The bigger and better-simulated brain regions will adapt and integrate with my brain just like this first batch did. Same thing will be true down the line, when hardware and simulations that are ten or a hundred times better come about. Each boost will become part of me, the same way new neurons do. The resulting Ada will still be me, and obviously conscious, even if she doesn't fully understand the how of it. It's not that different from how a baby turns into an adult over time."

I consider her incremental vision and realize she's right. The "baby me" reached my current state by growing new neurons in a process called neurogenesis. Even as an adult, I have neurons that die and get reborn as part of a slower neurogenesis process. Yet, from the moment I was born until now, I've always been *me*, no matter how much brain tissue got added. If my brain grows more neurons or a new region, I'll still be conscious and feel like myself. I'll just be smarter and more capable of interesting feats. The same is probably true for this virtual brain extension.

"But what if Mitya shuts down the servers?" I ask.

"What if I got a lobotomy right now? What if Stephen Hawking lost that special chair and his voice synthesizer? What if I got an infection and there weren't any antibiotics around?" Ada retorts. "It would obviously suck, but I won't hold back my potential over what-ifs."

"Going back to the scenario where you have the hardware that allows the non-biological half of your brain to exceed the biological half," I say, getting into the spirit of things. "Wouldn't that lead to a purely simulated version of you? And what's to stop that creature from spawning a whole race of Ada copies and taking over the world?"

"A girl can only hope." She fluffs up her Mohawk. "But seriously, as more hardware becomes available, such implementation details can be fleshed out. I can think of ways to keep myself a singleton, if that was what I wanted."

I sit in silence, pondering all this. I can picture these brain extensions morphing into something like brains in the cloud over time. Such technology has the potential of redefining the human condition so completely that the resulting beings would barely be recognizable as *Homo sapiens*.

Ada looks at me anxiously, and I realize I've been silent too long. Figuring we can discuss the future consequences in more detail later, I turn the conversation toward a more pragmatic direction. "I take it you asked for double STRELA cycles to do this brain boost for me?"

"Of course." Ada's unease disappears, and her eyes gleam. "It would be silly not to take advantage of the situation."

I now understand the reason for her sudden candor. Okay, maybe I understood halfway through eating my ice cream, but I no longer have any doubts. She wants me to become like her. She wants to give me all these apps and the intelligence boost. Actually, she already gave me some of it—hence her earlier statement of "here is a new custom OS, but I can't tell you why yet."

"It's already in my head, isn't it?" I say, looking at her.

"Yes," she says. "But it wouldn't work without Mitya's help, and you still have to launch an app to get it started."

"And the other icons?"

"Some are what your mom was going to have," Ada says. "I had help from my minions on those. A bunch of the others are utility apps I wrote for myself. I branched off some open-source projects when I had to, and now you have the basic necessities like a web browser, terminal emulator, email, texting, as well as a videoconference app, word processor, and the IDE I mentioned earlier—just to name a few apps off the top of my head."

"I think I want to go back to your office now," I say and get up. "Thanks for the snack."

"You're welcome." She leads me back to the beanbag chair I've started to view as mine.

Sitting down, I grab the controller and click the A button. The transparent shapes reappear, each representing one of the apps she just mentioned. They form a circle around the room, and I can guess their functions just by looking at them. Zooming in on one to my right, I ask, "That small sphere surrounded by tricolor swirly lines is your version of the Chrome browser, isn't it?"

"I actually branched off Chromium, the project Chrome draws its source from, so you're close," Ada says. "The codebase is mainly C++, my strong suit, so I figured why not make my life easier?"

"Let me try it," I say and use the controller to hover the white arrow over the 3D Chromium logo.

A slightly see-through screen shows up in front of my face.

"I think the folks who made *Minority Report* might sue you," I say, marveling at the apparition. The ghostly screen is the size of my seventy-inch TV. On the screen is an empty page with an address bar in that minimalistic style I associate with Chromium's popular progeny.

I use the remote to move the screen closer to my face and direct the cursor to the address bar, but then I realize I have no way of typing text.

"You'll have to learn how to control all this stuff with your mind," Ada says after I raise this issue with her. "For now, you can use this." She walks over to her desk drawer and fishes out a wireless keyboard.

After she does her magic to hook it up to my AROS, I put the keyboard on my lap, type *techno.com* into the address bar, and press Enter.

The official Techno website looks glorious in this version. The colors are sharper and the text is crystal clear, which makes sense since I'm not really seeing this stuff. The Brainocytes are making my visual center think I am, so the resolution can be anything the eye can see.

"Damn," I whisper after browsing the internet for a few minutes. "This is already better than Precious."

"Yeah," Ada says. "I now use my iPhone for video calls only, and then only for cover. For everything else, I use my head."

"I can't blame you. What do these other icons do?"

She walks me through the apps, and as we go, I log in to things like the email client, the calendar, and so on. Throughout, I feel something between kid-on-Christmas excitement and whatever a crack addict feels when scoring a new fix. This is a thousand times cooler than setting up a new computer or smartphone, even one as prodigious as Precious.

When we get to the music player, I ask, "Does hearing work the same way as vision?"

"The principle is the same. The brainocytes stimulate the right brain area," Ada says. "Oh, and by the way, you're stuck listening to my music library for now."

I browse through her eclectic collection until I find a song called "Where is My Mind?" by The Pixies and press play.

The song starts, and it's the next best thing to being at an actual concert. I again marvel at the entertainment possibilities of this technology. When Techno goes public, all its employees will be rolling in money, and my bank account might finally measure up to Mitya's. Actually, no. Mitya invested so much into Techno that if it grows, he's going along for the ride too. Oh well. It's never been a competition between us anyway, since he would've won many times over already.

"I don't envy the lawyers who'll have to figure out if having songs in someone's head violates copyright," I say. "Loving the music, by the way."

As I say it, I feel a spurt of guilt for enjoying music while my mom is suffering who-knows-what. With the guilt comes sickening worry, and the throbbing in my head comes back with a vengeance, as does the pain from all my injuries.

Taking a breath, I slowly release it and push the worry and guilt away. What I'm doing will help Mom; I have to believe that, or I'll go crazy.

Leaving the song playing in the background, I move on to more apps, trying to feel the enthusiasm this technology should generate.

"So," I say when there are only two unexplained icons left, "I take it the brain-looking thingy launches the brain boost, or whatever you call it, but what's this sphere with a half-moon shape and white halo around it?"

"That's a tongue and gray hair," Ada says, mischief returning to her face. "Just use it and you'll see. You'll like it, I promise."

I click the app and a figure appears, floating in the room. This time, it's the Star Wars franchise Ada is ripping off, because a blue-gray holographic version of the cartoony Einstein, the AI assistant, says, "Hello."

His German-accented voice is as clear as if he'd spoken from where he's floating.

"Einstein," I say. "Remind me to get a new car in a few weeks."

"He can't hear you," Ada says. "I haven't gotten around to hooking him up with speech recognition like I did with the VOIP stuff. But you can type to him, and I can tell you from experience, once you can do it mentally, it'll be better than speaking."

I type my request and watch Einstein walk over to the calendar app and launch it. The reminder is instantly filled out, though I guess Ada didn't bother creating an animation of Einstein actually writing it out, which would've been neat.

"Okay, Einstein, please go away," I type, and the hologram fizzles out.

"I'm officially impressed," I say, "and I haven't even boosted my intelligence yet."

"Strictly speaking, just using these tools boosts a person's intelligence significantly. But you're right. You're currently doing the same things someone with a very nice smartphone could do, but much faster—which is an important difference." Getting up, she walks over to me and puts a hand on my shoulder. "I think it's time to try the boost," she says with a smile.

Her hand on my shoulder seems to spread warm energy throughout my body, making it hard to concentrate on what she's saying. Straining to focus, I wonder if I want to try the boost. Part of me shouts a resounding yes. The appeal is the same as the reasons I went to MIT and continue to read scientific journals and pursue intellectual self-improvement. More important to the situation at hand, the smarter I am, the higher the chance that I'll figure out where Mom is, as well as who took her and why. I tell myself this as I hover the 3D pointer over the brain icon.

"You can turn it off if you don't like it," Ada reminds me and squeezes my shoulder before dropping her hand. "But I doubt you ever will."

I try to think of something appropriate to say and decide to use the legendary phrase uttered by Yuri Gagarin, the first Russian cosmonaut.

"*Poyekhali*," I say. I'm about to translate it as "let's go" for Ada, but she surprises me yet again.

"I think Armstrong's 'one small step' is more apropos," she says, smiling.

I think back to all the Russian I've spoken behind Ada's back and redden. "You speak Russian now?"

Her smile widens. "Just what I've been able to learn in the last few months. The boosted intelligence has helped."

"And how much Russian is that?"

"I little Russian speak," she says with a horrendous accent. "I better at understanding than speaking."

Shaking my head in disbelief, I repeat Gagarin's statement and activate the brain icon.

CHAPTER EIGHTEEN

Nothing happens.

I count to twenty and say, "I don't feel anything."

"Well, yeah," Ada says. "What did you expect to feel, exactly?"

"Smarter," I mutter, feeling like maybe the intellect boost went in the opposite direction. "Or at least something."

"I told you, your brain needs to adjust to this new state of being," Ada says. "The effects are subtle at first. Even as early as the second day, I did better on a slew of cognitive ability tests, even though I felt the same, aside from a certain sharpness that's hard to describe. The only noticeable thing was those weird pre-cog moments I had in the beginning."

"Pre-cog moments?" I frown at her. "As in, psychic?"

"No, but sort of. It was very strange." She chews on her lower lip. "It's like a vivid daydream or hallucination. You see what's about to happen." I look at her incredulously, so she clarifies, "I don't mean literally. The vision can easily be inaccurate. It's a side effect of the not-yet-integrated portions of the simulated brain regions anticipating the result of a decision or action but serving the information to your normal brain too quickly. Thanks to neuroplasticity, they later learn how to work together, so don't worry. It took a day or so before I stopped having these episodes, and since then, I suppose I've simply made better decisions, so no visions required."

"Still sounds strange," I say. "Are you sure you didn't eat too many magic mushrooms or peyote?"

"The effects of mescaline and psilocybin are very different from what I'm talking about," Ada says without blinking. "If you think about the brain's primary function in nature, this phenomenon isn't that odd. The brain tries to predict what's about to happen in its environment. If bushes rustle, the brain might predict a lion is lurking behind them and send the rest of the body into a fight-or-flight response. This is similar, only it's the new brain regions that are shouting 'lion,' and since your regular brain isn't used to it, it shows you a quick dream of a lion as a way to cope with the new experience. That's my theory, anyway."

"Having done neither of those drugs, I'll take your word for it." The nagging aches throughout my body and my overall tiredness make it hard to hide the hint of irritation in my voice as I add, "But this would've been great information to have *before* I enabled this thing in my brain."

"I didn't think it would matter." Ada takes a tiny step back. "It went away for me, and you can disable the whole thing at any moment."

I instantly feel bad for putting her on the defensive. "Sorry if that sounded accusatory." I blow out a breath. "I've had a long day."

"It's not a problem," she says, though I can tell she's still miffed.

"How can I make this process go smoother?" I ask, knowing that letting Ada geek out might improve her mood.

I was spot on with my question. Her bad mood forgotten, Ada rattles out, "My advice is to put a load on your brain. The bigger, the better. Double your reading material, check out those startup financials or whatever it is you do as a venture capitalist. Try your hand at programming again. You can create your own apps that'll run inside your head, and my IDE will make coding easy, even for a noob like you. At the very least, use games like Brain Age; they stimulate all sorts of brain regions and help you see your progress as you go. My Brain Age is 20, which is very good. Take IQ tests or the SATs and the GRE test repeatedly, and you'll see daily gains, for whatever that's worth. In general, any new intellectual pursuit is a good idea."

"Got it. I'd say I'm covered for a while, since just playing with this new toy in my head should keep my brain stimulated on multiple levels."

"You're one hundred percent right," Ada says. "To that end, I advise you to start getting rid of your reliance on the keyboard and controller."

"Sure," I say. "What do I do?"

Ada sets things up for me to learn how to use my mind instead of the keyboard. The protocol is identical to what the people in the study were doing yesterday, but because I can type around a hundred words per minute, the process is quicker and easier for me. I start by typing out predetermined text while the Brainocytes keep an eye on what happens in my brain. Afterwards, using the same text, I mime typing in the air, and the Brainocytes report to Ada an extremely high degree of correlation between "real" and "mimed" typing. I progress to needing less and less physical involvement and eventually just mentally pretend to type. Again, the Brainocytes prove something neuroscience has known for a while: many regions of the brain that activate during regular typing still activate when I mentally type. It's a lot like how athletes can mentally run through their exercises and achieve actual gains.

When I can type by thought alone, I picture what this aspect of the technology will do for people with disabilities and swell with pride at being a small part of it.

Dealing with the controller is even easier since I'm more proficient at video games than I am at typing. Ada isn't surprised and jokes that our generation of gamers might actually have a large portion of our brain dedicated to video game controllers.

"You know, it's possible," I say and mentally bring up the email app. "I read about neuroscience experiments that found the brains of pianists were noticeably different from the average person's."

"Anything you do changes your brain." Ada yawns the most contagious yawn ever and adds, "But yeah, very absorbing and challenging activities have an even bigger impact, and video games can certainly be that."

Unable to suppress my retaliatory yawn, I use the email client window hovering in front of my face to mentally type out an email to Ada, writing, "So is this that technologically enabled telepathy you spoke about?"

She looks distant for a moment, then gives me the widest grin I've ever seen.

In utter silence, I hear a ding in my head and check my email, finding an email response from Ada that says, "Exactly."

"The only issue is that the NSA can, in this case, intercept our thoughts," I joke out loud.

"Sure, having part of your thinking in the cloud could indeed expose your private thoughts to the NSA. That's a potential worry if you're the paranoid type," Ada says. "I say we can cross that bridge later, probably by using heavier encryption."

A text message arrives in my head in the form of a jumping green sphere with a little text balloon icon next to it. I mentally click on it, and the message reads, "I prefer using texting for telepathy rather than email, if you don't mind."

I notice Ada sometimes closes her eyes when she works with her version of AROS. For some reason, that makes her look even cuter, which I didn't think was possible.

Closing my eyes is a great idea, so I do it as I play with my mental apps for a few minutes. What I end up experiencing is icons hanging in the darkness without the distraction of the surrounding room. It's definitely a good way to use the system, but having my eyes closed has one big flaw: I instantly feel the weight of the crazy day press against my eyelids, and another yawn creeps up on me.

"Okay, I'll take that as a hint that you want to go to sleep," Ada says through yet another yawn. "I can't blame you."

"Let me call a cab," I say, opening my eyes and glancing around uncomfortably.

"Nonsense," Ada says. "You should stay here."

"Are you sure? I don't want to impose on you."

I'm deathly tired, so I was actually fishing for her to extend this exact offer, but now that she has, I find myself wondering what it means, if anything. Besides, where would I sleep? Her apartment is big, but—

"There's a couch in the library room," Ada says, and for a moment, I get the creepy feeling that the Brainocytes somehow let her glimpse my private thoughts.

"That'll work," I say, perhaps a tad too quickly. "Thank you."

The adrenaline that was covering up the pain from my injuries must be fully out of my system, because my shoulder's killing me and my legs feel so wooden I can barely stand. I contemplate taking pain pills but decide that might make me miss the alarm Ada set up for Mom's locator app. I just hope I can fall asleep as is.

"Alternatively, you can take my bed and I'll take the couch," Ada says, playing the role of mind reader once more.

"No." I step toward her. "I can't let you do that. I'll take the couch."

"I fall asleep on it with a book all the time," Ada says, looking up at me. "You're what, six-one, six-two? You probably won't even fit on the couch without having to fold your legs under you."

"Can you show it to me?" I shift from foot to foot. "I'm sure you're exaggerating."

She leads me into the library, and I realize she might've actually downplayed how unsuitable this sleeping arrangement is. The so-called couch is a glorified loveseat. Even with her barely above five-foot petite frame, she might feel cramped on it.

"It's fine," I fib and try to hide my disappointment by looking at the rows of books in the room. The subject matter varies greatly. There's a big philosophy of science tome on the shelf to my right, and adjacent to it are a bunch of science fiction novels that I've either read or always meant to. A row of computer science books sits below that. Sadly, I've read these or similar ones before. I have a flashback to the college years I'll never get back as I glimpse exciting titles like *Design and Analysis of Algorithms* and *Data Structures and Other Objects*. I chuckle when I spot the *Introduction to Ada* textbook, a volume that teaches Ada's namesake's programming language—not how to pick her up.

Ada doesn't buy my lie or my avoidance strategy of looking at her books. She waits until I catch her gaze and softly says, "Neither of us has to sleep on this torture device if you promise to be a gentleman."

Stunned, I notice her eyes are the same translucent smoky brown as the thousand-dollar cognac bottle I have sitting in my bar at home. I stare into them for a few moments before I remember she's waiting for a coherent response. "I can pretend to be a gentleman, sure."

She smiles, steps closer, and brushes the backs of her fingers over the extra swollen side of my face. "You poor thing."

I catch her hand and hold it. It's small in my hand and almost painfully warm against my battered face.

Ada waits a couple of beats, then steps out of my reach, pulling her hand away. "Let me use the shower first. I'll put some towels out for you," she says. "Do you want to wait here or go to the lab?"

"I'll wait here," I say, gesturing at the couch.

Ada leaves, and I take a seat, my world whirling from that brief touch.

As the pleasant haze of excitement fades, I feel all the aches and pains of the day again. It's as if I'm one hundred and seventy. Closing my eyes, I call up the AROS interface and use the apps I didn't get a chance to fully examine. When I tire of the apps, I set the alarm app to make sure I don't oversleep tomorrow and dismiss the interface.

Before I can open my eyes, I feel something moving on my leg, followed by a crawling sensation on my shirt, followed by a sudden stop and a small pressure on my chest.

Something just scurried up my body.

"What the—?" I exclaim in panic and open my eyes.

A giant pair of creepy pink eyes are staring me down.

And they look hungry.

CHAPTER NINETEEN

Okay, so on second thought, the eyes aren't giant. They're actually pretty beady, and they're not that creepy either, just those of an albino.

A white lab rat is sitting on my chest. Upon closer inspection, besides hunger, I also notice a glimmer of intellect in its gaze, though maybe that's just my jittery imagination.

"Mr. Spock," Ada says sternly from the doorway. "How many times have I told you to be mindful of my guests?"

The rat looks at Ada, then back at me, its eyes seeming to say, "I can read your thoughts, Mike, and I'm warning you, here and now, don't try any funny business."

Ada scoffs at Mr. Spock and comes toward me.

I ignore the rat long enough to notice what Ada is wearing, or more specifically, what she *isn't* wearing, which is pretty much anything other than a large towel. The towel is wrapped midway around her chest, and her breasts are perkier and lovelier than I imagined—and my imagination has worked overtime in this area. Even more interesting is the fact that the towel only extends a few inches past her bikini area.

I suddenly feel like I'm in a banya—a steam bathhouse Russians like to visit in winter. It's as if the temperature in the room just tripled.

Seemingly oblivious to my reaction, Ada gently takes the rat off my chest, and I glimpse even more of her flesh. To avoid breaking my promise about being a gentleman, I try not to gawk as she walks away. Still, I'm only human, and I can't help noticing her shapely legs and the dancer-like muscles of her back. I also spot a brightly colored tattoo on her shoulder.

"Let me feed you, my furry troublemaker," Ada says to the rat in a voice people usually reserve for babies or dogs. In a normal, or perhaps slightly playful tone, she tells me, "Come if you want to watch."

I'd watch her do her accounting, knit, or perform any other boring activity as long as she was wearing that outfit. I get up, suddenly feeling spryer, and follow her into the kitchen.

Putting her little charge on the floor, Ada reaches into a drawer and pulls out a box.

"These are lab blocks," she says, forestalling my question, and gives the box a shake.

I hear the scurry of many little feet on the floor as Ada takes out some blueberries and spinach from the fridge.

She pours the brown pellets from the box onto six tea-cup saucers and then adds a little fruit and veg. Each plate is instantly taken over by a white lab rat.

As I watch them eat, I notice the rats' fur isn't perfectly white. Someone, probably Ada, added colorful streaks on top, like a Mohawk. There's a green-streaked rat and a blue one, while Mr. Spock's streak is a very un-mister-like pink, though I guess the color does match his eyes.

"That's Kirk, McCoy, Uhura, and Scotty." Ada points at each rat. "That there is Chekov, and I bet if he could speak, his accent would be stronger than your uncle's."

"That's kind of racist, specist, and maybe ratist." I snicker, then add seriously, "They all had Brainocytes in their heads?"

"Not *had*. They still have them," Ada says and pours water into a big bowl. "It's all still up and running. Why do you think my babies are so smart?"

I examine the rat crew with renewed interest. When developing Brainocytes, Techno initially experimented on so-called brainbow rats—rats that were genetically modified to have a spectrum of florescent colors added to their neural cells, making them ideal for study under a confocal microscope. To see real-life versions of these famous critters, plus ones with a brain boost to boot, is a big surprise. It also makes me wonder if maybe I didn't imagine the intelligence I saw in Mr. Spock's eyes. Maybe he took better advantage of his rat version of the intelligence boost than I did.

"Can I pet him?" I ask, looking at the pink-streaked rat.

"He'd love that," Ada says. "But not while he's eating."

As though on cue, Mr. Spock stops eating, drinks from the water bowl, and scurries over, giving me an uncannily cat-like stare that seems to say, "I'll tolerate you, mortal."

I gingerly reach out and rub the fur. Spock graciously allows it, or at least he doesn't bite me, which I think is the rodent equivalent.

I guess I never inherited my mom's deep-seated fear of rats. Quite the opposite, I find this little encounter kind of soothing, and I wonder if rats can be employed as some sort of pet therapy. Then again, given the day I've had, it wouldn't take much to lower my blood pressure.

"Where's the shower?" I ask softly, afraid I'll spook Mr. Spock.

"I'll show you," Ada says and leads me down the corridor, past her office, and to the bathroom all the way at the end.

Since I'm still trying to be a gentleman, I primarily study Ada's tattoo as we walk. Unfortunately, I have to give up and look elsewhere, because the towel is hiding most of it.

"You can use those towels and wear those boxers once you're done." Ada points at the pile of fluffy towels and the pair of purple shorts.

"Where did you get those?" I ask cautiously. I don't want to come across as ungrateful, but if they belonged to her ex-boyfriend, there's no way I'm wearing them.

"I like sleeping in boxers," Ada says, and I worry I might start drooling at the image. "They're clean, and I don't have cooties."

"I definitely didn't mean to imply you have cooties."

The Enterprise crew in the kitchen might have something worse, but I don't mention that.

"Do you need help?" Ada asks, her expression unreadable. "With all your injuries, is it hard to undress?"

"I should be fine," I say quickly. Inhaling a breath, I discreetly swallow and add, "Thank you."

She nods toward the kitchen. "I'll go hang out with the gang. See you in a few."

"One moment," I say, and Ada stops in the doorway.

"What's your tattoo supposed to be?" I ask, and maybe it's my imagination, but I think I see slight disappointment flit across Ada's delicate features. Maybe she hoped I'd ask for her help undressing?

"It's the donkey and the dragon," Ada says. "I got it after watching *Shrek*. It's also why I never mix pot with alcohol anymore."

She turns around and lowers the towel just enough for me to get a good look at the ink. Now that she told me what it is, the big pinkish-purple head and the small creature next to it make perfect sense.

Then I realize something else, and a nervous chuckle accidentally escapes me.

The towel goes back up, and Ada gives me a stern look. "Are you laughing at me?"

"No," I say, but a new bout of laughter is on the tip of my tongue, itching to escape. "Don't you see what this makes you?" I gesture at her short haircut, which isn't sticking up as usual since it's wet. Then I mime typing on a keyboard.

"No." She narrows her eyes at me. "What does it make me?"

"The girl with a dragon tattoo," I say, grinning.

"You're clearly tired," Ada says, but her sneaky Mona Lisa smile touches the corners of her eyes again. "Shower so we can go to sleep."

She closes the door behind her, and I hear her chuckling down the hall.

Taking off my clothes is painful, but I manage it. Maybe I should've said yes to her offer.

The shower only hurts where my shoulder is stitched up, but the pain's tolerable. It might not have hurt at all if Ada had helped me get soaped up—assuming that was even on the table. I decide that the coconut shampoo is Ada's trademark scent, so I opt to wash my hair with baby soap instead.

After I finish and towel off, I put on the boxers. They're snug, and I wonder if that means Ada and I have approximately the same butt size. Given our height and weight differences, I figure my heinie is proportionally small, which is manly, while hers is rather curvy, which is awesome. I wisely decide not to discuss this with Ada, especially since I'm in her apartment and she could unleash her rats on me, like that Willard guy from the old horror movie.

Ada meets me outside her room, wearing comfy-looking PJs. Part of me hoped she'd decide to sleep in a pair of boxers, but I can respect her more conservative choice. Besides, it might help me be a gentleman as promised.

Her bedroom is dark, but I can still make out the stripper pole by the closet. I fight the urge to rub my eyes as they widen at the mental images of Ada using that thing.

The queen-sized bed is mixed news. At home, I sleep on a California king, and I've been contemplating getting an even bigger bed. Then again, a smaller bed means we'll be huddled closer together, and that has a certain appeal.

Ada gets under the blankets, and I get in from the other side of the bed.

"Good night?" I say, unsure what the gentlemanly protocol would say about me trying to kiss her.

"Will you hold me?" she whispers and wriggles under the blanket, nestling backward into me.

"Sure." My throat is suddenly too dry to talk.

In the next moment, we're in the classic spooning position.

My mind is whirling. She smells like summer and feels just as warm in my embrace. An almost healing energy spreads from her body into every injury I suffered today. Placebo or not, all the pain disappears as though I took a Percocet.

"Do you mind if we fall asleep like this?" Ada murmurs. "Does it hurt lying on your side?"

"No," I whisper. "Not at all."

After a few minutes of blissful peace, my eyes adjust to the dark, and I notice Mr. Spock and his kin lying in strategic positions around the bed.

As sleep steals over me, I have the eerie sensation that if I hadn't been a perfect gentleman, a pack of rats would've attacked me. Maybe it isn't called a pack, though, but a swarm or maybe a colony? Or perhaps a pride, or possibly even a plague? Knowing the question might keep me up for needless minutes, I use my newfound power to Google stuff in my mind and learn the proper term is actually a "mischief of rats." As odd as it sounds, it's kind of fitting.

I don't think I even turn off AROS before I drift to sleep.

CHAPTER TWENTY

I'm falling down a never-ending skyscraper in slow motion.

Frantically, I look through every window, searching for something or someone.

Suddenly, I spot my target, and instead of falling, I float in one place and squint through the window.

Inside is a white medical room, and I see Mom sitting on an ancient dental chair. She looks horrified as she stares at the dentist. He turns toward me, and I realize he isn't a dentist at all.

"I know him," I scream at Mom through the window. "His name is Anton."

Mom can't hear me, and neither can Anton. With an abrupt motion, he grabs one of those frightening metal picks and leans toward Mom.

One moment I'm floating outside the window, and the next I'm crashing through it, jagged pieces of mirrored glass flying everywhere.

The sound of breaking glass continues as I leap forward, just as Anton is about to stab Mom in the chest with the dental pick.

My enemy turns in time for me to punch him in the face, and I hope my desperation and hatred give me the strength required to break his monumentally large jaw.

I hear the distant sound of a phone ringing, but I ignore it and focus on my fist, which feels like I just hit an iron plate instead of a human face.

Before I can even think of throwing another punch, a giant fist connects with *my* face in a vaguely familiar arc, and I fly backward through the window.

Looking down, I see the pavement approaching at the speed of light. Though I should be terrified for myself, I'm more worried about leaving Mom alone with that monster.

The pavement approaches even quicker, and I brace for the impact.

CHAPTER TWENTY-ONE

Instead of hitting the pavement, I wake up and realize it was a dream.

Just like in the dream, I hear a phone ringing in the distance. Maybe that's what woke me up from that completely illogical Superman-like nightmare that only a sleeping mind wouldn't question.

I open my eyes and note the room is only beginning to brighten from the rising sun peering through the gaps in the shutters. I dismiss the AROS interface that I left on last night and wonder why I didn't see it in my strange dream. The ringing is coming from down the hall. I have to assume it's Precious, unless Ada also uses "I Like to Move It" as her default ringtone.

I get up, careful not to step on any members of the mischief of rats.

Precious is with my clothes in the bathroom, proving how fickle my love for my phone has become; once I got something better in the form of Brainocytes, I left the poor device in a moisture-rich environment.

According to the phone, it's 6:45 a.m., and it's Joe calling.

My sleepiness evaporates, leaving me feeling like I just downed a venti cup of coffee. "Hey. What's going on?"

"I talked with a few guys who work at that airport." Given the time of day, Joe sounds surprisingly alert. "You won't believe where that plane is headed."

By "talk," does he mean needles under nails or just waterboarding? I don't interrupt him to ask since what's about to follow must be extremely important, and I don't want to have a "talk" with him myself.

"Where?" I ask, trying to sound calm. "I know it didn't get there yet, so it must be really far."

"It's going to—"

A blast of noise that sounds like a computer notification cranked to the level of an air siren drowns out his words.

To avoid going deaf, I raise my hands to cover my ears. My phone slips out of my hands. My heart in my throat, I watch Precious hit the tile floor with a bang and shatter into little pieces. Glass from the phone flies everywhere, and a shard punctures my bare calf.

I stare at it, wanting to reject what I just witnessed. My phone is supposed to be impact proof.

Suddenly, I'm standing there again, not holding my ears, and the phone is inexplicably back in my hand. The pain in my calf is gone too, but the noise is still assaulting my eardrums.

Given how holding my ears turned out, I don't repeat the action. Instead, I tightly clutch the phone. Needless to say, it doesn't fall and I don't get cut.

The noise abruptly stops.

"Location application execution halted," a mechanical voice says, booming loudly enough to have come from Zeus or some other thunder deity.

Through the fugue of confusion, I understand what happened, or at least part of it.

The horrendous noise was from the alarm Ada coded as per my request. I asked for it to be hard to ignore, and she made sure of that. This means the noise brings good news.

Mom must've blipped on the app's radar.

The second thing that happened, which I'm a bit less sure about, tempers the flood of relief. What was the deal with the phone falling out of my hand, breaking, and then being back in my hand, unbroken? Am I going crazy? Because that felt like jumping back in time.

Then I recall Ada's warning about pre-cog events. She said something about seeing events that her simulated brain regions anticipated, so that must've been my first episode. Maybe the brain-boost regions realized I might drop the phone if I grabbed my ears the way I'd been about to do and gave the biological brain the input, which got turned into a vision of what might happen. Just like Ada explained, this wasn't a psychic prediction, but more of a forecast, and a faulty one at that, since my phone is impact resistant.

"Are you there?" Joe demands from the phone's speaker.

"I'm here," I say, trying to catch my breath. "I'm sorry, Joe, I almost dropped my phone. Where did you say Mom is?"

"Fucking Russia," Joe grits out.

I nearly drop my phone again, or for the first time— or whatever the proper terminology is, given that pre-cog moment.

The last thing I expected was for my mom to be in Russia. Then again, given how long the flight took, it does fit.

"Where in Russia?" I ask, sounding hollow.

"I just found out it's in Russia. I have no fucking clue where specifically." Joe's words are clipped.

My heart sinks deeper.

Russia has the largest area in the world. It's just shy of being double the size of the US. My mom is not a needle, but a grain of sand in a haystack.

Then I remember the alarm and say, "Thanks for letting me know. I was just working on a way to track her on my end, and if I'm lucky, I might have a clearer fix on her location."

"Oh?"

I do my best to describe what Ada and I cooked up with the app. After I finish, Joe asks a few surprisingly insightful follow-up questions. He ends with, "Sounds promising. Go get the data and call me back right away."

The line disconnects, which I guess is Joe's version of goodbye.

I stare at the bathroom mirror in confusion.

My face looks just as swollen, but the pain is more tolerable today. I feel it now that I'm focusing on it, but not as intensely as yesterday.

"Russia?" I ask my bruised reflection. "Really?"

I'm not my grandparents, in that I don't practice their reverse anti-Semitism. Having said that, if I were ever guilty of disliking a country wholesale, that country might be Russia. I mean you don't escape with a refugee status the way we did without developing some irrational—and maybe even rational—negative attitudes.

Thinking about it more, I realize I don't dislike Russians, and I have plenty of Russian friends whom I respect. I also find many famous Russian people admirable and very likable. I guess disliking a country can, paradoxically, be different from disliking its people.

"Mike?" Ada says groggily from down the hall. "The alarm went off."

This is when I realize a ringing is coming from somewhere else. I guess Ada didn't take any chances. Besides the crazy alarm going off in my head, she also created something external to make sure she'd know when the app did its job.

"Coming," I yell. "Can you put the GPS coordinates onto the map, like you did before?"

"On it," she shouts back. "Come to my office when you're done in there. I left out a toothbrush for you last night, in case you didn't notice."

I look at the edge of the sink and confirm there's indeed a sealed toothbrush there, the type dentists give out after a cleaning. I quickly prioritize and use the toilet first; then I wash my hands and brush my teeth.

I don't bother dressing and leave the bathroom wearing only my boxers so I can quickly learn what the app found out. I do bring Precious with me, though, just in case.

"You'll never believe this," Ada says when I enter her office.

I don't share what I already know, hoping against all hope that Ada says my mom is in Russia, but that Russia happens to be an oddly named town in Florida. It's not impossible—Florida has a city called St. Petersburg and another one called Odessa.

"This"—she taps the screen that's zoomed in on an image of a small airport—"is in Podmoskovye... as in Moscow Oblast... as in Moscow in *Russia*."

The tiny hope bubble bursts, and I feel the need to sit down.

"My cousin just called," I say and grab onto the back of Ada's chair. "His findings corroborate this."

She looks at me worriedly. "You should eat something. You're too pale. At least the parts that aren't purple."

"I'll be fine," I say, my injuries aching at the reminder. "What else did the logs reveal?"

"The cell service in Russia isn't compatible with Brainocytes," Ada says. "But that isn't a shock, since we didn't exactly expect these things to go roaming in the alpha stage of the project."

The cell service we currently use belongs to a company in Mitya's portfolio, and they don't have any cell towers in Russia.

"We can fix this with something like a firmware up-date," Ada says, "but only after I do some coding on my end and if your mom is on Wi-Fi, which she isn't right now. The log is full of connection attempts, and once she does con-nect to Wi-Fi, we'll get a new data point. Problem is, they must have fewer public Wi-Fi points in that part of Russia, or she's outside civilization at the moment."

"Of course she's outside civilization," I mumble. "She's in Russia."

"This is all the data we have." Ada brings up a map with a single dot. "She got onto Wi-Fi here." She points at a place on the map.

The town is called Khimki, and the street is named Babakina. On the satellite view, I see gray Soviet-era build-ings and a forest in the middle of the town. The public Wi-Fi my mom joined appears to be coming from a school imaginatively named "Number 2."

"That's something," I say, lifting my phone. "Let me call the detectives and give them all this information."

"Yeah," Ada says, "you do that, and I'll go make you a smoothie. Here, take my chair."

Ada leaves while I dial Detective Sawyer's number. He doesn't pick up, so I leave a voicemail describing the situ-ation in detail.

It is only 7:00 a.m., which is on the early side for some people. I contemplate calling 911, but it might be too dif-ficult to explain this emergency. Instead, I call Mitya and cross my fingers. If anyone can give me good advice, it's him.

"What?" Mitya sounds exactly the way he did back in the day after one of his all-nighters. "It's four in the morning."

"It's actually seven. You're on Eastern Standard Time now," I say, wishing I video-called him instead so I could see his expression. "I had to talk to you. I just learned more about Mom."

"Of course." Mitya sounds instantly awake. "What's up?"

I explain the situation, and as I expected, Mitya mutters curses when he learns where Mom is.

If I'm conflicted about my feelings toward Russia, Mitya is very secure in his open dislike of the place. As he told me in college, "You have to live there during your formative years to really get the taste of it."

I can't blame my friend. His bitterness is justified. When he finished the top lyceum in Russia, his parents sent him to get the rest of his education in the US, which is how we met. The Levin family was part of the emerging class of so-called New Russians—people who made their wealth after the fall of the Soviet Union. That status came at great peril, and before Mitya completed his junior year at MIT, he learned of his parents' murder. He doesn't like to talk about it, but the one time he did, he told me the reason he was gone a whole summer as a senior was because he went back to Russia—and now he can never go back there again. I presume he got some kind of revenge on his parents' killers, but I don't know for certain, and I'm not sure I want to know.

"The official route will be too slow," Mitya says after running out of choice words—a process that took a while since he moved from English cuss words to Russian, a language that prides itself on its rich profanity.

"So what do I do?" I ask, afraid I already know what he'll suggest and preemptively dreading it.

"I think you should go there yourself," Mitya says.

"Yeah?" Coldness spreads throughout my body, as though I'm in a Russian winter. "I don't know anyone there. What can I actually do?"

"I know someone there who can help you," Mitya says. "His name is Sasha, though he prefers to go by Alex. You might've heard of him. His last name is Voynskiy."

"As in Alexander Voynskiy?" I ask, not hiding my shock. "The one guy who's actually richer than you?"

"That's not a fact," Mitya says dismissively. "Have you seen the ruble-to-dollar conversion rate lately? With all the sanctions and embargoes, it's pretty bad."

I try to recall everything I've heard about the eccentric Russian. Aside from Mitya, who might come close, we don't really have Voynskiy's equivalent here in the States, but I guess he's like Steve Jobs, Bill Gates, Mark Zuckerberg, and Jeff Bezos all rolled into one. I heard that like Ray Kurzweil, one of Ada's heroes, Voynskiy takes a hundred and fifty supplements per day, some intravenously.

"I don't know," I say. "I mean, it's Russia."

"We both know you'd go to hell for your mom," Mitya says. "This is just a little worse."

"The center of hell in *Dante's Inferno* was very cold." I laugh, but there's no mirth in it.

"Luckily for you, it's summer, so unless she's in Siberia, you'll be warm," Mitya says.

"But how—"

"I'll arrange it for you," my friend says. "My jet can make the flight if it stops to refuel."

"When—"

"I'll need a couple of hours. Will that be enough?"

"I guess." I try not to sound as overwhelmed as I feel. "But don't I need visas and stuff?"

"I have a pricey team of lawyers who can do all the paperwork. I also know whom to bribe in Russia, and even in the US if need be. Don't worry. At the airport where you'll land, you can bring anyone to and from Russia, no questions asked. Hell, you can even kidnap some Russian citizens—say, the culprits—and bring them here, and my guys will still figure out a way to get them into the country, even if we have to issue them each an H-1B visa and give them a bullshit job at one of my companies."

I swallow. "What about talking to the authorities?"

"Do it from the cab or let your uncle handle it," Mitya says. "Don't worry. Ada and I can support you from here, and I promise to pull some strings with my connections in the government, as well as the media. Is your mom a US citizen?"

"Yeah, for many years now. You should've seen her study for that test."

"Good," he says. "That will help if the American government needs to get involved. I'll also contact my friends in the media, so the headlines will be screaming about US citizens being kidnapped and brought to Russia. The pressure will be on."

"Fine." I'm beginning to accept my fate. "Let me ring my cousin so I can let him know all this."

"Your cousin? You mean the psycho you told me about?"

I sigh. "Do yourself a favor and never call him that to his face. But yeah, that one."

"All right," Mitya says. "I'll text you where to go and meet you there."

"Thanks. I might run out of collectible items to repay you with pretty soon."

"Don't mention it," Mitya says. "See you soon."

I close my eyes and bring up AROS. The green box icon that represents text messaging dings with the address Mitya promised.

I dismiss AROS and realize I'm feeling a little different today. My mind is clear, as though I had a bunch of coffee and a ton of sleep—except I had neither. Maybe the intelligence boost is kicking in? I'll have to check with Ada about that.

Unable to delay the unpleasant task any longer, I call Joe and tell him what's going on.

"Your friend's right," Joe says. "We need to get there as soon as possible."

I nearly drop my phone for the third time today.

"What do you mean, *we*?" I try to sound casual.

"I mean I'm obviously going to Russia to get my aunt," my cousin says. "And it sounds like you're going too. Therefore, *we*."

CHAPTER TWENTY-TWO

I hold the phone in silence for a moment, then say, "Okay, Joe. Let me text you the address."

"Good," he says and hangs up.

Stunned, I make my way to Ada's kitchen.

Only the sight of Ada in her PJs takes me out of my daze. Well, that and the sight of Mr. Spock sitting on the counter.

I think I see recognition in the rat's eyes. He even seems friendly. If he could talk, I bet he'd say, "Hey, I know you. We've slept together."

"Take this," Ada says and hands me a gigantic plastic cup with something thick and green inside.

I sip the liquid gingerly and get hit with a surprisingly refreshing taste. The liquid is cold, sweet, and exactly what I needed.

"Yum," I say after I swallow my third icy gulp. "It tastes a lot like a milkshake. What's in it?"

"Frozen banana, silken tofu, and a little spinach for color." Ada pours herself another cup and looks me over approvingly.

I follow her gaze and remember I'm only wearing boxers.

Oh well. Since she doesn't seem to mind, I decide I'll get dressed after breakfast. I tell her what I've learned, concluding with the fact that Joe will be accompanying me on this trip to Russia.

"I can see why you don't want Joe joining you," she says. "But I think he might actually be of some help. His job is providing people with security, after all. What I don't get is your problem with visiting Russia." Ada takes a small sip of her green drink. "I'd love to see Russia if I could."

"You're not going," I say firmly, in case she was hinting at it.

"Of course not. I need to provide backup, and I'm best equipped to do that here," Ada says. "It still doesn't explain what your problem with Russia is."

"How can I explain it to you?" I savor my drink and say, "Picture every Russian movie villain."

Ada demonstratively closes her eyes and smiles.

Taking that to mean she's using her imagination like I instructed, I continue. "So, I bet you're picturing a Russian drug lord, or a weapons dealer, or a crazed Soviet spy, or an ex-military mercenary—"

"Actually"—Ada's eyes open, glinting amber in the morning light—"I was thinking of the guys who kidnapped and threatened to cannibalize the yellow M&M candy in that Super Bowl commercial."

"You know, that 'Boris the Bullet Dodger' actor in the ad is actually Croatian. His Russian was barely coherent during his monologue, but yeah, that'll work as far as the point I'm trying to make. Now, take that guy and his crew and picture all these villains multiplied millions of times and located in a spot roughly double the size of NYC."

"Okay." Ada's tone is serious, but her eyes roll slightly upward.

"You now have Moscow in your mind's eye."

"Sure I do. I can trust you, the guy who hasn't visited the motherland since the early nineties."

She has a semi-decent point. I don't watch Russian movies or shows like Mom does, and I haven't read a book in Russian for two decades. As a result, I don't have a clue what's really going on in Russia, outside of American news, and they definitely put a spin on things. So I know the picture I painted for Ada might be irrational, but it doesn't change how I feel.

"I hope you're right," I tell her. "And even if you're not, it's not like I have much choice."

"If it's as bad as you think, it's even more important that you get your mom back as soon as possible."

Either Ada's words or the air conditioning makes me shiver, so I say, "I'll go get dressed."

"Me too, and then I'll prep a bunch of stuff for you to take with," Ada says and reaches inside her fridge.

I leave to go put on some clothes, and by the time I return to the kitchen, Ada has already changed out of her PJs and is holding a backpack. She's wearing skinny jeans and a t-shirt with an internet meme on it. The meme is of

Patrick Stewart next to a quote that says, "Use the force, Harry," with an attribution to Gandalf.

"This is for you." Ada hands me the backpack. "I made you sandwiches for the flight and also put in some items that might aid in your brain development."

I take the backpack, thank Ada, and together, we leave her apartment. As we walk down a flight of stairs, I mentally activate Einstein and ask him to get us a car on Uber.

The car arrives a minute after we exit the building, and I get to play the gentleman once again by holding the door open for Ada.

"I'll work on a few apps for you," Ada says and whips out her laptop as the car pulls into traffic. "You should make sure to set up a mobile hotspot on your phone, and double-check you'll have cell coverage in Russia. This way, your Brainocytes will be able to connect to the internet through your phone."

Appreciating Ada's advice, I spend the next twenty minutes sorting out my phone. The whole process feels like it takes hours, but in the end, I'm satisfied. I even surprise the otherwise uncaring customer service rep by telling him their outrageous roaming prices are "fair enough."

Once I'm done, I look over Ada's shoulder to see what she's coding.

After I watch for a while, I can't help mumbling, "That's even less readable than before. How's it going to pass code review?"

"You can review the code on the plane if you want. Since this is just a little video game I'm writing for your entertainment, the review is optional," Ada says without looking away from her laptop. "Tell me something, does Russia have the same expression about looking a gift horse in the mouth?"

"There's a mare and teeth in the proverb, but yeah, there's something like that," I say. "Do you mind if I keep watching?"

"Why do you think I'm not writing this in my head?" she responds via a mental text message. "I want to encourage you to be able to do this for yourself someday."

"Thanks," I mentally type back.

My focus on Ada's work is so intense I don't notice the car stopping and get startled when the driver coughs to get our attention.

We're standing by an airport entrance gate. After a call to Mitya, we're escorted to a special golf cart that takes us to the plane.

Before today, I've only seen Mitya's custom version of the Boeing 747 on his Facebook page. Driving up to it now, I'm amazed at its sleekness and size. I've always pictured something smaller, but this is almost as big as a commercial jet.

My admiration is interrupted when Ada closes her laptop and says, "Okay, I finished and loaded the game into your AROS environment."

"Thanks," I say and resume gawking at the airplane.

When we stop moving, I get out of the vehicle and run into yet another surprise.

My cousin is already here.

"Hey, Joe," I say as Ada and I walk up to him. "How did you get through security?"

Joe doesn't respond, his lizard eyes boring a hole into something over my shoulder.

I follow his gaze and see a posh limo pulling up. It must be an electric, because I didn't hear it arrive at all. "It's probably my friend Mitya," I say. "This is his plane."

Joe crosses his arms over his chest and watches the limo with the same determined mistrust.

When the door opens, it's indeed Mitya who gets out.

I approach and reluctantly give him a Russian-style man hug, a gesture I reserve for close friends I haven't seen in a while. "Good to see you, man. Sorry we won't get a chance to hang out face to face."

Mitya assures me we'll get to chill once I return, and I make the introductions. Ignoring my cousin's suspicious glare, Mitya asks his driver to take my backpack up to the plane, but I protest, saying I'm still capable of carrying twenty pounds strapped to my back.

As we walk up the fancy airstairs, I can tell by Mitya's eager stride that he wants to show off his pimped-out air ride.

The place doesn't disappoint. We pass a high-tech 3D movie theater setup and a huge collection of parachutes and wingsuits. After he shows them off, Mitya leads us past uber-comfortable beds and lets us park our butts on couches that look twenty times more expensive than what I have in my apartment—and I splurged.

Happy his efforts to impress us succeeded, Mitya really pushes it by hollering for the two stewardesses who will accompany us on the flight. The women come out wearing cutesy uniforms that emphasize their ridiculously long legs and model-like facial symmetry.

I notice Ada frowning at them, but I don't feel comfortable reassuring her she has nothing to worry about, in case she's feeling jealous. They're not my type—not that it makes a difference, since I only have one woman on my mind these days, and that's Ada. Besides, if she was going to worry, it should be about the Russian girls I'll meet once I step off the plane. I've heard crazy stories of debauchery from almost everyone who's gone to Russia. In fact, I know men who go to Russia primarily for the effect they have on the country's female population. Vic, one of the analysts at my fund, got married to a Russian girl while visiting there—a girl who's so out of his league the rest of us are convinced she just wants him for his green card.

"Any problem with the Wi-Fi?" Mitya asks when Joe and I take our seats.

"Nope, all set," I mentally text him.

Mitya's phone plays Black Sabbath's "Iron Man" intro as his text notification. He looks at it and says, "Ada, can I get the Brainocytes as soon as we're done? Mike just convinced me I'd give my left kidney to have them."

"Sure," she says. "We'll need to get the backups first, but afterwards, we can do that. I assume you know or have access to a nurse?"

"No problem. Anything you need." Mitya pushes his power specs farther up his nose with his middle finger, a gesture that someone might mistake for getting flipped off. "Okay, Mike, anything you want to discuss before we leave?"

I'm tempted to tell Mitya in Russian to keep his grubby paws off Ada, but since she understands Russian now, I'd only sound like a jealous idiot, so I opt for something more practical.

"I have some app ideas that'll be useful when we're in Russia, particularly this gun app I have in mind," I say. "Can you guys help me out by developing these apps once Mitya gets what he wants?"

They wholeheartedly agree, and I feel a tiny spurt of guilt mixed with relief. The big coding project I gave them is, in part, to keep them busy so they don't get too chummy with each other. The rational part of me trusts Mitya. He knows I like Ada and wouldn't stab me in the back. However, the irrational, primitive part of me thinks no one can resist Ada. Either way, the apps will be useful, and if the request has the added bonus of girl-theft prevention, that's just gravy.

"So this is goodbye," Ada says as she comes up to me.

She looks like she wants a hug, so I stand up to give her one. I usually find this type of human interaction a little uncomfortable, but since it's Ada, I might actually enjoy it.

Ada glances at the blond stewardess, then at me, and then she suddenly rises on her tiptoes. She's looking directly into my eyes, and I feel like a fly caught in amber.

Ada's lips touch mine.

CHAPTER TWENTY-THREE

I have to admit, until this very moment, I fully expected something like a peck on the cheek. As I savor the reality of Ada's lips on mine, my eyes threaten to jump out of my head.

In contrast, Ada's eyes are closed, the skin around them creased in smile lines.

I return the kiss, noting she tastes like a strawberry vanilla milkshake. This is odd, since she's a vegan who avoids dairy. More random thoughts like that fly through my mind. I wonder if this kiss is how Ada always says goodbye to her friends. As unlikely as it is, there are precedents. In the Russian culture, even men will sometimes smooch each other on the lips. Brezhnev, the communist leader when I was a little kid, was famous for it.

I almost send Ada a mental message asking, "What does this mean?" but I'm glad I refrain, because at that moment, Ada's tiny tongue locates mine, dispelling any illusion that this is some kind of platonic gesture.

I close my eyes and enjoy the kiss. However, my Zen quickly turns into something primal as blood rushes from my head into other parts.

Somewhere far away, I hear someone, I assume Mitya, chuckle uncomfortably, and I realize my hand found its way onto Ada's bottom—and might be grabbing said bottom demonstratively.

Grudgingly, Ada and I part. Her face is flushed, and I imagine mine would be too if it weren't purple from all the bruises.

"We have to head out," I say hoarsely, my tone apologetic.

I hear a chime indicating a mental text arrival. It's from Ada, and it says, "To be continued."

"Let's go," Mitya says and leads Ada off the plane. Mitya's butler/driver bows and follows his employer.

I take a seat next to Joe. He reaches into his jeans pocket and takes out a small box with medicine.

"Ambien." He pops two pills into his palm and extends his hand to me.

Since I just woke up about an hour ago, I'm tempted to refuse the sleeping pills. However, I might change my mind mid-flight, so I take them and say, "Thanks."

Not wasting his breath on niceties like "you're welcome," or even a shrug, Joe dry swallows his pill and closes his eyes.

I pocket mine and spend a few minutes speccing out the apps I want my friends to work on. When I finish the email, I decide to check out the game Ada wrote for me, hoping it'll distract me from the departure—my least favorite part of air travel, aside from turbulence, landing, and being in the sky in general.

Closing my eyes, I bring up the AROS interface. The new icon is vaguely familiar. I launch it, and as soon as I hear the music, I recognize the game. I probably should've known it from the code I glimpsed.

The music is a Russian folk song called "Korobeiniki." I've heard it performed with the original lyrics about a thousand times as a kid. Now, though, since Gameboy borrowed the song for this game, it's much more famous and familiar to me as the theme for Tetris. I guess Ada thought a game originally developed in Russia while I was growing up would be a fitting gift for my trip back to the motherland.

A three-dimensional rectangle appears in my field of vision, reminiscent of the typical playfield in Tetris, except it's as big as the Empire State Building. The tetriminos—the pieces in Tetris—are the size of gas tankers as they fall from the top at speeds approaching fifty miles per hour. Though all this looks three-dimensional, I can only manipulate the tetrimino across the same axes as regular Tetris. The scope, colors, and movement are way over the top, and I think I prefer playing the game on my phone. Still, this just demonstrates the videogame potential of the tech—not that I had any doubts about that.

On the bright side, my scores are the best I've ever gotten, though I can't tell if it's from the intelligence boost or just a side effect of controlling the game with my mind, which is obviously more efficient. Another bonus is that I indeed missed the departure.

I write Ada a thank-you email in my head, dismiss AROS, and open the backpack she gave me to see what else I can find to entertain myself.

At the very top of the pile is a Rubik's Cube. I guess Ada really wants me to play with geometric shapes today. The cube is an interesting coincidence. Mom brought one, or its Soviet knockoff, on our momentous trip to the United States. I remember this because I was so bored on the flight that I decided to give the puzzle a shot, a decision I regretted after a few hours. Solving the cube intuitively requires patience, and patience was an alien concept to me as a teen. Now, though, I hope I can do better since I'm around the same age Mom was on our trip to America—a mind-boggling fact in itself.

I take the cube and begin twisting it.

An hour later, I decide that solving this thing intuitively will take way too long, and I still don't have the necessary patience. Bringing up my trusty mental browser, I search "speed cubing." I quickly learn it's possible to solve the cube in under a minute. Intrigued, I read some more and learn the most popular method for solving the cube is called the Fridrich method, sometimes referred to as CFOP. It's perfect for my purposes, since you only have to use intuition to make the cross on the bottom of your cube. After that, thinking is reduced, and you rely more heavily on pattern recognition and muscle memory. Though I don't know which skill sets got boosted for me, if any, pattern recognition should be the most basic thing to improve, since that's what brains are best at in general.

Following a cheat sheet from one of the websites, I solve the cube in ten minutes for the first time in my life. A few solves later, I halve my time. Eventually, I can do it in four minutes, but my hands ache so much I'm forced to stop.

Massaging my hands, I come to the depressing conclusion that speed-solving the cube won't tell me whether my intelligence got boosted, a question I'm pondering more and more.

I reach into the backpack, hoping Ada packed something I can use to better gauge my new and improved mental skills.

I quickly come across a manila folder, on which Ada neatly wrote "Tests" with a thick black sharpie. I take the folder out and spread its contents on the cushion next to me. As the label suggested, I find a slew of tests that include the SAT, the GRE, the MCAT, and a bunch more I don't even recognize.

I grab a pencil and the SAT test, figuring it could be useful since I can look up my old score for comparison. Then again, I scored very high to get into MIT, so my boosted intelligence doesn't have much wiggle room to show off.

I take the test, minus the essay. My first shock is how long it takes me to finish. I initially figured time flew by because I was busy, but as it turns out, it took me less than two hours to complete the test, which is nearly half the time you're given. The second shock is how many questions I messed up.

None. I made zero errors.

My test score to get into MIT was very good, but I still got a couple of English questions wrong, as well as a math one. What's key is that I took the SAT after my mom convinced me to take a year of Kaplan prep courses, which really helped, despite the SAT allegedly being an aptitude test.

So did I do so well because of Ada's boost? It sure looks that way. I understand my English score might've naturally improved over time; after all, I've been in this country longer now and learned my second language on a deeper level. A better math score is trickier to explain. If anything, I expected it to drop since I haven't used any math outside of tip calculations since my last calculus class back in college. When I do have to calculate something more complicated, I resort to Excel, the calculator app, Mathematica, and other similar tools. Yet instead of dropping, my math score improved. Then again, it only improved by one question, so I could argue that the one question I screwed up in high school was a fluke and not statistically significant anyway.

The solution is obvious: I need to disable the brain boost and take another SAT.

Hesitantly, I mentally click the brain-looking app icon and examine myself. I think I'm the same, but it's hard to tell right away.

I grab another SAT test, and as soon as I read my first math question, I can tell things won't go as well for me this time around. I find it difficult to concentrate on the question, and I have a hard time caring about solving the problem. I push through my reluctance and do my best to focus.

Halfway through the math section, I decide I've had enough. The English section doesn't fare much better, and I only end up doing about a quarter of the questions. This, in itself, proves something about the boost.

When I check my answers, it turns out I messed up three math questions and a whopping six English questions. So the boost is real and can, at the very least, have an impact on tests.

I bring AROS back up and enable the boost.

This time, I can actually feel the difference in my state of being. It's subtle, but my surroundings seem more solid, the edges of objects sharper and all the colors brighter. It might be an illusion, but I also feel as though I understand certain things that previously eluded me. I have a eureka moment when I think back to that tricky math question I stumbled on a few minutes ago. It's obvious to me now that a silo consists of a cylinder and two cones.

Another difference is that I no longer feel that strange mental fatigue when it comes to intellectual pursuits. To test out that theory, I decide now is a good time to do a little programming.

I mentally open Ada's pet IDE program and spend the next few hours reading the necessary documentation and mucking around with it. Once I feel up to it, I start writing my first AROS application.

The result is just a few lines, most of them dedicated to including the right API libraries. Still, I feel a glimmer of pride when I mentally press the compile icon and don't get any error messages. I build the app and send it into my head space.

A gray icon appears in my apps list, and I launch it.

A text window shows up in the air in front of me, just for a fraction of a second. I grin as I glance at its message. Honoring the tradition of all introductory programming tasks, it boldly states, "Hello, World."

I'll be the first to admit that the utility of the program is nonexistent. Still, it's a step toward almost literally expanding my own mind.

I check out the MCAT test next and decide I could do very well on it, especially if I cheat by Googling all the biological facts and other things beyond my educational background. Since I can do the searches lightning fast in my head, I could probably get a super-high score within the time limit. I don't actually take the MCAT, though, because I'm getting tired and hungry from all this mental work.

I contemplate summoning the stewardess but decide to check Ada's backpack first, since she said she packed me some sandwiches.

It takes me a second to spot the cardboard box at the bottom. As I pull it out, I notice there's a strange heft to it.

I place it comfortably on my lap and open the lid. I'm lucky I can't drop the box now, because if I could, I probably would have.

Two very non-hungry pink eyes stare up at me from inside the box.

1011000100101001001 11 001 1011010
10 0110110011101000010101001111101
1000111 000011011001110110011010
0111010 0100 1 110010 011000000
1101 011 0 1100000 101 010101101
00 0 001 0010 100 001 000 1 0101
010000 001 010010110 101 010 0 00 0
110 1 0 0 11 101000 00 00 0 100
00101 00 110 0 10 0 01 0 1
01010 011 010 0 1 0 1010
0 010 11 1111 0 0 1 10 1 111
010 1 0 0 1 01 1 011
00 1 0 0 1 1 1 100
011 0 0 0 0 1 11 001
0 0 0 1 0 00 000
1 10 0 0 0 0 10
1 0 0 1 1 10
0 0 1
1 1 01

CHAPTER TWENTY-FOUR

"Mr. Spock?" I say, spotting the pink stripe on the white rat staring up at me from the box. Inside is some sort of veggie wrap with a couple of rat bites in it. "What the hell are you doing here?"

Mr. Spock's whiskers move back and forth, and his perceptive little eyes seem to say, "What does it look like? I had some lunch and now I'm chillin."

Taking out my phone, I get onto the plane's Wi-Fi and video-conference Ada.

"Mike?" she says. "I see you're using your phone like a person without Brainocytes."

"I need the camera so I can show you this." I point my phone at the box.

"Mr. Spock?" Ada sounds more incredulous than I feel, an impressive feat given how shocked I was to find the stowaway. "Baby, what the hell are you doing there?"

"That's what I asked him a second ago," I say. "But I didn't call him baby."

Ada looks distant for a moment. "He's not scared. Best I can make sense of this is he likes you. Likes you enough to decide to go with you."

"How do you know how he feels?" I study the rat, wondering how he'd look if he was scared, or, for that matter, how he'd look if he liked me. "You don't think he came with me by accident? I mean, he ate the food you prepared for me. Maybe he was in the box when—"

"I get where you're going with this, but I highly doubt it," Ada says. "I can review his data in a bit, but I think he followed you willingly."

I look at Ada and then at the rat, hoping one of them will explain what she's talking about. Neither of them enlightens me, so I ask, "What data? How does a rat have data?"

"Okay, please don't judge me." Ada bites her lip. "It has to do with experiments I've been performing on my little darlings. More specifically, with the apps I'm running inside and outside their heads. These things are easier to implement in rats since their brains are extremely well studied and simpler to boot, plus their privacy is less of a concern."

"I'm not judging," I say when I see how distraught she looks.

"The data I mentioned is what I collect from Mr. Spock's sensorium. I store everything he and the others see and hear. I even have access to their whiskers' perception—"

"You can see everything the rats see?"

"Yes, and I can map out their basic emotions, as well as some of their bodily needs," Ada says. "And I have a way of communicating with them that's better than using verbal commands. I can also control their behavior using Augmented Reality constructs —"

"Wait, what?" I look at Mr. Spock again. "You created Virtual Reality for rats?"

"No. Though I could, in theory, create VR for them, I only augment their reality. For example, I can make them see the walls of a maze that isn't there. The tech is very similar to the way you see the AROS icons. This way, I can get them to run where I want them to, though I don't use it since they're now bright enough to avoid trouble on their own. Their brain boosts are far more advanced than ours—"

Ada keeps talking, but I don't hear her. Dread grips me, and it's not because I've had an animal rights activist awaken inside me. The Brainocyte technology is in its infancy, but Ada's already implemented the basics for perfect surveillance, as well as mind reading—not to mention mind control. All this would be very scary if done to a human brain instead of a rat's.

"—in any case, we are where we are," I hear Ada say when I bring my attention back to her. "Please, take care of Mr. Spock. I'll make sure to include some of the apps I mentioned to assist you."

"Of course," I say, shaking my head to clear the remnants of my paranoia. "Are you sure you don't want me to leave him here, on the plane?"

"No," Ada says. "Take him with you. He'll be lonely on his own or with strangers."

"Fine," I say. "I will. Now can you please explain why he's always chewing on something?" I point at Mr. Spock's jaw. It's moving up and down, and his nose is crinkling.

"He's just bruxing," Ada says. "He does it when he feels safe."

I mentally Google the word and find at least a dozen YouTube videos of rats serenely grinding their teeth.

Spock stops bruxing to clean his snout with his front paws.

"Okay, that's cute," I tell Ada. "But I hope he can hide. As cool as it would be to look like a pirate with a rat on my shoulder, the Russian people, or any people, might not understand."

"Mr. Spock," Ada says, her tone switching to baby talk. "Please hide in Mike's pocket."

Before I get a chance to raise any objections, the rat scurries up the side of the box into my lap. Then he jumps into my tweed jacket and hides inside the inner pocket.

"Wow," I say. "Can you give me the app that displays his emotions?"

"I'll get you that, along with one of the first apps Mitya and I put together for your trip," Ada says and closes her eyes—I presume to work with her AROS.

The world around me flickers in that signature AROS-update fashion. I bring up all the icons and see a couple of new ones.

"The one that looks like a mood ring is the one I call EmoRat," Ada says. "Try it."

I enable the icon, but nothing happens.

"Mr. Spock," Ada says soothingly. "Come out for a second so we can see you."

Spock peeks his head out from his hiding place. There's a subtle green aura around his head, like a halo.

"The basics are the same as a mood ring," Ada says. "The highlights include green, for average wellbeing, blue-green for somewhat relaxed, solid blue for relaxed and calm, and violet for very happy. Just like with a mood ring, you want to avoid amber, which means he's unsettled, the gray of anxiety, and especially the tension of the black moods."

I use a notepad app to create a mental reminder for the rat mood colors and say, "I'll try to avoid those."

"Oh, and there's special emoticon-like stuff you'll sometimes see. Like this one"—a circle with a toilet in the middle shows up as a bubble over Mr. Spock's head—"means the little guy needs to go to the bathroom."

"Got it," I say gratefully and take Mr. Spock to the bathroom.

"Now for the next app," Ada says when I return. "I want you to strap on the camera I left in the bag for you."

I rummage through the bag and locate one of those GoPro chest setups for people who are into extreme sports. "You mean this harness?"

"Yeah, that getup is to make sure Mitya and I can see what you see and hear what you hear," Ada explains. "Since you're a human being and not a rat, I figured you'd prefer a camera. I didn't realize you'd have Mr. Spock with you. The camera's less important now, since I can hear your surroundings through his ears, and if he peeks out of your pocket, I'll see through his eyes. But having him peek out could be problematic, and since we coded the camera solution already, we might as well test it out. So please, put that on."

I carefully take off my jacket and put on the harness.

"I probably look ridiculous," I say as I put the jacket back on without buttoning it.

Mr. Spock pops his head out to check what's happening. I think he decides I indeed look ridiculous, because his color changes from anxious to relaxed.

"You look fine," Ada says. "Now, launch the camera icon and the one that looks like an angel."

I locate the two icons and enable them one after the other.

"Awesome," Ada says from both my phone and to my right. "I can see through the camera and hear the roar of the plane."

I look toward the new source of her voice and nearly drop my phone again.

A small figure is floating in the air to my right. She looks like Ada—if Ada were ten times smaller and dressed as a Valentine's Day cherub. She has a halo, a white toga, and a pair of wings. Only the bow and arrows are missing.

"What's happening?" I ask.

"It's an Augmented Reality interface," the angelic Ada says, and I confirm that her voice is coming from the creature's mouth. "I can hear you through the camera just fine."

I study her closer and realize her outfit and facial expressions aren't as realistic as in the video conference. Still, they're pretty darn good, especially for a 3D hologram or whatever the proper term is.

"This is far too sophisticated even for you guys to have put together in a few hours." I try grabbing the flying Ada, but, obviously, my hand goes through her.

"Have you heard of Centaur censors?" Ada asks.

I nod, things already becoming clearer. She's talking about Mitya's company that developed special cameras optimized for reading facial expressions.

"Well, we combined it with something he still has in development and voilà." Ada flies a circle around me. "I can control the avatar with my mind, like a video game, but the facial features work via the Centaur interface and mimic mine."

Punctuating her point, she winks at me and licks her lips salaciously.

"Please don't do that," I say. "My mind just got flooded with the weirdest imagery."

"Oh." Ada's expression becomes foxlike. "If Mitya wasn't sitting next to me and privy to this conversation, I'd put worse ideas into your head."

"But I'm here," Mitya says from a distance. "So stop it. Now."

"Okay," Ada says with a pout. "I guess it's only fair for you to launch the little devil icon. And while you're at it, launch that instant messenger icon that looks like a tiny penguin wearing pince-nez."

I launch the icon and hear Mitya say from my left, "Before you ask, that instant messenger is based on Pidgin—"

"Dude," I interrupt, looking to my left. "Do you really think *that*'s what I was going to ask about?"

On my left, I see Mitya, only like Ada, he's ten times smaller than normal. Also like her, he's floating in the air and has wings that aren't actually beating. The difference is that Mitya looks like a little red devil with hoofed feet, horns, and a tail.

"Ada picked the theme," he says defensively. "I just kind of went with it."

"You guys are having way too much fun with this," I mutter and log in to the instant messenger, figuring I might as well test it out.

Making sure I have my friends added to my buddy list, I start a chat room and mentally type, "We can talk through this when I don't want people thinking I've gone totally insane."

"Sure," Ada says and flies closer to my right shoulder. "We'll play along with that deception if you want."

"I think she should've been the devil," Mitya says in Russian in the IM window. "That *Bedazzle* movie got the gender right."

"You look more natural when horny," Ada says out loud.

I snicker at Mitya's dumbstruck expression, then mentally type, "Ada learned Russian."

The angel giggles as the devil mutters Russian and English curses under his breath.

"So," I type into the chat, "what app are you working on next?"

"You guys already have a basic face recognition app," Mitya says out loud. "Your mom even used one. Ada is working on tweaking the app to pull data from a backend that Alex, the guy I mentioned earlier, provided. He helped us get access to Vkontakte and other popular Russian social network platforms, and he's now trying to get us access to all the major Russian criminal databases—a perk of having good connections."

Something clicks in my brain, but before I can say anything, Ada says, "I'll expand it to show you more data than what your mom would've had access to. Our work will take some time, and I think you should spend that time sleeping."

"She's right," Mitya says. "Eastern Standard is seven hours behind Moscow time. It'll be early morning when you land."

Crap. They're both right. I've been too busy to think about jetlag.

"My cousin gave me Ambien," I say.

"Take it," Mitya says at the same time as Ada says, "Be careful, those are addictive."

"Now you guys are getting into your roles," I say and push the button overhead to summon one of the hot stewardesses.

"I'm going to ask her for food and water," I find myself needing to explain to Ada.

In the distance, I see the blonder and longer-legged stewardess walk toward me with the grace of a ballerina.

"Just a reminder," Ada whispers next to my ear. "We can see and hear what you're doing."

I ignore Ada and make sure Mr. Spock is hidden as the woman approaches.

The stewardess gives me a thousand-watt smile. "How can I help you, Mr. Cohen?"

"I asked them to call him that," Mitya types inside the chat.

"Like he wasn't already full of himself," Ada responds.

They type more snarky remarks back and forth, but I ignore them as I ask about food and drink. This being Mitya's plane, I'm not surprised when the stewardess whips out a menu with obscene options that include escargot and lobster tails.

I choose a simple cheese sandwich and tomato juice for myself and a bag of trail mix and bottled water for Mr. Spock—without explaining there's a hungry rat in the equation. As the woman leaves to get the stuff, I have Ada teach me how to disable the mental app windows and icons I don't need, as well as how to disable her and Mitya's angel/devil avatars.

"Thanks," I say when I master the skill of manipulating the mental windows. "It's distracting having that stuff around when I'm talking to people, but I don't want to dismiss AROS entirely."

"I'm so jealous." Since I disabled his avatar, Mitya's voice is now disembodied. "I haven't even learned how to type with my mind yet."

An idea that was swirling in my brain since we talked about face recognition suddenly jells, and I excitedly type, "Mitya, this Russian database Alex provided for you, can we use it to look up the kidnappers?"

"Well, yeah," Mitya replies, "if you have a picture—"

"I have three." I forward the email my cousin sent me and cross my fingers.

"I got the images," Mitya says. "Running the first one now."

I'm on the verge of biting my nails when he says, "Sorry, the first one isn't working. Not enough of his face is showing for the algorithm to do its job." After a pause, he says, "Same problem with the second one."

I hold my breath because I know the ape-bison image is discernible.

"Finally," Mitya says. "This last one worked—and the first name is indeed Anton, as the nurse said. I'm looking at the data, and it's not pretty. You're lucky to be alive. I'm sending you the details."

In the silence that follows, I read the dossier on my new nemesis, whose full name is Anton Pintarev. His criminal career began when he murdered his elderly aunt, but because Anton was a minor at the time, he was sent to a special camp for violent underage criminals. According to what my mom told me about those institutions, they might as well have been called Crime Universities, especially since having a criminal record instantly disqualified you from active duty in the army and made it nearly impossible to find a job. Having a record was a more public affair in the Soviet Union than it is in the US. My understanding is that a criminal got a special stamp in his passport and an entry of "prison" in a special worker diary that functioned like a detailed resume back in that system. A year after Anton got out, he was promptly arrested for stabbing a man, tried as an adult, and placed in a real jail. When he was released in the post-Soviet Russia of the early nineties, he found himself in an environment where some of his unsavory skills were valuable, so he got to work and managed to avoid recapture and even thrive. There's a list of crimes he allegedly committed, but the authorities couldn't prove it was him.

As I read, my stomach churns with worry for my mom, because even if one percent of this list is true, she's in the company of a genuine monster. When I reach the graphic details about Alina Petrova, a fourteen-year-old Anton is believed to have brutally beaten, raped, and killed, I stop reading and take a couple of calming breaths.

"This is bad," I mentally type into the chat.

"I know," Mitya says. "But keep in mind, they need the people they took hostage, so your mom should be safe."

"Right," I murmur to myself. "Like Mrs. Sanchez was safe."

"Here you are," the stewardess says. I didn't even notice her approach, thanks in part to my dark mood. She pulls out the table expansion and sets down the tray with goodies. "Let me know if you need anything else."

"Thank you," I manage to say. "I will."

The sight of food lifts my spirits by a fraction.

"Tell her you want her to stop flirting," Ada says in a very un-angelic tone. I'm not sure if she's serious or trying to get my mind off Anton's file.

"Victoria gives an outstanding shoulder rub," Mitya says, staying in his devil character. "She's also an expert—ouch!"

Ada's angel avatar doesn't show it, but I bet Ada either kicked or punched Mitya in the real world. Somehow, even that kind of touch makes me jealous, which is ironic since jealousy led to Ada hitting him in the first place.

In an effort to reassure my friends I'm fine, and to take my mind off Anton, I type into the chat, "All right, kids, tell me about the other apps you're going to write."

Ada and Mitya give me the rundown as I start in on my meal.

"I have an idea outside the apps you requested," Mitya says as I chase down the sandwich with a gulp of tomato juice. "I think I can improve on Ada's brain boost stuff by creating a scheduling algorithm that would allow the three of us to better utilize the STRELA servers."

He proceeds to explain his idea, which reminds me of when I took the Operating Systems course back at MIT. In that course, the hardest part was learning about the clever ways people come up with for sharing limited computer resources. Those resources can be shared between processes running on the system, or, more applicable to our server problem, cleverly allocated between different human users so the users are unaware they're sharing anything at all.

"We should be able to test it on my babies first," Ada says toward the end. "Once we do, keep an eye out for any oddities in Mr. Spock's behavior."

"Great," I say disingenuously. I can tell she's impressed with Mitya's smarts, and I don't like it. "If you don't mind, I'm going to take my pill."

"Good day—or night," Mitya says.

I take my Ambien and give Mr. Spock his food and water.

As the rat eats, I decide to take a Percocet for the pain as well—no need for mental acuity while I'm sleeping.

Feeling properly medicated, I navigate my way to Amazon and use their cloud eBook app to do a bit of reading. I want to get the horrors of the dossier out of my head to avoid another nightmare. It only takes me a few chapters to realize that reading this way is yet another revolution the Brainocytes will bring to personal entertainment.

About ten minutes into the book, my lids grow heavy. I don't fight the drowsiness, opting instead to dismiss AROS altogether and close my eyes.

Despite my earlier attempt to chase away the bad thoughts, my sleep is interrupted by horrific dreams that feature Anton Pintarev committing atrocities against Mom and me.

CHAPTER TWENTY-FIVE

I wake up slowly. It takes me a minute to remember I'm on a plane and to realize that the motion I'm feeling doesn't mean my bed decided to move on its own.

Actually, for a plane, the ride does feel rather bumpy.

I open my eyes to a surprise. Instead of flying in a plane, I'm riding in a car. At least that explains the shaking—Russian roads are infamously bad.

I reach into my pocket to check on Mr. Spock and feel reassured when he gently nibbles on my finger. Satisfied I didn't lose the rat, I look around.

I'm in the back seat, and there's a gigantic bald woman sitting next to me—or at least I assume she's a woman based on her semi-feminine round features and D-size bosom. She's staring intently at the neck of an unfamiliar black-haired guy sitting in the front passenger seat. The only person I recognize is Joe, who's sitting behind the wheel.

In the back window, far in the distance, I see the airport I assume we landed at. On either side of the road is a bucolic Russian landscape, with its signature birch trees, oaks, and some pines. I spot a red squirrel climbing a tree—a sight that finally evokes something like nostalgia. I've always found the gray squirrels in NYC unsatisfactory compared to their cuter, pointier-eared, and more colorful cousins back in Krasnodar.

As I turn away from the window, I catch the woman looking at me with a stony expression. Now that I'm studying her closer, her lack of an Adam's apple and the hint of makeup on her face assure me she really is a *she*, though I can probably be forgiven for having doubts given her shiny shaved head and muscle tone that's about triple mine. A spiderweb tattoo adorns the rightmost side of her head, evoking stories of spider females feasting on their males during mating.

Without any emotion, in a voice you can only get after at least a decade of smoking unfiltered Russian cigs, she says in Moscow-accented Russian, "Looks like Sleeping Beauty is up."

"What happened?" I try not to gag as a wave of garlic breath mixed with stale nicotine assaults my nose. "How did I get here?"

"You walked," Joe says, his blue eyes glinting in the rearview mirror.

"I told you he was sleepwalking," the woman says.

Though I don't recall being woken up, I bring up AROS and do a quick search on Ambien side effects to confirm my hunch that my memory loss is due to the drug.

"Where are we going?" I ask, rubbing my eyes.

"Levin texted me the location of Voynskiy," Joe says, and it takes me a second to understand he means Mitya texted him where to meet Alex.

The front passenger guy turns around and grins at me. Looking at his weather-beaten face, I can right away tell he isn't Russian. With his hawkish nose and Stalin-inspired mustache, he looks Georgian—which in this context isn't the US state, but a country in the Caucasus mountains.

"I'm Gogi," he says in Georgian-accented Russian.

If his accent weren't enough, that name solidifies my theory on Gogi's nationality. "Gogi" is as common a name in those parts as Ivan is in Russia. In fact, a fictional Gogi is often the butt of derisive Russian jokes about Georgians.

"I'm Mike." I shake the man's hairy hand. "Though you can call me Misha if it's easier."

"Good to meet you, Mike," Gogi says, pronouncing my name as *meek*. "I can see the familial resemblance." He tilts his head toward Joe.

"I'm Nadejda," the woman says, but only after Gogi and I look at her expectantly for a few moments. "Regardless of whether it's easier, you can't call me Nadya, Nadyusha, or any other variant."

Nadejda means hope in Russian, a fitting name since hope is probably what everyone feels when they look at her—as in, they hope to never piss her off.

"How do you know my cousin?" I ask, aiming the question at no one in particular.

They look at each other. Gogi must lose the staring match, because he's the first to speak, saying, "It's a long story."

My prodding appears to have lessened their enthusiasm for socializing, and Gogi turns back toward the front while Nadejda resumes hypnotizing the back of his neck.

Re-enabling the avatars, I type into the mental chat window, "Are you guys up?"

Since it's 8:14 a.m. here, it must be 1:14 a.m. in NYC.

"Of course we're up," Ada says as she materializes near Nadejda's shoulder.

"Did you notice the new icons?" asks Mitya, who materializes outside the car window—not that it matters for his devil avatar.

I look closer at the AROS interface.

"There are new icons here," I mentally type into the chat window. "Where do I start?"

"Try the face recognition app on her," Ada says, pointing at the large woman next to her avatar. "You'll need to launch that googly-eyed emoticon that Mitya designed as an app icon."

I locate the icon and start the app.

Instantly, white ghostly lines crisscross every nook and cranny of Nadejda's face. I've seen this sort of animation in crime procedural movies and TV shows, and I suspect this is Mitya's flourish and has nothing to do with the actual way this face recognition app works.

Next, a box shows up in the air. It lists information, along with its sources, and I recall how Mom was reminded of the Terminator films when she had a similar process run inside her head two days ago. Thinking of Mom threatens to overwhelm me with worry again, so I focus on the information I acquired about my new acquaintance, Nadejda Vedrova.

Nadejda was born in Latvia, but according to her social media profile, she's "of Russian heritage," whatever that means. From the data in the Russian law enforcement databases, I learn she served in the SUV, a Latvian special tasks unit I've never heard of, where she was a sniper—something that surprises me, since she doesn't seem like the type who likes working from a distance. I also learn she's worked as a private security consultant all over Russia since 2009. In this context, it means she's been a bodyguard for oil oligarchs and the like. That might be her connection with Joe, since he runs a similar business in the States, at least officially. From the Russian Wikipedia, I'm impressed to find out that at the age of twenty-three, Nadejda won gold in Greco-Roman wrestling, which explains both her physique and the "I can crush you" attitude she's sporting. Finally, I discover she's thirty-seven, widowed, and that her husband was killed by a criminal kingpin, who was later shot dead by a high-powered rifle under mysterious circumstances.

"Gogi?" I say in an effort to capture the man's face. When he turns, I say, "Do you have any food scraps or water? I need to feed my little friend."

Mr. Spock takes that as his cue to poke his head out of my jacket.

Joe sees the rat in the rearview mirror and just raises an eyebrow, as if he's met people with white rats in their pockets before but didn't expect me to be one of them.

Gogi's reaction isn't as calm. His eyes visibly widen, and he looks on the verge of asking a dozen questions.

The face recognition lines scan Gogi's face, and a bio shows up in a comic-book balloon above his head. I don't get a chance to read the details, though, because I'm deafened by a noise that sounds like a rabid hippopotamus picked a fight with a horny cow.

Mr. Spock swiftly hides back inside my pocket, and I get the urge to join him as the screaming continues.

"Nadejda," my cousin grits through his teeth. "Shut it."

The woman stops screaming, but her feet stay up off the floor and her eyes bore a hole in my pocket. There's terrified fascination on her face, an expression that looks completely unnatural on her.

I note she stopped screaming as soon as Joe commanded it, so she might fear or respect him more than her rat phobia, or whatever that was.

"Here." Gogi hands me a handful of sunflower seeds, a very traditional Russian snack. "Just make sure you keep your pet away from the lady."

If looks could kill, Nadejda's stare would've slayed Gogi, perhaps after torturing him first. However, her pride must win out over her irrational fear, because after a moment, she places her feet back on the floor and crosses her arms high over her chest.

I drop the sunflower seeds into my pocket, and as soon as I feel Mr. Spock eating them, I study the information the face recognition app found on Gogi—which turns out to be very little. He was part of the elite Georgian Special Forces, and in the early nineties, he participated in the War in Abkhazia. Apart from that, he was discharged after something he did during the conflict in South Ossetia in 2008, but the Russian databases don't know what that something was, just that it was, and I quote, "an atrocity." He's deemed extremely dangerous and is on the Russian version of the no-fly list—only here, again, no explicit cause is given. Finally, no personal information is known about him, and not surprisingly, he has no social media footprint of any kind.

"Your cousin has nice friends," Mitya says, his avatar flying about a foot outside the car window.

I'm about to chastise my friend for goofing off when something happening outside the car window catches my eye.

Actually, it might be more accurate to say my mind scans our surroundings and tabulates what it sees at a speed so blinding I can only assume it's due to the brain boost.

Point number one is that we're currently on a narrow part of the road cresting a hill. Point two, there's a big ditch on either side. Point three, the critical one, is that despite these road conditions, a car is trying to pass us on the left.

Perhaps an unenhanced or less paranoid mind might dismiss all this and think the driver of the offending car is an idiot, but I don't think that's the case, so I let my mind continue with its assessment.

Point four and five are that the car is a large black Mercedes M-Class with four men wearing sunglasses in the middle of a cloudy day.

Then point six happens. The car in question turns its wheels toward us, and it doesn't take a brain boost to know what's about to happen.

The car is going to intentionally ram into us.

CHAPTER TWENTY-SIX

"Joe," I shout. "On your left!"

My perception seems to sharpen, and everything becomes more vivid. I watch the approaching car and try to swallow my heart back into my chest. From somewhere, I recall my body is currently experiencing the Law of Inertia; if we hit the other car, my body will attempt to keep moving in our car's original trajectory. With uncanny mathematical precision, possible scenarios play through my head, down to the number of tons of force I'll experience in different outcomes.

At the same moment, I see my cousin grip the wheel so hard his knuckles whiten. His head turns toward the offending vehicle, and he jerks the wheel.

We swerve.

I start calculating our chances of survival as I glimpse Gogi reaching into the glove compartment.

Nadejda is already holding an Uzi, though where she got it from is beyond me. She slides down the backseat toward me and aims the gun at the window.

Before I can blink or do another calculation, the big woman grabs me roughly by my neck.

"What—" The rest of my question is cut off by her pulling my head down in some sort of wrestling maneuver.

Though I would usually find humor in the way my face ended up in the crotch area of Nadejda's jeans, right now I'm too petrified for levity. I only have one overriding thought in my head.

I'm going to die.

A thunderclap booms above me.

Shards of glass fly everywhere, but Nadejda's body blocks me from the worst of it.

"I think you're being shot at," Ada says, her avatar visible to me even though my eyes are squeezed shut. Her face looks as shocked as I feel.

"No shit," Mitya says, his avatar sounding distraught despite his bravado.

"Shut up, guys," I inadvertently say out loud, but my voice is muffled by the mounds of flesh below my face.

More shots are fired from right next to me. I assume it's Joe and his friends, but I can't be sure since all I can see is Nadejda's zipper. Then again, it's a safe bet she's shooting, because I can feel the tension in her beefy thigh muscles with my cheek.

The car squeals to a jerky stop.

My position prevents whiplash, but I still feel woozy.

In a whirl of action, Nadejda extricates herself from under me, and before I can react, she's gone from the car.

The shooting resumes.

I try to peek through the rear window, but it explodes into shards.

Determined to at least see what's going on, I unhook the GoPro harness from my body and grip the camera tightly.

In the mental chat, I type, "Guys, can you feed me the camera input?"

"Of course," Mitya says. "Done."

I prepare to get shot in the arm and raise the camera like a periscope.

My friend delivers on his promise, and I stare at the video of what's going on outside the car.

Nadejda is still holding on to her machine pistol, while Gogi and Joe have slightly smaller guns. They're all aiming at the black car and walking toward it menacingly.

I point the camera at the vehicle and see that the bad guys' car looks like a pasta strainer.

Though no one is shooting back at my allies, the crew cautiously approach the vehicle. Then Gogi and Joe rip away the front and back doors and unload the rest of their bullets into whatever they find inside.

"All dead," my cousin says, and I detect a note of disappointment in his tone. Maybe he wanted to question the assailants but didn't get a chance to?

Well, I can learn something even if he didn't. I put the camera harness back on and exit the car on legs that feel like jelly.

"You should probably stay in the car, young man," Gogi says as I approach them. Then, probably figuring I didn't understand his Russian due to shock, he adds in broken English, "If you not see death up front like this, it can be very bad."

"He's probably right," Ada says in my right ear.

"At least get close enough for facial recognition to kick in," Mitya says in my left ear.

Gingerly, I take another couple of steps.

A strange kind of numbness overcomes me as I scan one shot-up man after another. I only stop once the face recognition data turns up. As I take it in, the numbness dissipates, and I find myself bent over, dry-heaving violently. My ribs ache with renewed fierceness, and my head reminds me it's only been a couple of days since the concussion.

"At least he hasn't eaten anything in a while," Mitya says from somewhere. "He'd lose it for sure."

"Shut up," Ada says. "Mike, sweetie, are you okay?"

I don't respond either vocally or mentally.

Gogi places a comforting hand on my shoulder, but I don't know how to respond to that either.

Eventually, I straighten, pulling away from Gogi's touch, and lumber back to our car.

Both the local and virtual crews follow me.

The car doors slam behind Gogi, then Joe, then Nadejda.

I just sit there, breathing heavily. Despite the cool air outside, sweat drips down my spine, and my ribs ache dully.

Gogi puts the gun back into the glove compartment without saying anything.

I gather some strength and look at Nadejda. She already hid the Uzi someplace, and in my current state, I don't care to guess where. As though feeling my gaze, the woman looks at me with a strange expression that might be compassion. On second thought, it could be worry about my rat, or maybe she's simply constipated.

Joe's expression, or lack thereof, is easier to read, since it's as emotionless as usual. Seeing he has my attention, he nonchalantly says, "How much do you trust them?"

"Who?" I ask, wondering if he means Nadejda and Gogi.

"Levin and your girlfriend," Joe clarifies.

"They know where we're heading," Gogi chimes in.

"And that didn't seem like a random attack," Nadejda adds.

"I trust them more than I trust any of you," I blurt out. When I see my cousin's blue icicles-for-eyes narrow, I swiftly clarify, "I trust them completely, Joe."

"If we wanted to hurt you, we'd use the Brainocytes to do it," Mitya says.

"Sure, tell them that," Ada says sarcastically. "Better yet, tell them we implanted a nuke inside your head that we can detonate at any time. That should relax everyone."

Glad only I can hear my friends bickering, I tell Joe, "Let's focus on the attackers. I can tell you who they are."

"You can?" Gogi's bushy unibrow tilts right.

"Don't tell anyone in Russia about the Brainocytes," Mitya warns. "Or else you might join your mom, and not in the way we want."

"I'm not an idiot," I mentally reply. Then I gesture at the camera on my chest and say out loud, "This took images of their faces and sent them to my friends. They looked them up and were about to share the information with me."

Gogi grunts approvingly, and even Nadejda looks a little less solemn.

Reassured, I take out my phone and pretend to read the bios from there instead of the Augmented Reality text boxes.

I rattle out the ages and the criminal records of the dead and finish with their personal connections, such as family members, friends, and other things gleaned from social media. Though my listeners don't seem to care, the social media information I read makes my chest tighten in empathy. I even feel a dash of remorse, an odd reaction since I wasn't the one who killed those men. I guess seeing pictures of their kids, wives, brothers, and sisters humanized them in my eyes, making their deaths register as the tragedy they are. True, this slaughter was in self-defense, but that doesn't make me feel better. I wonder if murders would still happen if everyone knew such intimate details about the people they were about to kill? Could this be yet another way the Brainocytes might improve the world? As soon as the thought occurs to me, I dismiss it. The likeliest suspect in a murder case is usually the spouse of the victim or some other acquaintance, so that rationale doesn't hold.

"They sound like your generic guns for hire," Gogi says, interrupting my inadvertent moment of silence.

"I agree," Nadejda says. "They could've been working for anyone with a large bank account."

"This is why you should've kept one alive." Joe throws out the words as an accusation, as though he wasn't doing a huge chunk of the killing.

Nadejda and Gogi don't respond, and after a moment of sullen quietude, my cousin starts the car and expresses his frustration by slamming on the gas pedal so hard we leave a streak of black tire marks behind us.

As we make our way to Alex's home, I mentally ask Ada and Mitya about improving the face recognition app based on some ideas I've come up with.

"I really like that," Mitya says after I explain what I want. "We can pick out certain markers in the person's profile and have Einstein alert you as needed."

"We can also give them a red halo," Ada says, getting into the spirit of things. "It'll let you spot any dangerous people in a crowd."

"Obviously, we'll leave you with the ability to use face recognition manually the way you do now," Mitya adds.

"You guys don't need to sell me on this," I mentally type. "I was the one who wanted the improvements in the first place."

"All right then," Mitya says. "We'll start coding."

"Okay." I draw in a heavy breath. "I'll just sit here alone, I guess."

"You have three other people in the car with you," Mitya says. "I'm sure they can keep you entertained."

Emphasizing that our conversation is officially over, Mitya's devil visage goes away.

"Don't mind him." Ada's angel avatar flies up to my face. "I'll go code a bit too, but I'll keep an eye on the chat window if you want to get in touch."

She flies even closer to my cheek, mimics giving me a kiss, and evaporates. I'm left marveling at how even a fake kiss from Ada has the power to make me feel all warm and fuzzy.

As the car ride continues, I take in the sights. We're passing through villages and fields of sunflowers and corn. After the dozenth sighting of herds of cows and horses, the rural vista begins to bore me, and I loudly yawn.

I surf the net with my mind for a while before realizing the sun outside isn't fooling my body's circadian rhythm. Somehow, it knows it's nighttime back home. Seeing no reason to fight the inevitable, I instruct Einstein to wake me up when we get to Alex's location and close my eyes.

From my perch on the second floor, I see Mom sitting on a metal chair in the middle of an abandoned factory. She's wrapped in duct tape from head to toe like a strange modern mummy. Anton—the ape-bison asshole—is standing next to her with a blowtorch.

I grab onto the rusty hook attached to a gigantic chain and swing toward Anton in a perfect imitation of Tarzan.

Anton turns to me and round-kicks me off the chain.

"Wakey-wakey," says a German-accented voice from far away.

Confused, I fall from the chain and land with a loud splat.

As I lie there, trying to catch my breath, Anton walks up to me and applies the blowtorch to my temple.

My head begins melting, and I realize I'm dreaming.

CHAPTER TWENTY-SEVEN

"**W**akey-wakey," Einstein's German-accented voice booms. "Eggs and Schnitzel."

As I struggle to regain my senses, I overhear Nadejda ask, "Does your cousin do anything else besides sleep?"

Joe says nothing, and Gogi chuckles.

"I'm awake," I mumble and rub my eyes, ignoring the twinge of pain in my ribs. "What did I miss?"

"We're almost there," Gogi says and points at a fence in the far distance. The fence looks inspired by the Wall of China.

"Alex calls this his Palace," says Mitya, his devil appearing almost on my left shoulder. "I call it the Monument to Alex's Ego."

I use my phone's GPS to pinpoint my location. Alex's house—or mansion or palace or whatever—is located close enough to Moscow proper to be stupendously expensive, but far enough to allow for a plot of land of this outlandish size.

"I can't see past the gate yet," I mentally respond. "Have you guys updated the face recognition app?"

"We finished that a while ago," Ada says, her angel showing up on my opposite shoulder.

"And we had time to sleep too," Mitya says.

"But not with each other," Ada clarifies hastily.

Instantly feeling wide awake, I launch the new version of the face recognition app. I'm prompted on whether I want to see Einstein's holographic image, and I decide against it; two illusory versions of my friends is enough Augmented Reality for now.

The gate we arrive at wouldn't look out of place in a medieval Russian castle. As we approach, it opens with a metal-on-metal screech.

"Sketchy person alert," Einstein says as soon as I glimpse the armed guards manning the gate. "Sketchy person alert. Sketchy person alert. Sketchy person alert."

"Sorry," Mitya says. "I set up the app so Einstein says that phrase every time he detects a new face that matches the predefined criteria. Those four guards are probably dangerous."

"I bet Mike could've figured that out just by looking at them," Ada says, her wings twitching nervously. "The AK-47s and the Neanderthal foreheads are dead giveaways."

"Mitya," I mentally type. "Does your friend know we're here?"

"I just texted him," Mitya replies. "And he's not my friend."

"He's not?" Ada asks as I type the same question.

"He's an old acquaintance who owes me a bunch of favors," Mitya explains. "If you knew Alex like I do, you'd know that's better than being his friend."

The burly security dudes examine each of us closely and suspiciously check their handhelds, but eventually, they allow us to proceed through the gate.

We slowly drive in and are greeted by a bunch of armed people. All but one raises the "sketchy person" alert. I look at the one man without a red halo and wonder how he ended up here. One manual face recognition scan later, I learn he's a cop.

"Not always a big difference between goons and cops in Russia," Mitya says. "The likes of Alex can hire cops just as easily as they can hire goons, and it's worth having a few on the payroll."

I shake my head and take in our surroundings. As we crest the big hill, we bear witness to the majesty of Alex's Palace—a name that might actually be an understatement. This thing is monstrous and dwarfs most mansions I've seen. It reminds me of a double-sized Winter Palace in St. Petersburg (the Russian city, never to be confused with the one in Florida), except it has many more gold-plated surfaces. Unlike the tsar's former residence, though, this place has some embellishments that seem tacky, the worst offender being the colorful peacocks roaming the gardens that are way too tropical for Russia.

We park on a driveway the size of a modest football stadium, and two armed men escort us to the Palace doors.

For people carrying machine guns, their manner is very polite.

A girl who looks like she stepped off the cover of Russian *Maxim* magazine greets us in the vestibule. In passable English, she says, "Hello, Mr. Cohen. I'm Anna. Mr. Voynskiy asked me to take you to the Lounge."

Nadejda gives Anna her signature Ice Queen stare, while Gogi checks her out appreciatively.

"We'd like to speak with your boss *now*," Joe says, and I get the impression he's itching to grab the girl by the neck to emphasize his point.

"He'll meet you in the Lounge shortly," Anna responds, unperturbed. "It's this way."

She turns and starts walking. As we follow her deeper into the Palace, I decide that Alex has a fetish for bling. The heavy chandeliers look like they're made of gold and diamonds, while the paintings and the ancient Russian icons on the walls are set in gold frames—adorned with copious amounts of jewels, of course.

"This sometimes happens when low-class people get money," Mitya whispers conspiratorially from my left. "It doesn't make it any less painful to look at."

"I didn't realize you came from old money," Ada says with a heavy dose of sarcasm. "And don't you own a race horse ranch?"

"Exactly," Mitya counters. "That just proves I know what I'm talking about."

I ignore their banter as we finally reach the Lounge. It's the size of the Bellagio hotel in Vegas—assuming that venerable place decided to turn itself into an opulent restaurant—and has the same feel.

"Please, take a seat." Anna points at a giant table, and we accept her offer.

On the table is a bottle of *Stoli Elit: Himalayan Edition*. A mental search reveals this brand of vodka costs three thousand dollars per bottle. The hors d'oeuvres include black caviar blinis, some strange golden fish roe on a tiny plate, little salmon roe sandwiches, and a slew of other high-end Russian culinary delights.

"May I get anyone anything?" Anna asks politely, and I get the eerie impression she included herself on the list of possible items she can deliver.

"Voynskiy," Joe says firmly.

"Tea if you could," says Gogi.

"Some plain water," I add. "And some nuts."

Nadejda gives me a panicked stare. She probably figured out that the food is meant for Mr. Spock.

"I'll be right back," Anna says and backs away. "Meanwhile, please try the gold caviar. It's Almas, from an albino Iranian Beluga sturgeon."

"Hello." A man emerges from behind one of the giant columns. "I'm Alex."

The man in front of us bears only a vague resemblance to the sharply dressed Alex Voynskiy I've seen in *Forbes Magazine*. In real life, he looks like a hybrid between Steve Jobs and Bill Gates. His clothes, particularly the black turtleneck, remind me of the Apple founder, while his kind face and the shape of his glasses are more reminiscent of Microsoft's former CEO.

"Except he wishes he was ten percent as brilliant as either man," Mitya says after I share my thoughts in the chat. "Alex is a poser. He can't code to save his life. Just another person in the right place at the right time."

"You mean next to you?" I type.

"Exactly," Mitya says. "Listening to me was the smartest thing he did, and this being Russia, he was able to monopolize the market."

A robotic contraption consisting of wheels, a stick, and an iPad on top rolls out from behind the column. I recognize it as one of those telepresence robots.

"That's me," Mitya explains. "So I'll turn off my avatar for now."

"Hi, everyone," Mitya says from the iPad on top of the robot. "I'm Mitya."

"Hi, Mitya. Thanks for letting us use your plane," I tell the robot, pretending I can't just mentally talk to my friend via the chat. Turning to our host, I say, "Nice to meet you, Alex."

After I introduce everyone around the table, Alex says, "Mitya filled me in on the situation, but I want to hear your version if you don't mind."

"We don't," I say, even though it looks like Joe feels otherwise. Between mouthfuls of multicolored fish eggs, I explain the situation, sticking as close to the truth as I can while omitting all mention of the Brainocyte technology.

Halfway through my story, Anna returns with the requested water and nuts. I combine this with the grapes and salad already on the table and sneak a meal to Mr. Spock.

"Just as I thought," Alex says when I finish. "We'll have to get help from Muhomor."

Nadejda and Gogi look shocked, while my cousin and I exchange blank stares.

"I take it he's not talking about the regular meaning of the word *muhomor*?" I type into the chat.

In Russian, muhomor is the name of a poisonous mushroom called *Amanita muscaria*, sometimes referred to as fly agaric. It's a toadstool with a bright red cap speckled with white, and I was always told to avoid it as a kid. A nifty mental Google search informs me this mushroom actually has hallucinogenic properties I wasn't previously aware of. This might explain why the caterpillar in *Alice in Wonderland* was so fond of sitting on it (and maybe why Alice needed to eat so many shrooms).

"No," Mitya replies from inside the chat. "It's a person. I didn't think he was real, let alone someone Alex might know." From the iPad, out loud, Mitya says, "Alex, stop building the suspense. Why don't you tell everyone who Muhomor is?"

"I don't like repeating rumors." Alex pours a shot of vodka with the air of someone who's certainly looking forward to sharing this particular rumor. "I'm sure you've seen certain articles in *Wired*, such as the one about Russia hacking into Pentagon emails, or Russia hacking Democratic National Committee, or the one about the Russian Dark Net marketplaces that allow one to buy illegal drugs, weapons, and stolen credit cards…" He downs the shot and chases it with a pickle. "If those stories have any foundation in reality, it's Muhomor behind the curtain pulling the invisible binary strings."

"And you know him how?" Mitya asks as the teleconference robot moves closer to Alex.

"Is it really relevant?" Alex pushes his glasses higher up his nose. "He owes me a few favors, just like I owed you."

"If this Muhomor helps Mike, we won't just be even," Mitya says. "I'll owe *you*."

"I can't guarantee he'll help." Alex sits down and faces the iPad. "I can only try to arrange the meeting."

"Fine." Mitya rolls the robot even closer to Alex. "Get in touch with him."

Alex pulls out his phone and types at a speed a tween would envy.

"Why do you assume Muhomor is a him?" Ada asks in our private chat window. "What if it's a her?"

"You have much to learn about the Russian language," Mitya types back. "The word *muhomor* is a masculine noun. A lady hacker would've called herself something like *lisichka*."

"I guess," Ada says. "But those are chanterelle mushrooms, right? They're way less cool than fly agaric."

"Ah," Mitya types back, "but that Russian word is also a diminutive of fox, which makes it kind of foxy, don't you think?"

"I think *muhomor* is cooler," I chime in. "It's a rare Russian word that can be written with letters that occur in both the Cyrillic and English alphabets."

Before anyone can comment further on options for hacker aliases, Alex looks up from his phone and says,

"Okay, I should hear back from Muhomor shortly. Now, let's all just relax for a minute." Holding on to the bottle, he walks over to Nadejda. "May I take care of the lady?" Without waiting for anyone to reply, he pours her a shot of vodka and asks, "Can I get you more chicken liver pâté?"

Nadejda looks at him as though he's about to harvest a liver from a chicken that's sprouting from his head. Then, to my utter shock, she smiles as coquettishly as her formidable frown lines allow and says, "Maybe a little."

"Such chauvinistic behavior," Ada comments.

"You're reading way too much into it," Mitya objects. "It's a Russian dinner table tradition for the gentleman to—"

I don't read the rest of the exchange because I notice how my cousin is looking at Alex, who's blissfully adding morsels of liver pâté to Nadejda's plate. His stare reminds me of the ice ball special move the character Sub-Zero enjoys throwing in the *Mortal Combat* games. In a voice as cold as his stare, Joe says, "We didn't come here to relax."

Nadejda, who must know Joe well, turns white, but I have to hand it to Alex. He doesn't flinch and just calmly says, "I understand and respect your position, Joseph Abramovich. The problem is there isn't much I can do. Muhomor is very eccentric. He'll take as long as he wants to reply. Also, I might as well warn you that it'll take even longer to set up a meeting with him."

"Will it?" I ask as Alex puts the *blin*—Russian crepe—that Nadejda refused into his own mouth. "Care to explain why?"

"Take it easy," Ada warns me in the chat. "Your voice shows an unusual amount of irritation."

"Well," I mentally type, "Joe is on the verge of either choking or torture-shooting our host to get answers, and that would be a bad move in this well-defended facility, no matter how tempting it might be."

Alex swallows his food and glances at his phone. Apparently seeing nothing on it, he looks up again and says, "Muhomor likes to include puzzles in his dealings, and that crap usually takes time to crack."

"So let's work with someone else," Gogi says, and I can tell he's also worried Joe might act out his displeasure.

Alex shakes his head. "He's the only such person I know," he explains. "Perhaps there's something we can do in the meantime? Did you want to change your clothes after your long trip? Or take a bath?" He looks longingly at Nadejda. "Or anything else?"

"We could use some weapons," Gogi says, and his unibrow does a jig on his forehead.

"That would be nice," Nadejda agrees and smiles widely, revealing a golden crown on her left canine tooth.

Alex looks like he's about to refuse, but then Joe stands, fists clenched and eyes set on homicide.

"Okay," Alex says a bit too quickly. When Joe unclenches his fists, our host smiles weakly, his relief apparent, and looks at Nadejda. "How can I resist, Nadechka?" he says in a smarmy tone. "Come, let me show you my armory."

To my utter shock, Nadejda lets Alex get away with the diminutive form of her name, and she's the first one on her feet, following him out of the Lounge. She walks next to him, eagerly chatting him up about something I can't quite hear. The rest of us follow with less enthusiasm.

"I'll disconnect now," my friend says from the telepresence robot behind us. "Don't worry about me."

No one shows the slightest hint that they heard Mitya as they continue through the maze of corridors after our host.

"It's in here," Alex says as he opens the large door to his left.

Gogi enters first and whistles loudly.

"It's bad luck to whistle in the house," Nadejda says, but then she whistles too. Even Joe looks pretty impressed, and with good reason.

The room reminds me of that iconic scene from *The Matrix*, when Neo is asked what he needs and he says, "Guns. Lots of guns."

The shelves in the hangar-sized space are overflowing with weapons of varying degrees of destruction. Some of these items look so deadly I suspect even the NRA might not want them in civilian hands. I estimate that about ninety-eight percent of these weapons are illegal in Russia and seventy percent would be illegal in the most gung-ho states in America. To my New Yorker eyes, these guns are obscenely shocking yet fascinating—like a porno scenario you think is sick but can't stop watching.

I walk through rows of plastic explosives, rifles, shotguns, and rocket launchers. Finally, I stop next to a few rows dedicated mostly to handguns, figuring I might as well pick one up while I'm here.

"I don't think you should get a gun," Ada says, appearing as an angel on my shoulder.

"If you're against him using a gun, why did you help me with the gun app?" Mitya asks, appearing in his devil form. "I think he totally should get a gun, maybe even a few. I recommend one of those 9mm Glocks." He points at the nearest shelf. "That one right there is something only cops and soldiers can have in the US."

"I only did the code review for that app." Ada tugs at her Mohawk. "That's far from actually helping, and it certainly doesn't mean I approve of gun use."

"I'm sorry, Ada," I type into the chat, "but I have to side with Mitya on this one." I pick up a gun for the second time in my life—the first time being when I went to a gun range in New Jersey about a decade ago.

"Does this mean the app is done?" I type into the chat. The app in question was the lowest priority on the list I specced out for them before flying out, and with all the other awesome software, I completely forgot about it.

"It's done," Mitya says. "I just sent it to your AROS."

A little 3D gun icon shows up in the air in front of me. The idea behind the app is to assist with aiming, so even a novice like me can actually hit a target. Since I now have access to a gun, I launch the app and grab a Glock to see how it'll all come together.

"Enter the gun model and make," a window asks, and I do.

"The app is querying several good gun databases," Mitya says as though he can see what I'm doing. "If it doesn't recognize the make and model, choose another gun."

"No, it has it," I say as the window spits out the exact data on my gun and disappears.

Faint lines appear and crisscross the gun, slowly zoning in on the rear and front sights. Eventually, a narrow line materializes in my vision. It comes out of the gun's barrel and goes straight into the floor where I'm currently pointing the weapon.

I wave the gun around, and the line moves with it. The theory is if I want to aim at something, I just need to point the tip of the line where the bullet should end up.

"We can market this to the army one day," Mitya says. "We'll call it Augmented Reality Aim Assist, or something."

"Great," Ada says sarcastically. "Our work will be used to take lives."

"Someone will come up with this anyway," Mitya says. "I think you're letting your angel avatar go to your head."

"How is this better than a laser sight?" I type into the chat, partly to stop them from bickering.

"Laser sight isn't perfect and only works up to a certain distance. This optimizes your accuracy at any distance," Mitya explains. "Plus, only you can see the AU sights, so it's stealthier as well."

Making sure the gun isn't loaded and that the safety's on, I aim the Augmented Reality pointer at Alex's head, who's about twenty feet away.

The line makes aiming ridiculously easy, and if the bullet really did fly down that path, the app would indeed make a marksman out of me.

"Hey, Alex," I shout as I close the distance between us. "Do you have a holster I can use?"

"And a couple of duffel bags," Gogi says.

"And a rucksack," Nadejda adds.

"I'll go ask Anna to locate whatever you need," Alex says, a little too eagerly, and leaves the room.

I take in the others' weapons. With my one Glock, I almost feel naked. Everyone else looks like they decided to star in an action movie, especially Gogi, who appears ready to singlehandedly start a small war.

Seeing that I'm armed, Gogi approaches me and gives me a few pointers so that I, in his words, "don't shoot his left nut by accident."

Alex returns and hands me a shoulder holster, telling the others, "Anna will bring the rest of your items shortly."

"Don't go near that," I whisper to Mr. Spock after I cover the gun with my jacket. "If I reach for it in a hurry, I don't want to end up grabbing you instead by accident."

Pink eyes glint from inside my jacket, and I get the feeling that if the rat could speak, he'd say, "Got it, boss. What am I, a Guinea pig?"

In the distance, Alex resumes his conversation with Nadejda. He tells her she's the quintessential Russian woman, straight from ancient poetry. He goes as far as quoting a verse from Nekrasov that roughly translates to, "A Russian woman can stop a galloping horse and enter a burning hut."

His flirting is interrupted by his phone's very nostalgia-inspiring ringtone—a line from the Russian cartoon

Nu, pogodi!, the Soviet answer to *Tom and Jerry*, only with a wolf and a hare.

"It's Muhomor," Alex says after a brief glance. He then frowns. "As I feared, he's sent another one of his dumb hacking puzzles."

CHAPTER TWENTY-EIGHT

Alex angrily presses a couple of keys on his phone and says, "I sent the puzzle to a team of experts on my payroll. It usually takes them a few hours to crack Muhomor's assignments, though last time it took a whole day."

Joe slams a fresh magazine into a ginormous black gun. I take it as a bad sign and say, "You mentioned puzzles before. Can you elaborate?"

"Sure, though there isn't much to explain," Alex says. "Muhomor never tells you the meeting location. He encodes it using a different method each time. Once, I got a cryptic text that was encoded; another time, he sent me a username and a server in Turkey to log in to. Though the details vary, the basic premise is the same. He wants you to do some work before he meets with you."

"But why would he do that?" Gogi asks. "I thought he owed you a favor?"

"I have no clue," Alex replies a bit too defensively. "Maybe it's his way of making sure it's me he's communicating with, or maybe he's just weird."

"He could be using you to hack stuff he's too lazy to hack himself," I suggest. "That Turkey thing sounds like it."

"Whatever the reason, I'm as annoyed with this as you guys are. Probably more so since I have to go through this more often." Alex glances nervously at Joe.

"Can I take a look at the problem he sent you?" I ask. "I'm good with puzzles." In my mental chat window, I add, "At least I hope I am, thanks to my brain boost."

"Sure," Alex says. "What's your email?"

"It's bigcheese@cohencapital.com," I reply.

Alex has me spell out the email and then plays with his phone some more.

I look at his message on Precious, mostly for appearance's sake, since I'd rather do it through the AROS interface in my head.

All the email contains is a picture of an attractive and very typically Russian girl with blond hair and blue eyes.

Now that they saw me look at it on my phone, I figure it's safe for me to close my eyes, so I do. I bring up the same image and maximize it in the AROS interface. When the face is nice and big, I apply the face recognition app to it. According to the results, her name is Lyuba Trupova. She has no criminal record, and most of her data comes from her Vkontakte social media account.

I forward the pic and my meager findings to my friends, and in my mental chat, I type, "Check your emails if you're willing to help me with this puzzle."

"I'm already trying some common passwords to get into her Vkontakte account," Mitya says.

"Good," I say. "Try things like her boyfriend's name, followed by a one or a zero."

"I just tried that," Mitya says. "I also tried 'password,' both in Russian and English, as well as 'god,' 'Minsk'—her city of birth—and 'Belorussian State University,' the school she attended."

"Try 'letmein,'" Ada suggests. "As well as 'love' and 'money.'"

"She wouldn't use love," I say but try it anyway to no avail. "Her name, Lyuba, is short for Lyubov, which means 'love' in Russian."

"Hey, that's actually a good clue," Mitya says. "Notice her last name is Trupova, which sounds like *trup*—Russian for corpse."

Even before Mitya has finished his sentence, I try "necrophilia" as a password and get in. Alex wasn't kidding when he said Muhomor was eccentric.

"Now that I'm in her account, I can see her email. It's skazka@mail.ru," I mentally type. "But I can't log in using the same password."

My friends suggest some very clever guesses for this new password, both based on their research into statistically common passwords and in a more targeted form by trying to backward engineer what someone with Lyuba's social connections would use. None of it pans out, though.

As we chat, the picture of the girl keeps staring at me, and I eventually notice something odd about it. "Guys, do you see something blurry or pixelated about this image?" I say. "I can't quite put my finger on it, but—"

"You're right. I think it's steganography," Mitya interrupts. After a pause, he adds, "Here's what I get when I remove all but the two least significant bits of each color component and perform a normalization. Check your email, Mr. Grandmaster."

Confused, I open my mental inbox. He sent me a picture of a chessboard with pieces arranged around it, which explains why Mitya called me a grandmaster. When I was a kid back in Russia, I belonged to a chess club for a few years, and I've made a habit out of beating Mitya in chess.

The board setup is oddly familiar, and after I stare at it for a few seconds, I remember where I've seen it. That makes me wonder for a second if Ada's brain boost is aiding my memory, but I decide that's unlikely.

A quick mental Google search confirms my recollection, and I type into the chat, "This is the next to last position of the conclusive match between Anatoly Karpov and Garry Kasparov in the World Chess Championship game in 1985. We covered it in the club ad nauseam. I bet the password is 'horseD4.' Horse is what the knight piece is called in Russian, and D4 is where the knight ended up during the finishing move of the game."

I then try the password, but it doesn't work.

"Maybe it's Kasparov?" Mitya says. "I just looked up that game, and that's who won."

I try Kasparov, then Kasparov with horseD4 before and after it, but it doesn't work. I then try a bunch of variations on the same theme, including the color of the last piece, black, and using the English word *knight* instead of *horse*—all without any luck.

"Wait a minute," Mitya writes in the chat. "Could he have done this again? The email was *skazka*, Russian for 'fairy tale.'"

"You're a genius," I type back. "Karpov comes from the word *karp*, Russian for—not surprisingly—carp, which means the password probably contains something along the lines of golden fish or maybe goldfish."

I try my earlier permutations again, adding the word goldfish into the mix, and when I try goldFishHorseD4, I finally get in.

In the chat, Mitya explains for Ada's benefit, "You see, there's a Russian fairy tale written in verse by Pushkin, who was a Russian author of Shakespeare's caliber. The story deals with a fisherman and a golden fish that grants him wishes, kind of like an aqua genie. And, of course, goldfish is a type of carp, so—"

"I'm in," I type and share the password with them.

"I'm in too," they both answer.

I scan Lyuba's emails but don't see anything that looks like a coded message.

"I've got it," Ada says out loud. "In the junk folder, the email from gyromitra@esculenta.com."

"Of course," Mitya says. "The guy's nickname is a type of mushroom, so he sent the email from an account that's the name of a mushroom that looks like a brain."

I Google "gyromitra esculenta," and it indeed looks eerily like a brain. Then I look at the email, dreading another roundabout.

To my relief, the message isn't encrypted. The email contains a Moscow address, instructions for what to tell the bouncers once we get there, and a reminder for Alex not to bring his mercenaries. Since there's nothing about *my* crew, I assume Muhomor will be okay with Gogi, Nadejda, and Joe coming along. I search the meeting place via Yandex (the Russian equivalent of Google), and it turns out to be Dazdraperma, a very exclusive establishment that's a blend of a casino, a strip club, and a nightclub. It even has a banya—the Russian sauna—on the premises.

I share my findings with my friends. Then I open my eyes and announce, "I know where to go."

I realize my mistake instantly. "I told you I was good with puzzles," I say in an effort to cover it up.

People are still looking at me with a mixture of suspicion and disbelief, especially Alex. Since Mom's rescue is on the line, I find it hard to care what they think, so I just explain where we're going.

"I know the place," Alex says after a long pause. "Sounds like somewhere Muhomor might be. I'll go make preparations so we can leave as soon as possible."

He exits the room, and I reflect on how this whole thing must've looked to him and the others. He emailed me; I glanced at his message, closed my eyes, probably had a look of concentration on my face, and then I opened my eyes a few minutes later and blurted out the answer to a puzzle his special team usually takes hours to crack.

"Make sure you get all the weapons you'll need," I tell Gogi, Nadejda, and Joe. "I'll go wait at the table."

No one says anything, so I plod back to the Lounge, cursing myself for not leaving before my friends and I started solving the puzzle.

"They probably just think you're wicked smart," Ada says when I complain about it in the chat.

"You shouldn't feel bad for fooling them." Mitya chuckles. "On a more serious note, and on the topic of getting smarter, I'm done with my STRELA resource allocation project, and the code is going to Ada for review. As soon as she's done, it'll be ready for testing."

"Then let me focus on it," Ada says. "I'm not as good as you at multitasking."

I don't get a chance to jealously check whether she meant Mitya or me when she said "you" because a new email arrives in my inbox.

I read the subject line, and my heart rate spikes.

It says: *If you don't go back to America, this will happen to your mother.*

There's no text in the body of the email, only a file named "play_me.mov."

As I forward the email to Joe, Mitya, and Ada, I pinpoint the icy, deadweight sensation in my stomach. As a kid, this was how I felt when I went to get my vaccine shots.

I start the video.

The camera is zoomed in on a shaved head, and because there aren't any objects around, it's hard to gauge the size of the person in the video, or their identity, or even something as basic as whether the head belongs to a man or a woman.

Then a hand appears in the frame.

The hand is clad in a blue latex glove, and it's holding a large yellow cordless DeWalt drill. A spindly sword-like drill bit is sticking out of its tip.

"No," Ada whispers out loud.

"This can't be heading where I think it is," Mitya echoes.

I suppress the urge to stop watching and brace myself.

CHAPTER TWENTY-NINE

The drill bit spins.

The video has no sound, maybe because the microphone wasn't enabled on the recording device used to film this atrocity.

I feel like I'm rooted to the floor and my roots are filling with a hundred pounds of ice every millimeter the drill gets closer to the back of the person's head.

When the tip of the drill bit penetrates the skin, my cursed imagination fills in the details not available to me, like the person's scream and the horrible bone-crunching buzz and the smell of—

I get violently sick on Alex's marble floor.

When I'm done heaving, my ribs sing in agony, but the video is over.

My friends are saying something, but I just stand there, gulping in air until I get sick again.

"Oh my," says Anna, Alex's model housekeeper. She must've witnessed me losing all that super-expensive caviar I ate on her earlier recommendation. "Are you okay?"

I get sick again. Both my ribs and my skull feel like they're breaking apart. "No, I'm the opposite of okay."

Anna grabs my elbow and starts dragging me away, saying something along the lines of, "Let me walk you."

She leads me to a bathroom to freshen up and rinse my mouth. Afterwards, she takes me somewhere else, and as I follow her, I'm truly glad I can communicate with my friends via the mental interface, because I don't think I can gather the strength to speak.

Into the chat, I type, "It must've been someone from the study."

"I'm so sorry," Ada whispers out loud.

"Yeah, man," Mitya echoes in a subdued tone. "Hang in there. Don't fall apart."

As they continue saying supportive nothings, I take out Mr. Spock and stroke the pink part of his fur, hoping a little pet therapy will help me pull myself together—something I have to do for Mom's sake.

Mr. Spock closes his eyes, which I take as a sign of pleasure. Confirming my guess, he begins bruxing and gently nibbling on my skin. All of that, combined with the violet aura he has from the app, means he's very happy and at ease. After a while, I also feel more relaxed and start thinking rationally enough to notice my surroundings. It turns out the whole gang is around me, with Nadejda staying far outside the rat-leaping range.

"Did you see it?" I ask Joe. "The email I forwarded?"

He nods, his expression unreadable. "Do we know who sent it yet?"

"I have my people on it," Alex says. "But I wouldn't hold my breath. It's from a free provider, so anyone with a Tor Browser could've created the account, sent the email, and remained anonymous as can be."

"Is that true?" I type into the chat. "We can't track it?"

"I'll take a look, but I'm afraid Alex might be right," Mitya replies.

"I don't know what to do," I say out loud to no one in particular.

"You should probably consider going back to the United States." Alex walks over to the nearby table, pours a shot of vodka, and offers it to me. "I saw the video. Those people aren't kidding around."

I shake my head, refusing the vodka (which is very rude in Russia, but I don't care), and grab a handful of grapes instead.

"Looks to me like they're showing their weakness." Gogi adjusts the shoulder strap on his heavy duffel bag. "They know we're on their trail, and they got scared enough to execute one of the hostages."

"But it's such a desperate move." I put all but two grapes in my mouth and feed the rest to Mr. Spock. "It worries me. Desperate people do irrational things."

"I agree," Alex says, knocking back the shot he offered me. "What if Mike's mother is the next victim? What if—"

Alex stops speaking because Joe demonstratively takes out his gun, flicks off the safety, and places the loaded weapon on the table in front of him. In the silence that follows, he stares at Alex until the billionaire looks away. With lethal finality, my cousin says, "We're going to Dazdraperma."

He doesn't need to add any niceties such as "and that's it" or "no more debate" or even "or else I'll shoot you," because it's clear he'd shoot anyone not on board with his plan.

Funny enough, I don't think I disagree with him. It doesn't take a brain boost to realize that if we fly back home, Mom's death is a certainty. True, it might involve something less drastic than a drill to the head, but her chances are slim nonetheless. On the other hand, if we stay, there's a possibility, however remote, that we might save her.

Thus determined, I carefully put Mr. Spock back in my pocket, grab a handful of food from the table, and say, "Let's head out."

As we drive through the congested Moscow streets in Alex's tricked-out Land Rover, I can't help gawking at the sights that range from the colorful onion-like cupolas of the Orthodox churches to monuments from both tsarist Russia and the Soviet days. When I was here as a kid, I didn't appreciate any of this, and I still don't, given my state of mind. But I glimpse enough wonders to understand why the real estate prices in Russia's capital are on par with those in New York, Shanghai, and Paris.

Dazdraperma isn't located in the center of the city for the same reason Alex's Palace isn't—it's huge. There's a block-long line, which is crazy in daytime. Lines in Russia shouldn't shock me, though. They're what I think of whenever I picture this country. In Krasnodar, around the late eighties and early nineties—when most of my perceptions of Russia were formed—you had to stand in line to get everything, even something as basic as bread or milk.

We bypass everyone standing in line and waltz up to the bouncers. Gogi tells them the password we got from Muhomor—*shmakodyavka frikadel'ka.*

"That's 'shorty meatball,'" Mitya types into the chat.

"I'm still reviewing the code," Ada replies. "Let me be."

Wanting to focus on my surroundings, I put away the chat window as I pass through the heavy doors.

The first thing we see upon entering is the casino, and it's themed to match the name of the establishment. In Russian, and to some degree in English, the word *dazdraperma* sounds funny, and not just because it sounds a bit like *sperm*. It comes from an infrequently used female name that only the most ardent communists or accidentally abusive parents gave their daughters during Soviet times. It actually stands for "*Da Zdra*(vstvuet) *Per*(voye) *Ma*(ya)," meaning something like "Long Live the First of May." That date was a big made-up holiday in honor of International Workers' Solidarity and reminds me of one of those Hallmark holidays in the US, like a sort of commie Valentine's Day. Incidentally, the Russian version of Valentine's Day is March 8th, though it's known as International Women's Day and kind of incorporates Mother's Day as well. When I was growing up, there were parades on May 1st, and I was often forced to participate in them with the other kids. In Moscow, the parades included soldiers marching down the

Red Square alongside rolling tanks, and I believe they recently reinstated the whole practice, though I can't be sure.

The casino has photos of Lenin, wheat husks, sickles and hammers, and other paraphernalia you'd see back in the day on May 1st, but I think it's meant to be ironic, since casinos were illegal back in the Soviet Union. Actually, speaking of legality, I'm not sure gambling is legal in Russia today. Then again, neither is marijuana, and I detect its telltale smell in the cloud of smoke I pass through.

"What do we do now?" I ask my entourage. "Every second we waste is a chance for them to figure out we didn't react to their threat."

"It's still not too late to leave," Alex says. Noticing Joe's jaw muscles tighten, he adds hastily, "Muhomor will send someone to approach us. That's how he always operates."

To stop myself from going crazy, I walk over to a table where a card game is taking place. There's a dealer and six players already at it, and it takes me only a couple of rounds to develop a theory about the rules—in part because it's a variation of poker. Curious if I'm right, I run a mental search. I learn I'm very close to knowing the rules and that this game is called Russian Poker—though I guess they might simply call it "poker" in Moscow. Based on what I've seen so far, I think I could make a killing if I played, though I don't know if it's because I've always had a propensity for poker or if my brain boost is striking once again.

I share my thoughts with Mitya via chat, and he warns me, "Don't even approach the table. Yes, you could make a figurative killing, but then it could turn into a literal killing—of you. You don't want the house thinking you're cheating, and casinos all over the world define being very good at a game as cheating. Even in Vegas you can get something broken for being too lucky—or at least that was the case in the past. This is Russia, so the bone they'll break is your skull."

"Hi," says a soft feminine voice. "You're Mike Cohen."

I turn around and see a familiar Russian face looking at me with a barely detectible smirk. It takes me half a second to place her as the girl from the puzzle picture Muhomor sent Alex.

"Hi," I say. "Is your name really Lyuba?"

"Why not?" the girl whose name is probably not Lyuba says. "It'll work for the purposes of my current assignment."

"Let's go then," I say. "*Lyuba.*"

"No funny business," Nadejda adds, her deep voice carrying over the pinging noise of slot machines.

Lyuba takes a good look at the former wrestling champion, and her smirk disappears. She turns on her heels, briskly walks through the casino, and opens a door into the next section of the club, which happens to be the dance floor.

Instantly, trance music envelops us, nearly deafening me, and I marvel at how good the insulation must be in the walls and doors. Just a moment ago, all I heard was the ambient casino noise. Still, I like the super-loud song enough to get Einstein to figure out what it is—"Resurrection" by a Russian group called PPK.

Lyuba pushes through the sweaty bodies on the dance floor and heads toward the giant DJ booth in the farthest corner. The DJ is wearing a shiny cosmonaut helmet, but as it turns out, he—or she—isn't our destination. To the side of the DJ's big podium is a door, and that's where Lyuba leads us.

A short corridor later, we stop at a big metal door, and Lyuba knocks.

A buzzing sound blares, and Lyuba pushes the door in.

Once we've all entered, she says, "He's inside," and slams the door behind us.

Joe reaches out and locks the door.

"Is it me, or is this a bit ominous?" I try typing into the chat but discover I can't.

I'm not feeling so great, and the AROS apps are shouting connection errors at me. My mind feels as though I just woke up with a hangover *and* a sleep-deprivation headache.

Teeth clenched, I look around the room for answers.

CHAPTER THIRTY

The room is all but empty, with the exception of a sleek desk and an office chair. In the chair sits a man with a haircut that could give Ada's hairdo a run for its money.

The walls have an odd metallic sheen to them, and I begin to suspect the cause of my mental state, as well as the reason for AROS bugging out.

I take out my phone to verify my theory, and sure enough, there are no bars or any hint of connectivity.

"Does your phone work?" I whisper to my conspirators.

One by one everyone checks their phones, confirming my suspicions.

So the errors of my AROS interface are due to a lack of connectivity. I got so used to the brain boost that without it, I actually feel like something is missing. I guess that makes sense since, in a way, it's as though an extra part of my brain suddenly went away.

"This room is a Faraday cage," the man behind the desk says without turning. "Hence why I use this." He dangles the network cable that snakes into one of those rugged, briefcase-looking laptops the military likes to use.

"A Faraday cage is an enclosure that blocks electromagnetic energy," I explain in case Gogi or Nadejda aren't familiar with the term. "Put your phone in a microwave oven, and it'll have the same effect. Microwaves have a Faraday cage built in to prevent—"

Alex puts a hand on my shoulder, interrupting me. When I turn, he simply shakes his head at me and says, "Muhomor, let me make the introductions."

"One moment," Muhomor says and types something so fast I wonder if he's just banging the keys randomly to look cool. The keyboard is arranged in JCUKEN (or ЙЦУКЕН in Cyrillic) formation, the Russian answer to the popular QWERTY layout. If Mitya could still communicate with me, he'd probably brag to Ada about his bilingual typing skills, which I lack.

Finally, Muhomor stops the banging and swivels his chair to look us over.

The guy has all the signs of being on a computer for more than twelve hours straight, the most telling of which are his red-rimmed, crusty eyes. Maybe to mask the wear and tear, or maybe to increase the air of mystery around him, he moves his dark shades from atop his head onto his nose. From the front, his spiky hair looks less like Ada's and more like he came out of an anime or Japanese RPG, a feeling heightened by the hint of Asian—likely Mongolian—heritage in his features. He's thin and clad in something like pajamas, which lend him a distinctly nonthreatening air, especially for the super-hacker/criminal Dark Net tsar I expected to meet.

Alex finally gets to the introductions, and Muhomor nods at each of us from his perch, but he doesn't get up to shake our hands.

"So," Muhomor says after Alex introduces the last person, me. "What can I do for you? And, more importantly, what can you do for me?"

Since he's looking at me, I say, "Whatever Alex usually pays you, I'll double it."

"Alex can't afford to just pay me." Muhomor toys with the arm of his sunglasses. "We barter in favors."

"So I'll owe you a big favor," I say evenly. "Time is of the essence here."

"I hear you pick winning companies for a living," Muhomor says, ignoring my plea for urgency. "Is that true?"

"It's an oversimplification, but yeah, that's roughly what I do."

"Good," Muhomor says, and I note some untraceable accent in his Russian. "How about I give you a portfolio of fifty Russian startups to check out, and you tell me which one you'd invest in if it was your money on the line?"

"Deal," I say confidently. "If your information leads to us rescuing my mom, I'll review your portfolio."

"Your mom?" Muhomor raises an eyebrow from under his shades. "I'd also like a million American dollars in addition to the investment advice."

"Done," I say, and low growls come from Gogi and Nadejda's direction. I wonder if they're rethinking how much they should've charged Joe to help him—assuming they're charging him at all.

"Okay then." Muhomor loudly cracks his knuckles. "Tell me how I can help you."

I take this as my cue to give him an edited version of the story, one that excludes any mention of Brainocytes. I finish with, "Maybe you know people who might know something? Or did anything in my story give you a clue about where my mom might be?"

Muhomor drums his fingers on the arms of his office chair for a few seconds, his forehead creased in thought. Then he rattles out, "I'd like to see the photos of all the people you've mentioned—the one called Anton Pintarev and the two you couldn't identify—as well as photos of the men who attacked your car."

"Sure, but I don't have any way of emailing you." I wave my disconnected phone.

"Here." He gets up, takes out a CAT-5-to-micro-USB adapter from his pajama bottoms, unplugs his laptop, and plugs the freed-up Ethernet cable into the converter.

I take his seat and plug in my phone. As soon as it gets on the network, my mind gets sharper, as though I just drank a triple expresso or popped an Adderall (something I'd done a few times back at MIT).

I restart the chat app and type, "Did you miss me?"

My friends begin speaking at the same time, and I tell them about the Faraday cage and that I don't have any time to talk because I need to email pictures to our helper. Not for the first time today, I notice how seamless this sort of mental typing has gotten for me in such a short time. It almost feels like a psychic phenomenon, like the words show up in the chat because I'm willing them to, and I love that. When it comes to using apps, the feeling is even stronger. The mental effort I exerted while using the imaginary video game controller has fallen away, and I feel like the emails go to Muhomor simply because that's want I want.

"Done," I tell him when the emails leave my outbox.

"Let me plug back in." Muhomor gets inside my space.

I warn Ada and Mitya that I'll be offline for a spell and internally cringe as I disconnect.

The dumbness, for lack of a better term, is much sharper this time, probably because I know what's happening to me.

Muhomor pulls the shades up on top of his head and plugs his laptop back in. I catch him looking at the photos first and then at the bios. He stares at the screen for a bit and then blocks my view as he begins frantically typing again.

I look at everyone else in the room. Joe looks stony, Gogi shrugs, and Nadejda and Alex seem to be two flirtatious words away from holding hands.

The typing stops, and Muhomor turns around and puts his shades back on.

"I'm sorry," he says, not sounding at all apologetic. "Given how little information I have, I can't help you."

"You what?" Joe takes out a gun and steps forward.

"Threatening me won't change the facts," Muhomor says so calmly you'd think Joe's gun shoots water instead of bullets. "Maybe if your cousin told me the whole story—"

"I did," I say.

"No, you did not," Muhomor says. "Nothing in your story even hints at why anyone in Russia would want a bunch of crippled Americans. There wasn't a ransom demand. This whole thing makes no sense."

"Tell him," Joe tells me. "Everyone else will wait outside."

Since he was present in New York, Joe knows about the technology part of the story, though even he doesn't know about the Brainocytes in my head. Still, he must've noticed my earlier omissions, and I bet he understood my need for caution. I also see why he made this suggestion—or more like demand. Given the gruesome video I received, I can't afford to play games with Muhomor. I have to risk telling him the truth.

"Thanks, Joe," I say as he unlocks the door and herds everyone out. "I'll be quick."

Joe closes the door, locking Gogi, Nadejda, and Alex out, and stands by the door like a sentry, arms crossed and face an emotionless mask.

"How much do you know about nanotechnology?" I ask Muhomor.

As it turns out, Muhomor knows quite a bit, so explaining the technology part of the story is pretty easy, though I still leave out the part about my own Brainocytes.

"I think I now have a better idea about what's going on," Muhomor says. "And I have a new deal."

"What?" I glance at Joe, who uncrosses his arms and balls his hands into fists. "We already have a deal."

"That was before you told me the whole story." Muhomor takes off his shades and rubs his eyes. "I have a theory now, and if it's correct, I have to either withdraw from our current deal altogether or ask for a new one."

I catch Joe's gaze. He seems to be offering to soften Muhomor up to make him more agreeable. Imperceptibly, I shake my head. It would be better to get Muhomor to cooperate willingly. Despite strongly suspecting what he'll request, I ask, "What do you want?"

"I want the Brainocytes," says Muhomor, confirming my guess.

I fleetingly consider letting Joe have him, then decide against it, at least for the moment. "For that, you'll have to do more than provide a theory," I say. "To get the Brainocytes, you'll have to basically hand-deliver my mom to me."

"Agreed," Muhomor says, his expression dead serious. "I'll do everything in my power to help you. How does that sound?"

"You'll also have to come to the US to get the Brainocytes," I say. "After this, I'm done with Russia for good."

"That's not a problem. I'll probably need to stay in the US afterwards anyway." Muhomor pulls out a pack of cigarettes, sees my horrified expression at the thought of second-hand smoke, and puts them back in his pocket. "If my theory is right and I help you, I'll have outlived my welcome in Mother Russia. In fact, I'll be lucky if they don't poison my sushi with polonium one day."

Stunned, I stare at him. "Wait a minute," I say slowly, wishing Ada and Mitya could overhear this conversation. "You don't mean it's the KGB that kidnapped my mom?"

For the first time in my life, Joe's expression approaches something remotely resembling concern.

"There's no more KGB." Muhomor cleans his sunglasses with his t-shirt. "But there *is* SVR."

"And you think they're behind this?" I ask incredulously. "Some Directorate T or whatever the modern equivalent is?"

Scenes from one of my favorite TV shows, *The Americans*, flit through my head. It's a show about KGB spies in the US during the eighties, and I love seeing the American side of that decade, since I was living in the Soviet Union at that time. It also helps that the Russian-speaking actors are outstanding, allowing me to enjoy the show on a level that non-Russian speakers miss out on. What's key, though, is that this show is the sole source of my knowledge about the former Russian intelligence agency, and there was definitely a Directorate T featured as an arm of the KGB that was interested in American advancements in science and technology.

"There's no official modern equivalent on the books." Muhomor looks at Joe for confirmation, gets none, and adds, "But old habits die hard."

"And you think they—"

"No." He gets up and starts pacing the small room, staying at least a leap away from my cousin. "Though this technology seems right up their alley, it sounds like this was done by someone who was looking to gain SVR's favor, or a group only remotely connected with them. Probably something like a subcontractor, if I were to use your American terminology."

"Why do you think that?" I ask, hoping he's right, since KGB subcontractor sounds less scary than KGB proper.

"Those brutes"—he waves at the laptop, where the pictures of Anton and his gang are still up—"aren't your typical agent material."

"True," I say, "but then, wouldn't they have to use people like them? No intelligence agency would want to get caught kidnapping people in the United States."

"The fact that you're alive tells me we're not dealing with the might of the agency itself," Muhomor says in a tone that has me wondering whether he's trying to convince himself as much as me. "I think someone somehow got a whiff of the tech you're working on. That person explained the possibilities to a more connected person and got the job—unofficially, of course."

"Who in Russia could 'get a whiff' of what we're doing?" I ask. "And how?"

"The who is a question for you to answer," Muhomor says. "As to how, I bet you filed papers with the FDA? Applied for a patent, maybe? You Americans are so cavalier with such information."

He's right. Off the top of my head, there's the Investigational Device Exemption filed with the FDA, as well as a million patents that add up to some useful information. Still, it would take someone watching everything from the start to piece it all together, and no one in Russia—or anywhere—should have paid Techno that kind of attention, unless they were tracking all the research and development of every startup company in America, and that seems hard to believe.

Muhomor makes the mistake of getting too close to Joe while pacing, and in a blur of movement, my cousin catches the hacker's slim upper arm in a vise-like grip. "I suggest you get back on your computer," he says softly, almost politely. "You have your new deal. Now tell us where my aunt is."

"Of course." Muhomor unsuccessfully tries to pull free from Joe's grip. "All you had to do was ask nicely."

Joe gives the thin man a push perfectly timed with him releasing his arm, and Muhomor violently plops into his chair. To his credit, he recovers quickly and opens his keyboard to resume that same frantic typing.

After about five minutes, I look at Joe questioningly. My cousin shrugs almost imperceptibly. I nod at Muhomor, and we approach the desk, something Joe manages to do quite menacingly.

"No point in standing over my shoulder," Muhomor says without a break in his typing. "If anything, you're distracting me."

"How much longer do you need?" I ask, fighting the urge to shut the laptop to get the guy's full attention.

"A couple of days," Muhomor says, his eyes never leaving the screen. "Three at most."

Joe slams the laptop cover shut, and Muhomor barely manages to save his fingers. Seems I wasn't the only one with that violent urge.

"Hey." The hacker glares at us. "If you break that machine or my hands, you'll just slow things down."

"We don't have a couple of days," I say. As gently as possible, I put my hand on Joe's shoulder to stop him from doing any more damage. "The video warned me to go back to the US. If I don't…"

Joe gives me a look that says, "Remove that hand or lose it."

I put my hands firmly inside my pockets.

Muhomor looks thoughtful for a couple of seconds and then asks, "Why don't you bluff them out? Go back to your plane. I'll email you an airport to fly to. We'll choose a backward town with nineties security, and I can make it so they won't know you landed there. We can then meet somewhere safe when I'm done."

"What do you think, Joe?" I ask. "It sounds doable to me."

Joe gives the hacker a onceover and says, "If you cross me, I'll lobotomize you." Matching his actions to his words, Joe pulls out a sharp, thin blade he must've borrowed from Alex's arsenal and jams it a few inches into the desk, a mere hair's width from Muhomor's elbow.

Muhomor visibly pales as he examines the blade. I bet he pictured the thing entering his brain.

Noisily removing the knife from the desk, Joe walks to the door.

"Try to hurry," I urge the hacker as I follow my cousin. "If something happens to my mom, the deal is off and you'll probably have to deal with the SVR—if Joe doesn't get to you first."

Not waiting for his response to that motivational threat, I slam the door behind me.

The world instantly feels richer, and I feel more alive. I have my brain boost back. I fleetingly wonder how long it'll take before I become as reliant on internet connectivity as amphetamine addicts are on their drugs, and decide it probably won't be long.

"Are you okay?" Ada asks worriedly.

"Seriously, what's going on?" Mitya echoes.

Though the music is back to an eardrum-shattering level, I can hear them perfectly well. I guess it makes sense since the Brainocytes are working directly with my brain, giving me the illusion of hearing.

I restart the chat window, and once it's ready, I mentally type, "I'm totally okay, but I'll explain everything in a minute."

Since Joe just started walking away, I take it upon myself to use gestures to explain to Gogi, Nadejda, and Alex that we want to exit the club before we discuss our plans. They understand, and we all follow Joe. By the time we come out by the DJ's podium, I have all my apps back up, with the AROS icons surrounding me in a surreal tableau that blends surprisingly well with the strobe lights reflecting off the nicely dressed people grinding on the dance floor.

Suddenly, I hear Einstein's voice, and I freeze, trying to make sense of the phrase the AI is repeating over and over.

"Sketchy person alert. Sketchy person alert. Sketchy person alert. Sketchy person alert…"

Einstein repeats that statement over and over, as if he's stuck on a loop, but then I realize the face recognition app must've scanned my surroundings for people with criminal profiles. Einstein is warning me there's a bunch of dangerous people around.

At first I wonder if they're Alex's people, but as much as I'd love for that to be the case, it's unlikely. Muhomor forbade Alex from bringing anyone, and Alex told us Muhomor takes that instruction very seriously. Also, I don't get repeat alerts, meaning I've never met these people before, and I'm certain I met the majority of Alex's guards when we were at the Palace.

Still, I have a small hope that the app is bugging out after getting disconnected, so I carefully scan the thousand faces around me.

The heavy music beat seems to grow distant, and despite the sweat gleaming on many faces, I feel like the temperature in the club dropped by several degrees as I note all the men with red haloes sprinkled around the room. Not a single one looks familiar, but I can tell they're dangerous men, hardened by life in ways I can't imagine.

The nearest one looks at me, then at his smartphone, and then gestures in my direction.

On instinct, I leap for Joe. Grabbing his arm, I scream into his ear, "Joe, we're being ambushed!" To highlight my words, I point at the guy who's gesturing.

For a second, I'm not sure Joe heard me, but then two things happen at once. Joe looks at the man I pointed out, and almost instantly, there's a gun in Joe's hand.

Before I can blink, several red-haloed men are holding guns as well.

"They can't start shooting in here," I type into the chat, almost instinctively. "It's too public. It'll be all over the news with a headline like 'Shooting in a Nightclub.' It'll draw too much attention and—"

I don't get to finish my thought, because the loud music is interrupted by a thunderous clap that causes my heart to jump into my throat.

I was wrong in the assessment I just gave my friends.

Someone just fired a gun in the middle of the dance floor.

CHAPTER THIRTY-ONE

All around me people begin screaming, shouting, and running in random directions.

Another shot is fired.

I freeze in place, unsure what to do.

Joe grabs me by the front of my shirt and throws me backward. Before I can hit the floor, strong, hairy hands grab me and shove me behind the DJ's podium. I recognize Gogi as the owner of the hands. As soon as he's done with me, he pulls out two guns with the speed of a gunslinger and fires.

I duck behind the podium and, in morbid fascination, watch Gogi aim his guns again. Dazedly, I wonder if his laser sights are useless in the ambient laser display in the club.

My question is answered instantly.

One moment I see two red dots on the forehead of the red-haloed man who first noticed me, and in the next, two shots blast out and the guy's head explodes like a brain-filled piñata.

Amidst the screaming, the people closest to the dead man freeze in place, and a few smarter ones drop to the ground, protectively shielding their heads with their arms.

Another round of shots follows.

Doing my best to stay hidden from our assailants, I examine my entourage.

Like me, Gogi and Nadejda are using the DJ's podium as cover. He's methodically aiming his two guns while she's preparing her Uzi. I don't know if it's the same one she used in the car or a newer, better model she got from Alex's armory.

Alex is crawling on the floor toward the hallway that leads to Muhomor. It occurs to me we got lucky the assailants didn't ambush us while we were in that room, as was probably their original plan.

I seek out Joe on the dance floor. He's using Gogi's cover fire, as well as the bodies of panicked people, to execute another gunman.

As I take it all in, I realize my allies have a big problem.

Unlike me, they don't know who the bad guys are, and they have to rely on visual cues, such as people holding guns and looking threatening. However, a few assailants are trying to blend in with the crowd, with only their red haloes giving them away.

I form a quick plan to deal with this problem and decide to shut down the music so my allies can hear me share my superior knowledge with them.

Taking out my gun, I approach the dumbfounded DJ.

"Take that off," I shout over the noise and wave my gun (with the safety still on) at the cosmonaut helmet in an up-and-down motion. In the curved, reflective surface of the visor, my face looks like a frightened caricature.

The DJ reaches for the headgear, but it suddenly explodes, shards of glass and plastic flying everywhere. A piece of glass nicks my earlobe, but the pain barely registers. Instead, I watch in horrified shock as the DJ's dead body crumples in front of me.

"Duck!" Mitya screams. "That bullet was meant for you."

My legs fold under me as if of their own accord. Finding myself on the floor, I start pulling cables out of the DJ's laptop, figuring one of them will cut the music. Thanks to Murphy's Law, the cable I need is the last one I pull, and the music stops, the sudden silence amplifying the terrified screams and the gunfire.

I sneak a peek at the mayhem and spot a red-haloed dude within a couple of feet of my cousin. Grabbing the DJ's microphone, I yell, "Joe, behind you!"

My voice booms across the dance floor, and Joe begins to turn. At the same time, the man pulls out his concealed weapon.

It's clear my cousin won't make it.

"Joe!" I scream, and then I hear the *rat-tat-tat* of the Uzi.

The man behind Joe falls. While I was dealing with the music, Nadejda exited the safety of the podium and got close enough to the action to put her Uzi to use.

Joe gives Nadejda the barest nod as thanks and runs toward the main exit, where the crowd is thicker and will provide him with good cover.

For the next minute, I use the mic to warn Joe and the others where the less obvious red-haloed guys are.

My gaze falls on Nadejda. A red-haloed man must've crept up behind her, because he has her in a headlock. I think I see Nadejda turning purple, though it's hard to tell from this distance and especially with these lights.

"Joe, Gogi, help Nadejda," I yell into the mic, but they have their own problems. Gogi is exchanging fire with three men, and my cousin is dealing with two assailants.

"You should shoot that guy yourself," Mitya suggests urgently. "Use the aiming app."

Something inside me snaps, and I don't even notice how I start up the gun-assist app. My weapon just suddenly has the aiming line. Just as automatically, I take the safety off the gun and use the assist app to line up the barrel with the leg of the guy behind Nadejda.

"If your hand shakes," Ada says, "or if the app doesn't work the way we hoped, you could hit Nadejda."

"If he doesn't shoot, she'll die anyway," Mitya retorts.

I wish I had time to think this through, but I don't. Going off my instincts, I squeeze the trigger.

The bullet bites off a chunk of the big man's thigh.

To my utter amazement, he doesn't let go of his victim's neck. Still, the wound weakens him enough to give Nadejda her chance. In what must be a wrestling maneuver, she rips free from the guy's grasp, and in a continuous motion, she lifts the wounded man into the air. To my eyes, he seems to hover over her head for a moment before his back lands over Nadejda's knee. I can almost hear his spine cracking from all the way behind the podium.

A bullet whines past my ear, and I switch focus from Nadejda to the bullet's origin.

The shooter is a blond guy, and he's still aiming at me.

I touch his right shoulder with my aim-assist line and pull the trigger.

The guy falls. He's twitching on the floor, so I assume he's alive.

"Stop shooting to maim," Mitya yells at me. "Shoot to kill."

"Don't listen to him," Ada retorts.

"Don't speak to me right now," I type into the chat. "I'll do what I have to."

What I don't say is that I'm siding more with Ada's viewpoint. I can't picture myself killing anyone, even though these people deserve it, both for trying to shoot us and because they're working with whoever kidnapped Mom. I'm not sure if it's the bios provided by the face recognition app or something ingrained in me, but I stick to shooting arms and legs, figuring I can analyze my reluctance to kill at a more opportune time. On the plus side—assuming it's a pro and not a con to be cold-blooded—I have zero qualms about the wounds I inflict.

I shoot the arm of a long-haired man aiming at Gogi while a speaker to my right shatters into small bits of metal and plastic.

Unperturbed, I hit the shoulder of a bald guy who was about to get Joe.

An odd sense of flow overcomes me, and I spend the next couple of minutes in a blur of aiming my Glock, pulling the trigger, rinsing and repeating, over and over again.

When my gun clicks empty, the concentration leaves me, and I take a look at the blood-soaked dance floor. Thanks to our joint efforts, the number of red-haloed men left standing is reduced to just a few individuals.

Since my extra magazines are in Alex's SUV, along with duffel bags full of other tools of war, I decide to leave the rest of our enemies to my cousin and his crew. It's time to get Muhomor and Alex and tell them we have to get as far away from this place as possible. It doesn't take a brain boost to realize a shootout in a popular nightclub means half of Moscow's police department is on their way. Dealing with the cops could easily turn deadly, and even in the best case, it could lead to a huge delay in rescuing Mom.

I turn and instantly get hit with the most intense fight-or-flight response of the last two days—a feat I wouldn't have thought possible until that very moment.

There's a guy behind me.

A guy with a halo and a comic book balloon with his bio above his head.

His gun looks like a medieval cannon, and its massive barrel is pointed squarely at my head.

CHAPTER THIRTY-TWO

Operating on pure adrenaline, I drop my gun and raise my hands. "Don't shoot! I give up."

My reaction seems to confuse my attacker for a moment, but then his face calcifies.

He's about to pull the trigger.

Suddenly, there's a whirl of motion.

The shooter grabs his head, and his gun flies into the air, landing two feet away from me.

Muhomor is standing behind the guy. Despite the sunglasses, I can make out the terror on the hacker's face. As I take in his tight grip on the briefcase-like laptop, I understand what happened.

Muhomor used his computer to club my attacker on the head.

The red-haloed man recovers and punches Muhomor in the stomach.

Muhomor doubles over, his sunglasses flying to the side.

I dive for the gun and bring it up, but there's no time to enter the gun's information into the aim assist app.

I have to shoot now, without hitting Muhomor.

Fortunately, I'm only a few feet away. Unfortunately, you could run a small town on the adrenaline in my veins.

"Shoot!" Mitya and Ada yell together.

The red-haloed guy sees my dilemma and pounces on Muhomor.

In a second, they'll be too intertwined for me to shoot safely, so I pull the trigger.

The gunshot reverberates through every cell in my eardrums, and the recoil makes my hands jerk.

A red stain on the man's leg proves I hit my target.

The pain must be bad, because the guy starts screaming, bends over, and clutches his leg.

Muhomor uses this moment to kick our opponent in the face. Blood sprays from the guy's nose, and he falls to the ground with a muffled grunt. Muhomor kicks the body a few more times, then looks at me, eyes wild. "What? Who? How?"

"No time," I say. Into the DJ's mic, I add, "We have to get out of here."

Muhomor closes the distance between us and unhooks the DJ's laptop. "It has a network card," he says.

I shrug and hobble away. Even with the adrenaline-induced numbness spreading through my mind and body, I feel a zillion aches and pains.

Joe meets us at the bottom of the podium. He's dragging Alex by the back of his shirt. The shootout must've been too much for Alex, because he has the composure of a ragdoll cat.

As we cross the dance floor, I focus on looking where I step and fighting my gag reflex.

"Is there another way out of here?" Gogi asks Muhomor. "Not through the casino?"

"Yes," the thin man replies. "The banya. Follow me."

He starts running, and we all follow as fast as possible without slipping on all the blood.

We exit the slaughterhouse of the dance floor through the southern door.

The once pearl-white tiles of the spa are covered in crimson footprints thanks to the mob that preceded us. We follow the grisly markers to a staircase on the opposite side of the large pool.

I move almost mechanically, occasionally fighting strange urges, like a desire to clean the blood from my shoes in the hot tub we pass.

A swift sprint later, we reach the stairs, and just as quickly, we find ourselves outside.

Muhomor clearly knew where he was going, because we're in a nearly empty parking lot.

When we reach the Land Rover, Joe says, "Alex, get in the back. Gogi, you drive."

Since I wasn't instructed where to go, I get into the middle seat, and Muhomor joins me. He puts his military suitcase on his lap and stacks the DJ's laptop on top. He then pulls out a sealed smartphone and unwraps it. He must be creating a hotspot for the DJ's laptop so he can get online, not unlike how I've been staying online all this time. I don't mention I have my own hotspot already available. The last thing I want is a hacker anywhere near a connection hooked up to my Brainocytes.

Gogi floors the gas pedal, and our tires violently screech as we surge forward.

As we approach the parking lot's exit, I make out the sound of police sirens.

"The cops are almost here." Muhomor confirms my guess about the hotspot by typing on the laptop in front of him. "And that includes OMON."

OMON is the Russian version of SWAT, so if they're here and see us as a threat, we're toast.

Muhomor opens a terminal session using Putty—a tool I'm familiar with from my programming days. I watch his bony fingers dance across the keyboard, and after a moment, he grins. "This should distract them," he says and presses the Enter key. Alarms suddenly blast from the Dazdraperma club.

Unfortunately, when we hit the street, only some of the cops are looking at the noisy building, and at least two heavily armored OMON officers are blocking our way, their assault rifles pointed at us.

"Over them," my cousin says, though I don't think Gogi needed urging given how confidently the SUV is torpedoing forward.

The officers in our way fly apart, and automatic gunfire rains down on our SUV from every direction.

I duck, but not before I see two police cars blocking the road ahead of us in a makeshift blockade.

Glass shards, bits of plastic, and metal fly all around me. Bullets whoosh by, and the only reason I don't tuck my head between my legs is my morbid curiosity over our possible cause of death. There are so many options.

We hit the fronts of the two cars with a world-shattering clang.

My head jerks back, and I wish I had tucked my head between my legs after all. It feels like my whiplash from the Zapo accident just got its own case of whiplash.

Straining to breathe, I realize my left nostril is bleeding again. I ignore it and check on how the others are doing. Gogi's knuckles are white on the wheel as our car surges forward. Alex is whimpering something unintelligible from the back. Muhomor's laptops are on the floor, and he's hugging himself and shaking like a frightened five-year-old. Nadejda split her shaved head on the dashboard. For whatever reason, she didn't buckle up when we left the parking lot.

Nadejda's reason for not buckling up soon becomes apparent. Oblivious to the blood trickling from the nasty cut on her forehead, she opens the window, leans out, and shoots at something behind us.

Muhomor calms down enough to execute my earlier idea for dealing with the surrounding violence; he tucks his head between his knees. Then he comes back up with both laptops, sets them up like before, and, to my amazement, begins typing again.

I chance a look back. The rear window is gone, allowing Joe to shoot at the swiftly approaching police cars. As I expected from the whimpering, Alex is on the floor in a fetal position.

The strange concentration I felt back in the club overcomes me again, making me wonder if adrenaline stimulates the brain boost in some positive way. With calm, methodical determination, I locate a magazine for my Glock and load it in with a click. I then turn all the way around so my knees are on the seat and my elbows are resting on the headrest. I aim the gun, and the Augmented Reality sight line appears. As I move the gun around, the AU assist continues uninterrupted, even when I point the barrel at faraway targets, like the nearest pursuing car half a block away.

I struggle to hold the line on the tire. Gogi must've just dodged another car or a pedestrian, because the car jerks and I lose my target.

"Can you drive smoothly for one second?" I say without turning.

Gogi grunts and we stop zigzagging, so I guess he's trying to accommodate my request.

I hold my breath, place the line on the tire again, and gently squeeze the trigger.

The cop car swerves off the road and crashes through the glass of a storefront.

Now that the lead car is gone, I see an even bigger vehicle behind it, and this one belongs to OMON, who are shooting at us with automatic weapons.

"Wow," I hear Mitya say as though from a distance. "I wonder if his shooting skills improved from the brain boost or just the aim app? Hand-eye coordination is—"

I don't hear any more of Mitya's musings, or even the gunfire erupting all around me, because my attention zeroes in on my gun and this bigger car's tire. The state I'm in is amazing. With the absence of all other stimuli, I realize how many distractions were around me. My wrists are no longer aching from the recoil, and I've stopped gagging from the smell of gunpowder. And though the smoothness of the ride is gone, I don't really notice it.

I intuitively raise my elbows off the headrest, adjusting to the back-and-forth motion of the car.

My finger waits for the right moment.

I don't know how I know it's time to take the shot, but when I fire, the faraway tire explodes and the OMON car violently veers off the road.

I keep the gun steady, ready to shoot more tires if I have to, but the road behind us is clear. Still, the sound of sirens is close, so I don't let myself relax. I do, however, pat my jacket pocket and confirm that Mr. Spock is within it.

"Are we safe?" Alex croaks, his voice so small it's barely recognizable.

"No," Muhomor says. "But I'm in their network." He raises the DJ's laptop from his lap. "Anyone without a line of sight on us will have a hard time keeping up. Still, we must switch cars as soon as possible."

"Great," Gogi says. "I'll just find the nearest car dealership."

"No need for sarcasm," Muhomor says after another few seconds of frantic typing. "Everything's been arranged. Take a left on Youth Street. There should be a Gastronom parking lot there."

I realize I'm still in a shooting position, and Joe is looking at me with what must be curiosity on his austere face, though it could just as easily be disapproval. Then he gives me a faint nod that seems to say, "Good shooting. Thanks, Mike."

I face forward again and buckle up, and it's a good thing I do. Gogi must've spotted the necessary street at the last second, because we nearly flip over on the turn.

With no reduction in speed, we fly into the parking lot of a big supermarket, and I reflect on how tragically ironic it would be if we got killed in a car crash right after escaping a war zone.

"Over there," Muhomor says. "The white minivan."

We screech to a tire-smoking halt next to the minivan, and I spot the familiar face of Lyuba, the girl from the puzzle, behind the wheel.

As our crew moves our stuff into the minivan, I calm down enough to pay attention to Mitya and Ada's conversation, and I overhear him say, "That's a Ford Windstar. It's clever using something like that. The back windows are tinted, and the car is so dorky the cops will think it's just a rich soccer mom behind the wheel."

As though to confirm his idea, Muhomor says, "Mike, as the least threatening-looking person, you should sit in the front."

I could argue that my bruises make me look tougher than his skinny ass, but I get into the front seat anyway. My hope is that a family car like this might have a passenger side airbag, a handy device in case Lyuba drives as dangerously as Gogi.

My cousin practically drags Alex into the back of the minivan and stays with him as Gogi, Muhomor, and Nadejda sit in the middle. I buckle up before Lyuba starts driving, but I quickly see I won't need that airbag. If anything, Lyuba drives annoyingly slow.

Her strategy pays off; the couple of police cars we pass simply drive by.

"The Gadyukino hideout," Muhomor says from his middle seat.

"On it," Lyuba says and makes a signaled, super-careful, almost slow-motion right turn.

Once I no longer hear sirens, I let myself breathe normally and reach into my pocket to check on Mr. Spock again.

When I take him out, the poor creature's mental aura is black. According to my notes, that means he's tense, nervous, or harassed. This time, I don't even need Ada's app to tell me he's frightened. His general haggard appearance is surprisingly telling.

"Does anyone have any snacks?" I ask and gently stroke the rat's soft white fur.

"Glove compartment," Lyuba says, reacting to Mr. Spock with a lack of curiosity bordering on indifference.

I open the drawer in front of me and see it's full of Russian-style junk food, which is actually a bit healthier than the American variety. I give Mr. Spock a few pine nuts and a piece of Alyonka chocolate bar. Spock gratefully eats his share, and I follow his example by consuming a much bigger handful of nuts and the rest of the candy. Once the worst of my hunger is satisfied, I gobble down a Tula Gingerbread—a treat from my childhood that tastes like pure nostalgia.

"He looks much better," Ada says when Mr. Spock's aura turns the blue-green color associated with a moderately relaxed state. "And he seems to be acting normal, just like his recently enhanced brothers and sisters."

"Wait," I type into the chat. "You already tested that resource allocation rigmarole on them?"

"I applied it when you went incommunicado in that room," Ada says. "Mitya and I flipped a coin, and I'm about to become the first official human test subject."

"Be careful, guys," I reply and watch Mr. Spock for any deviance in his behavior.

The little guy's color turns blue, and the only strange thing I notice is how intensely he's looking at the cup holder.

"Are you thirsty?" I ask him out loud, and again, Lyuba doesn't bat an eyelash, as though talking to your pet rat is as unremarkable as whipping one out of your pocket.

It could be my imagination, but I think Mr. Spock gives me a barely perceptible nod.

"Ada, do your rats know how to nod?" I mentally type into the chat. "Because I think he just did."

"Well," Ada says, "while I haven't observed that behavior before, I figure with the brain boost and all this human socializing, they might be learning things like that."

"May I?" I ask Lyuba as I reach for the water bottle.

"There are unopened ones in the back," the woman says. "But of course, you can also have mine."

Before I can retort something hopefully clever, Gogi's hairy paw shows up, holding a sealed bottle, and I take it from him.

Water bottles clearly weren't designed for rats to drink out of, and more water spills onto my jacket than into Mr. Spock's mouth. However, it must've been the final thing my furry friend needed, because his aura turns violet—the nirvana-like rat state.

I drink the rest of the water, and we drive contentedly for a while.

When the area turns rural and we're the only car on the road, I overhear Joe talking, which is strange, because he usually only speaks when he's about to hurt someone. When Joe falls silent, Alex says something, his voice sounding beyond terrified.

My heart rate speeds up.

Picking up on the same vibes, Mr. Spock scurries back into my pocket, and in the next instant, the car is filled with an inhuman shriek, followed by the smell of human feces.

I recognize the shriek as Alex's.

As far as I can tell, he just soiled himself and is screaming like a psychotic banshee.

CHAPTER THIRTY-THREE

A list of gloomy possibilities flashes through my mind, each more unrealistic than the other. Are the cops shooting at us again? Or is Alex watching another video where a hostage is brutally murdered?

I turn around and see it's something else.

Something to do with Joe towering over Alex and moving his arms around.

"Please, stop!" Alex shrieks. "Please, don't!"

I glimpse the point of Joe's knife piercing the tip of Alex's finger. Alex howls.

I finally comprehend what's happening, if not the why of it.

My cousin is torturing Alex while questioning him about something. The exact questions are hard to hear over Alex's screaming.

Muhomor's face is as contorted in fear as mine. In contrast, Gogi and Nadejda look utterly placid.

"Give him a chance to speak," Gogi says academically in the brief silence between screams. "He's probably ready."

Joe stops his grisly work, but it takes a few minutes for Alex to downgrade from shrieking to helplessly crying.

"You better talk," Nadejda says, her pseudo-friendly voice making me wonder if she's trying to capitalize on their earlier flirtations. "That isn't even a fraction of what Joe will do to you if you don't start speaking."

"Oh boy," Ada's angel form says. "If she's the good cop, I don't envy poor Alex."

"Yes," Alex whines. "It was me, but I didn't have a choice. Govrilovskiy has things on me. I had to tell them where you were landing and about the club, but I tried to stop you from going, remember? That's why I made the video—"

Joe slams his fist into Alex's head, cutting off the rest of his sentence.

My cousin's face is filled with more emotion than I've ever seen from him, but unfortunately for Alex, that emotion is wrath.

I cringe as I watch Joe deliver blow after hard blow, inflicting the kind of damage Alex might never recover from.

I know that I shouldn't be watching this, that I'll have nightmares for the rest of my life, but I'm hypnotized by the cruel precision of each strike and the sound of bones breaking.

In a surreal underscore to the violence, Muhomor starts typing on his keyboard again.

I'm in a strange stupor as the car pulls over to the side of the road, and Nadejda and Gogi restrain Joe. To me, it feels as if only a moment passed between Joe beating on Alex and my cousin's people holding him cautiously.

Slowly, my daze clears, and I process what happened. Just to make sure I'm not crazy, I share my revelations with my New York allies via the chat. "Alex confessed. He told someone, a guy named Govrilovskiy, where we were landing and about our destination—his residence. That was enough information for them to figure out what path we'd take. They also had enough time to dispatch the car that nearly drove us off the road. Since we survived that first encounter, Alex shared our plans to visit Muhomor at Dazdraperma. That's how the squad knew to ambush us there."

"I'm afraid you're spot on," Mitya says. "I'm so sorry I put you in touch with this traitor. I didn't think—"

"It's not your fault," I reply. "This Govrilovskiy was blackmailing Alex, a common occurrence in this country."

"But I should've figured this out," Mitya says. "The club thing could've had several explanations, but I should've considered that first attack. Besides you, me, Joe, and Ada, only Alex knew where you were going to land. True, there were your cousin's people to consider, but they seem very loyal to him, and they're also outsiders in Russia, so that only leaves Alex as the traitor—something Joe must've realized."

I recall Joe asking me if I trusted Mitya and Ada after the first attack and decide Mitya is right. Joe's paranoia made him realize the truth first.

"I just can't believe Alex could eat and drink with you in his home while planning to lead you to your deaths in the club," Mitya says in disgust.

"I don't mean to defend Alex," Ada says, "but he did try to stop you from going to the club. Before, and especially after the video, he insisted—"

"The video," I say out loud as another part of Alex's confession registers. "It was fake?"

"Yeah," Muhomor says. "Now that I had reason to suspect it, I checked it out and verified it's a clip from an obscure Russian horror flick called *The Handy Man*. Also, because we now know both the sender and the receiver, I should be able to link the email to Alex, though that would be overkill since he already confessed."

So this is what the thin man was doing on his computer during the beating. I feel a sense of relief mixed with a desire to punch what's left of Alex for making me think someone might put a drill to my mom's head. I also realize this is why Joe went berserk. In his own way, my cousin must've been worried about my mom, and when he learned Alex had created that video, he acted on the same impulse I'm currently suppressing.

"Let me go," Joe orders his allies, "or you're next."

Gogi releases Joe, and Nadejda follows.

They calmed him down enough that he doesn't resume beating Alex's limp body. Instead, he pointedly draws his gun and says, "Take him out of the car."

Gogi and Nadejda grab Alex and begin dragging him out.

"Wait," Muhomor says frantically. "Alex is a very high-profile individual. You can't just shoot him and leave him on the road. It's better if he disappears, and I know people who can make that happen. I can also make his digital trail look like he took a long vacation in Australia or some other faraway place."

Nadejda and Gogi stop, but Joe looks unconvinced.

"There's also your mission to consider," Muhomor adds. "We might still need Alex for that. If I don't get any hits when I search for this Govrilovskiy character, I might need more names."

"Fine," Joe says and gets into Gogi's seat. "Ride next to him."

The Georgian gets in the back, checks Alex's pulse, and says, "Alive for now."

Lyuba restarts the car, and we ride in sullen silence all the way to the village.

"This place isn't actually called Gadyukino," Mitya tells Ada when she comments on the discrepancy. "I realize why you thought so, given Muhomor's comments about the 'Gadyukino hideout,' but Gadyukino is just a nickname we Russians sometimes give to hole-in-the-wall places like this little community."

Gadyukino, or whatever the real name of this place is, is at its core a former *kolkhoz*, the dysfunctional Soviet collective farm. There aren't any paved roads here, and the village houses look exactly the same as when I visited a similar place all the way back in the eighties—poor and impossibly drab.

One structure stands out, however: the really worn-down and abandoned-looking warehouse we're heading toward.

"How do you feel, Ada?" Mitya asks in the chat. "Any insights?"

"Hold on," I interject. "You already got the resource allocation thing to increase your intelligence boost?"

"Yes," Ada replies. "Right before your psycho cousin went all Vlad The Impaler on Alex's ass."

"And?" I mentally type. "How do you feel?"

"I'm fine," Ada says out loud. "I feel a lot like when I first got the original boost."

"So, like nothing at all," I say. "At least that's how I felt."

"I wouldn't say nothing at all," Ada says. "I feel the potential, and the fact I'm feeling fine is a significant result in itself."

"I guess I'm next," Mitya says.

"Shouldn't it be Mike?" Ada asks. "He might need it more."

"Fine," Mitya mumbles, almost under his breath. With an exaggerated sigh, he adds, "I guess I can wait a little longer."

"You up for it, Mike?" Ada asks.

I think about it, then decide whatever extra advantage this boost might offer is welcome. "Okay, hit me."

"I'll set it up and let you know in a sec," she says. "You might want to pay attention to your surroundings for now."

I catch myself sitting with my eyes closed—a bad habit I'm developing when using the AROS interface. I open my eyes and realize we're already inside the warehouse and Lyuba is parking the car.

I look around.

If a twister decimated a couple of high-end datacenters, plus a RadioShack and maybe the computer department at Best Buy, the aftermath might look like the inside of this "hideout."

Muhomor exits the car, hands the DJ's laptop to Lyuba, and says, "The machine needs to disappear completely, and Alex needs to be kept alive for the moment."

Without waiting for Lyuba to reply, or even inviting us to follow, Muhomor prances toward the big wall of monitors.

Gogi shrugs and heads in the same direction, and the rest of us follow.

"It's all set," Ada says. "Just click on that little blue brain when you're ready."

"I'm crossing my breath and holding my fingers," I mentally jest while locating the icon in question. Initiating the app, I say, "This is it."

CHAPTER THIRTY-FOUR

Part of me thought this time would be different, yet I feel almost nothing again.

My vision might be slightly sharper, but that could be from the lights Muhomor just turned on. Also, my hearing seems keener, almost like I can tell which keys Muhomor is banging on his keyboard, but this could be an illusion as well. I guess I'll feel more as my brain adjusts to its new capabilities, like before.

"It might help if you get on a better connection," Ada says when I complain to her. "I had more effects than you described."

"Okay," I say, "but I'm not sure I want to get on Muhomor's Wi-Fi."

"Speaking of the devil, I think he has something," Mitya chimes in.

I look over and see everyone huddling around Muhomor as he turns around and says, "Govrilovskiy was a solid lead and proves I was right about the intelligence community connection."

At his audience's blank stares, he asks me to explain and resumes typing. I go through his SVR-contractor theory for those who had to leave the room and for my NYC friends. Since Muhomor is only paying attention to his computer, no doubt working on this lead, I guesstimate the answers to all their questions. I even go as far as proposing theories about the sinister applications the Russian government—and especially the KGB's offspring agency—might have for the Brainocyte technology.

I'm in the middle of discussing the benefits of having telepathic-like coms and various Augmented Reality overlays on the battlefield, when Muhomor stops typing and says, "Like I thought, Govrilovskiy is the head of a group that acts as a contractor for the agency. He has connections in the government, in business, and particularly in the criminal underworld. The good news is I just got into his organization's systems and located a few facilities where his people might keep important research subjects." He works on his computer for a few seconds, and maps of different parts of Russia appear on several screens. "The bad news is there are twelve locations." More maps show up on the screens. "The worse news is that each and every location is pretty much a fortress."

"Can you locate this Govrilovskiy?" Gogi strokes his mustache with his index finger and thumb in a movie-villain manner. "If we had him, we could find out where our quarry is."

Bile rises in my throat as I picture the methods they might use to find out this information. Alex's ordeal is still very fresh in my psyche.

"Let me try," Muhomor replies without turning. "This might take a while, so why don't you all stretch your legs a little?"

Given Joe's body language, it's clear he's considering making Muhomor work faster by putting a gun to the thin man's head. He doesn't actually get his weapon out, though, so maybe he decided that's not the best motivational tool at his disposal.

I locate a dingy chair a few feet from Muhomor and close my eyes for a second. It's a mistake, because it makes me realize how utterly tired I am. There's jetlag, and then there's jetlag combined with the crash you experience after a monstrous release of adrenaline. Despite all this, a spark of an idea—something that might avoid more torture and improve our chances at a successful rescue—keeps gnawing away at my weary brain, keeping me awake. I rub my temples as though trying to physically jumpstart my brain, and in a jolt of inspiration, a way to locate Mom comes to me.

Hopefully, Muhomor is as good a hacker as I think he is.

Before I speak up, I mentally share my idea with Ada and Mitya. When I'm done, Ada says, "See, the boost might already be working. That's a great idea. I'm ashamed I didn't come up with it myself."

"I feel like I would've suggested it with time," Mitya says, his avatar bashful. "I'll send you the specs you'll need."

"I have an idea," I say, walking back to Muhomor.

"This guy is very careful when it comes to his where-abouts," Muhomor tells me over his shoulder, and I suspect he didn't hear my soft-spoken proclamation. "No obvious calendar entries, no—"

"I know how to locate Mom without him," I say firmly. "Can you look at me, please?"

Muhomor turns around, and for the first time since the shootout, he looks like himself. He even located another pair of sunglasses, and they're back in place, sitting on his nose.

"According to an app I wrote with my friends," I begin, "my mom's Brainocytes aren't currently on any network, either Wi-Fi or cellular."

"Understood," Muhomor says. "Otherwise, we'd know where she is."

"Right," I reply. "But think about it. The Brainocytes are probably trying to connect to the Wi-Fi at these locations you mentioned. The network must be secure, and thus her connection requests keep failing."

Muhomor's eyes widen with excitement. "Of course. But if I hack into the Wi-Fi and leave the right ports open—"

"She'd connect and we'd know her location," I finish. "I'll send over the ports and the specs for the logins."

"Actually," Mitya mentally chimes in, "we could also communicate with your mom once she's on Wi-Fi. Given enough time, I can write something to piggyback on her current interface."

I don't mention what Mitya said to Muhomor because the hacker is already working on the problem, and I don't want to delay him. Instead, I walk around his hideout, collecting parts for another, much less defined idea I have.

It takes me half an hour to locate a small night-vision camera, and a few more minutes to find something I can use to make a tiny harness.

"I can modify this stuff into a camera like the one I'm wearing and turn Mr. Spock into a spy," I mentally type.

"Sure," Ada says. "That'll work great at night. During the day, we can capture what Mr. Spock sees through his Brainocytes."

"Yep," I reply. "I remembered that. I just know that rats have poor night vision, so—"

A noise that must've originally been meant to signal the start of a nuclear bombardment fills the hideout. Oddly, it sounds familiar, like the ding of a computer notification, except obscenely loud.

Then it hits me.

It's the alarm Ada put together to notify me when Mom gets online. The app was running in the background all this time. The fact that it just went off means Muhomor must've hacked the bad guys' Wi-Fi and opened a port for Mom's Brainocytes.

Confirming my realization, Muhomor yells, "Eureka!"

"I have the location." On her avatar, Ada's relieved eyes look as tired as I feel. "Sending it to you now."

I summon Joe and the others and send the location to Muhomor. Then we all huddle around the wall of monitors.

"They're in the Chelyabinsk facility," Muhomor says disappointedly. "It's one of the heavier-fortified locations."

On the screens, we see schematics of the buildings on the compound, as well as a very discouraging satellite view. This place is to a fortress what a fortress is to a wooden hut. Five thousand acres in size with barbed-wire-topped walls surrounding it, the place looks like a military base.

"This"—I point at a building in the middle of the facility—"is where Mom is."

Joe looks at Gogi expectantly, and the Georgian nods, saying, "I think I can devise a plan, but I'll need more details."

Muhomor provides Gogi with a ton of information about the facility and some of the resources we can use.

At the end of it all, Gogi explains the plan he formed based on all our data, and as he goes on, he breaks many of my expectations. I always thought when I located Mom there'd be something like a heist to get her out. If not a heist, then maybe a hostage negotiation. But what Gogi is proposing is neither.

It's more along the lines of a SEAL Team Six black op—something a venture capitalist like me can't even imagine participating in.

"You can take a nap en route," Gogi tells me when the preparations begin. "It's an hour drive to the supermarket, and half an hour more to get the other supplies from Muhomor's shadier connections. From there, it's forty minutes to the plane, and then a two-and-a-half-hour flight to Chelyabinsk."

Lyuba is driving again; this time, we're in a station wagon. She transferred all the weapons Alex provided into this car, but not the man himself. Him, she tied up and left behind. I don't dare ask what her plans are for him, because I probably won't like the answer.

As we leave the bumpy dirt road of Gadyukino behind, I try to sleep, but the remnants of adrenaline in my system thwart my attempts.

When we get to our first stop, the supermarket, I look around and can't help but be impressed by the very American abundance of items. Back in the late eighties, when the empty store shelves held only canned seaweed, Russians couldn't have even dreamed of this.

What's extra impressive is that the supermarket contains a bunch of businesses inside, similar to a Wal-Mart. Purely on a whim, I walk into the hair salon.

"How can I help you?" the hairstylist asks. Styles in Russia often lag behind, so she has a poodle-like eighties hairdo that reminds me of the cashiers from my childhood. However, her smile is genuine, unlike the horrific customer service back in the Soviet era.

"I'd like you to color him gray-black," I say in Russian and take out Mr. Spock.

The woman's composure cracks, and her eyes widen. Before she can decide to kick me out, I take out a thick roll of hundred-dollar bills.

Her eyes threaten to pop out of her head, but the cash does its job. Without a hint of hesitancy, she gently takes the little guy from my hands and asks, "Do you want me to leave this pink streak on top?"

"No," I say as seriously as I can. "He'll be doing something stealthy at night, so the pink won't be right for that."

If the woman thinks I'm dangerous or crazy—a fairly reasonable assumption at this point—she hides it well and proceeds to color Mr. Spock, who endures the whole process stoically, almost as though he understands the reason behind this human madness.

With the rat disguise complete, I get Mr. Spock a bunch of treats and head back to the car.

Once we start driving, I go over Gogi's plan in my mind and find that the very first step makes sleeping nearly impossible. I settle for trying to relax, using all my willpower not to think about the inevitable.

When we get to Mitya's plane, all my attempts to relax evaporate. I'm so terrified of what's about to happen I don't even notice the departure—what I used to think was the worst part of flying. That was before I knew what we're about to do.

Realizing I can't clench my teeth during the whole two-and-a-half-hour flight, no matter how justified that would be, I keep my eyes shut and do my best to stop myself from panicking. It's impossible, though, given what I know.

When the plane is over the Chelyabinsk facility, I'm going to do the craziest thing I've ever done in my life.

I'm going to jump out of the plane.

CHAPTER THIRTY-FIVE

I open my eyes and see Gogi looming over me, all geared up.

It's that time.

"You ready?" he asks and hands me a mess of harnesses, polypropylene-knit undergarments, warm clothes, and a slew of other gear.

"As ready as I'll ever be," I say, forcing the tremor from my voice.

To my right, Joe's already begun his prep, while Nadejda is as ready to go as Gogi.

Hands trembling, I let Gogi help me put all this crap on. He then examines and adjusts every belt and harness on my body and rewards me with a satisfied grunt.

In a panicked daze, I let him lead me toward the airlock.

"Breathe through this." He gives me one of those mask-hat things I've seen jet pilots wear in movies, and I put the contraption on.

As I breathe the slightly sweet air, I realize this must be pure oxygen. Just like after my car crash, I don't feel the high promised by Tyler Durden in *Fight Club*. Quite the contrary, this time around, I'm lightheaded and borderline dizzy.

The others also put on oxygen masks, and the atmosphere in the plane turns somber.

To distract myself from gloomy imaginings, I mentally research the purpose of this step. In the context of high-altitude parachuting, breathing pure oxygen for a half an hour flushes out the nitrogen from your bloodstream, helping to prevent decompression sickness.

"So, I guess I'll be nitrogen free as I plummet to my death," I mentally type into the chat. "Great."

"Don't be a wuss," Mitya writes back. "You're about to do a tandem HALO jump. I paid four thousand dollars for mine a couple of years back."

"Right, but you're crazy," Ada says out loud, her voice soothing. "Mike isn't."

"And you should be working on the piggybacking app anyway," I mentally chime in.

Since no one replies after that, I sigh and masochistically read more about HALO—high altitude low opening—jumps.

The more I learn, the more I question why I insisted on participating in *this* part of the plan. Gogi originally suggested I help Muhomor and Lyuba in their separate efforts and that only he, Nadejda, and Joe do the dangerous part. But no, I wanted to be there in person to make sure Mom's rescue went as smoothly as humanly possible. Now, thanks to my damn bravery and initiative, I'm thirty thousand feet in the air, mentally preparing for something completely insane.

When Gogi gets enough pure oxygen, he walks up to the airlock, mask still on, and opens it.

The noise is beyond deafening, and the cold air hits us like an icy sledgehammer. It must be negative fifty outside, and I'm unpleasantly reminded of that winter trip to Yakutsk—a visit that made me realize the most biting Krasnodar winters are like a trip to the banya in comparison to the weather near Siberia.

"Take deep breaths," Ada says from somewhere. "Don't panic."

"You'll be fine," Mitya echoes. "Once you're in free fall, the fun will begin."

I ignore their chatter. Every part of my body is frozen in terror, especially my amygdala, the region of the brain responsible for fear.

"Can Brainocytes de-stimulate someone's amygdala?" I mentally type into the chat, more so as a distraction. "Can we use them to make someone less afraid?"

"In theory, yes," Ada replies out loud. "In practice, though, it would be very tricky, and I haven't tried it on the rats."

"But that sort of brain stimulation is something I've been thinking about," Mitya says, his devil avatar shaking with pent-up enthusiasm. "Fear is small potatoes compared to figuring out how to increase attention span or trigger neurogenesis."

The implications of this train of thought would usually excite me, but under the current circumstances, they barely distract me from my overwhelming apprehension.

Gogi waves his head toward the black void that's our destination.

I nod, but my feet don't move.

As though leading me through icy molasses, Gogi drags me closer to the airlock. When he deems the distance right, he attaches us together for the tandem part of the jump.

I know I shouldn't, but I look into the dark night outside the plane, and my adrenal glands manage to produce another tsunami of adrenaline.

Before I even realize how it happened, I'm flying through the air.

At first, I do my best to suck my heart back into my chest, along with copious amounts of oxygen; then I can't help screaming into the oxygen mask.

If my Brainocytes hadn't disconnected from the plane's Wi-Fi, I would've told Mitya where to shove his promise of fun during free fall. If I survive this, I vow to tell him that people like him, who do this for fun, are insane.

Going from hypoventilation to hyperventilation, I begin feeling fainter than before and wonder—possibly with hope—whether I'm on the verge of passing out. The welcome blackout doesn't arrive, though, and we just keep plummeting.

The altitude meter on my wrist reminds me of a digital countdown clock in a movie, when the big explosion is only seconds away. Below me, the darkness is so complete I can barely make out the tiny specks of light that must be Gogi's destination.

Rationally, I know our free fall will last about a minute, but as often happens in near-death experiences, it feels like I'm falling a hundred times longer than that, reminding me of the time I got my teeth drilled by a Krasnodar dentist back in the no-Novocain Soviet days.

Suddenly, I'm violently jolted.

Scenes from my life flit before my eyes, and I'm in the middle of saying farewell to the world when I realize the jolt was due to Gogi deploying his parachute.

Now that the chute is open, the speed of our descent reduces about a millionfold, and I get a chance to figuratively pull myself back together.

The distant lights grow bigger, and I stare at them as I practice every relaxation technique I've ever learned. Below us is the whole compound, as well as our impossibly small destination—a meadow inside a park/forest reserve in the center of the compound.

Despite my efforts to calm down, the next few moments of the jump happen in a haze of anxiety.

The forest gets nearer and nearer.

The treetops are almost under our feet, and I fully expect a branch to impale us.

In the last second, Gogi corrects our descent, and we glide toward the edge of the meadow. When we're just a few feet off the ground, he pulls on the parachute with a conductor-like gesture.

I brace for the pain of impact, but it doesn't come.

Gogi's feet expertly anchor us to the ground, and my feet touch the grass with about as much force as if I simply jumped up and down. Still, my knees feel weak, and I have to lock them to stop myself from sinking to the ground.

When I recover a little, I look around the meadow. This greenery is probably meant to look pleasing for the scientists and goons who work here, but right now, in the middle of the night, the place looks like an enchanted forest from a grisly Russian fairy tale—an effect enhanced by the pale moonlight that provides the only illumination.

Gogi takes charge and helps me remove all the equipment. He then ransacks his backpack for Mr. Spock's specially oxygenated cage, as well as our mission clothes and gadgets.

I'm halfway to having everything on when Nadejda and Joe land on the other side of the meadow. She must not be as good at landing as Gogi, or had bad luck, because their parachute is tangled up. The Georgian has to go over and cut them loose.

As the new arrivals join us in suiting up, I use the credentials Muhomor provided to get onto the compound's Wi-Fi.

The instant I connect, what feels like a surge of soothing, focusing energy spreads through my mind. It must be how my brain is learning to react to the presence of its cloud extension. The feeling is stronger because I now have more resources and a higher bandwidth than on the cellular network. If we survive this, I can totally imagine becoming a sort of techno-hermit—someone who has to be within reach of the fastest connections at all times.

"Hey all," I type into the chat, and as I wait for my friends to answer, I check on Mr. Spock to make sure he's feeling good after our ordeal.

The rat starts off amber, for nervous, but as soon as I pet his dyed fur, he moves onto happier green and blue hues, though not all the way to violet. When I think he's calm enough, I pull out the night-vision camera and put it on him.

"See," Mitya types in the chat. "Isn't skydiving fun?"

I don't dignify his question with a response. Instead, I ask, "Is everything ready for the recon part of the mission?"

"Yep," Ada says from my right, and when I glance at her, I see that her avatar looks like her normal self. She's wearing a t-shirt with a red anarchy symbol, and this time, her jeans are tucked into Converse sneakers instead of boots. I guess she thought this situation was too dire for the angel avatar. "All set. Just press the icon."

I make the AROS interface visible and locate the new icon, which looks like a rat wearing spy-like goggles.

After the app loads, three big screens show up in my field of vision. One shows what the camera sees, the second what Mr. Spock sees with his own eyes, and the third one looks surreal, so I ask Ada about it.

"It's my best attempt at displaying whisking—the way rats use their whiskers to navigate in the dark," Ada explains. "As you can see, it's a work in progress."

I put Mr. Spock on the grass and let him run around. The whisker screen looks like something out of *Daredevil*. I can see 3D outlines of the grass Mr. Spock's whiskers touch and a map of the world he thus develops, but it's really disorienting. I have to agree that Ada needs to develop this part of the app some more before it becomes useful. What's more interesting is that I see yet another potential for Brainocyte technology—providing people with brand-new senses. It wouldn't be that hard to give someone a bunch of instruments to wear or carry and get the Brainocytes to feed their inputs to the brain, mimicking something like the echolocation of bats, or the sense for electricity sharks have, or heat vision, and so on.

Speaking of sensory expansion, though Mr. Spock's vision is poor even in the bright moonlight, he *can* see some things we humans can't, such as the ultraviolet spectrum. That allows him to spot an otherwise invisible puddle of something, most likely the urine of a small creature, possibly another rat or a squirrel.

The night-vision camera is the most useful view of the three and looks just like one would expect, green hues and all.

"You can send this URL to everyone," Mitya says. Copying Ada, he also looks like his usual hoodie-wearing self. "This way, they can see through the night-vision camera as well."

I do as he says, and shortly after, Joe, Gogi, and Nadejda are staring at their phones with varying degrees of curiosity.

"Are you sure you can control where your pet runs?" Gogi asks after a few moments. "If the guards see a rat with a camera stuck to its back, they'll raise an alarm."

"Absolutely," I say out loud, feigning confidence. Mentally, I ask Ada, "Are you sure you can do this?"

Mr. Spock springs into action and runs circles first around me, then Gogi, then Joe. Nadejda cringes, so Ada doesn't have Mr. Spock approach the big woman, highlighting the control she can exert over Mr. Spock.

The rat's movements are so precise, the circles so perfect, that Gogi raises his unibrow and says, "We could've used this kind of rat in Ossetia."

On my end, in the screen that shows Mr. Spock's vision—or more correctly, an interpretation based on the activity of his visual center neurons—I see how Ada is accomplishing this. As she explained before, virtual walls show up in Mr. Spock's vision in a makeshift maze. These illusory walls are what prompts him to run, which tells me she conditioned him via mazes and treats. What's really odd is what I see when Mr. Spock looks up at me. Through his blurry vision, I can sort of make out my face, only I look eerily ratty.

"He must see you as the alpha rat," Ada explains when I point this out. "I've noticed this quirk as well. My guess is it's a bit like when humans anthropomorphize other animals by seeing grins on dogs and stuff like that."

"He's rattumorphizing me?" I type and add a smiley face emoticon.

"No," Mitya says. "*Anthropo* in the word *anthropomorphize* is based on the Greek word meaning man, not Latin, since that would be *homomorphize*. Since rat in Greek is *arouraíos*, the term should be *arouramorphize*."

"I think you guys need to tweak Mitya's Brainocytes for pedantic side effects," I reply.

"I don't care what we call it," Ada says. "But when my babies look at my face, it usually appears even more like a rat's."

"Start the recon." My cousin's stern voice brings me out of the virtual chat window, precluding further wonderment about rat vision.

"We're on the clock," Gogi says, just as sternly.

"Should we get through some of these trees first?" I ask. "Then Mr. Spock can scope out the rest of the area."

As one, they start walking. Taking that as a yes, I pick up Mr. Spock and cautiously lead the team toward the edge of the reserve.

The others walk so quietly I have to turn a few times to make sure I didn't lose them.

Eventually, Gogi places a hand on my shoulder, silently telling me to stop.

I put the rat down, pet him, and whisper, "Go."

"Got it," Ada says and does whatever she needs to do to make Mr. Spock scurry forward.

As soon as Mr. Spock is a few feet away from me, I can no longer see him with my naked eye—a good thing since that means the guards won't see him either.

I can, however, see his digital mood aura, and a few moments later, it turns the blackest color of anxiety I've seen so far.

Scanning the screen, I see what he's frightened of, and I get scared both with him and for him.

On the rat-vision screen, the source of our angst looks like a true monster, a mountainous blur of teeth, fur, and muscles.

In the night-vision screen, I see the obstacle for what it truly is—two hundred pounds of running dog.

CHAPTER THIRTY-SIX

"**O**vcharka," Gogi whispers.

"That's Caucasian Ovcharka," Mitya tells Ada pedantically. "But I guess a man from the Caucuses can be excused for just saying Ovcharka. And in case you aren't up to that point in your Russian studies, Ovcharka means Shepherd dog, though these doggies don't just herd sheep. With their five-hundred-pound bite force and deadly ferociousness, they make lethal guard dogs, and they're so dangerous they're banned in some countries."

I mentally search the breed and see Mitya isn't exaggerating. Though fluffy and cute in some pictures, these dogs have been used to hunt bears and whole packs of wolves.

It's not just Mr. Spock who's in danger. It's the whole team.

The huge dog stops running a few feet from the rat.

Its giant head turns in Mr. Spock's direction, and its snout seems to sniff the air.

Mr. Spock's aura turns a paler color that I don't even have in my notes, though I'm sure it means something along the lines of, "I just soiled myself."

"Don't move," Ada whispers to Spock. "Don't even breathe."

Despite her words, or the Augmented Reality, or whatever Ada's using to control the little guy, it's obvious he's about to bolt, and if he does, the dog will spot him, leap on him, and probably eat him in a single gulp.

I resist the temptation to pull out my Glock. We're not using weapons during this part of the plan, because even with silencers (which the Glock now has), the guns will still make too much noise. Instead, we're all equipped with air-based tranquilizer guns that were carefully tweaked and deemed silent enough.

I grab my tranquilizer gun, but I'm aware of a problem. Due to the lack of ballistic data on this nonstandard weapon, my friends didn't get a chance to update my aiming app to work as flawlessly as it does with a regular gun. The aiming line appears, but it's worse than a laser point.

Seeing no other choice, I point the aim-assist line at the dog and pull the trigger.

If I did hit the Ovcharka, its thick fur must have protected it, or maybe the human tranquilizer isn't effective on canines.

Mr. Spock hasn't moved. I suspect it's because he's frozen in fear at the towering behemoth of a dog.

In both camera views, the Ovcharka's teeth are exposed, and saliva is dripping from its maw. Mr. Spock is about to feel like Ripley from *Alien*.

To my surprise, Nadejda springs into action.

Her tranquilizer weapon isn't a handgun like mine, but a rifle. She brings it to her shoulder and takes careful aim.

The shot is accompanied by a barely audible pop, but nothing happens.

The dog leaps and lands three feet from the rat.

I wonder if I'll see Mr. Spock's life play across the rat-vision screen as the dog comes toward him.

When the wooly monstrosity is just a foot away from Spock's head, it stops, tilts its head to the side in that "confused dog" manner, and falls down, its giant clawed paw missing Mr. Spock by a couple of inches.

I realize I didn't breathe the entire time, so I allow myself the luxury of inhaling air.

"Phew." Ada's avatar rubs her forehead in an exaggerated fashion.

"I can't believe she saved him," I whisper. "I thought she hated rats."

I guess I whispered too loudly, because Nadejda leans in and says in my ear, "He's part of the team. We came together; we leave together."

"Still," I reply softly. "Thank you."

Nadejda nods and looks back at her tablet screen.

I stop pretending to look at my phone and focus on the AROS screens in the most convenient manner—with my eyes closed.

Using my mind to place the mental screens all around me, I wait for Mr. Spock to resume his recon.

He doesn't.

It takes a few minutes of soft pleading from Ada before Mr. Spock twitches a single muscle. Eventually, Ada has to resort to a stronger motivation and makes a virtual rat appear (probably Uhura), and that does the trick. Mr. Spock starts crawling after his friend.

"It's a rat race," Mitya says.

"For someone who has important work to do, you sure comment a lot," I tell my friend, irritated. "Did you figure out a way to talk to my mom?"

"I figured out how to show her one of those air bubbles with text of our choosing," Mitya says, "but not a way to communicate back and forth. That would take hours to put together."

"We'll have to use what we have," I say. "Anyway, she's probably sleeping right now."

In the quiet that follows, I watch Mr. Spock make his way to the large two-story facility that's our destination.

Step one of the reconnaissance part of the mission is for the rat to walk around the building so we can see how many guards are around and figure out other critical details. Since we now know dogs are in the picture, this part will take ten times longer than we originally planned, but the precaution should be worth it.

We start by having the rat sneak into the facility parking lot, since it's near our current location and there aren't any dogs or guards in Mr. Spock's way. He discovers a large minibus parked there, proof that the hostages are nearby. This is likely how they were transported here. There are a couple of other cars in the lot as well, helping us estimate the number of guards within walking distance.

After he's done with the parking lot, Spock locates as many outside guards as he can. There are ten or so, which is less than what we estimated. According to Gogi, this is good news. I'm less sure, because this could mean there are up to ten people guarding the hostages inside the facility. On the bright side, Mr. Spock doesn't come across any more dogs.

"Let's move on to step two," Ada says and leads Mr. Spock toward the building.

It takes the rat only a minute to get into the drainpipe, but what feels like forever to crawl up it.

Once Mr. Spock is in the drainage system of the roof, Ada has him navigate his way into the air ducts of the air-conditioning system.

The rat is halfway to the first floor when Muhomor finally speaks through my earpiece. "In position."

Touching his earpiece like a Secret Service agent, Gogi replies, "You're behind schedule."

"I figured stealth trumps punctuality," Muhomor retorts. "Now leave me alone so I can do my thing."

The sounds of keyboard strikes are audible through the earpiece, and we listen to them for a minute before Muhomor says, "They don't have much in their systems, but I see purchases for beds and a lot of scientific equipment that has to do with the brain—fMRI and the like. Most of this stuff is in the target facility, so I can extrapolate that the hostages are sleeping on those purchased beds in the highlighted area."

An email arrives on my phone, and when I look at the attachment, I see a blueprint with red circles around a bunch of rooms on the first floor.

"I'll have Spock investigate," I whisper. Into the chat, I type, "Did you get all that?"

"On it," Ada says, and Mr. Spock changes direction in the air duct, crawling toward the nearest room in question.

Even though the room is dark and the vent blocks most of the rat's vision and the camera's view, I can make out the bed.

I squint at the blurry picture and recognize Mr. Shafer's sleeping form.

"You're right," I tell Muhomor in an excited whisper. "Let's locate my mom and complete this mission."

For the first time, I let myself hope Gogi's plan will actually work as seamlessly as he envisioned.

Mr. Spock crawls to the next room, and I recognize another test subject. Then another and another.

With each participant, I'm relieved we found yet another person, but I'm also disappointed that the person isn't Mom.

As the rat discovers more people, my elation and disappointment grow.

When Mr. Spock discovers the next to last hostage, who annoyingly isn't Mom either, I mentally type, "This is it. She has to be in the last room down the hall. There are no other people left."

"I'm so glad everyone's alive," Ada says in subdued tones. "After what happened to Mrs. Sanchez, I feared the worst."

She stops talking because Mr. Spock scurries up to the final air vent.

When I look at the night-vision screen, my blood pressure rises.

"No," I whisper and examine the rat-vision screen, hoping against all hope I'll somehow see a different image.

The result is the same, however.

Mom's bed is empty.

CHAPTER THIRTY-SEVEN

"Where is she?" I mentally type into the chat. "Where's my mom?" I whisper for the benefit of the people on the other end of the earpiece, as well as those near me.

When no one responds for a couple of beats, I step up to the edge of the trees, but Gogi's rough hands grab my shoulders, keeping me in place.

"Mitya," I frantically type into the chat. "Do you have a way of speaking with her yet?"

"No," Mitya says. "I can only show her a textbox, but no back-and-forth communication."

More desperate ideas ignite and flicker out in my head, and I say, "Ada, can we pinpoint her location with the help of her Brainocytes?"

"It's a bit like using one of those 'find my phone' apps," Ada says. "We know she's in this building, probably on the south side, but a more detailed location would require a brand-new app. And even if we did develop it, that app would have to run off your mom's AROS, meaning we'd need your mom's cooperation, which is a catch-22 since we have no way of contacting her."

"Muhomor," I whisper into the earpiece. "Is there a lab or control center in the facility? Maybe they're studying her or questioning her."

I hear a flurry of keystrokes through the earpiece; then an email arrives from Muhomor with a picture attachment. Through the earpiece, he says, "There, on the second floor, is where the fMRI machine is."

The email contains the blueprints with the room in question circled in red. I forward this to Ada and type, "Can you get Mr. Spock over there so we can have a look?"

"On it," Ada says, and the rat starts crawling through the air ducts again, only, to my deepest annoyance, he's moving as fast as a turtle overdosing on Xanax.

"There," Ada finally says. She's stating the obvious since we can all see the large ventilation grill a foot away from Spock. "That'll give us a view into the room."

On my night and rat vision AROS screens, the video changes from a view of the air vent to that of the room. Unfortunately, only a portion of the large room is visible from this angle.

All I can see is a single guard—not a complete failure since a guard indicates *something* is happening in the room. There are also some sounds, but they're even less useful. All we can pick up on are some muffled voices talking in the distance.

I subdue the urge to punch the innocent birch tree in front of me and scan the screens again.

"Muhomor," I whisper a little too loudly in my excitement. "There, in the left corner, you see that camera?" I start to gesture at the screen in front of me before I recall that Muhomor wouldn't be able to see it even if he were next to me, which he isn't.

"I see it," the hacker says, and I hear his crazy typing again. "I'm tapping into their video surveillance system now."

After what feels like an hour, Muhomor sends me a link. I click it and get a view into the room from that camera.

My first reaction is a wave of relief, because I see Mom very clearly, alive and well. But right on the tail of that relief is a flood of adrenaline, chased by a huge dose of anger.

It's the other four men in the room who bring about these new emotions.

In addition to the guard I saw earlier, there's a pudgy, gray-haired man who's busy speaking with Mom. I can't see his face because his back is turned to both Mr. Spock and the security camera. Aside from standing a little too close to Mom, this guy isn't the source of my concern. That would be the two brutes who aren't looking at Mom. I glimpse their faces and right away guess who they are, thanks to the fifth and final person I see.

My blood begins to boil because it's Anton, the man who abducted Mom over my knocked-out body—the man who, if it were up to me, wouldn't survive the night. Logically, the other two guys must be the people whose pictures we couldn't identify.

I run the face recognition app on them and on the guard, and I learn their names are Denis, Yegor, and Ivan. I also glance at their bios, but I'm not sure why I even bothered. In a nutshell, their profiles say, "Highly dangerous dirt bags. Steer clear."

"So, what do we do?" I ask, looking at Gogi as the man with the plan. "We have to get her out of there."

"We could also wait," Gogi suggests. "They'll let her sleep at some point."

"We don't know how long that'll take," Nadejda replies, and it's clear her smoke-damaged vocal cords have trouble whispering. "Why don't we use the gas I brought, like they did in the Dubrovka Theater?"

"No to the gas, unless there's no other option," I say after a quick mental Wikipedia search. The Russians used that solution during the infamous 2002 Nord-Ost siege. "Mom's health isn't perfect, and the gas harmed some of the hostages."

"Some of those damage reports are propaganda," Nadejda says, though she doesn't sound as confident as usual.

"If we can somehow cut the power to the room," Gogi says, "we can come through those windows." He points on his screen at the two windows in the camera view. "If we also storm through the door, we can make this work quietly enough."

What he doesn't need to say is that a single gunshot could alert all the guards in this facility, and that would be the end of us.

"I think I can take care of the lights," Muhomor says, "but they have this annoying redundancy system I'm having trouble with. The best I can do is keep the lights off for about a minute. We're lucky they're still in the middle of setting up the security in this building, or else the lights would simply flicker and come back on."

"A minute is enough," Gogi says and scratches his neck. "Still, I vote we wait."

"They might detect my activity in their system at any moment," Muhomor says. "You know the deal with the plane, and you know about the explosives that are just waiting to get discovered. I vote we go in."

"We also don't know *when* and if they'll let her sleep," I chime in. "Or when the guard might change. I guess we can wait a few minutes, but after that—"

"We're going in," Joe says with a finality that reminds everyone our mission isn't a democratic one. His unblinking lizard stare is focused on his screen, and his other hand is white-knuckled around the grip of his tranquilizer gun.

I think I understand what's going on. As I suspected, he didn't just come on this expedition because of his warm feelings for his aunt. He probably wants to make an example of the people who, as he put it, dared to fuck with his family.

"Right," Gogi says, all hesitation forgotten. "We start by taking care of all the guards we find."

He proceeds to explain the finer details of the plan, and once he's done, Muhomor prepares to turn off the lights at the most opportune moment, while Gogi, Joe, and Nadejda slither away to put tranquilizer darts into the guards Mr. Spock located.

"Can you use Mr. Spock to find the guards inside the facility?" I type to Ada. "Then, given what's about to go down, you should have him evacuate the building."

In response, I see movement on my mental rat screen.

"I can't believe they didn't let me help with tranquilizing the guards," I whisper, both for Muhomor and my New York team.

"The app doesn't work well with these dart guns," Ada reminds me. "And you can't move as stealthily as they can."

Muhomor sends me an email that proves Ada's right.

Using the links, I open mental screens to see what's happening via Joe's, Nadejda's, and Gogi's head cams. Their movements are indeed stealthy, though stealthy doesn't really cover what they do, especially Gogi. His movements remind me of Snake, a badass character from the *Metal Gear* video game franchise, where a master spy has to save the world.

I spread every view around me, using the AROS interface to tame the out-of-control screens, and as my allies work, I forget my other worries.

A guard on the northwestern side of the building gets a dart in his neck; then his southeastern colleague gets a dart in his left butt cheek. Immediately after, Nadejda and Joe run into a problem.

Instead of being at their separate posts, two guards are smoking together by the entrance.

Nadejda and Joe exchange a few hand gestures, crouch, and then slowly make their way toward the guards.

When they're halfway to their goal, I understand their plan. Sure enough, they grab the guards in identical choke-holds, in unison.

Muscles bulge on Nadejda's and Joe's arms, and the two guards don't get a chance to exhale the fumes stuck in their lungs before falling to the ground.

"Mike," Gogi says, intruding on my voyeurism. "There are no more guards around. Meet us in the parking lot."

I knew that before he said it; I just thought they would return to the trees instead of having me meet them out in the open.

"Mr. Spock only found one guard on the first floor," Ada says in case I wasn't following that screen. I was, but only with a fraction of my attention. "I emailed the guard's location to your cousin."

"Thanks," I type back. "Can you get Mr. Spock to the parking lot?"

"I actually started on that when I heard Gogi tell you where to meet him," Ada replies. "You be careful."

Her encouraging words have the opposite effect. Though I know Muhomor disabled all the pressure sensors, laser fields, auto-feeders for crocodiles, or whatever else my imagination can conjure up, an iceberg of fear forms in the pit of my stomach as I exit the relative anonymity of the forest and walk down the large grassy field before me.

Mimicking Gogi, I do my best to stay out of the lamp-light and walk far away from the incapacitated dog, just in case. As I approach the parking lot, I decide the walk isn't that bad compared to something like the HALO jump.

When Joe sees me, he puts a finger to his lips, emphasizing the need to be quiet, and I fight the urge to whisper something like, "I'm not a complete moron," because if I did that, I'd disprove my statement in the process of making it.

I glance around and locate Gogi, who's using something like a coat hanger to fiddle with the minibus doors. Similarly, I find Nadejda working on the locks of another car. It takes them less than a few seconds to beat the locks.

Then I catch the familiar glow of Mr. Spock's aura near the drainpipe.

The rat made it out in one piece.

A minuscule dose of tension leaves my shoulders, and I run to him as fast as stealth will permit. I get on one knee, and he eagerly jumps into my outstretched hands.

Getting up, I turn to find Gogi right next to me and have no clue how he snuck up on me so silently. He points at the minibus and leads me to it.

When we reach the vehicle, Gogi gestures at the minibus's glove compartment and then at Mr. Spock. I take that to mean, "Put him there."

I nod and give the rat a quick rub. I then take out a small handful of sunflower seeds and leave them in the compartment with Mr. Spock.

"Will he be okay?" I type into the chat. "I assume rats don't get claustrophobic?"

"They can live in literal holes in a wall," Mitya types back.

"I can soothe him from here," Ada says out loud. "Don't worry."

Gogi shakes his head as I reach to close the door, and I notice Nadejda left the doors open to the other car.

Gogi puts his bag into one of the cars, and he and Nadejda begin pulling climbing gear out of her rucksack. I swallow hard, picturing them using those ropes to climb onto the roof.

Joe must decide that the prep is done, because he stalks toward the building entrance, and I'm forced to follow.

My cousin slides a worm-like device with a camera on its tip into the small opening between the door and the floor and stares intently at the video feed on his phone's screen. I look over his shoulder and see that the guard Mr. Spock spotted didn't make his way to the entrance. When Joe deems the entrance clear, he quietly pulls the doors open, allowing me to go in. He then slowly closes the doors behind us.

When Joe slithers forward, I try to both follow him and orient myself in reference to the blueprints and Mr. Spock's air-vent recon.

This place looks like a Manhattan loft that used to be a warehouse. It'll take a lot more work to turn it into a full-fledged medical facility, assuming that's their goal.

The first bedroom, the one with Mr. Shafer, is to the right, so that's where I start turning, but at that moment, my upper arm is caught in a crushing hold that sends a blast of pain through my nerve endings.

CHAPTER THIRTY-EIGHT

A hand covers my mouth, and just in time too, because I was about to scream.

I look at my attacker and feel a smidge of relief, because both the hand over my mouth and the claw-like grip on my arm turn out to be Joe.

"Where are you going?" my cousin says in a barely audible whisper. "The stairs are in the opposite direction."

"I'm going to wake up the hostages," I whisper back, my voice shaking. "Where else?"

"The hostages?" Joe asks. He looks as close to confused as it's possible to get while also appearing homicidal.

"Right," I say, trying not to cringe. "To save them."

"Why?"

"Because they're sick, kidnapped people?" I whisper a bit too loudly. "Because they'll get their heads cracked open and die if we leave them here? Because they're Americans stuck in Russia? Because—"

"Shut up." Joe's whisper is like a punch, and I'm fairly sure he would've accompanied the words with a real punch if we weren't related. In a softer but actually creepier tone, he adds, "They don't matter."

I look at those emotionless eyes.

He really doesn't care.

We've been working under a misunderstanding this entire time. I took it as a given that we'd save everyone, but Joe was only thinking about my mom.

"Look," I whisper. "I'll wake up Mr. Shafer. His condition is the least severe of the bunch. I'll tell him to quietly wake the others and put them in the minibus. It'll only take a few seconds and shouldn't affect our plan in any way." My cousin looks unimpressed, so I try appealing to his inner monster by saying, "If something goes wrong and we get shot at, the extra people could provide cover. Also, once we get to the US, the police won't ask questions about—"

"Fine," my cousin whispers, and I'm not sure whether he agrees so he won't have to punch me, or because I actually convinced him. "You have a minute while I walk ahead and deal with that guard."

We split up, and I continue to Mr. Shafer's room, my footsteps barely audible—a pleasant surprise given the good acoustics in this place.

I turn the corner that, according to the blueprints, leads to the first bedroom. The room should be just a few feet away.

A pair of surprised eyes stares at me in the semi-darkness of the hall.

It's the guard.

Looks like he moved from his original location after all.

The blast of terror causes my pupils to dilate, and despite the poor lighting, I can clearly see his arm lifting his weapon.

CHAPTER THIRTY-NINE

My right hand propels the tranquilizer gun up and fires, seemingly before the conscious part of my brain reacts at all.

The dart does its job, and I grab the gun from the man's limp hand as he drops to the floor, afraid the weapon might make an unwelcome clanking sound if it hit the ground. Though I already have a Glock and the tranquilizer gun on me, I stuff this new weapon into my waistband behind my back as a precaution.

Once my thinking catches up with my actions, I wonder if my sudden quick-draw skills are from the brain boost. Could the Wi-Fi, plus the extra brain resources, be behind my faster reaction time? Since I've never been in life-or-death situations like this before, I have no idea what my normal reaction time is, but I doubt it's this quick.

Trying to steady my overly fast breathing, I walk up to Mr. Shafer's room and turn the door handle.

The door is locked, but the solution occurs to me right away, and it's only two feet behind me.

I go back to the guard and search him for the keys, finding them on his belt.

Armed with the keys, I open Mr. Shafer's door.

It takes a gentle shake to wake the old man, and I resort to holding his mouth shut, Joe style, to make sure he doesn't scream once he comes to his senses.

At first, Mr. Shafer looks like he's about to turn a shade grayer, but then I think he recognizes me because the initial desperation in his rheumy eyes turns into a glimmer of hope.

I let go of the old man's mouth, and he instantly whispers, "Thank God you're here. They—"

I cover his mouth again and whisper, "Sorry, we don't have much time."

I proceed to explain what he needs to do, going as far as pulling up the blueprints of the facility on my phone to show him where to go—not that the instructions are complicated. The parking lot is near the entrance, and that's just a corridor away from where we are.

"I know how to get there," Mr. Shafer whispers. "They didn't blindfold us when we—"

"Okay," I interrupt again. "I have to go help my mom. Make sure everyone gets to the car as soon as possible and leave the front seats empty so we can jump in quickly."

Mr. Shafer nods, but then he looks at something behind me and his eyes widen.

The hair on the back of my neck stands up. Spinning around, I aim my gun at whatever Mr. Shafer just saw—and exhale sharply.

It's Joe.

My cousin is in a half crouch, dragging the unconscious guard behind him.

Mr. Shafer cringes at the sight of the knocked-out guard.

I'm not sure if Joe notices the old man's reaction, but he takes out a knife and kneels as if to tie his shoe. Before either of us can utter a single word, Joe slices the guard's throat with all the emotion of someone cutting up a melon.

I forget how to speak for a second and look at Mr. Shafer as though he might explain what just happened. What I actually see raises a warning bell in my head.

The old man is about to scream.

Except Joe is already next to Mr. Shafer, his hand covering the old man's mouth in a much rougher way than mine did.

My cousin wipes his knife with his left thumb, and the blood lands at Mr. Shafer's feet. Joe then whispers something into the old man's ear. Mr. Shafer's lips tremble, and he turns so white he looks like a ghost.

"Will there be a problem?" Joe whispers loud enough for me to hear.

"No, sir," Mr. Shafer whispers, eyes wide. "I'll get everyone into the car. I'll be quiet. You don't have to—"

"Then get started." Joe's whisper sounds like the crack of a whip as he rips the keys out of my hand and throws them at Mr. Shafer.

Ignoring Mr. Shafer's frantic nods, Joe heads out of the room. Numbly, I follow him, trying not to think about the literal blood on his hands. Out of the corner of my eye, I see Mr. Shafer walk determinedly toward the room adjacent to his. Whatever Joe told him was clearly effective.

I hurry to catch up with Joe, and we make our way to the staircase that will lead us to the second floor.

Joe's movements remind me of a stalking predator as he exits the staircase into a corridor.

When we reach the target door, Joe puts his finger to his lips, indicating the need for silence. He then points at the earpiece and then at my phone.

Instead of using the phone, I mentally compose a text message to Muhomor that states, "We're in position."

"Good," Muhomor says in our ears. "Gogi and Nadejda are almost ready, but I need a few more minutes with the lights. Please stand by until I say go."

Joe looks at his phone, checking on the room in front of us. Suddenly, his grip on his tranquilizer gun tightens, and his features contort in animalistic fury. He takes a small step toward the door, but then checks himself.

My heart goes from pounding to thrashing violently as I focus my attention on the AROS view that shows me the video feed from the surveillance camera Muhomor hacked into.

The gray-haired man, the one who was near Mom, is now within touching distance of her.

I stare unblinkingly as he touches Mom's face with the familiarity of an old lover.

She cringes at his touch and tries to pull away, but her action seems to irritate the man, and he steps even closer.

This time, when he reaches out, his hands go for Mom's bosom.

She tries to slap his face, but he catches her wrist and leans in closer.

Though there's no sound, I can see Mom's lips moving. It seems like she's yelling at the other people in the room for help. The guard and the three other bastards act as though they're not even there.

I didn't think I was capable of this kind of fury. The rage clouds my mind. I can barely think, and it's almost impossible to understand what I'm seeing at first, but then I extrapolate the revolting direction this interaction is heading.

"This asshole is trying to rape my mother!" I mentally type into the chat, without even meaning to. "He's so fucking dead."

I don't know what my friends respond with because my blood is pumping in my ears, and the red mist of anger overwhelms every cell in my body.

Teeth clenched, I reach for my Glock and step toward the door.

CHAPTER FORTY

In a blur of rage, I kick open the door.

As soon as there's a wide enough gap, I shoot the tranquilizer gun at Ivan, the guard who's been in the camera's view the entire time.

Then I spin around and aim my gun at Denis, one of the two assholes who assisted in the kidnapping. Using the aiming app, I put a bullet in his right shoulder.

Both men fall, though Denis hits the ground with a lot of screaming.

I hear movement behind me, and in my view through the room's camera, I watch Joe jump in and put a bullet in Yegor's chest—the second of the two previously unidentified kidnappers.

My cousin also spares a dart for Denis, stopping the bigger man's halfhearted attempt at aiming the gun with his left hand and silencing his pained cries.

The older man—the one whose blood I'm truly after—leaps for Mom. Before I can react, he's holding a gun to her head.

For the first time, I see his face—and almost wish I hadn't. It's covered in scars, burns, warts, and open wounds oozing pus. Combined, it makes him look like a cross between Freddy Krueger, Jabba the Hutt, and the right side of the Phantom of the Opera. It's as if he was raised in the heart of the Chernobyl accident.

"Don't move," the monstrosity says through what passes for lips, and green saliva sprays in a fountain around him. "I'll shoot the bitch, I swear."

I freeze at his threat, but in the video camera feed, I see Joe raising his tranquilizer gun. Before I can cry out for him to stop, he pulls the trigger.

The guy tilts Mom's body at the last second, and Joe's dart hits her instead of its intended target.

Mom goes limp in the guy's arms.

Time, which already seemed to crawl, slows further as I watch the monster-faced man squeeze the trigger of the gun pointed at Mom's head.

"No!" I scream over the boom of the shot.

Mom's head detonates from the inside, spraying blood all around the room. It reminds me of the worst parts of the atrocity I witnessed at the club.

A heartbeat later, her body falls to the floor.

I feel a stunned sense of déjà vu, because she looks exactly like the headless Mrs. Sanchez did when I mistook her for Mom back in New York.

Now there's no mistaking whose headless body that is.

Mom is dead.

A tsunami of grief wells inside my chest, but I channel it into something more productive—anger. I force myself to morph my pain into icy revenge.

I raise my hand and shoot Mom's killer with the tranquilizer gun—not because I don't want him dead, but because I don't want him dead *yet*. I want to make sure he lives so I can unleash Joe on him and let my cousin do as he pleases for as long as he pleases. I don't want this man to die from the merciful quickness of a bullet.

Something calls my attention to the camera view, and I see Anton, the ape-bison fucker who punched me in the hospital, aim a giant gun and shoot.

I expect pain, and almost welcome it as a relief from my grief, but Anton wasn't aiming at me after all.

In the camera view, I see a huge bloodstain cover Joe's chest. My cousin clutches at his wound and crumples to the floor.

Before I even register my intentions, I aim the app-assisted Glock at the very center of Anton's forehead and spasmodically squeeze the trigger.

Anton falls.

Suddenly, another shot is fired.

In horror, I look at where the monster-face guy fell and see my dart sticking out of the wall, not the man.

The man must've pretended to be hit.

Smoke is spreading from the barrel of his gun—the gun that's currently pointed at my chest.

The melting-hot freight train of the bullet finally reaches my chest, and I fly backward.

My heart stops, and I'm dead before my head hits the floor.

CHAPTER FORTY-ONE

Instead of finding myself in the afterlife, I'm standing outside the door, my emotions in turmoil and my mind confused.

Joe is standing there too, very much unharmed and looking at me.

In the room's camera, I see Mom is also alive. She pulls away from the monster man's latest harassing gesture.

Stunned, I try to process it all. Didn't we all just die? Wasn't I just in that room?

Then I comprehend what happened.

I never actually rushed into the room. It was that weird brain-boost side effect, like my phone that broke but didn't break in Ada's bathroom—the phenomenon Ada calls a pre-cog moment.

It makes sense. It's only been a short while since I got the newer and better brain boost, courtesy of Mitya's resource allocation algorithm. Plus, to make better use of the new resources, I'm also on a Wi-Fi network. Just like when I first got the brain boost, I experienced a side effect. Ada said the new boost made her feel like she did in the beginning. I bet she got this weird side effect as well, something I can verify later.

My brain's cloud extension must've showed the rest of my brain what might happen if I gave in to my overwhelming anger. It seems my biological brain isn't yet accustomed to this new extension and reinterpreted this overflow of data as a dream-like scenario. Or, more specifically, a part of me warned the rest of me what might happen if I stormed into the room without waiting for Muhomor to disable the lights and for Gogi and Nadejda to assist us through the windows. My brain gave me a vision using the available information and even utilized my existing memories for assistance, causing me to relive that horrible headless Mrs. Sanchez/Mom moment.

"We need to go in now," I text Muhomor, realizing I'm just standing there, wide-eyed. At the same time, I type into the chat, "Mitya, when we go in, show Mom a text box instructing her to run into a corner and lie on the floor. I don't want anyone using her as a hostage or one of us accidentally shooting her."

"I have everything set up to send that message," Mitya types back. "Let's hope she catches on when she sees it."

As I read Mitya's reply, I hear Muhomor respond to my earlier comment with, "I'm not ready yet. I'm trying to make sure the lights don't come back on prematurely, so I need to work on this a little longer."

On the screen, the monster guy is leaning over my mom as she cringes away, and it takes every effort of will to stop myself from repeating the scenario the brain-boost side effect warned me against.

As time crawls onward, I remind myself that the monster guy has to take his pants off before something truly unthinkable can happen, but this line of thinking, even if it's somewhat rational, makes me feel like the lousiest son in the world. I also keep telling myself that my brain-boost vision was probably an accurate estimation of what will happen if I just storm in—and that makes me feel like the most cowardly son in the world.

I spare Joe a glance, and it seems like similar thoughts are battling in the dark place that's his mind. If a look at a phone screen could castrate someone, the gray-haired man inside the room would be squealing in a high falsetto.

"I want to change the plan," Joe whispers through his teeth. "I want to deal with this gray fucker myself."

"Joe," Gogi says softly into our earpieces. "Mike should handle him."

In my rage, I forgot the plan, and particularly the part where, by a stroke of fate, Gogi said I should tranquilize the gray-haired guy when we storm the room. His logic for doing things this way was sound. Even if I miss, since the man might not be armed (while the others are visibly armed), I can shoot at him a second time in relative safety.

At first, I want to tell everyone that the monster guy is indeed armed, but then I realize his gun was part of my vision, which isn't proof he actually has one. I'm not psychic, and the vision wasn't prophetic, but rather a hypothesis with the same validity as my favorite recurring dream where I'm walking naked in the middle of Times Square.

"Fine," Joe grunts. "But we have to go in—now."

"Nadejda and I are set," Gogi says. "We're waiting on Muhomor."

"Muhomor," I mentally type. "If you don't want Joe to do to you what he did to Alex, you'll tell us everything is all set."

"Fine," Muhomor says hesitantly. "I guess you can go in. The lights will turn off in ten, nine..."

As Muhomor counts down, Joe pulls down his night-vision goggles and stands in front of me, ready to kick the door in.

I lower my goggles onto my face and tense as the world turns different shades of green.

"Lights out," Muhomor says, and the lights from below the door, as well as the AROS view through the security camera in the room, go black.

"Go," Gogi says, and through the two views that represent his and Nadejda's cameras, I see them scaling the side of the building, SWAT style.

Joe springs into motion and gives the door a powerful kick.

CHAPTER FORTY-TWO

Joe runs in and shoots a dart into the disoriented guard's neck—as per Gogi's plan.

I follow him and briefly take in the green-tinted room.

As we hoped, Anton and his goons can't see us in the dark, but they don't look as disoriented as would be ideal, and their guns are out.

I turn toward my objective—the asshole next to where Mom was. Thanks to Mitya's message, Mom is in the corner of the room already, only she didn't get a chance to lie down yet, or maybe she isn't planning to because of the darkness.

My mind gets laser-focused on my goal, but at the same time, I'm able to pay close attention to the many events in the room. I wonder if it's from the brain boost assisting me. I also feel as though time slowed to the point where I can think many more thoughts per second than usual. I've heard of time distortion happening to people in stressful situations, but I doubt it was to this extent. What I'm experiencing reminds me of an altered state of consciousness that has more to do with hallucinogens than stress.

In the next instant, the two windows shatter, and Nadejda and Gogi fly in, spraying shards of glass all over the floor and bringing a draft of fresh air into the stuffy room.

The monster-faced guy isn't facing the back of the room anymore. Reacting to the sound of breaking glass, he turns, and I get a good look at his face.

If I needed proof that my earlier vision wasn't prophetic but a product of my imagination, I get it now. The man's face doesn't have warts and doesn't resemble Freddy's. He looks like an accountant, or maybe, given the context, a scientist. The worst thing I can say about his face is that he has an overbite. The weirdest part is that this guy looks vaguely familiar, but I'm pretty sure I've never met him before. He clearly isn't a thug, or my face-recognition app would've alerted me—assuming face recognition can work in this green-tinted environment.

His identity isn't important, though. As far as I'm concerned, his name is Shoot Me.

I raise the tranquilizer gun and do my best to aim. The assist app must have a problem with the lighting conditions, because even the flawed version doesn't appear.

I pull the trigger unassisted.

All of a sudden, a green sun flare erupts around me, and I can't see a thing.

"Fuck," Muhomor says through the earpiece. "The lights came back on too soon." When the others shout obscenities at him, he replies with, "If you'd only given me time to—"

I ignore the rest of his monologue.

That this green super flare is from the lights coming back on is preferable to what I originally thought—that I was going blind or having a stress-induced stroke.

Though I can't see much with my eyes, I have an alternative. Since the lights are back on, the AROS screen with the security camera feed is no longer black, and my eyes' condition is irrelevant to AROS, which works with the vision center of my brain.

In that camera view, I see I missed my shot at the scientist again, or for the first time depending on whether the vision counts. At least I assume I missed, since he isn't on the ground.

I'm worried I'll find it impossible to navigate my way around the room using only the camera input, so I rip off the night-vision goggles.

The bright light blinds my green-adjusted eyes, so I take my chances with the camera feed and leap for the corner where my mom is.

My plan is straightforward. I'll put myself between Mom and the rest of the people in the room. If anyone wants to take her hostage like in my pre-cog vision, they'll have to get through me. As a bonus, I get closer to the scientist asshole, so once my eyes recover enough, I'll have a better chance at shooting him.

Navigating by camera turns out to be harder than I thought, and I bump into a chair, causing my kneecap to scream in pain. Gritting my teeth, I vow to learn how to walk around rooms based on a security camera video feed.

Suddenly, I see a blur of motion coming toward me in the camera view.

I squint and make out a fist flying at my face.

The punch connects, and the pain in my knee seems like a tickle in comparison.

As somewhat of a developing expert on getting hit like this, I have to say, pain aside, the punch isn't that bad. I think it only hurts this much because my face is already swollen from my previous adventures. I do see a few stars as I drop the gun, but—and this is critical—I'm still standing. As a side benefit, the hit shocked my vision into recovering, and I can see my opponent quite well. It's the damn scientist guy.

"Come on, Mike," Mitya yells. "Wipe the floor with this old fart!"

"Shut up," Ada tells him sternly. "Don't distract him."

I throw a punch at the guy's cheek, but he dodges it.

Either my movements are slow due to the earlier hit, or the old man is spryer than he looks.

"Felix," my mom screams from behind me. "That's Misha you're fighting!"

If Mom's goal was to distract my attacker, she succeeded spectacularly. Wide-eyed, he looks at me as though he's trying to use x-ray vision. I don't need a brain boost to take advantage of this. Seizing the moment, I plant a satisfyingly hard punch on his jaw.

Something seems to break in my knuckles, but it's worth it, because something also seems to break in the guy's face as he reels back.

I don't get to gloat, though, because as he falls, he grabs me by my belt, and I topple with him in a heap of flailing limbs.

Once on the ground, I recover enough to straddle my opponent and smack him with my forehead. Sparks explode in my vision, and the strike goes on my list of movie fight moves to never repeat again. I'm convinced the blow hurt me more than him.

Next, I try punching him with my fist, but he dodges, and I hit the toilet-white floor tiles. If my knuckles weren't broken before, they might be now.

Through the pain, I make myself another promise: once I master moving around using a camera feed, I'll also learn how to fight. Maybe shooting a tranquilizer gun without any apps should go on that list as well.

Though blood is trickling from a cut in his forehead, my opponent's eyes gleam with fear and malice. In general, he looks much too lucid for my liking.

With my left hand, I punch him in the chest, a move that causes my hand to feel as though a mob of angry bees stung each knuckle. Air whooshes from my opponent's mouth, and I get a tiny bit closer to my goal of knocking him out so he's no longer a threat to Mom.

Then the bastard tries escaping from under me.

I hit him in the face this time, then his ear, and then I knee him in the stomach with my still-recovering knee.

In a haze of pain, in the middle of this bout of almost mindless pummeling—and probably thanks to the boost—I take in the rest of the room through the camera view.

Similar to me, Gogi is on the floor. Unlike me, instead of punching Denis—his opponent who's the bigger one of Anton's flunkies—he's wrestling with him. Gogi must've jumped the man to stop him from using his gun and alerting the nearby guards, though I'm not sure whether I know this by using the evidence I see, or if some brain-boosted part of me was paying attention to what was happening to Gogi without me being consciously aware of it. Looking at the big mess of glistening limbs clawing at each other, it's hard to know who's winning the fight. For Gogi's sake, I hope Nadejda taught him some wrestling moves—an activity I decide to add to my quickly growing list of future self-improvements.

I land another blow on my attacker's face and see blood. As the metallic scent fills my nostrils, I realize I can't tell whether the red liquid is coming from the cuts on my fist or a wound on my opponent.

"Misha, stop!" someone yells. It sounds like Mom, but I must be imagining it. It makes no sense for her to defend the guy who was about to rape her.

My fists scream in agony, yet my victim is still squirming underneath me, meaning he's still dangerous and I need to hit him some more.

In the camera view of the room, I spot Nadejda locked in a fight with Yegor. She has hold of his gun hand, and they're struggling for control of the weapon. Her tranquilizer gun is on the floor, and I vaguely recall seeing her lose it via the camera feed, back when Yegor disarmed her when the lights came back on.

"Misha!" Mom's voice intrudes again. "You're going to kill him."

I don't get a chance to tell Mom something like, "That's a sacrifice I'm willing to make," because my attention zooms in on what Anton is doing—aiming his gun at Joe.

"Mike, he's your father!" my mom screams, but her words don't register as Nadejda also spots Joe's predicament and does something I've only seen in a UFC fight.

With her huge muscles rippling under the strain and her neck veins bulging, Nadejda grabs Yegor by the waist and throws him at Anton.

The two Russian brutes collide with the smack of a slab of meat hitting the butcher's counter, just as Anton's gun goes off.

My eardrums feel like they might pop out of my eyes.

A rush of relief hits me when I see Joe is still standing—meaning Nadejda's ploy worked.

Of course, the gunshot also means our attempts at stealth were for nothing. It's now a matter of minutes before an army of guards descends on our asses.

This is when my mom's words finally register.

She called the man I'm currently hitting *my father*.

CHAPTER FORTY-THREE

"**D**id she really just call him my father?" I hysterically type into the chat, in part as a sanity check, but also to frame the question for myself.

"She did," Ada replies. "I know it's very *Empire Strikes Back*, but you have to pull yourself together and quick."

My mind is a beehive of thoughts as I try to piece it all together. Mom also referred to this guy as Felix. According to my grandparents, that's indeed the name of the asshole who got Mom pregnant all those years ago.

Slowing my punching, I study the battered face in front of me and realize some of his features are similar to the ones I see in the mirror every day. That's why he looked so familiar. Still, to be extra sure, I manually run the face recognition app. Since the lights are back up, the app runs without a hitch and confirms what I already knew.

This is Felix Rodinov, which are the first and last names of my father. I only get a glimpse of his bio. His real family includes kids, my half-siblings, and a wife he's been married to for about forty years, meaning he was married before and during his affair with Mom. There's a laundry list of scientific accomplishments and posts at various Russian universities and agencies.

An insight flashes through my brain—a vague notion of how his presence answers a number of questions I've had about this whole affair—but I put the thought aside.

More confused than I've ever felt in my life, I stop hitting my father and wonder what to do.

My attention is stolen by what's happening in the camera view.

Joe makes his move.

With his real gun, he aims in Anton and Yegor's direction. Joe must have switched weapons because stealth is no longer a factor, and he might as well give Anton the piece of lead he deserves.

His silenced shot is much quieter than Anton's, but it's still loud enough to hurt my damaged eardrums.

Unfortunately, Anton doesn't fall, but Yegor does get a bullet in his eyeball, or so I assume given the bloody fountain of gelatinous goo that sprays from his face and the bits of brain matter that fly out the back of his head. The nauseating smell of blood mingled with gunpowder fills the room, followed by something far worse.

As Yegor falls, two last things happen in his life. His bowels release with a sickening stench, and he drags Anton to the ground with him.

The ape-bison Russian doesn't let the fall put him at a disadvantage. He lands in a kneeling position with his gun outstretched and pointed at Joe.

Anton's forearm muscles twitch. He's pulling the trigger.

In a flurry of movement, Nadejda dives and pushes Joe out of the way.

Anton's gun goes off, and the bang scrambles my brain through my ear canals.

The bullet hits Nadejda square in her left breast.

Blood sprays out, and Nadejda clutches her chest as if to force the blood back in.

Eyes wide with horror and shock, Nadejda collapses to the ground, her bald head smacking loudly against the floor tiles.

Despite the push, Joe doesn't lose his footing. Catching himself, he glances at Nadejda, and a frightening, guttural sound escapes his mouth at the sight of her crime-scene posed body. Like a jaguar, he leaps at Anton. His fist connects with Anton's jaw, and their guns clank against the floor.

Joe's attack looks like something out of a slasher movie. He bites Anton's ear, Mike Tyson style, then spits the blood and flesh into Anton's ever-whitening face.

Anton screams like a terrified cornered animal. Almost in slow motion, I watch as his big, sweaty fist lands a devastating blow to Joe's right eye, and my cousin's head ricochets backward.

As someone who received that same blow, I fear Joe might've gotten knocked out. Acting as quickly as I can, I turn and draw my silenced Glock.

In the blink of an eye, I realize my aim assist is back—at least something good came out of the lights coming back on.

I point the oh-so-helpful line at the only place I can without hitting Joe—Anton's right shoulder.

Squeezing the trigger, I feel the gun kick in my wounded hands.

The bullet rips through Anton's shoulder, and he yelps in pain.

Joe manages not to lose consciousness. Instead, he sticks his fingers into the bloody mound of meat I just created and twists them back and forth, as though trying to find the bullet to keep as a souvenir. At the same time, he claws at his enemy's face with his other hand, and I wince as I glimpse Anton's eyes popping like squished slugs.

Anton's cry is no longer recognizable as human.

I fight the temptation to puke and keep my gun on Anton, but after another moment, the precaution isn't needed.

Joe takes out his knife and repeatedly stabs Anton in the chest.

The blood coming out of Anton's mouth garbles his wails and sprays the room like gruesome fire sprinklers as he collapses to the floor.

Holding in a surge of bile, I check the video view to see if I should shoot Gogi's opponent, but Gogi is already getting up, having won the fight.

Something pulls on my waistband from behind, and with a sinking feeling, I realize my father just snatched the guard's gun I stuck there earlier.

A shot rings out, and I expect to feel a blast of pain. Instead, I see Gogi grab his left upper arm.

I spin around to deal with my father, but my mom is already kicking him in the temple. Felix reels back, his head snapping to the side.

As someone who's played soccer with her, I know her kick is freakishly strong.

Felix looks too dazed to shoot again, but I club him on the nose with the butt of my gun for good measure, and I'm rewarded with the crunch of his nose breaking.

My father goes limp underneath me, finally losing consciousness.

I take away the gun he stole and slide the magazine out, mentally noting to do this earlier in the future—if the future involves the type of events we've experienced today, that is.

Gogi offers me his uninjured hand, and I let him help me up.

Though my legs are wobbly, I manage to stand straight.

"Mishen'ka." Mom rushes to me, and Gogi moves out of her way.

I'm caught in a huge mama-bear hug that instantly makes me feel better. In the next moment, however, she begins sobbing, and my fleeting comfort evaporates, replaced by that feeling I've known since I was a little kid—the despair of having to hear my mother cry.

"We have to get out of here," I tell her forcefully in Russian, pulling back. "Can you run?"

"I think I can," Mom says between hiccups and sobs. Her round face is blotchy, and she looks dazed. "I can't believe you're here, in Russia. And Joseph. Please tell me my brother isn't here—"

"Uncle Abe is in New York," I answer as I grab Mom by her elbow and unceremoniously usher her to the door. It looks like stress sharpened her memory, or at least her awareness of her surroundings.

"Take her outside," Joe tells me. "Gogi and I will go through the window."

As I field Mom's panicked questions, I lead her out of the room toward the stairs.

In the camera view, I watch as Joe walks over to Nadejda's body, kneels, and checks her pulse.

Gogi, who's in the process of bandaging his arm with his ripped sleeve, approaches them and looks solemnly at Joe. My cousin shakes his head, almost imperceptibly. Gogi's shoulders droop, and while Joe's bloodied face is an emotionless mask again, I swear I see sorrow somewhere deep in his icy-blue eyes.

My grief hits me then. I try not to show it since I don't want to burden Mom. Even though I didn't know Nadejda very long, I somehow became fond of the big woman. It just doesn't seem right that such a courageous, tough-as-nails person is dead, that she died saving my cousin.

Joe jumps to his feet, walks up to Anton, and rips out the knife he left in the man's chest with a violent jerk. I mentally zoom in the camera view, trying not to trip on the stairs as I lead my mom down.

Joe approaches Ivan, the guard, and stabs the knocked-out man in the heart.

A moment later, he's looming over Felix's unconscious form.

"Wait, Joe, don't," I mentally text my cousin.

He bends over.

"Please, Joe, stop," I whisper into the earpiece. "He's—"

Joe either doesn't hear me or doesn't care. His knife cuts into my father's neck on the left and slides all the way to his right ear. A pool of blood forms on the floor.

I'm on the verge of losing the contents of my stomach again, but for Mom's sake, I breathe in deep, fighting the nausea. My father, whom I just met, is dead, and I have no idea how to process that. What should I feel for a man who shared half of my genes yet was capable of such evil? How should I view a stranger who did such horrible things? The cocktail of emotions boiling in my chest is overwhelming, but I know whatever I'm feeling is just the tip of an enormous iceberg I'll have to confront at some point, Titanic style.

"What about Joe?" Mom asks, looking confused. Unlike me, she didn't watch the murder on the camera. "What did you not want him to do?"

"Nothing, Mom," I force myself to say as we clear the turn in the staircase. Swallowing the acid rising in my throat, I lie, "I was asking him if I could sit next to you in the car."

"Of course you're sitting next to me," Mom says, frowning. "Why would he mind?"

"Safety," I say as we get to the first floor and head for the exit. "But don't worry. Everything will be fine."

Through Gogi's camera, I see him slide down the rope like a fireman and run for the second car while Joe gets behind the wheel of the minibus.

My jaw drops as I watch Gogi take explosives out of one of the bags he's had with him since the HALO jump. I mistakenly thought all the explosives were in Muhomor's possession, but it seems like Gogi kept some for himself.

I belatedly shudder at what we risked during the jump. If Gogi's parachute hadn't opened, our deaths would've been violent on a much larger scale than I thought.

When Mom and I are halfway through the first floor, Gogi sets up the explosives around the doomed car, shoulders the bag with the leftover explosives, and puts the car into neutral. He then exits the car and pushes it closer to the facility wall.

Making sure his guns are on him, he runs for the minibus.

As Mom and I approach the building exit, Gogi jumps into the car, and I glimpse the rest of the terrified hostages already inside.

"Mr. Shafer came through," I mentally type into the chat.

Before my friends can respond, gunshots ring out outside.

CHAPTER FORTY-FOUR

"Stay behind me," I tell Mom in a hopefully commanding voice.

Mom listens, proving this ordeal must've had an impact on her usual "eggs don't teach the chicken" philosophy. Normally, she never would've let me risk my life on her behalf—not that we've ever been in a situation like this before.

I open the door a sliver to see where the shots are coming from. Two guards are running toward us from the east.

Fortunately, they're shooting at something that isn't me.

I raise the Glock and aim the assist line at the rightmost man's leg. Suddenly, the minibus crashes into my target, causing him and his buddy to fly in opposite directions and sparing me a bullet.

The minibus violently turns in our direction, grass and dirt spraying from under its tires.

I pull Mom through the exit.

Joe stops the van, and Gogi opens the door.

I help Mom inside, and she scoots toward the middle. I jump in after her and sit by the window, behind Joe.

The hostages look shell-shocked, but they're not screaming or panicking.

Our tires spin in place, spitting grass; then we rocket forward.

I hear shouting and engines revving somewhere nearby.

The guards are almost here.

"Muhomor, the plan has changed," Gogi says into the earpiece. "I want you to blow half the distraction. Just make sure the exit point isn't part of that." At the same time, Gogi presses the detonator in his hands and carefully puts it into his bag.

The ground, along with the minibus, shakes violently as the car next to the facility explodes.

The view from the security camera in the room goes static and dies, so I dismiss that AROS window. I'm guessing about half the facility is now in ruins.

About a dozen more explosions ring out in the distance, and Muhomor says, "That's round one, as requested."

We were originally going to detonate the explosives all at once to create a distraction as we escaped the compound. Muhomor and Lyuba snuck around and placed the explosives around the compound's walls. Of course, in that original plan, we were supposed to be next to our exit point when the explosions went off. Now we can only hope the havoc this batch of bombs created is enough to minimize the number of guards about to swoop down on us.

"I'm also trying to mess with their comms," Muhomor says into our earpieces. "Oh, and you guys might appreciate this—it wasn't part of the original plan, but I was able to improvise."

Loud alarms go off from every direction. Muhomor must've hacked into the alarm system. He's clearly trying his hardest to make up for the lights debacle.

"Keep this up, and Joe might not kill you after all," I text him reassuringly, and he mutters a bunch of choice Russian curses into my earpiece in reply.

The literal and figurative ear assault continues as we move from grass onto asphalt.

A pair of confused guards shows up in our way. Joe's hands tighten on the wheel, and he floors the gas pedal. The guards' bodies thump against the front of the minibus, and I swallow thickly as we leave them broken behind us.

As we approach an intersection, a Humvee, or its Russian equivalent, appears on the road perpendicular to us.

Joe speeds up.

The car does the same.

The driver must be truly insane to play a game of chicken with Joe of all people.

Joe grips the wheel firmly.

The Humvee doesn't slow down.

In a chorus of voices, Gogi, my mom, and the rest of the study participants beg Joe to stop or turn or do *something* to avoid the inevitable crash.

"Joe," I scream over everyone, my voice going hoarse, "even if we T-bone him, which is the best case scenario in this madness, we'll all break our bones or worse. We have older people in the car, including your aunt—"

Without any sign that he heard us, Joe rolls the window down further, draws his gun, turns the wheel, and slams on the brakes.

Maybe it's a trick from the brain boost, but I suddenly understand Joe's plan. In case I'm right, I take out my gun and prepare to assist him.

Victim to the laws of physics, the minibus spins almost ninety degrees and skids to a stop parallel to the Humvee's direction a few feet from the intersection.

As the Humvee passes us, Joe sprays it with a torrent of bullets.

Doing my part, I use the aiming app to shoot the Humvee's front tire.

In a fierce jerk, the Humvee veers off the road. Either Joe hit the driver, or I got the tire—or we both succeeded.

When the big vehicle hits the bushes, it flips over and rolls into the ditch.

Joe turns the wheel all the way to the left and floors the gas pedal.

As we get back onto the road, I notice another car far behind us.

Joe drives like a rabid maniac, and at last, I see the wall looming in the distance. Our target shouldn't be far off.

Mom gasps, and I follow her gaze. Several cars are blocking the road in front of us. We'll never get through them.

I guess Joe wasn't planning on driving in a straight line anyway. With a sudden jerk that makes at least eight of our passengers squeal, the minibus veers off the road and heads straight for the part of the wall we originally planned to escape from.

The wall grows bigger and bigger, the moonlight illuminating the rusty barbed wire across the very top.

Driving on dirt is an art Joe hasn't mastered. A big rock causes me to literally bite my tongue, and I taste blood for the umpteenth time today, while the miniature hill we drive over causes me to hit my head on the minibus roof.

Only a dozen seconds pass before someone in the back throws up, and a sour smell permeates the air, which, combined with the sound of someone heaving, initiates a horrible chain reaction. It takes all my willpower not to join the puke circle, and I can tell by Mom's green face that she's in the same boat.

The car that was behind us and a couple of swifter cars from the blockade aren't just following us; they're closing the distance. They must be better equipped for off-road driving than our piece of junk van.

Our destination, the wall, gets ever closer, but it might as well be miles away, because someone starts firing at us from behind.

Gogi opens his bomb bag and fiddles with something inside.

The first bullet shatters the right-side mirror. The second hits the back window, and someone moans in pain.

My heart skips a beat, but then I see my mom is unharmed. I feel a wave of relief mixed with a hint of guilt, partly because I'm glad for someone else's misfortune, but also because of what I prophetically told Joe earlier—that the participants we saved could be used as a buffer if we got shot at.

Gogi finishes whatever he was doing with the explosives. Rolling down his window, he throws the bag out.

I block my ears, expecting to hear an explosion upon impact, but nothing happens when the bag hits the ground.

Another bullet strikes the back window, but the screams that follow don't sound like cries of pain.

His hand clutching the detonator, Gogi looks intently behind us.

"Phase Two, on my order," he barks, his finger on his earpiece.

"Got it," Muhomor replies.

Gogi's jaw muscles tense.

I look behind us and see our pursuers almost level with the bag.

Unfortunately, we're less than a minute from hitting the brick wall.

"Now," Gogi says and squeezes the detonator.

CHAPTER FORTY-FIVE

The bag explodes in a blinding flash of fire, and the pursuing cars blow up with it, metal shards and glass flying everywhere.

At the same time, a sequence of explosions goes off in the distance.

I look through the front window. The wall is so close and we're driving so fast that I picture us turning into a human/car pancake.

Suddenly, a chunk of wall in our way explodes in a fireball that makes the bag explosion look like a cheap Fourth of July firecracker.

Once my vision clears, I see a jagged, charred gap where the wall once stood, and we fly through the blaze still covering the edges of the hole. The smell of smoke is acrid in my nostrils, and I feel the heat on my face.

We speed up, and the open windows clear the stench of fire, as well as the nauseating fumes of stomach juices from the motion sickness disaster.

Gulping in fresh air, I enjoy the breeze on my face as we drive in silence for a while. Even the wounded person stopped wailing.

We're probably all thinking of the same questions. Will they continue chasing after us now that we're outside the compound? Did Gogi get all the cars? Was the commotion Muhomor created enough to throw them off our track?

Holding my breath, I look back.

Two bright lights hit my eyes, and my heart sinks.

There's at least one car behind us.

"Wasn't that awesome?" Muhomor says into all our earpieces. "If I had more explosives planted, I'd blow them up right now."

"I assume it's you and Lyuba driving behind us," Gogi says grumpily.

"Of course it's us," Muhomor answers to my utter relief. "Who did you expect it to be?"

As Gogi curses Muhomor in his native Georgian language, I hear a man in the back moan, "My shoulder… I've been shot. Oh God, I'm going to die…"

I recognize the voice.

"You'll be fine, Mr. Shafer," I reassure him. "Here." I rip the sleeve off my shirt and pass it behind me. "Someone use that to bind his wound."

I use a mental search to learn as much as I can about impromptu bandages like this and walk Mrs. Stevens—Mr.

Shafer's closest seat neighbor—through the process of bandaging him as best I can.

"No one is following us," Muhomor says, precluding a question I was about to ask. "I'm looking through the cameras, and they're running from one explosion site to another like ants in a squashed anthill."

"Good," I text Muhomor. "Mitya," I mentally type into the chat. "Do the flight attendants have any first aid training?"

"More than that," Mitya replies with unusual seriousness. "Natalia is a registered nurse, and my plane has a fully stocked first aid kit. I already told her to prepare."

"Thank you," I type. "I don't know how I'll ever pay you back."

"Brainocytes are a gift beyond my wildest dreams," Mitya says with the same unusual seriousness. "Even after all this, I feel like I owe you guys."

"If all this madness is over, I think I'll go change my pants," Ada says. "That was some crazy driving, and the fighting before it—" Her voice breaks. "I thought you were a goner, Mike."

I'm in the process of coming up with something suitable to tell Ada, when Mom gently grabs my chin and tilts my head toward her. She says, "Okay, now that no one's tried to kill us for a whole minute, you better tell me what happened to your face. You already had those horrible bruises when I first saw you today."

"Oh, I got those at the hospital," I say in Russian, in part to make sure our conversation remains understandable only to Joe and Gogi. I proceed to tell Mom the whole story, minimizing the danger I was in when I can get away with it, and I don't go into too much detail when it comes to some of Joe's actions, since he's listening and might not appreciate it. I particularly avoid telling her about my father's fate. Thinking of him, I again feel that confusing mixture of emotions: sorrow, rage, bitterness, and resentment. How could my father—a man I only heard stories about—be behind all this?

"Mom," I say tentatively, realizing I have to ask some very unpleasant questions.

She looks at me intently.

Unsure how to proceed, I blurt out, "About Felix. He didn't hurt you before this evening, did he? I mean, do you remember him doing anything—"

"No." Mom's face simultaneously darkens and turns red. "I remember everything, and we just talked, or more like, he talked about himself the whole time."

"So you didn't get—"

"No," Mom interrupts. "Felix is the same as he was all those years ago—an asshole, but not a monster when sober. It's just that he drank vodka today, and he becomes an absolute fucktard as soon as any alcohol enters his system."

What she said is not only a record amount of information about my father, but also a record amount of cursing. If I were to sum up what Mom has told me about my father throughout the years, it would boil down to him not being a good man and me being better off without him. My grandparents used more colorful language to describe him, but the overall gist was the same. Of course, I'm only human, so sometimes I did wonder about the man, especially when I was younger. As I grew up, I thought about him less and less, to the point where, as I now realize, I never even bothered Googling his name, even though it's something I routinely do with mere acquaintances.

"I can't believe I share DNA with him," I say, nauseated at the thought.

"He isn't all bad." Mom rubs her eyes with the tips of her fingers. "You have to realize I wasn't completely insane when I decided to have an affair with a married man all those years ago."

"He was your boss." The words come out harsh, and to make sure Mom doesn't think I'm being hostile toward her, I add softly, "In America, what he did to you is called sexual harassment."

"Well," Mom says sadly, "something wonderful did come out of the whole mess." She looks at me warmly. "You couldn't be more different from Felix if you tried."

"Did he say anything about me?" I ask, wondering if some of my guesses are correct. "Something to explain how he knew about the Braincyte project?"

"Yes," Mom says. "I already knew he was keeping tabs on me, but as it turns out, out of fatherly pride as he called it, he kept tabs on all your accomplishments too, including your work."

"So my earlier insight about the kidnapping was right," I say, less to Mom and more so to say it out loud. Even as I used the face recognition app on his face, I knew, somewhere deep down, that Felix being behind all this made the puzzle pieces fit together. "This answers the biggest question of all: how did someone in Russia learn about Brainocytes in the first place?"

"I guess it does," Mom says. "To corroborate something your friend Muhomor suggested, your father indeed mentioned the FDA papers you filed, as well as patents, but it was really my memory condition that clued him in."

"So he figured out what we were working on," I whisper. "Hell, he might've understood more about it than most, since you two worked together in that company where theories of nanotechnology were discussed."

Mom nods. "He claimed he wanted to use this as a chance for us to reconnect, but I knew it for the bullshit it was. My guess is, he understood enough about your technology to get tempted by the possibility of fame and fortune. The man has an ego bigger than his head. From there, he must've reached out to someone who eventually introduced him to the right people, and things escalated from there."

"I think you're right," I say. "I think he eventually started working for a man named Govrilovskiy, a man who's still out there, now that I think about it. He's probably a threat to us—"

"About that," Muhomor says into the earpiece, making me realize the conversation is less private than I thought. "Didn't Gogi tell you? I continued searching for this Govrilovskiy guy since that was our contingency plan, and around the time you jumped out of the airplane, I found him and passed the information on to Gogi."

Gogi turns around and hands me his phone, saying, "I called in a favor with some fellow Georgians and told them there's a million dollars in it for them. Joe said you were good for it."

I take the phone, dreading what I might see, but I look anyway, hoping I'm sufficiently desensitized to violence by this point.

Sure enough, a brutally beaten man is sitting in front of the phone's camera. He's staring down the barrel of a gun.

"*Turizmi,*" Gogi says loudly in what I assume is Georgian.

The word must mean something like "go," because the gun on the other end goes off, and the man—who I presume is Govrilovskiy—falls to the ground with a substantial hole in his head.

Mom must see me flinch, because she puts her hand on my arm reassuringly.

I hand the phone back to Gogi, and Joe says, "A couple more million will take care of his associates. I can put up a portion—"

"No," I say, catching my breath. "I'll cover all that too. I like the idea of no one being left to try this again."

As soon as the words leave my mouth, I realize what this offer is—a commission for assassinations. It makes me, the person paying for it, directly responsible for ending their lives. Nevertheless, my conscience doesn't raise any alarms. I feel as much guilt as I would if I offered to pay for Joe's medical or legal bills.

"There's still your father," Mom says, taking me out of my ruminations. "If anyone might try this again, it'll be—"

She notices my expression and stops speaking. I take in a breath, unsure how she'll react, and say, "I don't think he survived, Mom. I'm sorry."

"I see," Mom says, her voice even, but her face is paler than I've ever seen it. Her throat works as she swallows; then she mutters, "I guess he dug that hole himself."

She looks away, and I spot her wiping tears from her eyes.

We ride in silence for a while, and I wonder if the fact I'm not crying over my deceased father and all the people who died today means I'm morally bankrupt or empty inside.

As I try to sort through the tangle of emotions again, I discover the most prevalent one is numbness. It blankets me, covering everything in a soothing fog. Behind that layer of numbness, I feel like I've been shattered into pieces that someone put back together the wrong way. I have no idea if I'll ever be the same again, but I suspect I won't—not after seeing so much death and violence up close.

Determined to escape my dark thoughts, I decide to get some pet therapy and ask, "Gogi, can you please pass me Mr. Spock?"

As a bonus, this distracts Mom from her brooding. When I told her about Mr. Spock's assistance during the rescue, she reacted well—at least on a purely intellectual level. Now, though, she'll have to tackle the reality of having a live rat in her proximity.

"Hmm," she says, catching me looking at her expectantly. "If he's going to be your pet, I'll try not to freak out around him." Her uncertain tone doesn't match her words, and she ends weakly with, "Especially if he's as well behaved and clean as you claim."

As though he waited for her to be okay with it, Gogi opens the glove compartment. Before he can grab the rat, Mr. Spock jumps onto Gogi's arm, then scurries up to the big man's shoulder and leaps right into my outstretched hands.

"He looks a bit like a squirrel, or maybe a guinea pig," Mom says, sounding like someone unsuccessfully trying to convince herself of a falsehood. "I hope it's okay if I never touch him."

"I don't think he likes anyone but me and Ada touching him," I say, though I don't know if that's actually true. "So it's preferable if you don't touch him."

"Good," Mom says, as though touching the rat was an important debt she had to pay, and she's relieved she doesn't have to pay it.

"Now for the most important part," she says, her tone suggesting she's about to teach a big moral lesson or complain about a grievance. Once she has my full attention, she firmly says, "If I'm ever kidnapped again, I want you to promise to let law enforcement handle it. That goes for you too, you hear me, Joseph?"

Joe grunts something unintelligible, and I say, "I'll make sure your Brainocytes allow us to consult with you if you're ever kidnapped again. How does that sound?"

"Oh, about that," Mom says. "I almost had a heart attack when I got your message in my Terminator interface."

"We call that the AROS interface, Mom," I say, finally managing a smile. "And you can thank Mitya for that message when you meet him."

"Speaking of Mitya... is that his plane?" Mom points into the distance.

Her eyes are wide, and I can't blame her.

Mitya's plane is a sight to behold, and where it's parked is just as awe-inspiring as the aircraft.

There's a huge abandoned Soviet-era warehouse by the road, with a parking lot covered by cracked, winter-beaten asphalt. It looks like it was originally meant to store trucks and the like. The shiny new plane is standing on the lot, looking as out of place as fried chicken liver inside a birthday cake.

It takes ten minutes to load everybody onto the plane. As soon as everyone is on board, we roll out of the parking lot to use the empty highway as a runway—one of the million reasons why our mission had to be done in the dead of night.

Natalia, the flight attendant nurse, tends to Mr. Shafer first, Gogi second, and me last. As I look at the bandages on my hands, I have to hand it to Mitya's wisdom, assuming there was wisdom involved in hiring her. Having a model-hot nurse tend to injuries cuts down on male whining considerably, even from me, a person who isn't interested in Natalia's charms.

"Do you want us to fly you back to Moscow?" I ask Gogi and Lyuba.

"Actually, if it's possible, I'd like to visit the United States," Gogi says.

"I need to go back to the Gadyukino hideout," Lyuba says.

"Okay, I think that can be arranged," I tell them, trying not to think too hard about what Lyuba needs to do back there with Alex. Getting up, I walk over to the pilot's cabin and make the appropriate arrangements. As I come back, for Mitya's benefit, I mentally type into the chat, "Your lawyers need to start working on those H-1B visas."

"Already on it," Mitya replies out loud. "I'll give them real jobs too if they want. Gogi can be your bodyguard or mine, and Muhomor—"

"No more business talk," I mentally reply. "Need sleep."

As though on the same wavelength as me, Joe hands out his Ambien to anyone who wants one, like it's candy. I bet my cousin's generosity is calculated and meant to incapacitate this rowdy bunch so he can get some sleep. I ask for a pill too, but I don't take it right away, because I need to call Uncle Abe and tell him Mom's okay. After that conversation, I call the authorities and explain everything as well as I can, promising that yes, we'll come down to the station to make a statement, that we'll obviously bring everyone wherever they want us to, et cetera, ad infinitum.

The one good part about the unpleasant phone calls is that they sufficiently distract me from the much worse unpleasantness of the liftoff. When I'm done with all the calls, and since Mom and the others are already in Ambien dreamland, I swallow my pill and wait for the drug to kick in.

Instead of counting sheep, I think about everything that's happened and examine the scabby wound that is my biological father's fate. For now, my turmoil has settled into a deep numbness. Given how little I thought or cared about the guy before I met him, that might be a normal reaction. Alternatively, this could be a psychological defense mechanism hiding a deep sense of loss of something I never thought I'd value. It's hard to introspect the truth. What I do know is that I'm the least qualified person to examine my feelings. I was never good at it, even under better circumstances. Maybe, despite my negative view of psychiatry, I'll give therapy a shot after things settle down. I might need it to properly deal with the gruesome things I've seen these last few days.

On the bright side, given my experience with Brainocytes so far, I have no doubt this technology will help Mom's condition. If she wants, she can even end up with a mind superior to the one she had before the accident. Judging by her extremely lucid behavior since the kidnapping, Phase One might've already had some positive effects.

As for me, even though I haven't fully adjusted to the bigger brain boost, I already feel like I could never go back to not having it. In fact, I want more. I guess I'll need to speak with Ada and read up on transhumanism, because in the very near future, I foresee us getting smarter and more capable than the smartest human being currently alive.

"Good night," Ada's voice says softly in my ear, interrupting my sleepy musings. "When you wake up, I'll probably be there in the flesh."

I'm not sure if it's Ada's soothing words, the drug, or the post-adrenaline crash—or even the feeling of a warm rat bruxing next to me—but my eyes get pleasantly heavy and I close them, sinking into sleep.

I wake up to people leaving the plane.

"I was worried," Mom says. "I called out to you, but you didn't answer."

"This is nothing." Gogi chuckles. "Upon his arrival into Russia, I helped him sleepwalk to the car."

"Whatever," I say groggily. "I'm going to the bathroom. You're welcome to sleepwalk me there if you want to hold something for me."

Gogi and Mom laugh, and then she says, "I'll meet you outside."

They follow the rest of the research participants off the plane, and I head in the opposite direction to one of the dozen bathrooms.

By the time I wash up and use the facilities, I feel like a slightly more lucid approximation of myself, though a triple espresso wouldn't hurt.

As I exit the plane, I feel like I've aged a couple of decades on this trip. Every bone and muscle in my body is aching all at once. Then I see Ada, and all my discomfort evaporates. It's as though I drank that triple espresso, and it was spiked with a shot of vodka to boot.

Maybe to make an impression on me—at which she succeeded—or maybe as a trick to make sure my mom doesn't think she's a boy again, Ada is wearing a strappy pink summer dress. It still manages to look punky somehow, though that could simply be from her attitude.

I increase my pace and Ada does the same, but she's forced to hold down her skirt, Marilyn Monroe style, because of the wind.

"Oh, you poor thing," she says when she sees my mummified hands. "And your face." She touches my left temple, probably my only non-swollen part. "I didn't think it could get worse than the injuries you had after the accident, but I was obviously wrong."

Instead of replying, I gently clasp her waist and pull her to me.

"Wow," she whispers as she looks up at me. Her amber eyes twinkle, giving her the charm of a mischievous puppy. "All that danger must have—"

I press my lips against hers, channeling all my gratitude for her help, as well as all my longing for her, into the kiss.

She responds with an unexpected fierceness, and to my surprise, her small hands grab my buttocks, giving them a noticeable squeeze.

We're at it for what feels like hours, and I fully expect someone to say, "Get a room, you two," but no one dares.

After the kiss, I take Ada's hand and let her lead me to the limo, where Mitya, my uncle, Muhomor, my cousin, Gogi, Mom, and JC are waiting for us. To my shock, JC is holding my mom's hand—a development I'll have to process later. My friends and family smile at me knowingly, and I know a lot of girl talk—and teasing from Mitya—is coming my way. I don't care, though. My steps are light, and despite the lingering tightness in my chest, I feel like I'm floating on post-kiss endorphins and oxytocin.

The numbness is still with me, shielding me from the worst of the turmoil, but underneath that, I'm aware of a strange contentment, a feeling I never expected to experience after all the horrors we've been through. For that matter, I didn't think I'd feel this hopeful after being repeatedly beaten and shot at and having the person closest to me kidnapped. Yet, paradoxically, that's exactly how I feel—hopeful. Hopeful for my future. Hopeful for Mom's future. Hopeful for the future of the study participants, and that of Alzheimer's patients, paraplegics, and other people we'll soon help. I even feel ambitious enough to feel hopeful for the future the Brainocytes will bring to the whole human race—though that might be a delusion brought on by my post-kiss high.

In a gentlemanly fashion, I let Ada enter the limo first and then follow, ready to share my feelings of hope with these people, who, in one way or another, for better or worse, are now my closest companions in the world.

"*Poyekhali*," I say to the driver, echoing the Russian cosmonaut again for Ada's benefit. Then, on the off chance Mitya's driver doesn't speak Russian, I clarify, "Let's go."

SNEAK PEEKS

Thank you for reading! If you would consider leaving a review, it would be greatly appreciated.

If you'd like to know when the next book in the Human++ series comes out, please sign up for my new release email list at www.dimazales.com.

Other series of mine include:

- *The Last Humans* — futuristic sci-fi/dystopian novels similar to *The Hunger Games*, *Divergent*, and *The Giver*
- *Mind Dimensions* — urban fantasy with a sci-fi flavor
- *The Sorcery Code* — epic fantasy

I also collaborate with my wife, Anna Zaires, on sci-fi romance, so if you don't mind erotic material, you can check out *Close Liaisons*.

If you enjoy audiobooks, you can find this series and our other books in audio format at www.dimazales.com.

And now, please turn the page for a sneak peek at *Oasis (The Last Humans: Book 1)*, *The Thought Readers (Mind Dimensions: Book 1)*, and *The Sorcery Code*.

EXCERPT FROM *OASIS*

My name is Theo, and I'm a resident of Oasis, the last habitable area on Earth. It's meant to be a paradise, a place where we are all content. Vulgarity, violence, insanity, and other ills are but a distant memory, and even death no longer plagues us.

I was once content too, but now I'm different. Now I hear a voice in my head, and she tells me things no imaginary friend should know. Her name is Phoe, and she is my delusion.

Or is she?

Fuck. Vagina. Shit.

I pointedly think these forbidden words, but my neural scan shows nothing out of the ordinary compared to when I think phonetically similar words, such as *shuck, angina,* or *fit.* I don't see any evidence of my brain being corrupted, though maybe it's already so damaged that things can't get any worse. Maybe I need another test subject—another 'impressionable' twenty-three-year-old Youth such as myself.

After all, I might be mentally ill.

"Oh, Theo. Not this again," says an overly friendly, high-pitched female voice. "Besides, the words do have an effect on your brain. For instance, the part of your brain responsible for disgust lights up at the mention of 'shit,' yet doesn't for 'fit.'"

This is Phoe speaking. This time, she's not a voice inside my head; instead, it's as though she's in the thick bushes behind me, except there's no one there.

I'm the only person on this strip of grass.

Nobody else comes here because the Edge is only a couple of feet away. Few residents of Oasis like looking at the dreary line dividing where our habitable world ends and the deserted wasteland of the Goo begins. I don't mind it, though.

Then again, I may be crazy—and Phoe would be the reason for that. You see, I don't think Phoe is real. She is, as far as my best guess goes, my imaginary friend. And her name, by the way, is pronounced 'Fee,' but is spelled 'P-h-o-e.'

Yes, that's how specific my delusion is.

"So you go from one overused topic straight into another." Phoe snorts. "My so-called realness."

"Right," I say. Though we're alone, I still answer without moving my lips. "Because I *am* imagining you."

She snorts again, and I shake my head. Yes, I just shook my head for the benefit of my delusion. I also feel compelled to respond to her.

"For the record," I say, "I'm sure the taboo word 'shit' affects the parts of my brain that deal with disgust just as much as its more acceptable cousins, such as 'fecal matter,' do. The point I was trying to make is that the word doesn't hurt or corrupt my brain. There's nothing special about these words."

"Yeah, yeah." This time, Phoe is inside my head, and she sounds mocking. "Next you'll tell me how back in the day, some of the forbidden words merely referred to things like female dogs, and how there are words in the dead languages that used to be just as taboo, yet they are not currently forbidden because they have lost their power. Then you're likely to complain that, though the brains of both genders are nearly identical, only males are not allowed to say 'vagina,' et cetera."

I realize I was about to counter with those exact thoughts, which means Phoe and I have talked about this quite a bit. This is what happens between close friends: they repeat conversations. Doubly so with imaginary friends, I figure. Though, of course, I'm probably the only person in Oasis who actually has one.

Come to think of it, wouldn't *every* conversation with your imaginary friend be redundant since you're basically talking to yourself?

"This is my cue to remind you that I'm real, Theo." Phoe purposefully states this out loud.

I can't help but notice that her voice came slightly from my right, as if she's just a friend sitting on the grass next to me—a friend who happens to be invisible.

"Just because I'm invisible doesn't mean I'm not real," Phoe responds to my thought. "At least *I'm* convinced that I'm real. I would be the crazy one if I *didn't* think I was real. Besides, a lot of evidence points to that conclusion, and you know it."

"But wouldn't an imaginary friend *have* to insist she's real?" I can't resist saying the words out loud. "Wouldn't this be part of the delusion?"

"Don't talk to me out loud," she reminds me, her tone worried. "Even when you subvocalize, sometimes you imperceptibly move your neck muscles or even your lips. All those things are too risky. You should just think your thoughts at me. Use your inner voice. It's safer that way, especially when we're around other Youths."

"Sure, but for the record, that makes me feel even nuttier," I reply, but I subvocalize my words, trying my best not to move my lips or neck muscles. Then, as an experiment, I think, "Talking to you inside my head just highlights the impossibility of you and thus makes me feel like I'm missing even more screws."

"Well, it shouldn't." Her voice is inside my head now, yet it still sounds high-pitched. "Back in the day, when it was not forbidden to be mentally ill, I imagine it made people around you uncomfortable if you spoke to your imaginary friends out loud." She chuckles, but there's more worry than humor in her voice. "I have no idea what would happen if someone thought you were crazy, but I have a bad feeling about it, so please don't do it, okay?"

"Fine," I think and pull at my left earlobe. "Though it's overkill to do it here. No one's around."

"Yes, but the nanobots I told you about, the ones that permeate everything from your head to the utility fog, *can* be used to monitor this place, at least in theory."

"Right. Unless all this conveniently invisible technology you keep telling me about is as much of a figment of my imagination as you are," I think at her. "In any case, since no one seems to know about this tech, how can they use it to spy on me?"

"Correction: no Youth knows, but the others might," Phoe counters patiently. "There's too much we still don't know about Adults, not to mention the Elderly."

"But if they can access the nanocytes in my mind, wouldn't they have access to my thoughts too?" I think, suppressing a shudder. If this is true, I'm utterly screwed.

"The fact that you haven't faced any consequences for your frequently wayward thoughts is evidence that no one monitors them in general, or at least, they're not bothering with yours specifically," she responds, her words easing my dread. "Therefore, I think monitoring thoughts is either computationally prohibitive or breaks one of the bazillion taboos on the proper use of technology—rules I have a very hard time keeping track of, by the way."

"Well, what if using tech to listen in on me is also taboo?" I retort, though she's beginning to convince me.

"It may be, but I've seen evidence that can best be explained as the Adults spying." Her voice in my head takes on a hushed tone. "Just think of the time you and Liam made plans to skip your Physics Lecture. How did they know about that?"

I think of the epic Quietude session we were sentenced to and how we both swore we hadn't betrayed each other. We reached the same conclusion: our speech is not secure. That's why Liam, Mason, and I now often speak in code.

"There could be other explanations," I think at Phoe. "That conversation happened during Lectures, and someone could've overheard us. But even if they hadn't, just because they monitor us during class doesn't mean they would bother monitoring this forsaken spot."

"Even if they don't monitor *this* place or anywhere outside of the Institute, I still want you to acquire the right habit."

"What if I speak in code?" I suggest. "You know, the one I use with my non-imaginary friends."

"You already speak too slowly for my liking," she thinks at me with clear exasperation. "When you speak in that code, you sound ridiculous and drastically increase the number of syllables you say. Now if you were willing to learn one of the dead languages…"

"Fine. I will 'think' when I have to speak to you," I think. Then I subvocalize, "But I will also subvocalize."

"If you must." She sighs out loud. "Just do it the way you did a second ago, without any voice musculature moving."

Instead of replying, I look at the Edge again, the place where the serene greenery under the Dome meets the repulsive ocean of the desolate Goo—the ever-replicating parasitic technology that converts matter into itself. The Goo is what's left of the world outside the Dome barrier, and if the barrier were to ever come down, the Goo would destroy us in short order. Naturally, this view evokes all sorts of unpleasant feelings, and the fact that I'm voluntarily gazing at it must be yet another sign of my shaky mental state.

"The thing *is* decidedly gross," Phoe reflects, trying to cheer me up, as usual. "It looks like someone tried to make Jell-O out of vomit and human excrement." Then, with a mental snicker, she adds, "Sorry, I should've said 'vomit and shit.'"

"I have no idea what Jell-O is," I subvocalize. "But whatever it is, you're probably spot on regarding the ingredients."

"Jell-O was something the ancients ate in the pre-Food days," Phoe explains. "I'll find something for you to watch or read about it, or if you're lucky, they might serve it at the upcoming Birth Day fair."

"I hope they do. It's hard to learn about food from books or movies," I complain. "I tried."

"In this case, you might," Phoe counters. "Jell-O was more about texture than taste. It had the consistency of jellyfish."

"People actually ate those slimy things back then?" I think in disgust. I can't recall seeing that in any of the movies. Waving toward the Goo, I say, "No wonder the world turned to this."

"They didn't eat it in most parts of the world," Phoe says, her voice taking on a pedantic tone. "And Jell-O was actually made out of partially decomposed proteins extracted from cow and pig hides, hooves, bones, and connective tissue."

"Now you're just trying to gross me out," I think.

"That's rich, coming from you, Mr. Shit." She chuckles. "Anyway, you have to leave this place."

"I do?"

"You have Lectures in half an hour, but more importantly, Mason is looking for you," she says, and her voice gives me the impression she's already gotten up from the grass.

I get up and start walking through the tall shrubbery that hides the Goo from the view of the rest of Oasis Youths.

"By the way"—Phoe's voice comes from the distance; she's simulating walking ahead of me—"once you verify that Mason *is* looking for you, *do* try to explain how an imaginary friend like me could possibly know something like that… something you yourself didn't know."

───────────

Oasis is currently available at most retailers. If you'd like to learn more, please visit <u>www.dimazales.com</u>.

EXCERPT FROM
THE THOUGHT READERS

Everyone thinks I'm a genius.

Everyone is wrong.

Sure, I finished Harvard at eighteen and now make crazy money at a hedge fund. But that's not because I'm unusually smart or hard-working.

It's because I cheat.

You see, I have a unique ability. I can go outside time into my own personal version of reality—the place I call "the Quiet"—where I can explore my surroundings while the rest of the world stands still.

I thought I was the only one who could do this—until I met *her*.

My name is Darren, and this is how I learned that I'm a Reader.

Sometimes I think I'm crazy. I'm sitting at a casino table in Atlantic City, and everyone around me is motionless. I call this the *Quiet*, as though giving it a name makes it seem more real—as though giving it a name changes the fact that all the players around me are frozen like statues, and I'm walking among them, looking at the cards they've been dealt.

The problem with the theory of my being crazy is that when I 'unfreeze' the world, as I just have, the cards the players turn over are the same ones I just saw in the Quiet. If I were crazy, wouldn't these cards be different? Unless I'm so far gone that I'm imagining the cards on the table, too.

But then I also win. If that's a delusion—if the pile of chips on my side of the table is a delusion—then I might as well question everything. Maybe my name isn't even Darren.

No. I can't think that way. If I'm really that confused, I don't want to snap out of it—because if I do, I'll probably wake up in a mental hospital.

Besides, I love my life, crazy and all.

My shrink thinks the Quiet is an inventive way I describe the 'inner workings of my genius.' Now that sounds crazy to me. She also might want me, but that's beside the point. Suffice it to say, she's as far as it gets from my datable age range, which is currently right around twenty-four. Still young, still hot, but done with school and pretty much beyond the clubbing phase. I hate clubbing, almost as much as I hated studying. In any case, my shrink's explanation doesn't work, as it doesn't account for the way I know things even a genius wouldn't know—like the exact value and suit of the other players' cards.

I watch as the dealer begins a new round. Besides me, there are three players at the table: Grandma, the Cowboy, and the Professional, as I call them. I feel that now almost imperceptible fear that accompanies the phasing. That's what I call the process: phasing into the Quiet. Worrying about my sanity has always facilitated phasing; fear seems helpful in this process.

I phase in, and everything gets quiet. Hence the name for this state.

It's eerie to me, even now. Outside the Quiet, this casino is very loud: drunk people talking, slot machines, ringing of wins, music—the only place louder is a club or a concert. And yet, right at this moment, I could probably hear a pin drop. It's like I've gone deaf to the chaos that surrounds me.

Having so many frozen people around adds to the strangeness of it all. Here is a waitress stopped mid-step, carrying a tray with drinks. There is a woman about to pull a slot machine lever. At my own table, the dealer's hand is raised, the last card he dealt hanging unnaturally in mid-air. I walk up to him from the side of the table and reach for it. It's a king, meant for the Professional. Once I let the card go, it falls on the table rather than continuing to float as before—but I know full well that it will be back in the air, in the exact position it was when I grabbed it, when I phase out.

The Professional looks like someone who makes money playing poker, or at least the way I always imagined someone like that might look. Scruffy, shades on, a little sketchy-looking. He's been doing an excellent job with the poker face—basically not twitching a single muscle throughout the game. His face is so expressionless that I wonder if he might've gotten Botox to help maintain such a stony countenance. His hand is on the table, protectively covering the cards dealt to him.

I move his limp hand away. It feels normal. Well, in a manner of speaking. The hand is sweaty and hairy, so moving it aside is unpleasant and is admittedly an abnormal thing to do. The normal part is that the hand is warm, rather than cold. When I was a kid, I expected people to feel cold in the Quiet, like stone statues.

With the Professional's hand moved away, I pick up his cards. Combined with the king that was hanging in the air, he has a nice high pair. Good to know.

I walk over to Grandma. She's already holding her cards, and she has fanned them nicely for me. I'm able to avoid touching her wrinkled, spotted hands. This is a relief, as I've recently become conflicted about touching people—or, more specifically, women—in the Quiet. If I had to, I would rationalize touching Grandma's hand as harmless, or at least not creepy, but it's better to avoid it if possible.

In any case, she has a low pair. I feel bad for her. She's been losing a lot tonight. Her chips are dwindling. Her losses are due, at least partially, to the fact that she has a terrible poker face. Even before looking at her cards, I knew they wouldn't be good because I could tell she was disappointed as soon as her hand was dealt. I also caught a gleeful gleam in her eyes a few rounds ago when she had a winning three of a kind.

This whole game of poker is, to a large degree, an exercise in reading people—something I really want to get better at. At my job, I've been told I'm great at reading people. I'm not, though; I'm just good at using the Quiet to make it seem like I am. I do want to learn how to read people for real, though. It would be nice to know what everyone is thinking.

What I don't care that much about in this poker game is money. I do well enough financially to not have to depend on hitting it big gambling. I don't care if I win or lose, though quintupling my money back at the blackjack table was fun. This whole trip has been more about going gambling because I finally can, being twenty-one and all. I was never into fake IDs, so this is an actual milestone for me.

Leaving Grandma alone, I move on to the next player—the Cowboy. I can't resist taking off his straw hat and trying it on. I wonder if it's possible for me to get lice this way. Since I've never been able to bring back any inanimate objects from the Quiet, nor otherwise affect the real world in any lasting way, I figure I won't be able to get any living critters to come back with me, either.

Dropping the hat, I look at his cards. He has a pair of aces—a better hand than the Professional. Maybe the Cowboy is a professional, too. He has a good poker face, as far as I can tell. It'll be interesting to watch those two in this round.

Next, I walk up to the deck and look at the top cards, memorizing them. I'm not leaving anything to chance.

When my task in the Quiet is complete, I walk back to myself. Oh, yes, did I mention that I see myself sitting there, frozen like the rest of them? That's the weirdest part. It's like having an out-of-body experience.

Approaching my frozen self, I look at him. I usually avoid doing this, as it's too unsettling. No amount of looking in the mirror—or seeing videos of yourself on YouTube—can prepare you for viewing your own three-dimensional body up close. It's not something anyone is meant to experience. Well, aside from identical twins, I guess.

It's hard to believe that this person is me. He looks more like some random guy. Well, maybe a bit better than that. I do find this guy interesting. He looks cool. He looks smart. I think women would probably consider him good-looking, though I know that's not a modest thing to think.

It's not like I'm an expert at gauging how attractive a guy is, but some things are common sense. I can tell when a dude is ugly, and this frozen me is not. I also know that generally, being good-looking requires a symmetrical face, and the statue of me has that. A strong jaw doesn't hurt, either. Check. Having broad shoulders is a positive, and being tall really helps. All covered. I have blue eyes—that seems to be a plus. Girls have told me they like my eyes, though right now, on the frozen me, the eyes look creepy—glassy. They look like the eyes of a lifeless wax figure.

Realizing that I'm dwelling on this subject way too long, I shake my head. I can just picture my shrink analyzing this moment. Who would imagine admiring themselves like this as part of their mental illness? I can just picture her scribbling down *Narcissist*, underlining it for emphasis.

Enough. I need to leave the Quiet. Raising my hand, I touch my frozen self on the forehead, and I hear noise again as I phase out.

Everything is back to normal.

The card that I looked at a moment before—the king that I left on the table—is in the air again, and from there it follows the trajectory it was always meant to, landing near the Professional's hands. Grandma is still eyeing her fanned cards in disappointment, and the Cowboy has his hat on again, though I took it off him in the Quiet. Everything is exactly as it was.

On some level, my brain never ceases to be surprised at the discontinuity of the experience in the Quiet and outside it. As humans, we're hardwired to question reality when such things happen. When I was trying to outwit my shrink early on in my therapy, I once read an entire psychology textbook during our session. She, of course, didn't notice it, as I did it in the Quiet. The book talked about how babies as young as two months old are surprised if they see something out of the ordinary, like gravity appearing to work backwards. It's no wonder my brain has trouble adapting. Until I was ten, the world behaved normally, but everything has been weird since then, to put it mildly.

Glancing down, I realize I'm holding three of a kind. Next time, I'll look at my cards before phasing. If I have something this strong, I might take my chances and play fair.

The game unfolds predictably because I know every-body's cards. At the end, Grandma gets up. She's clearly lost enough money.

And that's when I see the girl for the first time.

She's hot. My friend Bert at work claims that I have a 'type,' but I reject that idea. I don't like to think of myself as shallow or predictable. But I might actually be a bit of both, because this girl fits Bert's description of my type to a T. And my reaction is extreme interest, to say the least.

Large blue eyes. Well-defined cheekbones on a slender face, with a hint of something exotic. Long, shapely legs, like those of a dancer. Dark wavy hair in a ponytail—a hairstyle that I like. And without bangs—even better. I hate bangs—not sure why girls do that to themselves. Though lack of bangs is not, strictly speaking, in Bert's description of my type, it probably should be.

I continue staring at her. With her high heels and tight skirt, she's overdressed for this place. Or maybe I'm under-dressed in my jeans and t-shirt. Either way, I don't care. I have to try to talk to her.

I debate phasing into the Quiet and approaching her, so I can do something creepy like stare at her up close, or maybe even snoop in her pockets. Anything to help me when I talk to her.

I decide against it, which is probably the first time that's ever happened.

I know that my reasoning for breaking my usual habit—if you can even call it that—is strange. I picture the following chain of events: she agrees to date me, we go out for a while, we get serious, and because of the deep connection we have, I come clean about the Quiet. She learns I did something creepy and has a fit, then dumps me. It's ridiculous to think this, of course, considering that we haven't even spoken yet. Talk about jumping the gun. She might have an IQ below seventy, or the personality of a piece of wood. There can be twenty different reasons why I wouldn't want to date her. And besides, it's not all up to me. She might tell me to go fuck myself as soon as I try to talk to her.

Still, working at a hedge fund has taught me to hedge. As crazy as that reasoning is, I stick with my decision not to phase because I know it's the gentlemanly thing to do. In keeping with this unusually chivalrous me, I also decide not to cheat at this round of poker.

As the cards are dealt again, I reflect on how good it feels to have done the honorable thing—even without anyone knowing. Maybe I should try to respect people's privacy more often. As soon as I think this, I mentally snort. *Yeah, right.* I have to be realistic. I wouldn't be where I am today if I'd followed that advice. In fact, if I made a habit of respecting people's privacy, I would lose my job within days—and with it, a lot of the comforts I've become accustomed to.

Copying the Professional's move, I cover my cards with my hand as soon as I receive them. I'm about to sneak a peek at what I was dealt when something unusual happens.

The world goes quiet, just like it does when I phase in... but I did nothing this time.

And at that moment, I see *her*—the girl sitting across the table from me, the girl I was just thinking about. She's standing next to me, pulling her hand away from mine. Or, strictly speaking, from my frozen self's hand—as I'm standing a little to the side looking at her.

She's also still sitting in front of me at the table, a frozen statue like all the others.

My mind goes into overdrive as my heartbeat jumps. I don't even consider the possibility of that second girl being a twin sister or something like that. I know it's her. She's doing what I did just a few minutes ago. She's walking in the Quiet. The world around us is frozen, but we are not.

A horrified look crosses her face as she realizes the same thing. Before I can react, she lunges across the table and touches her own forehead.

The world becomes normal again.

She stares at me from across the table, shocked, her eyes huge and her face pale. Her hands tremble as she rises to her feet. Without so much as a word, she turns and begins walking away, then breaks into a run a couple of seconds later.

Getting over my own shock, I get up and run after her. It's not exactly smooth. If she notices a guy she doesn't know running after her, dating will be the last thing on her mind. But I'm beyond that now. She's the only person I've met who can do what I do. She's proof that I'm not insane. She might have what I want most in the world.

She might have answers.

The Thought Readers is now available at most retailers. If you'd like to learn more, please visit www.dimazales.com.

EXCERPT FROM
THE SORCERY CODE

Once a respected member of the Sorcerer Council and now an outcast, Blaise has spent the last year of his life working on a special magical object. The goal is to allow anyone to do magic, not just the sorcerer elite. The outcome of his quest is unlike anything he could've ever imagined—because, instead of an object, he creates Her.

She is Gala, and she is anything but inanimate. Born in the Spell Realm, she is beautiful and highly intelligent—and nobody knows what she's capable of. She will do anything to experience the world... even leave the man she is beginning to fall for.

Augusta, a powerful sorceress and Blaise's former fiancée, sees Blaise's deed as the ultimate hubris and Gala as an abomination that must be destroyed. In her quest to save the human race, Augusta will forge new alliances, becoming tangled in a web of intrigue that stretches further than any of them suspect. She may even have to turn to her new lover Barson, a ruthless warrior who might have an agenda of his own…

———————

There was a naked woman on the floor of Blaise's study.

A beautiful naked woman.

Stunned, Blaise stared at the gorgeous creature who just appeared out of thin air. She was looking around with a bewildered expression on her face, apparently as shocked to be there as he was to be seeing her. Her wavy blond hair streamed down her back, partially covering a body that appeared to be perfection itself. Blaise tried not to think about that body and to focus on the situation instead.

A woman. A *She*, not an *It*. Blaise could hardly believe it. Could it be? Could this girl be the object?

She was sitting with her legs folded underneath her, propping herself up with one slim arm. There was something awkward about that pose, as though she didn't know what to do with her own limbs. In general, despite the curves that marked her a fully grown woman, there was a child-like innocence in the way she sat there, completely unselfconscious and totally unaware of her own appeal.

Clearing his throat, Blaise tried to think of what to say. In his wildest dreams, he couldn't have imagined this kind of outcome to the project that had consumed his entire life for the past several months.

Hearing the sound, she turned her head to look at him, and Blaise found himself staring into a pair of unusually clear blue eyes.

She blinked, then cocked her head to the side, studying him with visible curiosity. Blaise wondered what she was seeing. He hadn't seen the light of day in weeks, and he wouldn't be surprised if he looked like a mad sorcerer at this point. There was probably a week's worth of stubble covering his face, and he knew his dark hair was unbrushed and sticking out in every direction. If he'd known he would be facing a beautiful woman today, he would've done a grooming spell in the morning.

"Who am I?" she asked, startling Blaise. Her voice was soft and feminine, as alluring as the rest of her. "What is this place?"

"You don't know?" Blaise was glad he finally managed to string together a semi-coherent sentence. "You don't know who you are or where you are?"

She shook her head. "No."

Blaise swallowed. "I see."

"What am I?" she asked again, staring at him with those incredible eyes.

"Well," Blaise said slowly, "if you're not some cruel prankster or a figment of my imagination, then it's somewhat difficult to explain…"

She was watching his mouth as he spoke, and when he stopped, she looked up again, meeting his gaze. "It's strange," she said, "hearing words this way. These are the first real words I've heard."

Blaise felt a chill go down his spine. Getting up from his chair, he began to pace, trying to keep his eyes off her nude body. He had been expecting something to appear. A magical object, a thing. He just hadn't known what form that thing would take. A mirror, perhaps, or a lamp. Maybe even something as unusual as the Life Capture Sphere that sat on his desk like a large round diamond.

But a person? A female person at that?

To be fair, he had been trying to make the object intelligent, to ensure it would have the ability to comprehend human language and convert it into the code. Maybe he shouldn't be so surprised that the intelligence he invoked took on a human shape.

A beautiful, feminine, sensual shape.

Focus, Blaise, focus.

"Why are you walking like that?" She slowly got to her feet, her movements uncertain and strangely clumsy. "Should I be walking too? Is that how people talk to each other?"

Blaise stopped in front of her, doing his best to keep his eyes above her neck. "I'm sorry. I'm not accustomed to naked women in my study."

She ran her hands down her body, as though trying to feel it for the first time. Whatever her intent, Blaise found the gesture extremely erotic.

"Is something wrong with the way I look?" she asked. It was such a typical feminine concern that Blaise had to stifle a smile.

"Quite the opposite," he assured her. "You look unimaginably good." So good, in fact, that he was having trouble concentrating on anything but her delicate curves. She was of medium height, and so perfectly proportioned that she could've been used as a sculptor's template.

"Why do I look this way?" A small frown creased her smooth forehead. "What am I?" That last part seemed to be puzzling her the most.

Blaise took a deep breath, trying to calm his racing pulse. "I think I can try to venture a guess, but before I do, I want to give you some clothing. Please wait here—I'll be right back."

And without waiting for her answer, he hurried out of the room.

The Sorcery Code is currently available at most retailers. If you'd like to learn more, please visit www.dimazales.com.

Made in the USA
Columbia, SC
30 December 2018